The Undiscovered

The Undiscovered

Paul Hinton

Published by Oneoff Publishing.com
www.oneoffpublishing.com

First Published by Oneoff Publishing.com 2008

British Library Cataloguing in Publication Data.
A catalogue record for this book is available from the British Library

ISBN 978 0 952 2603 63

Published by Oneoff Publishing.com
11 Farmers Heath, Wirral, CH66 2GX, Great Britain.
www.oneoffpublishing.com

To Jenny, thanks for believing. To Sara, Samantha and Shannon, thanks for knowing how to react when Dad had the 'Do not disturb' sign on his forehead!

Foreword

The war was over, peace had finally been declared!

The few remaining survivors had decided enough was enough. Nobody was sure which government had fired the first missile, released the viruses and poisoned most of the planet. Only one thing was certain, mankind had lost. From the original seven billion inhabitants, only a few million were left alive world-wide, the decimation completed in under two years! Scattered over the continents, the survivors may have felt lucky at first, Governments were quickly reformed, law and order re-established, communications between countries re-built. Every society newly formed was fully based on democracy. No one person would ever be allowed to decide anything again.

For a while everything had gone well. Villages were re-built, cities began to grow out of the rubble, the people left alive carving an existence out of an abused planet. Scientists worked to improve farming techniques, so mankind could feed themselves again. Trade began between communities, eventually between lands. Life was returning to normal, the planet was recovering, they had survived.

No-one could have imagined what was about to happen.

In the year 2016, three years after the war had ended, the first incident took place. Contact with a small farming community in France was lost. After a week of silence, soldiers were sent to investigate. What they found, horrified the world. Over two hundred men, women and children had been killed, no apparent cause. Once again talk of war surfaced!

Scientific teams were flown into the area to establish what exactly had happened. After weeks of apparent tests and autopsies, it was reported to the public that a virus type weapon, left over from the war, was responsible for the tragedy. The world breathed again, but one week later a second incident took place, this time in Germany. As this was being investigated, reports came to light of similar incidents in Spain, Belgium and England. Once again the world stood on the brink.

Eventually Scientists announced that the use of weapons could be ruled out in every case, a more sinister explanation was suggested. Facts held back from the initial investigation of the first incident, led the Scientists to believe the people had been killed by something non-human. Unknown DNA samples collected from the scene of the first massacre had been tested and seemed to confirm this theory. The evidence even suggested that some of the victims had been partially eaten! Rumours of cannibals or mutants circled the globe, panic ensued, communities were reinforced until the truth started to surface. During an 'attack' on a small village in Belgium, one of the villagers had managed to radio for help. Before being killed he had told of an apparent raid by, what he described as, monsters! The attacks became more regular, what few soldiers that were left were deployed to combat the problem, but more often than not they too came under attack. The facts were slowly pieced together. The creatures, now attacking them, had been on our planet for centuries feeding!

Every year before the war, tens of thousands of people had disappeared without trace. Flimsy attempts were always made to find them, but usually without success. The reasons why, now slowly became clear. They were all victims of these monsters. With the population of the planet around seven billion, the vanishing of a few thousand had never seemed important or mysterious enough to worry about for long. They had learnt to ignore it! Now with the population decimated, every death or disappearance would be investigated, they could not ignore it any more.

They had survived the last war, but would the rest of mankind survive this one . . .

Chapter One - Ambush

"I heard that noise again, John," Stephanie whispered.

"Shit! Head for that house. Until we know what it is, we'd better play it safe," John said, a sense of urgency unmistakable in his voice.

They ran the fifty yards up to the house door John had pointed towards but it was locked. John took a step backwards and kicked as hard as he could, the door giving a little but staying closed. He kicked again, this time the door exploded inwards. They ran inside.

"Do you think it's them?" Stephanie asked, sounding a little panicked. "Or something else?"

"I'm not sure, keep your head down," John replied, re-closing the door he had just destroyed. "If it is them, try to keep calm and don't waste your shots. If there are too many, get away as best you can. I'll be right behind you."

"If there are too many, we won't have that many places to run to, they'll be all over us in seconds," Stephanie argued. "Out in the open we don't stand a chance, especially if there are more of them in the area."

John stared at her, knowing she was right. Getting caught inside the house he had singled out, by too many of the creatures, might prolong the inevitable but it wouldn't change the end result. He had been careless and that annoyed him. In his haste to reach the castle stronghold they had been told about, he had pushed their luck. He knew very well that travelling at night was dangerous, that was the creature's time! That's why the couple had mostly rested at night, hidden away somewhere safe from the roaming groups of creatures but he had felt the gamble this time was necessary. Now it seemed they might have to pay the price for his stupidity. Suddenly unsure about what to do, he was about to suggest they move when the reason for their hiding appeared at the end of the street. It was too late, all they could do now was wait.

There were twenty of them that John could see but he knew there were probably more hiding nearby. They were bigger than people, on average over seven feet tall, powerfully built, with an almost lizard-like appearance but lizards that walked on two legs.

Each of the creatures were equipped with razor-like talons on both their 'hands' and 'feet' and an impressive jaw full of lethal looking teeth. They were formidable-looking. Whenever they stopped to taste the air with their snake like tongues, they blended to the background, making them almost invisible. This chameleon-type camouflage had tipped the balance in their favour during the last few years of fighting and had helped them to remain undiscovered in the centuries before. John had often wondered what naturalists would have made of them, all those years ago when such programmes had been popular on television. The thought of Steve Irwin chasing and wrestling one of them to the ground, always brought a smile to his face. As the creatures ambled down the street, it reminded John of scenes out of the old zombie films from the 1990s. Their movements were slow, almost comical looking but both John and Stephanie had witnessed this behaviour before. They were searching for evidence that people were still hiding in the area. Anybody found would be in immediate danger of becoming food for these deadly predators, the comical looking parade suddenly turning into a lightning fast attack.

"Oh, shit," Stephanie whispered. "If they pick up our scent, we're in trouble."

"We're lucky they haven't picked it up already. The next time I suggest travelling at night, kick my arse, will you," John said, not taking his eyes off the gathering creatures.

"I will do that, Mr Stewart, with pleasure," Stephanie whispered. "That's if we live through this."

He turned to look at her, worried about her comment but she was smiling.

The creatures had stopped twenty yards from the house, John held his breath. If any of the monsters realised they were there, the attack would be ferocious. They both quietly checked their weapons, realising the next few seconds would be critical. Neither of them carried a rifle because the fighting was always at close quarters, instead they were both armed with automatics. John had always considered the nine millimetre Beretta to be one of the best handguns ever produced. He carried two of them, one in a shoulder holster, one tucked in his waistband. Stephanie also had two of the pistols. Fully loaded each weapon had sixteen rounds. Normally speaking it was enough firepower and the two of them were very adept at fighting with the powerful handguns but they both carried Japanese Samurai swords as back up. These were sheathed safely on their backs but always within easy reach. Both of them had been martial arts instructors, working with and training members of the Special Air Services in the handling of edged weapons before and during the Third World War. During the very first years they had spent training the elite fighting force, they had met and fallen in love. They had been inseparable ever since.

After the war against these marauding bands of monsters had started, they had witnessed a steady increase in the number of attacks being made. The country was once again a battlefield. People had tried to fight back but, against the massive numbers of attackers, the fighting had not gone well. What was left of the military had greatly underestimated the capabilities of the creatures they were fighting on several occasions and had suffered disastrous defeats. At that point, John had decided it would be better for them to head out on their own. They had been travelling the country ever since, trying to find a place where they might be safe but it was proving harder than he had anticipated. Through careful planning sometimes combined with luck, they had, more often than not, managed to avoid the monsters that were systematically wiping out the human race. On the few occasions they had encountered the creatures, they had managed to fight themselves out of trouble but the group standing in the street outside was too big for the two of them to handle, especially in the confines of the house. John was trying to find a way for them to survive the attack if it came, when the creatures passed by the house, going further down the street. They had not picked up their scent.

"John, they're leaving," Stephanie whispered.

"We were lucky. We'd better stay here tonight. You get some sleep, I'll take the first watch. Wake you in four hours," John said.

"Okay, but call me if anything happens," Stephanie replied.

"I will," John said, already going to check the back door was secure.

She went upstairs and, after checking the rooms, picked one and tried to sleep. She could not remember the last time she had really slept, every night the same nightmare, that night would prove to be no exception.

They were cornered, she was wounded, John hopelessly outnumbered. Unable to help him she must witness how he is killed and partially devoured. Terrifyingly, the creatures then turn towards her and start to advance. Usually at that point she always woke up but that night, for some reason, the nightmare

11

was lasting longer. The creatures were almost touching her as she screamed and awoke!

She heard him rushing up the stairs to rescue her, the thought warming her. He strode through the door into her room, his Berettas in his hands, ready for anything.

"It's alright, I was dreaming again. Sorry, I didn't mean to scare you," she said.

"You didn't," he replied. "But the thought of something happening to you terrifies me."

She kissed him, he responded at first but quickly backed off. She understood why. It had been three weeks since they had last felt secure enough to enjoy each other. She secretly wondered if a time would ever come again. Making love to him was something she missed terribly but the danger of being surprised whilst doing so was too great.

"What should we do now?" she asked.

"First we'll try to find something to eat, then we'll keep heading north," he said.

"We're still trying to reach this castle then."

"If it exists, yes. Maybe we'll find our own - I'm tired of running," he said.

"What's the matter?" she asked, worried about him.

"I'm alright, I'm just tired."

At that moment she realised it was light outside, he had let her sleep all night again.

"John, I thought we'd talked about this. You need your sleep as well," she told him, slightly annoyed.

"I'll get a few hours later, don't worry about me," he argued.

"But I do worry, John. You're always going without, making sure I get enough of everything. Answer me this, who is going to do that when you're dead?" she asked.

"I've no intention of dying just yet," he argued.

"Lack of food and lack of sleep will dull your senses. You've read the manuals, you know exactly how dangerous the game you're playing is. You can't keep doing this, it's stupid. If anything ever happened to you, I'd hate myself and I certainly wouldn't want to go on on my own."

"Okay, okay, you win," he said, smiling.

"Good. We eat and then you sleep. We'll leave at midday, that still gives us a good five hours daylight. I won't take no for an answer," she said, firmly.

John laughed. "What made you so tough?" he asked.

"You did, John Stewart, just you," and she kissed him lovingly on his cheek.

They went downstairs and found a little food in the kitchen, tins of baked beans, peaches and carrots. The tins were out of date and it made a strange meal but it was the first food they had had in days. Afterwards John slept, just as he had promised.

At midday they left the house as planned. Everything was quiet, almost too quiet. They had walked for a couple of hours when they came across a farmhouse with a barn and a garage. John decided it was worth a look, maybe they would be lucky and find something useful.

With Berettas drawn they approached the garage first, both knowing that what they were doing was highly dangerous. The creatures mostly seemed to hide during daylight hours and empty buildings offered them the security they sought. If any of them happened to be hiding in the garage then, as soon as the door was opened, they would attack. This in turn, would bring any others in the area running but the remote chance of finding a car seemed worth the risk. A few miles travelling in relative security was a luxury they had seldom had.

"You stay back," John said. "I'll open the door and jump out of the way, you nail anything that moves. If there are too many of them, then get as far away from here as possible. Don't wait for me. Don't hesitate, just run."

"I won't leave you, John!" Stephanie said stubbornly.

He could tell by the look on her face he would not win the argument.

"Okay. Are you ready?" he asked.

She nodded, both her pistols aimed at the garage door. She was as ready as she always was.

He turned the door's handle slowly, from experience knowing the noise would cause any hiding creatures to react. As the door swung upwards, he dived to his left out of the way, rolled and came up on to his knees poised for action, his Berettas seeking out a target almost independently of him but the garage was empty. Empty apart from the almost antique Landrover Freelander parked within it. A stroke of luck, they held hands for a second but would it run? Luckily the four wheel drive was open but there was no key in sight.

"Can you start it without a key, John?" she asked, half expecting the answer to be no, frightened their stroke of luck would be short lived.

The answer was yes, he could start it, no problem. John checked the fuel tank. There was petrol, not much but enough for a few precious miles. After ripping out the necessary wires, John started the engine. It coughed and spluttered into life. Stephanie beamed, the idea of driving for even a short while was a luxury she had never expected to experience again. With the engine running, John was checking out something on the dashboard.

"What are you doing?" she asked, worried that his antics might kill the battery.

"Checking if the navigation system still works," he said, a smile appearing on his face. "If it does, we might be able to find this damned castle on the map. It might make all the difference."

Understanding straightaway that he was right, Stephanie held her breath. After a few seconds John disconnected the wires he had used to start the vehicle, a disappointed look on his face.

"What's the matter?" she asked.

"It doesn't work," he answered. "Either it's knackered or the satellite system that it requires to function was damaged or destroyed during the war. We're on our own."

She leant over and kissed him on the cheek.

"We do alright on our own anyway," she smiled. "We'll find what we're looking for with or without help. I have faith in you, John Stewart."

He smiled. She always found a way to make him feel better, always had.

"Okay, what about the house?" John asked.

"What do you mean?" Stephanie said.

"Do we cut and run or push our luck? There might be supplies, guns, who knows what in there. Granted there could also be creatures but I don't think so. We go in quick, look around, take anything useful and leave. Ten minutes tops, what do you say?"

"Okay but ten minutes, not a second longer. I want to get as far away from here as possible. In a couple of hours it will get dark. They'll come!" she said, giving in.

The house had been deserted and after a short time they left, having found a shotgun, several cartridges and a small amount of food.

As they drove along the narrow country lanes, it was hard to believe what was happening. They could have been a normal married couple out for a Sunday drive, except they were not married and nobody could consider anything about their situation normal.

After about twenty miles the car ran out of petrol. Taking everything they could comfortably carry they continued on foot.

"It will be dark in about an hour, we need to find a place to rest up," John said.

"Yes, I know but where?" Stephanie asked. "We haven't seen a house or anything suitable for the last hour and out here in the open, our chances aren't exactly good."

"We could try the radio. Maybe there are people out here hiding who can help us or even a village or settlement we can reach in time. What do you think?" John asked, trying to sound optimistic.

"Okay," Stephanie replied. "But hurry. If there's no answer, then we need to get out of here quickly and find some kind of defensible shelter for the night."

John took his pack off and quickly assembled their radio. Because of the amount of fallout after the Third World War, communication had been a problem. Without the help of very powerful radio equipment, it had been almost impossible to set up a communications network. The survivors had eventually mastered the problem but the resulting size of the equipment needed to do so had made it impossible for John and Stephanie to take a reliable radio along with them. The only realistic option had been a short wave radio. This fact naturally limited the range of the signal they could send. John had, from the beginning, understood that this problem could prove deadly for both of them, especially if they found themselves in a desperate situation. The situation now was not desperate but if they could not find shelter for the night it would very quickly become so. He smiled at Stephanie, trying to appear calm and confident that they would be alright, but the look on her face told him she understood exactly what the next few minutes might mean.

"Can anybody hear me? Is anybody receiving this signal? We are travellers in need of shelter. Over."

Only static came back on the radio and Stephanie sighed. It seemed they had pushed their luck with the farmhouse too far. Now when they really needed a break . . .

John tried again.

"Can anybody hear me? Over."

Static . . .

"Forget it, John, there's nobody. Come on, we need to move fast, otherwise . . ." she let it hang.

Suddenly the radio came to life.

"Identify yourselves please. Over."

Startled for a moment, John and Stephanie just stared at each other, the radio speaking again.

"Persons who just radioed for help, please identify yourselves. Over."

"This is John Stewart and my fiancée, Stephanie Jones. We are travelling northwards, trying to find a castle supposedly in this vicinity. I'm afraid we've misjudged daylight hours and run the risk of being caught out in the open. Could do with a bit of help, mate. Over."

The radio stayed silent for what seemed like an eternity but, after a few seconds, crackled into life again.

"Mr Stewart, how do you know about the castle? Over."

John looked at Stephanie and whispered "The castle's real." She smiled and kissed him.

"We've been on the road for months now, just wandering really. About seventy miles from here, back down the country in a southerly direction, we came across a number of soldiers who had been ambushed by the creatures. As we arrived two of the men were still alive and fighting, we went to their aid. We managed to fight off the attacking creatures but only one of the soldiers was still alive at that time, a Sergeant-Major O'Connell. We tried to help him but he was severely injured. Before dying he told us of the castle, where it was approximately located and suggested we'd be safe there. Over."

The radio was again quiet for a few seconds but then it spoke with a new voice.

"This is Major Robert Jones, commanding officer of the castle you're looking for. Can you tell us where you are, we'll try to get to you. Please be as specific about your current location as possible and please hurry. It will be dark in forty-three minutes, I expect you know what that means. Over."

"Major, I'll be as specific as I can be. We found an abandoned farm about twenty five miles back down the country, eight miles north of a small settlement called Churchtown, where we sheltered last night. We liberated a vehicle there and travelled due north. It ran out of fuel about an hour ago. At this moment we are in a wooded area still travelling northwards. Over."

"That could have been the Lewis's farm, they are amongst the survivors here. The son had a four wheel, a Landrover I believe. He's moaned about leaving it behind often enough. Was the vehicle a Landrover? Over."

"Yes, yes it was," John said, excitely. "But as I said, it ran out of petrol a few miles back, we are now on foot. Over."

"That should put you south-east of us, maybe not too far away. We'll try to get to you. I suggest you change direction, head North West, but be advised this area is seriously compromised. There are creatures in significant numbers surrounding us at all times. I won't compromise my men or our situation here. If we have difficulty getting to you then we'll break off the attempt and you're on your own. Is that understood? Over."

"Thanks, Major, we'll start moving towards you. Hope to see you soon. Over and out," he turned to Stephanie. "Come on, we need to move fast."

With John reading his compass and their weapons at the ready, they started off in a north westerly direction just as the Major had suggested.

"Do you think they'll reach us in time?" Stephanie asked, obviously worried.

"They are military, that much is obvious. If we can stay alive long enough, I'd say yes, they'll find us. They must have experience in dealing with these things, otherwise they wouldn't have survived this long. It's down to us, we have to stay alive as long as possible to give them a chance, okay."

"John, if it's a choice between you leaving me and living or us both dying, I want you to go," Stephanie said, seriously.

John stopped, turned and looked at her. He reached out and gently took her by the hand.

"Listen very carefully, I won't leave you. Either we both make it or nobody gets to go, do you understand? If you were killed, then I wouldn't want to go on. God knows how sick I am of running from these things but as long as we're together, it's bearable. We've lived through everything they've thrown at us up to now and we'll get through this. I won't die and I sure as hell won't let you die either. Do you understand?"

She looked into his eyes and noticed a tear running down his cheek.

"God, I love you," was all she could manage to say.

"Come on," he said. "Let's keep moving."

They moved off again, John wondering if the soldiers would reach them in time.

It happened just as it always did. In the forest that was now surrounding them, they could hear the creatures moving through the undergrowth. They had picked up John and Stephanie's scent and were closing in on the couple. A look of panic took over her face, she knew this time everything was different. They had killed the creatures before, plenty of them but they had always been able to control the situation. Out there in the woods they would be attacked on all sides. Who knew how many creatures would be involved. What had the Major said, 'considerable numbers'. What did that mean, tens, hundreds or even thousands? She shivered at the thought.

Suddenly, there was a loud noise and she realised John had already opened fire, his pistols barking, dispersing death towards the creatures now attacking them. She looked in the direction he was shooting and almost screamed. They were moving too fast for her to be sure but there were a lot of these things hunting them. She stopped counting at thirty. She checked behind her, on the other side of the track they were following, creatures were there as well. She opened fire. 'Control, breathe' she kept whispering under her breath. The Beretta in her left hand came up empty. She reloaded, the empty magazine falling to the ground, lost to her. She continued firing. They had learnt how to kill the creatures early on in the beginning of the conflict, wounds to the head area always proving effective at stopping them. She concentrated on that now, aiming for their heads. She had always been a good shot, with any weapon but the speed at which the creatures moved sometimes made accurate shooting difficult. She was firing constantly in an attempt to keep the attackers at bay and could not help wondering how long their supply of ammunition would hold out.

"John, what about ammunition, we haven't got that much?" she shouted out above the noise of battle.

"Don't worry," he shouted back. "Go on the assumption the soldier boys have got plenty. We just need to get through this. Watch it to your left," and he turned and fired.

The creature was only hit in the shoulder with his first shot and kept coming. John's second shot though, a head shot, dropped it.

They were killing creatures on both sides of the track but there were too many and their ammunition supply was already getting low. She heard John unsheathing his Samurai sword; she looked over in his direction. With a pistol in his left hand and his sword in his right, he was holding the attacking creatures at bay. She wondered how much longer they could survive against such odds? She drew her sword. She was also down to her last few magazines and realised they would go quickly.

"I'm out," John shouted.

They both had reserve ammunition in their packs but could not reach it at that moment, it would just be the swords. They had mastered this art of fighting during time spent working in Japan, had gone on to teach the Martial Art during and after the war, mostly to the military. The skill had saved them on numerous occasions but, against this many creatures, Stephanie wondered if it would be enough?

She fired her last shot, a kill, one less of the monsters to worry about but already more were coming, the noise of battle drawing them in. She holstered her pistol, the sword coming alive in her hands. With well practised Katas, she began to eliminate the creatures, John already doing the same but she quickly realised there were too many this time and although her arms were working like pistons, they were losing the fight. More and more of the creatures were appearing out of the darkness, the odds terrifyingly high. Suddenly she stumbled, having missed her step and fell, screaming John's name, as the creatures pounced. She closed her eyes expecting the worst but shots rang out! She searched for the source, the heads of the attacking creatures exploding around her. She looked behind her where John was standing with one of his Berettas again drawn.

"Found a little ammunition," he shouted, shooting again as two more of the monsters lunged at Stephanie. "Are you going to just lie there and let me do all the work?" he shouted, smiling.

She got up and moved towards John who, panting heavily, shouted, "Run for that outcropping over there, at least then our backs are covered."

Without hesitation she started to run, at the same time reaching for her pack. If she could just reach the spare magazines they might stand a chance. As she reached the outcropping she had found eight fully loaded magazines. Quickly reloading her pistols, she turned and started to fire, peeling the creatures off John, giving him the chance to run to her. Already the creatures were massing again for another onslaught.

John was almost to her when he slipped and disappeared from view, her heart almost stopping but then he was up again, blood pouring from a wound to his head. He limped towards her, one of the creatures reaching for him from behind; she shot it just as it was going to strike. Another jumped for him; she nailed it in mid-air. The spare magazines were almost spent, another minute or two and it would be the swords again. John was by her, dazed but okay, still able to fight. He had also found a few more magazines in his pack but in her heart she felt it would not be enough, not this time. As he opened fire, she thought she heard something but was not sure.

At that moment somebody shouted, "Get down!"

She knew better than to hesitate. She dived for cover, dragging John down with her. Suddenly, there was gunfire all around them and explosions, grenades, she thought but not certain. The gunfire was deafening, M-16 fire and heavy.

After what seemed like an age the gunfire stopped. As she looked up she saw the creatures, those still alive at least, withdrawing into the darkness. At that moment three fatigue-clad figures came running up.

"Can you move?" one asked, the others keeping watch.

"Yes, we're okay," she replied.

"We have to go now, they'll be back in minutes once they've re-organised," the soldier said, urgently.

She got up and helped John who was still a little dazed and they followed the men up the trail. As they moved, she noticed at least another four fatigue-clad men, also heavily armed, guarding the way. After about two minutes walking they reached their obvious destination. Helicopters! She could not believe it; she had seen nothing flying for months.

"Get in quickly," ordered the soldier accompanying them.

Already from behind she could hear gunfire, the creatures had regrouped quickly and were again attacking. The three soldiers who were providing the rear guard were already retreating towards the helicopters. As they approached, she wondered how they would manage to board the waiting aircraft. Then, as soon as they stopped firing, the creatures would rush the helicopters and nobody would get away.

As the three soldiers made it into the clearing where the helicopters had landed, the soldier who had done all the talking up to then, shouted "Cover!" The three men dived to the ground as the last ten yards of the forest surrounding the clearing erupted into flames.

A second later the three men were up and running for the helicopters. Fires were raging all around the clearing where they had landed, the take off proving easier than she had anticipated. When they were in the air she looked down, the fires already starting to die back. The creatures were appearing again but, seeing that their prey had escaped, they were disappearing back into the forest.

"You're okay now, miss," the soldier shouted to her over the noise of the helicopter. "How is Mr Stewart doing?"

"I don't know," she replied. "He got a knock on the head during the fight."

"He'll be okay, our Medic will fix him up. You guys were doing okay, you've obviously had a lot of experience fighting these things," the soldier said.

"We've held our own for a long time now," she replied, thoughtfully. "But today was a close call, too close! If you hadn't come along when you did . . ." she paused. "Where are we heading?"

"There," the soldier replied, pointing out of the window.

As she looked, she realised they had found exactly what they had been looking for. Hopefully it would be worth it, for coming into view below them she could see a castle.

Chapter Two - The Castle

As the helicopters touched down in the castle compound, Stephanie realised how enormous the place was. There were vehicles parked everywhere, several of the ones she could see were armoured. There were at least two more helicopters, one of which appeared to be an Apache attack helicopter. Hidden amongst the vehicles in view was at least one huge tank and a couple of fuel tankers.

Upon landing the soldiers vacated the helicopters, medics approaching to treat any wounded. John, being the only person injured, was examined quickly and then carried off on a stretcher, she presumed to hospital. She wanted to go with him but her attention was drawn to the friendly soldier who had done all the talking during their short flight. He was apparently making some kind of a report to an officer. After giving a short salute, he disappeared into the main building of the castle, the officer then walked over to where Stephanie was standing.

"Miss Jones, I'm pleased you and Mister Stewart made it. My name is Major Robert Jones," he said smiling. "I'm the commanding officer here."

"Major Jones," she began. "Thank you for rescuing us. If your men hadn't arrived when they did, then . . ." she paused, again realising just how close they had been to being killed.

"We can talk later. I dare say you are worried about Mr. Stewart's condition," he said. Calling over a nearby soldier, he continued, "The Corporal will escort you to the med. tent. Please give Mister Stewart my compliments. We'll continue our conversation in the morning, when he's recovered."

"Thank you, Major," she replied and followed the waiting soldier.

As she entered the medical facility, she could see John sitting up and talking to a doctor. His face lit up with a smile as he saw her walk in.

"How are you feeling?" she asked, showing her concern.

"I'm fine, no concussion, nothing. It just dazed me for a minute. You saved me again, didn't you?" he asked, smirking.

"They saved us both! I've never seen so many creatures working together. What do you think is going on?" she asked.

"It's this place and the people hiding in it. I should have known better than to bring you here," he answered.

"Why? I've seen some of the equipment they have. They are well armed, they have helicopters, armoured vehicles and, as we touched down, I saw considerable numbers of soldiers. It has to be one of the biggest military units left in the country. The castle itself is massive! We are a lot safer in here than out there on our own."

"You're probably right but those facts will keep the creatures very interested in trying to get in the place. The people here will never be allowed to leave. That probably means we can't either."

"What do you mean?" she asked.

"There'll be enough of 'them' to make sure we can never get out and there'll be more coming every day. You're right, this place is without doubt, one of the last strongholds in the country. That fact alone will make the place irresistible to the creatures. It will attract them like a magnet attracts iron filings. Hey, don't worry about it, we are safe for now. We'll find out more in the morning. This will be the first good night's sleep we've both had for ages. The doctor said I've got to stay here tonight for observation but I'm sure he'll allow you to join me in the next bed. Tomorrow we'll go and see the guy in charge."

With that they had slept long and sound, both of them having been exhausted.

After they had woken they were amazed to find they could shower and were even more impressed when one of the nurses brought them both breakfast. Feeling almost human again, they walked out into the castle grounds and were approached by the soldier that had led the rescue mission the night before.

"Major Jones's compliments, would you please join him in his office for debriefing."

"Certainly, Sergeant Major," John replied, noticing the soldier's rank.

"No need for that, Sir. My name's Mark, Mark Roberts to be exact. Me and the boys were very impressed with the way you handled yourselves on the outside last night."

"Thanks, Mark," John replied. "But I'm pretty certain if you hadn't come along when you did, we'd have wound up as a snack for those things. What's your situation here?"

"It's better you speak to the Major, we can talk afterwards. If you'd follow me, please," and he led them to the Major's office.

After knocking, they followed Mark in and found the commanding officer sitting at his desk, going over a report of the rescue mission.

"Major Jones, we spoke shortly on the radio yesterday, my name is John Stewart. Stephanie, I believe, you met last night. Thanks for the cavalry, I realise it was dangerous for the men you sent out. I'd like to thank them all if that's possible."

"Certainly, John, the men will be eager to talk to you as well. We've had no contact with the outside world for some time now. Any news on the war will be welcomed."

"The news isn't good, Major, we are losing! The creatures seem to be getting stronger, while we are definitely getting weaker. Looking at some of your hardware here, I'd say yours was one of the strongest military units left on the face of the planet. You might make a difference out there, the forces that are still fighting could definitely use your help."

"John, we have two operational helicopters, three armoured personnel carriers, six sixteen toners, a handful of jeeps and a bridge repair crane. At the moment, we have fuel enough to be able to keep small operations going. Other equipment you might have seen here is, at this time, non-functional. I have one hundred and sixteen fully fit soldiers and a medical unit consisting of three doctors and six nurses. I also have two hundred and thirteen civilians, villagers, farmers and locals. Some we picked up on the way here, some were already here when we arrived. Even if we wanted to leave, we haven't enough transport for everyone. I can't expect these people to walk, not with those monsters out there. So you see John, we are stuck here, just like you are now. Finding enough food to keep everybody fed is difficult enough, finding a way for everybody to leave here safely just isn't feasible. Taking my men out of here and leaving everybody else behind, is something I won't even consider. I'm afraid our contribution to the war effort is over. We did our bit."

"I apologise, Major, I didn't mean to imply anything. I had no idea of the situation here. Up to now we have only seen military personnel."

"The civilians stay indoors at night, for obvious security reasons, no doubt you'll meet some of them today. Now, have you heard any information about how the war's progressing in other countries?"

"Not really," John replied. "We've just been trying to stay alive. The last news on the war from abroad was months ago. France was basically lost, Germany as well. From the smaller countries nothing has been heard for months. Russia, America and China were still fighting but struggling. More and more of the creatures appear every day, the odds are greatly stacked in their favour. In America they apparently managed to catch a couple of the creatures. They wanted to know more about them, feeding needs, how their camouflage works, how we could better combat them but, before they could even begin, the things killed themselves somehow. They learnt nothing! We are fighting a war against an enemy we know practically nothing about. I'm sorry, Major, we can't help you that much, we could barely help ourselves out there."

"From what I've been told, John, that's not exactly true. What about your journey up the country? Did you travel through any towns or cities that hadn't been destroyed or looted? Any information along those lines could be of great help to us. Please take your time and think carefully."

Stephanie spoke for the first time since entering the Major's office.

"John, the town where we found the soldiers, the ones that told us about the castle. It was deserted but basically intact. If I remember correctly, we passed a huge looking precinct and at least two smaller supermarkets. They all appeared to be untouched."

"You're right," John agreed. "Major, that was a town about seventy miles away, almost due south of here. I can't remember its name but it looked as if it had been evacuated early on. No looters had been there at the time we passed through but that is almost a week ago. The situation could be different now."

Looking on a small hand drawn map of the general area, the Major suggested the town in question could have been Hadlee, a large trading centre built shortly after the end of the war. John said he was not sure but after checking on the small map, agreed it was the only town in the area big enough.

"Why is it important for you to know that, Major?" John asked, puzzled.

"Food, John. Quite simple really. I need to find food for three hundred and thirty nine people every day. In fact, now with your arrival, it's three hundred and forty one. As you will appreciate, we can't just wander around outside the castle walls. That gives us limited space in here to grow our own food. We have a small garden and do produce, quite successfully, a small amount of fresh vegetables but nothing like the quantities we actually need.

We have only one option open to us; every so many weeks we have to go on a food raid. We have enough supplies at the moment for the next week, maybe ten days but then we'll have to go shopping again. Surrounding towns have already been visited and stripped of everything we can use. The longer we stay here, the further we have to travel from the castle to find what we need. Your town could give us the opportunity to re-supply for a longer time. The only hiccup, it's a long way away. Any problems that crop up have to be dealt with by the raiding team. Because we only have two operational helicopters at the moment, the number of personnel we can send is limited. Even transporting the supplies back to the castle, once they're secured, isn't as straight forward as one might imagine. All told, it's complicated and very dangerous for my men."

"I can appreciate that, Major. Why don't you send the helicopters, enough firepower and scout the area first?" John suggested. "It would limit the danger and maybe forewarn of any unexpected problems."

"The tactic's sound, John. Have you got a military background?" the Major asked, suddenly very interested.

"Yes," replied John. "Both of us have. We have been involved a lot with the military, usually as instructors but sometimes as operatives. The last few years, up until we left, we were mainly with Special Services, working as martial arts instructors and weapons specialists, specialising in edged weapons. Since we've been on the road, that particular skill has saved us on numerous occasions."

"Yes, I noticed the swords, John," replied the Major. "Very interesting. This castle, being as big as it is, had a small museum before the war and a considerable collection of edged weapons. The museum area has been turned into sleeping quarters now but the weapons are still here, stored in the castle's cellars. Maybe you would both like to examine them, in fact come on, we'll talk more later. Let me give you a guided tour of my castle."

With that the Major led the way out into the courtyard.

"These are some of the vehicles we came here with. Over there we have two fuel tankers, so for the moment at least fuel is not a problem."

"What about ammunition?" Stephanie asked.

"When we decided to head up here from our base, we spent weeks flying up equipment. During that time the castle was manned by a small complement of my best men and sealed from the outside. We were constantly flying in supplies, so it was important the place was secure. Survivors started arriving soon after that, they were obviously allowed to enter but my men did a good job of keeping any creatures out. When we finally got here we also brought a small convoy of supplies and equipment with us, so from the point of ammunition and explosives we have more than enough. Feel free to take what you need to re-supply. We have installed generators, so power's not a problem, at least as long as we have fuel. We've installed pumps and filter systems, meaning we can use the castle's underground springs, so water isn't an immediate problem. We had stored tons of food, but we didn't reckon with so many civilians being picked up on the way here. It went quicker than expected, now it's our only problem."

"Impressive, Major," John remarked. "How many of these creatures are now in the area? Up until last night, we'd never seen so many grouped together."

"We don't know exactly. We used to send out reconnaissance patrols but they came under attack more and more. We lost quite a few good men in the early days of being here. The only reconnaissance performed now is with the helicopters but we don't bother that often. I know more and more creatures arrive every day; we seem to attract them but as long as they can't get in here, it doesn't really matter."

"How can you be sure they can't get in here, Major? We've found they can solve problems quite successfully. I'd be worried they were trying to find a way in. Old castle's have secret tunnels, who knows?"

"John, please call me Robert. I play down the rank situation nowadays, there doesn't seem to be much point. Let me show you why they can't get in here," and he led the way up on to the old battlements.

On the top, Robert showed John and Stephanie the layout of the castle.

"First," he started, "we have cleared the ground for two hundred yards all around the walls; that gives us a good killing zone. On every wall, at all times, we have snipers positioned. They are excellent marksmen so nothing approaches the wall. We have a moat around the entire castle, it is twenty five feet deep and forty feet wide. Tunnelling underneath it would require machinery, which they don't possess, so they aren't getting in that way any time soon. We have a drawbridge and a working portcullis but, just in case, we have added inner doors. They are made from wood reinforced with steel and are over one foot thick. These are barred at all times. As to tunnels and the like, the soldiers who originally took the place over checked it with ultrasonic, radar, in fact everything we've got. They found one secret passage leading down under the moat, with an exit coming out in a cave system to the north of the castle. It must have taken years to dig. The exit is hidden, difficult to find. We have modified the tunnel by building, every thirty yards or so, steel doors into the walls. The passageways between the doors are monitored by cameras at all times. Altogether there are ten sections built into the tunnel, the last five of which are fitted with robot sentries. They are something we brought with us, left over from the war. They have one thousand rounds of armour piercing ammunition each, are censor controlled reacting to movement. They are battery powered and work independently of us. They'll kill anything that's moving through the tunnel. As extra insurance, we've planted explosives in the section of the tunnel running under the moat. They can be detonated using remote control if at any time the tunnel defences fail and creatures are moving through. The sender is always in the control room where the monitoring equipment is installed, the soldier in charge there is under standing orders to blow the tunnel if the need arises. One second after the explosives are detonated, the tunnel will be filled with water, drowning everything in it. The door at the castle end of the tunnel is solid steel, two feet thick and built into the castle walls. It can easily withstand the water pressure after the moat is blown, so there's little or no danger to us. We thought about blowing it when we found it but decided having a second exit could prove useful at a later date. I think you'll agree, John, we're perfectly safe here."

"Impressive, very impressive," John stated. "They can't get in but it seems we can't get out. It's stalemate. Don't get me wrong, Robert, we are very grateful that you rescued us yesterday but I can't help wondering how our lives will be locked in this prison, because, whether we like it or not, that's what it will become."

"What do you suggest, John?" the Major asked, seeming a little annoyed by the statement.

"I don't know, I just don't know," John replied.

Chapter Three - Settling In

The Major left them standing out on top of the castle battlements. Stephanie turned to face John.

"What are we going to do?" she asked.

"We are going to enjoy a few days of sleeping, without having to keep one eye open. We are going to eat regularly, without having to wonder where the food is coming from, at least for a while. We are going to make love," he said, his eyes sparkling, "all night! Then we'll see. We need to re-supply anyway, ammunition at least, before we decide anything. Whether we stay here or try to leave, is a question I can't answer at the moment. We could stay here forever but I'm not sure we'd be happy. I don't think the decision will be ours to make, the food situation will eventually dictate the way this plays out. Eventually we'll all have to leave, either that or starve! It might be months or even years from now but at some stage we'll have to travel too far to find the necessary supplies. At that point, there will be no other option available to us but to leave. The only trouble is, by then, they'll be so many of these creatures gathered outside the castle walls, leaving might not be possible."

"I'll stay here with you, John. I'll leave with you, if that's what you decide but we can't run forever. At some stage we will have to find another alternative. I don't know what but, if we give it a little time, maybe an answer will come to us," she suggested.

"Time is something we're going to have a lot of, at least for now," John said, smiling.

He leant over and kissed her on the mouth.

"What do you say? Let's see if we can get a room in this motel."

After finding a room, they made love, showered and then made love again. Afterwards they both slept deeply. It was the first chance in months for them both to completely relax and sleep, without the risk of being discovered and attacked. As John awoke, it was four o'clock in the afternoon. He showered again, enjoying the novelty. It had been weeks since his last shower and that had been cold water. The opportunity to wash under warm water was a luxury he could not refuse. After dressing he left Stephanie still sleeping, confident he could leave her without worrying for the first time in months. He went outside to get some air and have a look around the compound, the castle and its inhabitants intriguing him. After only a few minutes, he bumped into the Sergeant Major who had led the rescue team the night before.

"How are you feeling, John?" Mark asked.

"Fine thanks," John replied. "Have you got time for that chat now?"

"Time is one thing we've all got plenty of, John. There's never a great deal to do here. How do you fancy a coffee?"

"Love one. Lead the way," John said.

"We'll see if the canteen staff are in a good mood today," Mark smiled. "That usually dictates the flavour of the coffee," he laughed.

After fetching two cups of the normal looking coffee they sat down together.

"Well, what do you think of our little set up?" Mark asked.

"I don't know enough to be able to comment. You certainly seem organised enough. Stephanie was impressed with the way you and your men handled yourselves last night. One thing worries me though . . ." John said.

"What's that? Your fiancée's attraction to me!" Mark interrupted.

"Not exactly," John smiled. "I'm wondering how long we are going to stay here. The longer we stay here, the more creatures are going to gather outside the walls. If at any stage we were forced to leave, it might prove to be impossible to break through their lines."

Mark considered John's question for a second, before telling him about the soldiers that he and Stephanie had tried to help in Hadlee. The Sergeant who had told them about the castle before dying, had been a good friend of Mark's. He had also expressed concerns about their future locked inside the fortress. He and a group of his friends could not stand the thought of being prisoners for the rest of their lives so they had asked for permission to leave. The Major had allowed it, had even flown them out of the immediate area by helicopter. Twelve soldiers had gone in total, all of them heavily armed. They had wanted to know what it was like, out beyond the castle walls. The castle occupants had heard from other survivors how bad things were supposed to have become, the soldiers wanted to know for definite. If possible, they wanted to return and let the Major know the real story. It had been a massive disappointment to everyone in the castle to hear that they were dead. Mark explained that with everybody locked in the castle twenty four hours a day, under no real threat, it was easy to forget how desperate their situation was really becoming. The news about the soldiers' demise had spread through the castle's population like wildfire. It had brought home the truth. Up until that point, many of the castle's occupants, soldiers and civilians alike, had expressed an interest in leaving. Since the sad news of the deaths of the soldiers had spread, a lot of the civilians who were unhappy with their situation, had resigned themselves to the fact they would probably never be able to leave.

John explained in detail what he and Stephanie had witnessed out on the road since beginning their travels. He suggested that whatever horrors the people in the castle had heard or imagined were, in fact, more than likely true. He went even further, explaining that even if they managed to break the siege, a large number of people travelling across country would be an irresistible target for the creatures. It would be a running gun battle that, without adequate transport, would result in extremely high casualties.

Mark agreed but added that certain units from the garrison stationed there were still willing to try. The civilians were frightened but he was sure, given a realistic chance, that most of them could be persuaded to consider another option.

After talking for an hour they both agreed that without the right plan and enough transportation, an attempt to leave at that time would prove as fatal to them as it had to the soldiers who had already died in Hadlee.

Other personnel had joined them in the meantime, the conversation becoming a little more relaxed. Many of the men asking John about what he had done before the war, his training and his martial art skills. Theories about the creatures' origins were also hotly debated, ranging from the sublime to the ridiculous. Time passed but slowly. Although John enjoyed the debating, sometimes even laughing out loud, a thing he rarely did, he could not imagine living that kind of life for years or even decades. He was sure it would drive him quite mad.

At that moment Stephanie walked in, looking totally refreshed and beautiful. Some of the soldiers sitting around the table moved to make room for her. She had barely introduced herself when an alarm bell started to ring. The soldiers sitting around in the canteen sprang into action. They were grabbing weapons and heading outside.

"What's happening, Mark?" John asked, standing up.

"It's dark," he answered. "The creatures are coming out of the tree line. Usually nothing happens but we like to let them know we're still here. Breaks the monotony."

Mark led them outside and up on to the castle battlements. As they reached the top, John spotted Major Jones on the wall.

"What's the story, Major?" he asked.

"Take a look," the Major replied, handing John a pair of night vision binoculars.

Looking through them he could see the reason for the excitement. There were creatures surrounding the entire castle, hundreds of them! He realised there were probably hundreds more hidden, maybe thousands. The sight of so many gathered together was scary and it proved to him how desperate their situation really was. Outside the castle walls they would be dead within minutes. Now he understood Major Jones's decision to stay put, anything else would be crazy.

One or two of the soldiers opened fire, Sergeants shouting orders to cease fire immediately. John looked at Major Jones, a puzzled look on his face.

"Unless they approach the castle walls, John, we don't open fire anymore. We let the snipers practice now and then but otherwise it's basically a waste of ammunition, they can't get in," Major Jones explained. "When we first occupied the castle we killed anything that moved out there, in the meantime I consider it unnecessary."

"Major," John said. "I've been talking with some of your men and it would seem many of them would still be interested in trying to leave here. Some civilians also. Would you be prepared to consider our options?"

"In my office, please," the Major replied abruptly and walked off, John and Stephanie following.

As they sat down, Major Jones closed the door behind them. He sat at his desk and stared at the couple.

"With all due respect, John, Stephanie, what I don't need here is a pair of troublemakers. I can understand my men unloading on you, they've been here a long time. I fully accept that some of them are unhappy with our situation. I'll go even further and say that if we'd have known beforehand that coming here would be the equivalent of a life sentence for all of us, we probably would have reconsidered. Unfortunately, we didn't know and the rest is history. Whether my men believe it or not and frankly I don't give a shit either way, I have considered trying to leave here many times. As I explained to you this morning I am not prepared to

32

leave anybody behind. Now, until somebody comes up with a realistic way of transporting everybody safely away from here, we are stuck. Don't misunderstand me, I hate it as much as the next man but I am responsible for the lives of every man, woman and child living here. I take my responsibilities very seriously, John, you should remember that. The twelve soldiers you came across in Hadlee were my men, my responsibility. I let them go with the hope they could bring back information that might enable the rest of us to leave. Now they are dead and God knows how much they suffered before they died! I will not risk another life without knowing our situation warrants it, or we have a damn good chance of succeeding. Do I make myself clear?"

"My apologise, Robert. I can see now I've misjudged the situation. I thought everything here was stagnating but after what you've just said and what we witnessed outside the walls tonight, I realise you are absolutely correct in your assessment," John replied, humbly.

"When you were both serving in the military, what ranks did you have?" Robert asked, his tone friendlier.

"We were both Captains," John answered.

"Good. Apart from me you both have the highest rank here. I would appreciate your help in any matters concerning the safety and well-being of the castle's population. However, I must insist we follow the normal chain of command. I might play down the rank situation but I am in command nevertheless. Anything on your mind, you come to me first, we will discuss it and find an answer between us. I know the enlisted men here are desperate to do something but talking about impossible escape plans will not help their situation or ease their suffering. It only makes it worse. We have had enough trouble with the rumour wagon running wild in the past. I would like to avoid such incidents if it's at all possible," Robert said.

"We'll be pleased to help where we can, Robert," Stephanie said.

"I'm not sure we're the right people for the job," John added, his days of responsibility for others, apart from Stephanie, well and truly over as far as he was concerned.

"With your experiences on the outside and your backgrounds, I'm sure you are," Robert said. "Now, I think we've all had enough excitement for today. We'll have plenty of time to talk more over the coming days and weeks. I don't know about you but I'm starving. I believe the cooks have excelled themselves again and have concocted some kind of dumpling stew for this evening. Personally, I can't wait. Would you both care to join me?"

"Certainly, Robert. It sounds interesting," John said smiling.

"Oh it will be that, I can assure you," Robert laughed.

They walked to the canteen and ate together, the meal proving to be quite edible, the mood at dinner relaxed and enjoyable. Afterwards John and Stephanie went back to their room and made love again, this another one of their new-found luxuries John could not get enough of. Spent and exhausted they had eventually fallen asleep in each others' arms.

This time the dream was different. They were still fighting against high odds but no longer alone. Surrounding them were also numbers of soldiers locked in combat with the creatures. She even recognised one of them, it was Mark, the Sergeant who had befriended them. He was wounded but still in the thick of things. They were all in some kind of a building she did not recognise but in the confined space the noise of the gunfire all around was deafening. She awoke, sweating. John was still asleep. She leant over and kissed him gently on his cheek. He murmured but slept on. She showered again, the luxury she had also never expected to be able to enjoy again. Mark had explained that everything was powered by the generators. Electricity and running water again an everyday thing, showing how adaptable the soldiers had become. The engineering skills needed to accomplish this feat something normal military personnel were not capable of. She dressed and decided to go exploring, leaving John to sleep. She left their room and noticed straightaway there were people milling around all over the place. This time there were not just soldiers but civilians as well. Three children in particular caught her attention. They were staring at her, obviously wondering who she was. She smiled at them, one of them smiling back. The other two seemed a little unsure of the stranger who was confronting them.

"Hello," Stephanie said, quietly. "What are your names?"

The biggest boy, seemingly the bravest of the bunch, spoke first.

"I'm Billy, this is John and that's Sarah," he said, pointing to the other children in turn.

"My name's Stephanie. What are you doing?" she asked.

"We're going outside to play," the boy called John said. "Hide and seek. Do you want to play with us?" he asked, hopefully.

"Maybe later," she said. "I have to go somewhere now but you play nicely and be careful."

They smiled at her and ran off laughing.

She could also understand Robert now. How could anybody risk the lives of such adorable children, so innocent and trusting.

She walked to the canteen and was sat drinking her second cup of coffee as John joined her. She told him of her chance meeting with the children. She desperately wanted children of her own but accepted that bringing children into the world, as it currently was, would be irresponsible. Helping to protect those that were already there would go someway to making up for her not having any of her own. John promised her they would do whatever was necessary to ensure the safety of everybody living in the castle, especially the children. Whether he liked it or not they were, as of that moment, part of the castle's community and he knew their fate would be linked with the fate of everybody living there.

Chapter Four - Food Raid

The next several days passed quietly, everybody was relaxed and happy. The creatures did not cause them any problems and everybody fell into a lazy routine of filling their days any way they could. John and Stephanie spent hours talking and getting to know more of the castle's population.

After a week where it was easy to forget they were at war, fighting for the right to exist, John was called into the Major's office. Once there, Robert explained that their food supplies were starting to run low and it was time to start thinking about re-supplying. He knew for a fact that the surrounding towns had already been stripped, so they had no choice but to go further afield. He had the town of Hadlee in mind. When John and Stephanie had passed through the town, the place had seemed intact. He hoped the necessary supplies would be there waiting for them. The only question now was how to acquire them with minimum risk to the forces involved. John asked how past raids had been conducted. Robert explained that the raids conducted up to that point had always been in small towns that were basically deserted, the few creatures appearing, easily dealt with by his men. The missions had gone so well that they had never suffered a single casualty. One helicopter had landed, the other keeping watch on the surrounding area from the air. Once the men in the raiding party had secured the supplies, both helicopters had flown them back to the castle. The big problem with Hadlee was its size. They had not attempted a raid in anything much bigger than a village. In comparison Hadlee was a city. That would probably mean many more creatures were in the area, maybe too many for their men to handle safely. By the time this fact was established, it might already be too late for the men on the ground.

John had agreed with Robert's assessment and suggested, again, a reconnaissance mission was the right way to deal with the problem. Fuel was apparently plentiful at that moment, at least, so they had nothing to lose by flying over and checking out the town before committing ground forces. The town was seventy miles away, easily reachable by helicopters in about twenty minutes. John suggested both helicopters take part as usual, both carrying an eight-man team. The men should all be heavily armed and prepared for every contingency. If everything checked out from the air then one helicopter should land. The men on board would scout the area further from the ground, the other helicopter and team acting as back up in case of difficulty. Robert found the plan excellent and asked John if he would be interested in leading the mission, John accepting straightaway.

"Pick your teams yourself, John. You've been here a week now and have got to know quite a few of the lads. I'll trust your judgement. Take any weapons or explosives you think you might need to get the job done. It's too late today; I suggest you go tomorrow at first light, then at least you won't have any problems with daylight."

"I'll take Sergeant Major Roberts, if that's okay? He's got a cool head, he proved that the night he rescued us in the forest. He can help me pick the rest of my team. I'd like Stephanie to come along in the second helicopter, she'll pick her own team. Our first objective will be intelligence. If the place doesn't look too hot then we'll land and try to bring back some supplies with us but we'll basically be in and out. It could well be we have to return with a stronger force. I'll take no risks, Robert, you have to understand that," John said.

"I wouldn't have it any other way," Robert agreed.

"We'll leave at first light then. If you'll excuse me, I have to find Mark and get my team together," John said, standing up.

"John," Robert said. "No heroics, I want you all back here in one piece."

"Hey, I've still got to talk to Stephanie. She might not let me go!" he laughed. "Don't worry, Robert, we'll be careful."

As he walked back to their room he smiled to himself. At last he had the opportunity to test his theory. The week in the castle with Stephanie had been wonderful but he had gradually realised he could not live like a caged animal forever. He had not voiced his feelings to her on the subject, because she had been so happy playing with the children, her life suddenly normal again but, if everything worked out in Hadlee as he hoped, he would have to. If it did not, then at least he had the opportunity to see action again. As every soldier knew, the everyday stress and adrenaline rush that they experienced during battle was something it was hard to forget. The excitement of battling the creatures was unfortunately something he felt he needed, at least every now and then. The idea of sitting in the castle and vegetating for the next thirty or forty years was something his mind rejected. He would find a way for them to escape the confines, he had to.

After finding her, he told her of the mission planned for the following morning. She had reacted well and was happy for him to take part in it, as long as she was there to watch his back. She had left him in the shower, wanting to pick and organise her team straightaway. John had sent for Mark and, just as he finished dressing, there was a knock at his door.

"Come in," he shouted.

"What's up, mate?" Mark asked, walking in.

"We're going to Hadlee, have a look around. Nothing too grand, maybe pick up a few supplies if we get the chance. I've had an idea for a day or two but it involves going back to Hadlee to check on a few things. Without knowing it, Robert's given me the opportunity to do just that," John said.

After he had explained the mission in more detail, Mark left to select and organise the rest of their team. In the meantime, Stephanie returned, her team already picked. She had also organised the helicopters, they would be fuelled and ready to leave at 0700 hours the following morning. It seemed that his fears of Stephanie reacting badly to their involvement in the forthcoming mission were totally unfounded, she was really getting into it. She also told him that the soldiers she had picked for her team were buzzing with anticipation at the thought of long-awaited combat. She had left them happily preparing for the following morning's mission.

They both cleaned and checked their weapons. They had already restocked their supply of ammunition but decided it was wise to take along more with them the following day, just in case. John did not want to get down to swordplay again, if he could help it. They went through the details of the plan one more time together before retiring for the night. Needing to be fresh for the morning, it seemed appropriate to get a good night's sleep. She had drifted off quickly, as usual but John could not sleep. He lay awake thinking about his idea. She knew nothing of his plan, he felt it better to keep it that way until they got back. Once he knew for sure that what he had in mind was feasible, he would tell her. In a few hours he would know and if it was possible then... He slept.

At 0700 hours the two teams were gathered by the waiting helicopters. John was feeling a little nervous. It had been a long time since he had commanded a mission of any sort. He looked at the men he would be leading. They were ready, he felt confident of that much. He felt sure that, once they were in the area, his nerves would disappear. He hadn't wanted to lead men again but his interest in what was in the town and the possibility of escaping their confines dictated that he do so again, if only for a short time.

Robert was there to see them off.

"John, remember, no unnecessary risks, bring your teams back."

Giving Robert a playful salute, he turned to Stephanie and kissed her. He pointed to the headsets they were all now wearing.

"See you later. Stay in touch and watch my back."

She nodded and replied, "Always."

They boarded the helicopters and, after giving Robert a final wave, took off heading due south.

Flying over the countryside, everything looked just as it always had, there was no evidence of the danger lurking there. John wondered if there would ever be a time again when children could play amongst the trees and run in the meadows, without having armed guards watching over them.

"Can you hear me, John? Over."

"Yes, Stephanie, I can hear you loud and clear. What's up? Missing me already? Over," he replied, smiling.

"We'll be there in a few minutes. Promise me you'll be careful. I need you. Over."

"I'll be careful. You just watch our backs and be there if we need you. Over."

"We'll be right there the whole time, you needn't worry about that. See you later. Over and out."

Minutes later they were flying over Hadlee. The town appeared deserted.

"Pilot, fly once over the town and then circle over the precinct," John said using his headset.

"Roger that," the pilot replied confidently.

With the second helicopter shadowing their every move, they inspected the area from the air, looking for signs of creatures or anything else that might present a threat to them. They saw nothing.

"What do you think?" John asked Mark, as they were hovering over the precinct. "Everything looks quiet enough."

"I don't like it, John," Mark stated. "The building is too big. Without power it will be dark inside, any number of creatures could be hiding in there. There's not enough of us to safely contain a building of that size. If we ever want to attempt it, we'll need more firepower."

John agreed and told the pilot to fly over the two smaller supermarkets to the east of the massive precinct. They were about three hundred yards apart and both looked to be untouched. The building to the left was slightly smaller but both had flat roofs that, at first sight, looked solid enough for a helicopter to be able to land. John decided the building to the right, the bigger of the two, was their target. He asked the pilot if landing on the roof would be feasible? The pilot, not having any way of knowing for certain, suggested they try it. John spoke to his men.

"Okay, listen up. We are going to attempt to land on the roof of the building to the right. When we are safely down, everybody out and form a perimeter around the rooftop. Clear?"

Seven voices replied as one, they understood.

"Did you copy that, Stephanie? Over," John said.

"Copied you, John. We'll stay above and keep the surrounding area under observation. Shout if you need us. Good luck. Over and out."

"Pilot," John said, his voice filled with anticipation. "Land."

The helicopter settled slowly on the roof of the supermarket and for a second everybody held their breath but the pilot reported no apparent problems. The roof had proven to be strong enough.

"Okay, let's go," John shouted.

Both doors slid open, his team exiting the helicopter and taking up positions around the roof. It was obvious from the fluidity of their movements that they had done this before and, to anybody watching, it would have looked impressive and formidable. Once the roof was secured, they found an entry point into the building below them. It was a skylight with a ladder leading down into some kind of a storeroom. John suggested it was probably a means for the staff to perform maintenance on the roof area.

"You and you," John said, pointing to two of his men. "Stay here and guard the helicopter. If anything other than us comes back up, then take off. Don't wait for us. Is that clear?"

Both men nodded and took up positions around the helicopter.

"The rest of us are going down that ladder. There won't be a lot of room in there, so stay calm, okay? Any creatures we meet, take them out quickly. Remember, aim for their heads. If there are too many of them, then get out as best you can. If it's possible, we will secure the building, then get all the food supplies we can up on to the roof. We can divide the load between the two helicopters, so get plenty. Concentrate just on tinned goods, everything else will be useless to us. Understood?" he asked.

His men all nodded.

"Mark, open the skylight. Let's go."

The skylight was quickly opened and they climbed down into, what they then realised, was really a storeroom full of everything they needed. Tinned soups, tinned vegetables, tinned meats, in fact everything they had hoped to find. In that one room there was more than they could carry, even with the two helicopters.

"Alright," John said. "Three of you stay here and start taking the stuff up on to the roof. Get the helicopter's cargo net unloaded and ready for transport. The rest of us are going downstairs to have a look around. Barricade this door behind us but don't panic if you hear shooting. We'll be using the headsets, if I say get out then don't hesitate. Take what you've already got and leave. Don't worry about us. Okay, let's do this. Mark, you're with me, pick one more."

Berettas drawn, John opened the door that led out of the storeroom and edged into the small corridor that appeared to lead to the shop floor. On both sides of the corridor were several doors, all closed.

"Leave the doors closed. If one of them even starts to open, then nail whatever is coming out of it," he said.

With that he started along the corridor, ready for anything. At the end of it there was a stairwell, two flights of stairs leading down, he assumed, into the store itself. He stopped and listened. There was nothing.

"Get ready. I'm going to fire a couple of shots. Any creatures hiding in here will come running. We can deal with them here easier than in the store itself. If there are too many, we back out quickly and make a run for it."

He heard the answering noise of rifle safeties being disengaged. He fired three shots in quick succession, then he waited. For a few seconds nothing happened, then it came. He could hear creatures moving through the store, but could not tell how many. The three men edged back from the stairwell. However many creatures were coming they were coming fast. John risked a quick glance down the two flights of stairs and spotted six of the monsters rushing up to greet them. He opened fire. Mark and the other soldier were already firing from behind him. The noise, although almost deafening, only lasted for a few seconds. As suddenly as it had started, it stopped again. The original six creatures were already dead but, as he checked, he could see another ten, at least, still coming. He continued firing, his two companions doing the same. After thirty seconds or so all firing stopped. All of the attacking creatures were down, apparently dead. He reloaded his two automatics and waited.

"What do you think, John?" Mark asked.

"I think we're lucky these things just react on instinct. God help us if they ever get organised. I think we got them all."

Using his headset, he informed the rest of his team that they were alright and the creatures in the store had been dealt with. The three men proceeded down the stairwell, stopping now and then to listen, just in case.

"We have to shut and lock the front doors. Mark, go and find the office, check for any keys. Be bloody careful, any trouble shout. We'll come a-running."

Along with the other soldier, a corporal called Ian, John walked slowly through the store to the front doors. To his relief they were already closed and, even better, the security gates were down and locked in place. That meant the creatures had found another way into the building, probably the back door. As Mark returned having found the office and a key chain containing several keys, they headed back through the store towards the rear entrance. It was open, just as John had suspected. Looking out of the back door, they could see the entire rear car park was surrounded by a high steel fence. The only way in to the area was through the open gates.

"If we could lock those gates, this place would be pretty secure. To get inside the supermarket itself, the creatures would have to break a window or something. That should be easy enough to spot from the air. The next time we need to go shopping, it will be a lot easier to check whether any company is waiting for us. What do you think?" John asked.

"Good idea. Even better, the place has an alarm system fitted. It can run off battery power for weeks. I'm pretty sure it will still work, if not, then we'll rig it. That way we wouldn't even need to land, we could see the alarm lights flashing on the exterior of the building if anything had broken in. We'd know straightaway."

"Perfect, mate, well done. All we need now are the keys to the backdoor and the gates. How many keys have we got?" John asked.

"Fourteen," Mark answered, having quickly counted them.

"We find the backdoor key first," John suggested. "Then we can concentrate on the gates."

It did not take long to find the key that locked the backdoor. Taking it off the chain, they left it in the lock. Now all they needed was the key to the gates.

"Wait a second," John said. "Stephanie, can you hear me? Over."

"Yes, John, I can hear you. What's the problem? Over."

"No problem but do me a favour. Fly over the area surrounding the car park at the back of the store. See if anything is moving towards us. Over."

"On our way, give us a second. Over," she replied.

After only a short time she reported everything looked quiet, there were no creatures in sight.

"Okay, guys," John said. "Let's go. Mark, you find the key. We'll cover you."

John went to the left, Ian to the right, Mark straight up the middle. In less than two minutes the gates were locked and they were safely back in the store.

"Let's go shopping," John said. "Mark, get a couple of guys down here from upstairs, they can help us carry the stuff."

He heard Mark over the headset, one minute later the soldiers Mark had sent for appeared. As the supplies were being carried back up to the waiting helicopters, John was talking to Mark about the store.

"Now it's reasonably secure, we can come back anytime and take more," Mark said.

"Did you see the trucks parked out back?" John asked, deep in thought.

"Yes but they are probably empty," Mark said.

"I was thinking of the trucks themselves, not what might be inside."

"I don't follow you, John. What are you getting at?" Mark asked.

"They are steel bodied and pretty big. They'd be perfect as transport," John said, casually.

Mark's face lit up as he finally understood what John was driving at.

"They'd be bloody perfect, mate. The Major would have the final say on what you are suggesting but he might just consider it."

"Come on, let's get back to the castle," John said.

He could not help wondering if Robert would seriously consider it. It was only a piece of the complicated puzzle they would have to complete before the possibility of leaving the castle could become a reality. He smiled to himself. It was a bloody big piece!

The mission had been a complete success, both of the helicopters carrying cargo nets full of supplies, the nets hanging below them. John had wondered about the weight but both pilots had agreed their aircraft could take it. The flight back to the castle proved to be uneventful. As they touched down, Robert was waiting for them. John wondered if he had even moved from the spot since they had left early that morning. As he jumped down from the helicopter, Robert ran up.

"How was it?" Robert asked.

"Piece of cake. No problems at all," John said. "The town was basically empty of creatures. I would hazard a guess they've either gone South or they are all up here with us."

"Then we could go back again when necessary and re-supply," Robert said.

"No problem. One of the supermarkets is now relatively secure and still pretty full. Mark even got the alarm system working, so we can go back at any time and quickly determine whether it has been compromised or not. I can't see any creatures going to the trouble of breaking in there, not when there are so many other empty buildings in the town for them to hide in. The only possible danger would be looters but I'm pretty sure we can count that possibility out. So yes, we can go back anytime."

"Great. Get some rest and some food. You and your men have earned it," Robert said.

Stephanie walked up and hugged him.

"Are you alright?" she asked.

"I'm fine, it was easy," he replied. "Come on, I need to talk to you."

Hand in hand they walked away from the helicopters. The supplies they had brought back would last the castle inhabitants about four weeks. John wondered if it would be enough time?

Chapter Five - The Plan

The morning after the successful raid in Hadlee, John awoke early. He had not slept well, tossing and turning most of the night, his idea keeping him awake. He had decided to discuss it with Robert that morning, he just needed the right approach. It was important that the Major listened to the whole plan. The last time he had broached the subject of leaving, Robert had not reacted well to the suggestion. He had to avoid annoying the Major before he had heard the whole idea. He showered and dressed, he could not wait any longer. He left Stephanie sleeping and walked to Robert's office. He knocked but there was no answer. A Corporal asked John if he was looking for the Major, explaining that the commander liked to work out in the mornings before anybody was really awake. John thanked the enlisted man and headed for the gym. Sure enough, Robert was there lifting weights.

"Morning, Robert. Can I have a word?" John said cheerfully.

"Of course, John. Just let me get a quick shower and I'll be right with you."

After ten minutes Robert was showered and dressed.

"What's up, John?"

"Can we go to your office? I think this needs to be done privately," John answered.

"Sure. Come on," Robert said, looking puzzled.

Five minutes later they were sitting down, drinking coffee Robert had reheated.

"What's on your mind?" he asked.

"When I first arrived here, we had a conversation about the possibility of trying to leave. At that time you said . . ."

"I know exactly what I said," Robert interrupted. "I will not leave anybody behind and we haven't got enough transport to be able to take everybody with us!"

He sounded annoyed.

"Yeah, that was about the gist of it. What if there was a way we could take everybody out of here? Would you be interested?" John asked, hoping for a positive answer.

Robert seemed to relax a little.

"What do you have in mind?" he almost whispered.

"Okay. Now hear me out, please," John said. "I've had the idea for a while now but I needed to check a few things out in Hadlee first. I had the opportunity to do that yesterday and now I'm sure my plan is feasible."

He had been closely watching Robert's face, looking for a reaction. There was none, at least up to then. He continued.

"What's our biggest problem if we ever wanted to leave here?"

Robert stared at John, shaking his head.

"You mean other than those things wanting to kill and eat us! You know as well as I do, transport. We can't expect the civilian population to fight their way through on foot, it would be a massacre."

"Exactly," John said. "We need a way of transporting three hundred and forty one people, all of the supplies we will need, weapons, ammunition, other equipment. In fact, everything we might need on the way and anything else we might need at a later date. We also need a method of transport that offers a certain degree of security and safety."

"Tell me something I don't know, John," Robert said, losing his patience. "With the vehicles we have at our disposal we can't address any of the problems you are listing. It's already been suggested, thought through and dismissed as impossible."

"What about the delivery trucks parked in Hadlee?" John asked.

Robert stared at him for a second or two, then he spoke.

"Okay, you've got my attention. Questions. Are they strong enough to withstand an attack from the creatures? How do we get them from Hadlee to here without losing the men involved? Do we know that they're driveable? What about fuel? The idea is very interesting John but there are a lot of questions that would need to be answered before what you're suggesting proves to be viable," Robert said.

"I've not finished yet. I have given it a lot of thought ever since the notion popped into my head. I can go a long way to answering a lot of your questions, not all of them, granted but, between us, we can work out any problems and solve them. You said yourself transport was the biggest problem. If we can solve that, the rest will fall into place," John argued.

"Alright, John, just exactly what are you suggesting?" Robert asked.

"Bear with me okay. This is still rough. As we left the supermarket yesterday, the parking area was secure. In the car park at the back there are six trucks, the big ones, eighteen wheelers I think. The other supermarket had the same and behind the precinct there were at least thirty odd. Now these vehicles are big inside. I reckon forty people could live in one. It wouldn't be the Hilton but it's better than walking. You've got the two fuel tankers here, so fuel wouldn't be an immediate problem. We never checked the whole town yesterday but we're bound to find fuel of some kind there, if not then on the way. All told, keeping the vehicles moving shouldn't be too much of a headache. Food supplies we pick up on the way out of here. The odds are high that once we're ready we'll head south. That takes us right through Hadlee again, where our supplies are waiting for us. The supermarket from yesterday is secure, as I explained. While we're picking up the trucks, we'll secure the other one and eventually the precinct. It seems crazy to fly the gear back up here when we could drive through and pick it up. After emptying all three buildings we just keep on heading south. Now we already have your sixteen toners, they can make fifty miles an hour so they are plenty fast enough to come with us. We pack ammunition, weapons, generators, spare parts, in fact everything we are likely to need into them. The trucks we liberate can be kept just for personnel. With regards to safety, we have tools here, parts, manpower and a few guys who seem to be excellent at improvising. What they've accomplished within the castle since you came here proves that. Those same men can help us modify the trucks. We can probably armour them to an extent. We weld the backdoors shut and reinforce them. We can cut new entrances into the roofs. We can mount machine guns on the roofs, build shooting platforms up there, sniper holes in the sides. Hell, Robert, we can do all kinds of shit to make them safer. We'd have to watch the weight but I don't see a problem."

It was obvious to Robert that John had given his plan a lot of thought.

"I'm impressed," he said. "But how do we get the trucks from Hadlee to here?"

"Okay. It's seventy miles from Hadlee to the castle. I know for a fact that most of the roads are still intact, because we followed them a lot of the time on our way up here. Driving the trucks back won't be a problem once we've captured them. The two helicopters need to be fitted with heavy calibre machine guns, it's time they had more to do anyway. They drop off the teams just like yesterday and then cover us from the air during the journey back to the castle. Eight men per helicopter, sixteen total. Four-man teams per truck means we can bring four trucks per trip. It will take about one and a half hours to drive from there to here, so two trips a day should be possible. We need to make six trips in total, three days work. That gives us twenty four trucks if we get them all back in one piece. If we lose a few on the road it doesn't matter, we'd still have more than enough to safely transport us all away from here. We modify the trucks we need, then strip down the rest for spare parts to use along the way. On one of the truck roofs we build a platform strong enough for a helicopter to land and take off. We take one with us to be our eyes in the sky, the other gets broken down for spare parts. If it is possible, it would be nice to get the Apache flying again. You have considerable stores of munitions for it here, having it along would considerably increase our firepower. If we could manage to repair it, then we would have to modify two of the trucks so it could also land and take off."

Robert lit a cigarette, his first in nearly a week. He offered John one, who declined saying he did not smoke, at least not yet. They both sat there, the silence deafening.

"One problem," Robert suggested. "What about them? The minute we open the doors to let the trucks in or out, those creatures will be all over us."

"I realise that but I think we can do something about it. It's time to start making their lives difficult," John said, seriously. "You said there was an old museum here before, I never did get the chance to look at the weapons they had stored there. It's time I did. We'll need some of the edged weapons for my men."

Robert looked as if he had missed something. How had they jumped from planning to leave the castle to swordplay in a heartbeat. He was puzzled to say the least.

"Don't panic, Robert, I'm not flipping out," John assured him. "Did you ever see the old film 'Zulu'?"

"About the British soldiers fighting the Zulus, yes I've seen it. I don't suppose there are many soldiers who haven't. What the hell has it got to do with our situation here?"

"It was always one of my favourite films, always shown at Christmas. I must have seen it twenty times, at least. One of my favourite scenes is the one where the commanding officer organises a platoon of good bayonet men to plug any gaps appearing in their defences. That's exactly what I'd like to do. It's my idea to leave, I expect to lead the raids on Hadlee using a team of hand-picked men. Mark will be my second in command and he'll help me to pick our boys. I want guys with martial arts skills to begin with, then with Stephanie's help, I propose to teach them how to fight with edged weapons. Their martial arts backgrounds will enable them to learn quickly. I'd guess a couple of weeks training and they'd be pretty lethal. We would then be in a position to take the creatures head on, my men filling the gaps, just like those in the film. It gives us an edge, especially in any hand-to-hand situations that might crop up along the way."

"Why's that so important?" Robert asked. "We are all heavily armed and can deal with these things anyway."

"I suggest a small group of better trained soldiers who can deal with these creatures at close quarters takes the pressure off the rest. Remember, Robert, we have to secure the second supermarket and the precinct. Inside those buildings, especially the precinct, it can quickly get down to hand-to-hand fighting. The guys we train would be able to handle a situation like that. In time we can train more but at the moment time is short."

"Why is time short?" Robert asked.

"Because we have enough food for maybe four weeks. We have that long to prepare. When the food runs out we leave. The longer we stay here, the more creatures we have to get through when we decide to go. As soon as possible we need to go on the offensive anyway. No more watching these things, we start killing them! They need thinning down for when the trucks arrive and for when we're ready to leave," John argued.

"We can increase the number of snipers on the walls. They have night vision technology so even in the dark, when the creatures are mostly about, we can engage them. We have mortars that can easily reach the tree line and then some. The helicopters can deliver munitions from the air and if we manage to repair the Apache, it's missiles are deadly. Yes, all told, I would say we have the capability to considerably thin them down. Up until now it would have been pointless but your idea might be just the reason we've been waiting for to turn up the heat," Robert said.

"With a little luck we could get everybody away from here and start again," John said, finding it hard to hide his excitement.

At that precise moment Robert looked straight at John, he suddenly seemed sceptical.

"Let's say everything goes approximately to plan and we manage to get away. I have just one question but unfortunately it's damned important. Where the hell do we go?" Robert asked.

"I've given that a lot of thought as well," John answered. "The British Mainland is lost, at least I've seen no evidence to the contrary. I imagine the whole European continent is gone, it belongs to them. Any pockets of humanity that are left will be just like us, surrounded and prisoners fighting for the right to exist. If we make it out of here, we should head for one of the harbour towns, best bet would probably be New Hull. We'd be more likely to find a vessel big enough to carry us and our equipment there, one of the old car ferries for instance. There should be somebody here with enough sailing experience to handle one. If not, then we'll have to work it out on site. We head for an island. I'm not sure where. Somewhere in the North Sea, or maybe Jersey, or maybe down around Spain into the Med. I haven't got all the answers, not yet anyway."

"I don't know, John, there's a lot of ifs. I don't think we have the right to make such a decision on our own. It's too important. We should probably call a meeting, explain it all and let everybody decide. After all, if everything that could go wrong went wrong, we could all wind up dead! What do you think?" Robert asked.

"Call the meeting," John almost whispered. "We've probably forgotten a thousand things at least. Everything would be better discussed out in the open. That way we might be able to refine a plan that's even better. I've always found the more input, the better the results," he said smiling.

Chapter Six - The Meeting

The meeting had been called for 2100 hours in the great hall. Everybody was gathering there, all wondering what was going on. In the time they had been at the castle, there had never been a meeting to discuss anything. The civilians were all a little bit frightened about what it could mean.

John was talking to Mark, who already knew about the plan to leave the castle.

"Do you think they'll go for it?" Mark asked John, a hint of doubt in the way he asked the question.

"I'm not sure," John replied. "But over the last few days Stephanie and I have been talking to some of the families here and we both came to the same conclusion. For the couples with children, this isn't living, it's existing. Their children have no future at all! I seriously believe that, given another viable alternative, at least the parents amongst us would definitely consider it. As for the rest of them, I've no idea. You're a soldier, you decide. Is this what you spent all your time training for, to hide behind stone walls and eventually just fade away? Is the danger of leaving here, finding a new home, where we can all make a new life, too great? A new life that would actually mean something again, where children can play and grow up without having to know how to fire a gun. I think you know the answer and I'm certain the same goes for every soldier here. If we treat this democratically, then I think we've got a great chance but it has to be that way, everybody's decision. We're not in the position to play God, deciding everybody's fate. The pratts who were in charge before the war, they decided for everybody and look where that got us. Afterwards, when peace was finally declared, for a time we did okay, we all had a say in everything. Maybe that was the difference. Then they appeared," and he gestured beyond the castle walls. "Since then, we've been up shits creek again."

"Where the hell did they come from, John?" Mark asked.

"You're asking the wrong guy. While we were with Special Services we were privy to a lot of information not released to the public. There were theories they'd always been here, going right back to prehistoric times. Another theory was that they crawled out of the same sludge as we did, except evolution took them up another route. If that were true, then they'd be our distant relatives, crazy, yeah. One thing's for certain, they are the perfect survivor. We know how difficult it is to kill them, even with our weapons. Imagine how difficult it would have been for our race hundreds of years ago. Their life span is unknown. They could be hundreds of years old, maybe even thousands. One theory was very interesting and could now explain why there are so many of them, it was based on a cycle. Every year different ones awake, feed, and disappear again. It was suggested that maybe they feed once every so many years, that would help to explain why we never noticed them before. You can imagine how many there might actually be. For whatever reason, probably the combination of nuclear weapons and viruses released in the last war somehow changing them or their cycle, they've all awoken at the same time. Only now food's in short supply. One thing I'm sure of, whatever they are, we can't beat them, there are too many. They'll outlast us. The only hope for us is a place, where there aren't any of them."

"Can we find such a place?" Mark asked, obviously doubtful of the answer.

"As we're suggesting, the only real chance is an island. They'll more than likely be there but maybe not too many of them. We hunt them down and clear them out. We've enough manpower to do that, if we get that far. Once the island's clear, they've no way to get to us. Their apparent fear of water is a weakness we can exploit. We'd be okay."

"The plan is sound, John, I hope they go for it," Mark said sincerely.

At that moment the Major called the meeting to order. He had asked John to chair the meeting because it was his idea but John had suggested it was better coming from somebody the castle community knew well. With John being a new member of the group, he was afraid it might have a negative effect on the outcome.

After about an hour, Robert, having explained the idea in full detail, opened the floor to questions and comments.

To start with the civilians just sat there discussing the plan amongst themselves, not so the soldiers attending the meeting. They voiced their opinions straightaway. They were all in favour and thankful to have a chance to leave the castle, just as John had expected.

He looked at Mark who, smiling, gave John the thumbs up sign. Now it was down to the civilians to decide.

Slowly one or two stood up voicing their opinions, mostly very positive, however raising one or two minor questions that Robert managed to explain away.

One of the more respected civilians then stood, a Mr. Smythe. He held a lot of influence over the community and his opinion would be very important to the outcome. He basically asked why they should risk everything to undertake such a dangerous journey, when they could live out their years in the castle, in relative safety.

Robert attempted to answer this question but was obviously struggling. He looked over to John, his eyes asking for help. John stood and walked over to the stage where Robert was sitting. Very deliberately Robert introduced him as the man who had developed the idea.

"Well, what's your answer?" Mr. Smythe asked smugly.

John realised straightaway he didn't like this man. He was one of the old breed, partly responsible for everything that had gone wrong in the world and only interested in themselves. They didn't like change, only felt secure with people they had known all their lives, treated anybody else poorly and always got their own way.

Smythe was sitting there, arms crossed, looking conceited.

"How old are you, Mr. Smythe?" John asked, knowing he was being rude.

"I don't see what that's got to do with anything," Smythe replied, his tone full of contempt.

"Humour me, please," John said, trying not to sound too serious.

"Very well, I'm sixty seven years old," came the answer.

"Now, another question for you ladies out there. How many of you are, at this moment, pregnant?"

Slowly, several women raised their hands.

"Okay, thank you all for being so honest and congratulations. For those of you who don't yet know me, my name is John Stewart. This is my fiancée, Stephanie Jones. We will also at some time have children," he looked over at her for a reaction, she was smiling. He continued. "If necessary within these walls. My point, ladies and gentlemen, is, that no matter how difficult our circumstances are, life goes on. That's a fact. The ladies who are currently expecting babies amongst us prove it. This means our population here will keep on growing. From the three hundred and forty one at the moment, it will climb. In five years, as many as four hundred maybe, in ten years more than that."

"What exactly is your point, Mr Stewart?" Smythe asked, confused.

53

"My point sir, is that we can't stay here, not realistically anyway. The place is too small, or at least it soon will be. We have great difficulty in feeding ourselves now, with more mouths to feed it will only get harder. I would estimate and I think Major Jones will agree with me, that at the most, in one year we won't physically be able to. We currently have to travel seventy miles to find the amounts of supplies we need. That means a round trip of one hundred and forty miles, every four weeks or so. As you can well appreciate, the risk to those involved in such an undertaking is, at best, great. We would only have to have one accident, or a stroke of bad luck and lose one of the helicopters and we'd be in big trouble. The next town, big enough at least, where we could get our supplies is probably two hundred miles away. That means a round trip of four hundred miles, this would not be possible, considering the quantities we require. So you see, Mr Smythe, whether we like it or not, eventually we will have to leave here or we'll just starve to death. The longer we wait the more creatures we'll have to deal with when the time comes. At this moment, we are strong, well armed and in the position where we can deal with the creatures quite successfully. Now is the time! Or we take the easy road - Mr. Smythe's suggestion and stay. Only his life is coming to an end. For our children yet to be born and those already amongst us, there is no chance of life, not here, not ever. Only a slow unavoidable death if we stay!"

John looked straight at Smythe and continued talking, this time just at him.

"I dare say that doesn't interest you, not your kind, anyway. You're safe and that's just how you'd like it to stay."

Smythe started to protest but John continued.

"I'm sorry to sound abrupt but the people with the most to gain should make this decision, those that deserve a future and are prepared to fight for it. I can't help you decide but I can promise you this. If your decision is yes, then every feasible precaution will be taken to ensure you and your children's safety. Please understand, no matter what your decision is today, at some point we have to leave here, if we want to live."

John left the stage and went back to his room with Stephanie. He was angry with himself, he had made it personal with Smythe. Had he gone too far? He didn't know. Stephanie tried to re-assure him but he was worried. Had he blown it and condemned them to life imprisonment without the chance of parole?

After what seemed like forever but in reality was only thirty minutes, there was a knock at their door. Stephanie opened it to find Robert and Mark standing there.

"How did it turn out?" John asked urgently.

"They went for it, John. Your speech swung it, even old Smythe voted yes. Crazy thing is, John, do you know what Smythe did for a living before the war?"

"No idea," he replied.

"He owned and operated a couple of car ferries. Knows how to sail them and everything, funny eh?"

"Shit!" John gasped.

"Get some sleep," Robert said. "We start tomorrow."

Both of them said goodnight and left.

"You did it, John," Stephanie stated. "I love you."

John laughed.

"Now the hard work really starts. We'd better make love, I might not get a lot of time free after tonight."

Chapter Seven - Finalising

They made love, afterwards falling asleep. Stephanie had not dreamt for nearly a week, that night she did.

It was the castle just as it always was. Children running around playing, soldiers doing odd jobs, anything to keep busy. Everything looked so quiet and peaceful. There was suddenly a loud noise, somewhere in the background. She could not place it at first but then she realised what it was. Motorbike engines and lots of them. She could hear gunfire all around, even the odd explosion. The crazy thing was the picture of the castle had not changed. It still looked peaceful. There was just this loud noise somewhere out of picture, she did not know where. She awoke, not understanding what the dream could possibly mean.

"What was that all about?" she whispered to herself.

"What was what about?" John asked, now also awake.

"I had a crazy dream, it was weird."

"What about?" John asked.

"Ah nothing, it was stupid. It didn't make any sense. Make love to me again," she pleaded, pulling him on top of her.

At 0900 hours John, having made love to Stephanie before showering and dressing, knocked on Robert's office door. Upon entering he saw Mark was already there, along with two other Sergeant Majors, Bill Young and Simon Gates. After being introduced properly, he sat down and they began to finalise the plan to leave the castle.

John would train his team, the members of which would be informed later that day as Mark already knew who they were. They would train intensively in the castle for a few days and then return to Hadlee to retrieve the first trucks. The team would continue to train afterwards but John felt the experience gained in the field would prove invaluable.

As soon as the first trucks were brought back, the modifications would begin. Several of the civilians had expressed the wish to help, some of them turning out to be engineers, others designers and several that had working experience with the big trucks. A meeting was organised for that afternoon between Bill, the Sergeant Major in charge of modifying the vehicles and his team to discuss what they were going to do. Bill made a very important point, suggesting the trucks they acquired should only have steel bodies. The canvas sided trucks would not offer enough protection, especially for people travelling inside. They would also prove harder to modify.

John reminded Bill that the two helicopters needed to be fitted with machine guns before the trip back to Hadlee. This should be considered a priority by his team and needed to be completed as soon as possible. The repairing of the Apache attack helicopter should also be undertaken as quickly as possible, as its firepower would help them in the conflicts to come. It was not clear where the problem lay with the machine but it needed to be airworthy as soon as humanly possible.

They would start, immediately thinning down the number of creatures outside the walls. The first action was already planned for that evening. Sergeant Major Gates was in charge of the operation and promised it would be quite a show.

They would start loading straightaway the sixteen tonners with the equipment they were taking along. Ammunition supplies could also be packed away. Anything that would not be needed for the modifications but might prove useful at some later date, would also be taken along.

They decided they should be a little more careful with the food supplies they had at their disposal, just in case it took longer than the anticipated four weeks to get ready.

Where to head for when they left was also discussed at length. The city of New Hull, travelling the route they would be forced to take, was over six hundred miles away. Since the war, certain parts of the country had been deemed too lethal to inhabit. One such area was the Dead Zone. It stretched down the country from the east coast almost into the Midlands and back to the east coast just above New Hull, basically forming a large V. This area of land had been saturated with nuclear fallout during the Third World War to such an extent that travelling through it would be fatal. If they decided to head for New Hull it meant travelling down under the V and back up on the other side, thus making the journey much longer. However, after the war finished, New Hull was the only ferry port still operating and seeing as they needed a ship big enough to carry all their vehicles, the logical choice seemed to be a car ferry. They decided that until a better alternative presented itself, they would head for New Hull. Mr. Smythe had already been asked if, in his opinion, a car ferry could make the trip down around Spain into the Med. He believed it was possible, although they would need a bit of luck with the weather during the attempt and they would have to re-fuel along the way. Possible end destinations were suggested. Parma, Corsica, Sardinia, and Crete amongst the alternatives. They had enough choice, but onsite surveillance would have to help them make the final choice.

They spent another hour troubleshooting, one of them suggesting problems, the others trying to solve them. They imagined all kinds of scenarios, from punctures to mass attacks by the creatures but everything panned out. They could always find an answer between them. The only possible problem was brought to the table by John. Other survivors. He explained that during their trip up the country they had come across motorbike tracks several times, lots of them, as if a big gang was moving through the area. If they were unfortunate enough to run into that gang or any other group of survivors, it could be a complication that no amount of planning could help. Any survivors still out there would be desperate. Maybe even desperate enough to try and get their hands on what the convoy of trucks would be carrying, by any means necessary, including attacking and killing the convoy inhabitants! They decided they could not prepare for every eventuality and such problems would have to be dealt with as and when they occurred.

As John got back to his room he felt tired, it had been a long meeting. Stephanie was waiting for him.

"How did it go? I was beginning to wonder if you'd ever finish," she said.

"Great," he replied. "The only problem left on the table is something unexpected happening."

"Like what for instance?" she asked.

"No idea, that's why it would be unexpected, you wally," he said, playfully. "For instance, what would we do if a gang of bloodthirsty bikers attacked us? That kind of thing. You can't prepare for it because the odds of it happening are minimal."

"That's weird," she whispered.

"Sorry?" John said, unclear what she meant.

"I said it's weird. Last night I dreamt about here and motorbikes. There was shooting and all kinds of noise. It was mixed up somehow but I got the distinct impression we were being attacked. I guess it's just a coincidence."

"You know I don't believe in coincidences," John said. "We'd better re-think the possibility through, just in case."

Chapter Eight - So It Begins

That evening, extra snipers were positioned on the battlements with new instructions to shoot anything that moved. Mortars were set up in the castle grounds, both helicopters on standby.

John was on the wall with Robert, Mark and Stephanie watching the tree line. At twilight the first creatures appeared but nobody fired. They all understood the rules of the new game that was about to begin. They waited because, with every minute, more and more of the creatures came into view. It did not matter how dark it became, they were all using night vision goggles and sights, so they could see perfectly well.

After waiting nearly an hour they could clearly see that the edge of the clearing, between the castle and the forest, was teeming with creatures.

Confidently, Robert gave the order that the first attack should begin. Upon his command, the two helicopters immediately took off and flew out over the clearing. As soon as they were hovering over the tree line to the west and east of the castle, John could see that they dropped suitcase sized objects down into the trees. John expected them to blow up, but nothing happened. The helicopters then flew off to the north and south and did exactly the same. They then returned to the castle, landed and the pilots left their machines to join everybody else on the battlements. Obviously their part in the coming offensive was over, at least for the time being. Robert looked at John. With a mischievous look on his face, Robert waved a box-like object in John's face. The scene reminded John of a spoilt child, showing off a new, wonderful toy to friends who couldn't afford to buy it themselves. He waited for Robert to go 'nah nah, nah nah, nah' but he didn't.

Robert, still smiling, shouted, "Get ready."

John heard the answer to the order, in that all the soldiers on the wall ready to fire, de-activated the safety's on their rifles. With an audible click, they were ready. John still couldn't quite understand exactly what they were ready for.

At that moment, Robert pushed a small button on the box-like object he had been holding. John realised it was a remote control, because all four objects the helicopters had dropped around the castle simultaneously exploded. It appeared to be an advanced version of Napalm, all around the castle the woods were on fire. The creatures appeared to do exactly what Robert had hoped they would do - they moved out of the trees further into the clearing and at that moment Robert ordered the mortars and his men on the battlements to open fire. All the snipers fired at once and kept firing. The mortar crews also opened fire, pounding the creatures. The noise was deafening.

Firing had been continuous for about twenty minutes, when Robert suddenly shouted to cease fire. The order was repeated around the walls and firing duly stopped.

The fires around the castle started to die back and the smoke started to clear; they waited with baited breath. Everybody knew how important this part of the plan was. They had to thin the creatures down, to be able to bring the trucks safely into the castle and be in a position to leave without great difficulty when they were ready.

After about ten minutes it was clear enough to see out over the battlefield. There were bodies everywhere. Snipers were detailed to watch out for wounded, and where necessary to finish off the creatures. Other soldiers were detailed to count the fallen bodies, giving them an idea of how successful the operation had been.

Robert, John and Mark retired to the Major's office. Upon entering, John congratulated them on a well planned attack.

"I'm impressed," he said. "Considering that, up until yesterday, you were never going to leave this place, you put that attack together pretty damned well. If I didn't know better, I'd say that part of the plan had been made for quite a while now. You don't just throw that kind of operation together in a couple of hours."

"You're right, John, we've had the idea of leaving this place in the back of our minds for months now. We just couldn't work out how. You were the catalyst, providing the missing pieces in our little puzzle," Robert said, smiling.

"You Berks," John said. "The meeting was just a sham or what?"

"No, mate, that was genuine. If the vote had gone against us, we would have stayed put, at least for a while. We hadn't formulated a plan that seemed to have a good enough chance of succeeding, you did that," Robert said, smiling.

John shook his head.

"That's why you allowed that patrol of soldiers to leave! They were supposed to get the lay of the land and if possible, report back. Fill in the gaps so to speak. That's why you were so interested in what we'd seen on our travels."

"Exactly. I was hoping you'd seen something, anything that could help us. I never imagined you'd come up with the solution, at least not all by yourself but you did, John. I thank God you were sent to us."

"You could have told me from the beginning," John argued.

"I know, Mark said we should. I decided against it, it was my decision. I hope the fact that I didn't doesn't change anything between us."

"Of course not, I'm just a little pissed off because you guys didn't trust me. I can also understand why but, if you had, we wouldn't have wasted as much time. I've had this idea practically from the start of our stay here."

"Well, now we are committed," Robert said. "We'll trust each other until the plan is carried through, or we die trying."

At that moment, there was a knock at the door, Robert shouting, "Come in."

Simon, the Sergeant Major in charge of operations concerning the creatures, came in to report.

"How's it looking, Simon?" Robert asked.

"Good," came the confident reply. "We estimate over six hundred dead, maybe more, but we can't get an accurate figure because of the way the bodies are clumped together. It could be as many as one thousand, sir."

"Not bad for a beginning, eh," Robert gloated.

"Pretty good," John agreed. "But they won't fall for the same tactic again. We'll have to work out another couple of ways to get to them. I presume the snipers will be staying on the walls at all times now with orders to engage."

"Yes," Simon confirmed. "We've worked out a rota. There'll be at least ten per wall at all times with orders to take out targets of opportunity."

"We'll keep chipping away at them," Mark added. "When do we want to fetch the first trucks, John?"

"We start training in the morning. I want at least a couple of days with our men, they won't be completely ready but at least better prepared than they are now. The second supermarket shouldn't be a problem but the precinct worries me. It's obviously massive and, as Mark pointed out, there could be hundreds of the creatures hiding inside. We'll be sixteen guys against God knows what. If everything went belly up in there, then you can forget the trucks and everybody would be stuck here. We should be thankful these things can't organise themselves, at least in battle. They seem to be driven purely by hunger or hate, I don't know which. That fact makes it easier for us during battle, we can basically predict what they're doing. There's possibly one problem and unfortunately it might be major. I don't know if you've noticed it but when you get a couple of miles away from this place there aren't any creatures. They are definitely drawn to us, or places where we might be. Unfortunately, that could work against us."

"How, John?" Robert asked.

"Going on what we know and what Stephanie and I have witnessed ourselves several times, after checking towns and buildings are uninhabited, the creatures move on. That should normally work in our favour but our returning to Hadlee several times could very well draw them back into the town. That's obviously bad for us and could complicate the mission. Plus, if I'm right, it shows a certain degree of intelligence. They might not be mindless zombies, as was suggested by some scientists. Whichever way you look at this, there's a part of the puzzle missing. I can't figure it out, not yet anyway but I think we will do before this is over."

"John, if I didn't know better I'd say you admired them," Robert stated.

"No, you're wrong Robert, admire's not the right word. Whatever they are, wherever they came from, they've been around a hell of a long time. During my time working with Special Services, I learnt to respect all adversaries. It keeps you sharp. I've always found that if I can understand a problem properly, then it's much more likely I'll find a solution and a safer one at that. This is one puzzle I can't quite understand and that annoys me. I've killed a lot of these things but only because they wanted to kill me. Self defence if you like. To stay alive, mankind has always pushed the envelope. Trying to win a war, the German's developed rockets and split the atom. It didn't help them but seventy odd years later it nearly destroyed the planet. Everything we've ever done has always had repercussions. Why should our situation now be any different? If we win this fight, we get away and find our paradise, will our children's children wonder why we did what we did? Will we be able to justify everything that has happened, or what is about to happen."

"John, I'm not sure what you're suggesting but, one thing's for sure, we didn't start this war with the creatures. They attacked us! There's been no attempt at contact, no attempts to communicate with us, just blood. If they were anything other than mindless animals, we would see some proof of it but we don't. They just attack and kill us on sight. I can't explain them but one thing's certain, they want us gone. Let's give them what they want, let's go. We'll hopefully find our place in the world and maybe they'll have theirs but I can't see a future for us together," Robert said.

They talked together a while longer then retired for the evening. There was a lot to do and they wanted an early start the next day.

Chapter Nine - The Prisoner

It was the morning after and John did not feel any different, the philosophical discussion the evening before had not answered any of his questions.

That morning, the first training session for the men who had been carefully selected to join John's team of specialists was planned. After consultations with Mark, Bill and Simon, John was confident they had only picked soldiers with considerable experience in the martial arts. Several of the men were so highly qualified that John felt sure their skills outmatched even his own. The fact that they all had experience was important because the handling of edged weapons involved several of the martial arts, from Karate to Kendo.

At 0800 hours the men who had been picked were gathered in the castle grounds, eager to begin. Introductions were made, after which John explained in detail the thinking behind the new unit. He and Stephanie gave an impressive demonstration of the techniques involved before the training finally began.

The men involved trained all morning, John and Stephanie putting them all through a very intensive programme designed to hone their current skills and prepare them for the techniques involved in fighting with swords. The two instructors showed no mercy in driving on the men beyond their normal capabilities and to the point of exhaustion. John explained, just before the group stopped for lunch, that this was necessary because fighting with a sword not only involved great skill but also tremendous levels of stamina. Holding a sword that weighed up to ten pounds for a length of time was difficult enough. Swinging it around, defending yourself against numbers of attackers was obviously far harder and not to be underestimated. The men had to be fit and strong. He apologised for the intensity of the training but reminded them that they did not have all that much time to get ready. It would be a crash course that none of them would ever forget but it would guarantee that they could successfully deal with the creatures, even when the situation seemed hopeless.

After a break for lunch, the men were allowed to pick their weapons. It turned out that the armoury in the castle had a very impressive collection, ranging from Broadswords to Samurai blades. John helped every man pick his personal weapon, making sure that the choice made was sensible. He explained in detail the advantages and disadvantages of all the weapons that were available to the men. Several of his pupils showed an interest in some of the Broadswords but he steered them all skilfully on to weapons that were lighter in weight. He explained that although the Broadswords would definitely take care of a creature, swinging one around for lengths of time required great strength. Even the strongest members of his team could not hope to manage the feat for more than five minutes. Although it was an impressive looking weapon, he assured the soldiers interested in it, the experience of using one would be short lived, especially in a combat situation. The soldiers all listened intently and bowed to John's experience and knowledge of the subject, quickly picking more appropriate weapons. The training session continued all afternoon and because of John and Stephanie's vast experience and the prior training of the soldiers themselves, the men all learnt very quickly.

Before dismissing them for the day, John congratulated them all, saying how pleased he and Stephanie were with their progress, and apologising for all the aches and pains the men were having to suffer. He promised that the next day would be equally as hard but again assured the men it was necessary. Dismissing the hard work as something that made a welcome change to what they had all been used to for the last two years, the men retired for the evening, agreeing to meet at the same time the following morning.

Hand in hand, John and Stephanie walked back to their room. It had been a long time since the couple had trained so hard, they were also feeling stiff and tired. The long hard day's training seemed to have affected Stephanie especially, she was feeling exhausted and went to bed as soon as they got back to their room. After assuring John, she was alright, just tired, he showered and joined her but John could not sleep. He could not forget the discussions from the day before.

After waking and making sure she was feeling alright again, John asked Stephanie if she could start the training with the men alone, as he wanted to talk to Robert about something.

Sitting in Robert's office, he gave a short report of their progress, saying how pleased he was and that no problems were arising from the training of the men. They would be ready. The Major, however, sensed this was not the real reason for John's visit and asked what the real problem was?

John explained he could not forget their conversation about the creatures and that the missing puzzle pieces were still bothering him. He then made a suggestion that astonished Robert, at least at first. It was a dangerous and maybe unnecessary risk but he wanted to take his team outside the castle walls and attempt to capture one of the creatures. Robert, for a minute, sat there in disbelief. This was the craziest notion he had ever heard. He asked why? Why should they risk the entire plan, perhaps even their actual existence doing such a foolish thing? If they were crazy enough to attempt what John was suggesting and lucky enough to pull it off, just what exactly would it prove?

John suggested that it might help to answer all of the questions that existed, since the beginning of the conflict with the creatures. He could not really explain why but felt sure it was something they had to do. The Americans had tried without success but maybe it had been right to try.

Robert argued against the idea as best he could but John remained adamant. He had to know if there was a way to avoid further conflict, even at this late stage. The only real way to be sure, was to capture one of them and then try to communicate with it. Eventually the Major, almost relenting, asked him how he suggested they capture a creature without risking the entire population of the castle?

"We use the tunnel," John explained. "I'm sure we have the capability of installing cameras outside the exit door. With luck, they might already be there. We wait inside until an opportunity presents itself. I'll use my team, we strike quickly and using some kind of drugs, bring one of 'them' alive into the castle. We keep it drugged until it's safely secure, then we allow it to wake and try to communicate with it."

"Is your team ready for such an undertaking? They've only been training for a day," Robert asked.

"I think so. They all learnt very quickly yesterday. I'm confident we can handle it, Robert," John argued.

Robert asked what made John think they could communicate at all? The risk to everybody involved would be for nothing if they couldn't. John explained that it was unlikely that the creatures, being so old, had not developed some kind of communication skills.

"If we could talk to them, then maybe, just maybe, we can find a peaceful solution to our situation," he said, hopefully.

"What exactly are the odds of these things being able to speak English?" Robert asked.

"I'll admit it's a long shot but I'm certain we should explore the possibility," John said.

Robert sat there obviously contemplating something. John was puzzled.

"What?" he asked, sensing Robert had something on his mind.

"Go and talk to Bill. Tell him what you've got in mind to do and listen to what he tells you. Afterwards, if you're still convinced you want to try, come back to me and we'll discuss it further," Robert said.

"But why Bill?" John asked.

"That will become obvious when you talk to him, John. Just do it. It might get you to see sense and realise there's no point to what you're suggesting."

"You want to do what?" Bill said.

"I want to take my team outside the castle walls and capture one of the creatures and try to communicate with it," John explained.

Bill just sat down. He was obviously disturbed somehow by what John was suggesting.

"I suppose Robert sent you to talk to me. I'm supposed to make you see sense," Bill said.

"That was the general idea but I don't understand why," John argued.

"You wouldn't," Bill said. "Wait here a minute. I've got something I need to show you."

Bill disappeared into the castle and re-appeared a few minutes later carrying a small box. John wasn't sure and he didn't like to ask but it appeared as if the box was blood stained. Bill sat back down next to John and slowly opened the box, removing its contents. What he was holding looked like one of the old fashioned transistor radios but a modern version. He held it up so that John could see it clearly.

"I don't understand," John said. "It looks like a radio."

"It does, doesn't it?" Bill said smiling. "It's a translator."

"It's a what?" John said, not believing what he had heard.

"It's a translator, at least that's what it's supposed to be," Bill said.

"A translator as in French to German or something similar," John said, unsure as to whether he should believe what Bill was trying to tell him.

"No. A translator as in monster to English," Bill said smiling.

"Where the hell did you get it?" John asked.

"I came across it while we were at Fort William. There was a specialist unit stationed there for a while. They were responsible for developing it. It's an advanced version of the device used by computers to talk to each other, at least that's how it was explained to me, only this is infinitely more powerful. It is designed to register the monster's language, if they have one, decipher it and then translate it," Bill explained.

"Does it work?" John asked, fascinated by the notion.

"I've no idea," Bill said. "The unit that developed it were all killed by the creatures during an attempted field test. This was all we found so, if I had to guess, I'd say no, it doesn't work."

"But you can't be sure?" John argued.

"No, we can't be sure of anything other than the men who were trying to do what you're now suggesting we do, were eaten. They didn't stand a chance."

"They could have been killed before they even had a chance to test it," John argued. "This might make the difference."

"John, either way those men died, these creatures won't give you a chance to use this, they'll be all over you."

"Not if we do it right. Besides, we're not taking the device to the creatures, we're bringing a creature to the device," John said. "Can you give it the once over and make sure it works."

"If you mean change the batteries, then yes, I can do that, anything else and you're on your own," Bill laughed. "I have no idea how the damned thing works."

John stood up.

"Where are you going now?" Bill asked.

"Back to Robert's office to clear the mission with him," John said.

"You're still going ahead with it?" Bill said. "Shit, he'll kill me."

"You're still determined to go ahead with this!" Robert said, slightly irritated that John's conversation with Bill had not persuaded him to see sense.

"Robert, the people who designed and built this translator device obviously thought an attempt at communicating with the creatures might pay off somehow. I do as well," John said, stubbornly.

Robert stared at him, shaking his head.

"Your team would have to volunteer, I won't order men to risk their lives unnecessarily, John." Robert stated.

"Of course, I wouldn't have it any other way," John agreed. "But if they do volunteer, will you allow us to try?"

"Yes but minimum risk. And I mean it."

"Thank you," John said, getting up.

"Don't thank me yet, John, this has got to be one of the craziest things we've done since we came here. Don't make me regret my decision."

"I won't. Just don't give Bill a hard time. He did his best to talk me out of the idea," John smiled.

Robert laughed.

"What if this translator doesn't work?" Robert asked.

"Then we lose nothing but at least we tried. I can live with that," John said.

"In that case, we all can," Robert said.

John went back to his team and explained his conversations with Robert and Bill. If he got enough volunteers, he could attempt to capture one of the creatures. Just as he had hoped, to a man, the whole team volunteered.

"Thank you all," he said, then turning to Mark he asked him who had been involved in the work on the tunnel when they had first moved to the castle.

"That would have been Paul Jennings and his guys, they were basically the first unit here and prepared everything. When we arrived here most of the work had already been completed, including the tunnel modifications," Mark explained.

"Okay, we need to talk to Mr. Jennings, where will he be?" John asked.

"I'll send for him straightaway," Mark replied and sent one of the men off to fetch him.

It had taken about ten minutes to locate Corporal Jennings but he finally appeared. John questioned him about the tunnel construction and the cameras. It turned out exactly as John had hoped, cameras had indeed been fitted outside the exit door. They had not been used for sometime but Corporal Jennings suggested that they would probably still work. He ran off to check.

"Right, Mark, we need a strong tranquilliser and a way to deliver it. It has to be strong enough to keep one of the creatures unconscious for at least a couple of hours. That gives us enough time to get back through the tunnel and secure it somewhere here inside. We need some strong chains to hold it. It's bound to be stronger than we are but chains should do the job."

Mark ran off with his shopping list, first stop would be Bill Young.

In the meantime, Corporal Jennings returned to report the cameras were still in working order, just as he had expected. John asked if it was somehow possible to see the camera pictures but from just inside the door where they were mounted. The Corporal confirmed it would be no problem, they just needed a portable receiver plugging into the camera cables inside the tunnel walls. He would make sure John had everything he needed within the hour.

Mark came back, drugs and everything John had requested would be ready and waiting. Bill had also sent a message regarding the translation device. Its batteries had been replaced and all the lights that should be blinking were doing so. More than that he was not prepared to say. John laughed. It was possible, as long as they were careful. It would work, John was sure of that. The experience for the men would prove invaluable and give them the confidence that could only be gained in combat.

It was midday, they broke for lunch. They ate in silence, each of them wondering how their mission outside the castle walls would turn out. Everything was ready, his men were ready. John sensed they were nervous but, in the meantime, he knew how capable they all were and had no doubt they would be successful. In a few hours, the robot sentries would be de-activated and they would make their way down the tunnel. John told his men to relax for the rest of the afternoon. They would meet again at four o'clock and make their way to the tunnel exit; they needed to be there just as it was getting dark. The creatures would be active then. They would wait there until a suitable group of them was passing by. At that moment they would pounce. John went with Stephanie to their room, he also wanted to get a couple of hours rest. He didn't know how long they would be stuck in the tunnel before a suitable group of creatures appeared. It could prove to be a long night. Stephanie did not want to disturb him but she felt she had to.

"John, I didn't say anything in front of the men but is this absolutely necessary? I mean, it's a hell of a risk you're all taking. If it were to backfire, then I hate to think what could happen to them or you. Are you sure you're doing the right thing?"

"Stephanie, I can't really justify it but it's something we have to do. I need to know we've done everything that we could have done. If there's the slightest chance to end this war, then I feel we have to try. I hoped at least you'd understand it."

"I understand you, John, I always have. I should have realised you'd want to try something like this but I don't have to like it!" She left, she needed some air.

Sometimes he was impossible but she knew he was only trying to do the right thing. That was his weakness. Everything always had to be fair and above board, she loved him because of it.

At 1600 hours they gathered outside the tunnel entrance and started down. Each of the steel doors would be closed behind them and the sentries re-activated, just in case. After about thirty minutes they reached the exit door. Using the portable receiver Corporal Jennings had given him, John tapped into the camera feed from the outside cameras. They waited. Using the headsets they could, quietly, talk to each other and the men monitoring the tunnel cameras in the control room. John asked if the camera angles could be split, one pointing to the right and one to the left. This would greatly improve their field of vision and enable them to pick groups of creatures moving in either direction, while making sure the opposite direction was free.

They had waited for almost an hour, several groups of creatures passing by in the time but John had held back, the groups too big. The resulting confrontation would maybe take too long, allowing other creatures to join the fray. He knew they could very quickly be outnumbered. What had Robert said, minimum risk?

After another quarter of an hour, a small group of creatures appeared to the right of the exit door, the camera to the left showed everything clear. John tensed, this was it. There were five of the creatures and he reminded his team they needed one alive.

Weapons were readied, the door unlocked. Each man knew his part in the dangerous task they were about to undertake. As the creatures drew level with the cave entrance where the tunnel exit was hidden, the trap was sprung. John threw the door open and the men stormed out of hiding. They had decided on silence, no guns except for the tranquilliser gun which was silent anyway. Proper guns would only be used if things were getting out of hand.

With swords drawn, they charged the creatures who, totally surprised by the action, had no chance at all. In no time at all, four were dead and one lay sleeping on the ground before them. Quietly, the bodies of the dead were carried away and hidden in the undergrowth, this way they hoped no attention would be brought to the cave system where the tunnel exit was hidden. The whole operation had taken just minutes. Four of the men carried the creature back into the tunnel, John closing the heavy door behind them and securing it again. Using the cameras, they checked the immediate area outside the door for any signs they had been seen by other creatures. There were none. It had worked perfectly.

They carried the heavy prisoner back along the tunnel, taking about thirty minutes, again Mark under strict instructions to kill the creature if any problems arose.

Having made it back into the castle without incident, the creature was secured, using the heavy duty chains Bill had provided them with. John, Robert and Mark were now the only ones present in the room where the creature was imprisoned. They were waiting for it to awaken, Mark covering it with his pistol at all times. He was still under orders to shoot it at the first signs of it breaking free of its bonds. They were taking no chances. After about thirty minutes, the creature started to stir.

After another ten minutes had gone by, it seemed to be fully awake. It had tested the strength of the chains holding it and apparently realising they were too strong, had given up. Now, it lay there quietly looking around, it seemed frightened. John slowly approached it. Placing the translation device on a table near to the creature, he spoke.

"Can you understand my words?" he asked quietly, trying not to panic the monster lying in front of him.

It seemed to register that he had said something but didn't react to him further. It struggled against the chains holding it, speaking out loud in a language that had nothing to do with anything any of them had heard before.

John tried again.

"What are you?" he asked.

"We don't even know if it can understand us. That stupid machine obviously doesn't work, John," Robert suggested.

"The translator needs time Robert. It's picking up every sound we or the creature makes."

"Kill it! At least we tried it your way."

John ignored him, and tried again.

"Where do you come from?"

Nothing, no reaction.

"Why do you hate us?" he said, not giving up.

To this question he thought he saw an understanding in the creature's eyes. He tried again.

"Why do you want to kill us?"

72

To their utter surprise, especially Robert's, the translator burst into life. The language coming out of it sounded at least similar to the creature's. So similar in fact, the creature stopped struggling and appeared to listen to the machine. It looked up at John, a look of astonishment clearly definable. John repeated his last question.

"Why do you want to kill us?"

The creature listened to the question in it's own language and spoke. The machine digested its answer and repeated it in English.

"We kill you because you chose to kill us."

John looked at both Robert and Mark. He had been right, they could communicate.

"What do you mean, we chose to kill you? I don't understand," John said.

The machine did its job and after a second the creature spoke again.

"We have existed for thousands of your years, preying only on your weak and ill. We chose not to interact with you because we've seen your weaknesses. You are violent and disrespectful of everything you touch, of all life, including your own. Without warning, you attacked us, killing millions of us. Others of us were changed. We didn't understand why. We fought back."

"What's it mean, we attacked them? They started this war, we did nothing," Robert argued.

"Don't you get it?" John asked. "The war. All the bombs we dropped on each other. All the poisons and chemicals we unleashed. They think we were attacking them!"

John turned back to the creature and spoke deliberately into the translator.

"We didn't attack you, we were fighting amongst ourselves. We had no knowledge of your existence. This is all a terrible mistake!"

The translator again changed the statement into the language the creature could understand. It replied immediately.

"No mistake," the creature said. "You have hunted us throughout your history. We are your Sasquatch, your Yeti. Each of your tribes has legends based on our existence. We always managed to hide using our camouflage. It is only because of this you could never find us but you wouldn't give up. You sent the rockets, the bombs, the poisons. We had to retaliate, now it's too late for you. We will win, you will die."

Listening to the electrical sounding voice of the translator making this threat seemed strange but there could be no mistake that the creature lying in front of them believed what it was saying. John tried to stay calm but found himself panicking at this statement, it seemed so final.

"This is a misunderstanding between us. We never meant to harm you or your kind, you have to believe us, then maybe we can live in peace together," John said, hopefully.

The creature's reply devastated him.

"There can be no peace between us. Too many have died. We will fight on until every one of you is dead and your memory is erased from this planet."

Robert and Mark had not said much since the creature had began to speak through the translator but the realisation of the truth showed on their faces.

"My God, John, what should we do?" Robert asked, the finality of the creature's statement scaring him as well.

"I don't know," John replied, then he turned back to the creature and tried once more. "Could there be peace between us?"

The answer came just as he had half expected.

"No!"

At this the creature went very quiet then started to convulse violently. John shouted to Robert and Mark, "Hold it down." but the convulsions were too violent. After a few minutes it seemed to stiffen, then lie still. John checked for a life sign, a pulse, anything but it was dead. Somehow it had killed itself, right before their very eyes, just as the American scientists had reported.

At least now, they understood more, they could even sympathise with the creatures they had unknowingly terrorised but the one fact that remained chilled them. Nothing could ever change, they would fight and live, or fight and die.

"I don't get it, John," Robert said. "If they eat us, what will they do when we're all dead?"

"They obviously don't just eat us," John replied, smiling. "We can compare them to the big cats in Africa. They are predators that hunt whatever they can catch. One day a Gazelle, the next a Wildebeest, basically whatever's available. These things, with their ability to hide, are most definitely the deadliest predator on the planet. Normally speaking, we'd have no chance against them. If the war hadn't happened, we wouldn't have known about them, they would have continued picking us off. Remember what it said, they only preyed on our weak and ill. It was talking law of the jungle, something we used to witness every day of our lives. In their minds, they weren't doing anything wrong but we did when we attacked. Now the answer to your question, Robert, is very simple, if we were exterminated, the planet would very quickly recover. We have always destroyed, the creature was right about that, rainforests, eco-systems, the oceans. You think how much meat and other foodstuffs we eat in a year, every year. Once we were gone, the animals would multiply quickly, the oceans would replenish themselves, the forests would grow again. Without mankind to destroy everything, they'd have more than enough food."

Robert and Mark just stood there staring at the dead creature. They had nothing to say, the creature had said it all.

Chapter Ten - Doubts!

The next morning, rumours were all over the castle about the events that had transpired the evening before. How a creature had been captured and brought into the castle endangering everybody. How it had been able to talk and had told its captors all manner of things before committing some kind of ritual suicide.

Robert decided that to avoid all kinds of hysterical behaviour it was important to publish an exact account of what had happened, so that the entire truth would be known. He hoped that this would stop the rumour wagon from running out of control and help to prevent any hysteria that sometimes accompanied it. He had written the report himself and posted it in the great hall where considerable numbers of the civilians had read it.

The creature had been buried in the castle grounds. Some people had objected to this but Robert and John both felt it was the right thing to do. It had, after all, died as a prisoner of war in their custody. The doctor had asked if he could perform an autopsy, insisting they could learn something that may prove to be important at a later date but Robert had flatly refused. He felt that the creatures should be seen as enemy soldiers and handled accordingly. No autopsies would ever be performed by somebody under his command. The conflict was now officially a war and would be fought following normal military guidelines.

Sitting together in Robert's office, everybody in the planning team felt that, although their situation had not changed, somehow everything was different. Their resolve was un-wavering but they now knew for definite the only chance to escape certain death was to carry their plan through to completion. However, on one thing they all agreed, it suddenly seemed wrong to carry on killing the creatures indiscriminately. After all, they had basically done nothing wrong. Somehow continuing to murder them felt immoral but nobody could suggest a suitable option. The drug they had used successfully against the creature had worked well but drugging hundreds, maybe thousands of them, seemed impossible. Or was it?

What about gas? They had such weapons stored at the castle in abundance. Could they be modified to render their opponents unconscious instead of killing them. After all, they only needed minutes to get the trucks through and into the castle. The same story when they were ready to leave. Once on the road, the creatures would be left quickly behind. Everyone agreed it should be tried. They would kill when they had to but only if absolutely necessary.

With their consciences appeased, they carried on with the preparations for the next part of the plan. They now all understood how desperate their situation really was. These things would not stop, would never surrender, unlike a normal adversary, who at some stage might reconsider his actions. It was a fight to the death, and to win they had to be better than good.

The next day they were going back to Hadlee to acquire the first trucks. There was not much time, not much time at all.

Chapter Eleven - Back to Hadlee

The next morning his men were ready and waiting for him, the helicopters idling on their landing pads. He was almost ready to leave but Stephanie was not going with him. She had had a couple of restless nights, not sleeping well and was feeling under the weather. John, obviously worried, was insisting she went to see one of the doctors under Robert's command. She had promised she would but insisted she was only coming down with the flu or something. She had made him promise to be extra careful, seeing as she would not be there to watch his back. He seriously suggested they postpone the mission. He had become used to the two of them working together and knew he could rely on her, especially in dangerous situations. She, however, suggested he could rely on Mark to back him up equally as well as she could and insisted if they were going to be able to stick to John's theoretical timetable, postponing was not an option. She would be fine, he did not need to worry. The quicker she recovered, the sooner they could get back to normal. He relented to her logic, kissed her goodbye and went to join his men. As soon as he left the room, Stephanie ran into the small bathroom and was ill.

"Where's Stephanie?" Robert asked, as John appeared on his own.

"She's not feeling too well so she's sitting this one out. I think it's just the flu or something but I've told her to go and see the doctor just in case. Do me a favour, Robert, make sure she does."

"Consider it done," Robert smiled. "If need be, I'll carry her there myself."

John smiled. It was almost worth cancelling the mission just to stay behind and watch Robert attempt to manhandle Stephanie. The last man to try that had soon realised it had been a mistake. He considered telling Robert to go careful but thought better of it. He would have to learn the hard way. John turned to address his men with Robert standing nearby.

"Guys, we're going back to Hadlee. First job today is the first supermarket, we're taking the trucks parked at the back. Four men per truck, backed up by the helicopters. Remember to check the fuel tanks. There are six trucks parked there altogether, so we should be able to scrounge up enough fuel. If everything goes well, then we'll be travelling back in daylight, we shouldn't see too many of the creatures until we approach the castle. The new weapons are ready to be used and will be if needed. We have to make it back without stopping, so the better prepared we are before we leave the less trouble we'll have on the way. Use your headsets at all times, a unit that communicates well together, operates well together. A lot of people are counting on us, let's get the job done."

He shook Robert's hand and climbed into his allotted helicopter. They took off and once again headed south.

The journey to Hadlee was quiet, the men speaking but not excessively. John was going through the operation with the pilot of his helicopter, discussing options if anything were to go wrong. They both felt that every possible precaution had been taken. Confidently, John turned to his men and once again told them how competent they had become. He was sure things would go well, they just needed to believe in themselves. Mark spoke to him.

"Where's the Mrs.?" he asked.

"Not feeling too well. She's been off colour for the last few days. I don't know what's going on," John said.

"I wouldn't worry about it, mate, it's that place. When we first moved up there, we all got the flu. It's the damp and the cold. Bloody castle! I'll be glad to see the back of it," Mark said.

After twenty minutes flying, the town of Hadlee was once again beneath them. Both helicopters headed straight to their target, supermarket one and hovered overhead. John could see from his seat in the helicopter that all doors and windows were still intact, the steel gates at the back still appeared to be locked. He spoke into his headset.

"Mark, everything looks okay. Do you agree?"

"Yes, John, nothing's changed, otherwise the alarm would be going off. There's been no creature activity, at least inside the place, since we were here last time."

"Okay, let's get down there. Pilot, land on the roof, then take off and hover. Keep in touch at all times and report anything that looks even remotely suspicious. Clear?"

"Got it, John," the pilot answered, confidently.

They landed, exited the helicopter and took up defensive positions on the roof, waiting for the second helicopter to land. As it took off again, Mark ran over to John.

"Everything's clear, John," he said.

"Okay, in through the store," John replied.

"Wait a minute," Mark suggested. "The store's all locked up at the moment, let's leave it that way. We go down over the wall, into the parking lot from here. We open the gates, start the trucks and we're away. I've got the gate key here in my pocket, that way we don't even have to risk the store or mess with the alarm system. The next time we come back, everything's just as it is now, plus it's quicker. A couple of guys go down first, we cover them from the rooftop, in case we've missed something, if not, we all go down. Saves time."

"That's not bad, mate. Okay, we do it your way. Get a couple of guys organised," John said, patting Mark on the shoulder.

"Guys, we're going over the wall, I need two volunteers to go first. The rest of us will cover you," Mark shouted to the men.

Six of the soldiers stepped forward to volunteer.

"Okay, Jimmy and Phil, over you go and be careful," Mark said, having picked his two men.

They attached ropes to the roof struts and lowered the other ends into the parking lot. The two soldiers who had volunteered, rappelled down the wall and stood in the parking lot, ready for anything but nothing moved. They waited for a minute, just in case but the situation didn't change.

"Let's go. Everybody down but stay alert," John said.

It took barely two minutes and everyone was down in the parking lot, automatically assuming a defensive posture. John and Mark went to control the trucks, while the rest of the men kept watch. After checking all six, they confirmed all fuel tanks had enough fuel, and all trucks were drivable.

"Okay guys, mount up just as we discussed. Mark, open the gates, I'll cover you. You ride with the first truck, I'll re-lock the gates and catch the last one," John said, starting to move.

"Wait a sec., John. Why not take them all? It means four trucks with three guys riding them, and two with two guys. The trucks with only two riding in them go first, the rest follow in case the others need backup. We've got the helicopters watching our backs. We can do it easy."

"It's tempting but I don't want to spread us too thinly. Anything could still happen," John argued.

"We haven't seen a thing all the way over here, not one creature. If we take all six, then we save at least a little time, it gets us ahead of schedule. That's got to be a plus. The only possible problem will be getting into the castle but it's going to be midday when we get back. Those things are rarely out and about in the midday sun and we have the gas bombs just in case. Punching a way through shouldn't be a problem. We can do it, John."

"What do you think, guys?" John asked the rest of his men.

They were unanimous, go for it.

"Good, you win," John said. "Bravo One, do you copy?"

Bravo One and Two were the call signs of the two helicopters.

"Loud and clear, John. Over," came the reply.

"We will be leaving with six, I repeat, six trucks, shortly. You're our eyes, guys. One of you leads the way, one stays at the back. Once we get to within three miles of the castle, fly ahead and drop your loads. Inform the Major we're approaching. He knows what to do. Everything clear? Over."

"Crystal, John, ready when you are. Over and out."

The men were divided amongst the trucks, everything regarding the plan and the route checked and re-checked. Mark was sitting in the first truck. John was to open and re-lock the gates, making life difficult for any nosy creatures, or looters for that matter that might show an interest in their supermarket and then ride with the last truck.

"Let's go," he shouted and opened the gates.

The first truck left the lot, turned right on to the main street and slowly started driving out of town. The second, third, fourth and fifth truck quickly followed, the convoy quickly starting to pick up speed. John was trying to lock the gates, the sixth truck waiting for him, when suddenly the pilot of Bravo One spoke over the headset.

"This is Bravo One, we've got some activity on the street, over to the left of your position. There's a group of creatures coming your way. I can see at least ten, there may be more concealed. I seriously suggest you get the hell out of there! Over."

The gates were not locked yet but John did not want to leave them open, it could complicate their plan later. He made a decision and signalled the last truck to leave, without him! The guys in the truck hesitated for a second but eventually they drove off. All six trucks were away and safe. Mark, hearing everything that was happening over his headset, spoke.

"John, where the hell are you?"

"Don't worry about me. I've locked the gates and will catch another ride out of here. Just keep going, I'll be right behind you."

"We're coming back for you!" Mark almost screamed into his headset.

"Negative. Bravo One can pick me up. We'll rendezvous on the road. Keep going, those trucks are important."

The gates finally locked, John started for the ropes leading to the roof.

"Bravo One, come in. Over."

"Reading you John. Over."

"Pick me up on the roof a.s.a.p. Over."

"On the way. Over and out."

They were coming. He hoped they would be quick enough. As he started up the wall, he could hear the creatures were already at the locked gates. Trying to concentrate on climbing, he could not help wondering if they would hold. As he got to the rooftop, he realised they had not. The two ropes tied to the roof struts, were both being used. The creatures were climbing up and quickly. Where was the bloody helicopter?

He could see it coming to his aid but it wasn't going to reach him in time! The first two creatures were already clambering on to the rooftop. His two Berettas were in his hands, safety's off. Turning to face the onrushing creatures, he shot the first two, both head shots, both kills. They fell from the roof. Already the next ones were coming. John, edging backwards, shot again. Both pistols bucked in his hands, again both creatures fell. This time however, only one stayed down. The other, only wounded, lunged at him again. He fired twice more, this time nailing it but another two were almost upon him. He thought of the sword strapped to his back but he realised he would never reach it in time. He made to fire again but suddenly lost his balance and stumbled backwards. He realised this was it and closed his eyes, waiting for the pouncing creatures to strike. He thought of Stephanie, how he would miss her. It was weird, he had always heard that your life flashes before your eyes just before you died, had not really believed it. Now he knew better!

As he landed on his back he heard shots. Heavy concentrated fire, coming from behind him. He dared to open his eyes again and witnessed how the creatures, one by one, fell to the withering fire. After another few seconds the last creature fell down, dead.

He turned, resting on his elbows, and saw one of the helicopters hovering at roof level, its cargo door open. Kneeling in the open doorway were Mark and another member of his team. They had disobeyed orders and come back for him. If they had not . . . He shivered at the thought. He had underestimated the creatures and it had nearly cost him his life. He vowed there and then never to do it again.

The helicopter landed and picked him up.

"Okay, John?" Mark asked.

John felt like kissing his friend but instead said, "Yes, thanks guys. It was close, almost too close."

"Yes, well that's the last time we ever split up. You know the Major's rule, nobody gets left behind. Any problems with that, John?" Mark asked.

"No, not any more. You live and learn. I just learned the hard way. You keep reminding me, mate. Okay pilot, let's catch the rest of the trucks up, as quick as you can, please," John said.

He leant back against the helicopter's fuselage and sighed deeply. He had been close to dying. He knew that he had made a mistake he never intended to make again.

After ten minutes, they had caught up the small convoy and were all sitting where they should have been. They experienced no further difficulties and, about ninety minutes later, reached the point where the helicopters were due to leave them. They would both fly on ahead, deliver the new gas weapons and then provide covering fire if required. The trucks would wait until evidence of the attack on the creatures was visible, then drive through. The pilots also had to inform the castle defenders that the trucks were on their way using their more powerful radios. The headsets were useful but only had a limited range. Once informed, Robert would also organise covering fire from the castle battlements.

After what seemed like seconds, Mark could see the gas had been delivered. He informed John who was sitting in the last truck. John ordered the men to put on their gas masks and told the drivers to punch their way through. If everything worked as it should, then any creature coming into contact with the vaporous cloud that was filling the forest in front of them, would be rendered unconscious. At least that was the theory. The gas had been put together using a combination of the tranquilliser, used so successfully in the operation to capture the creature and a gas left over from the war. Bill had felt confident it would not kill the creatures but they would be disabled enough that they could not attempt to interfere with the small convoy driving through their ranks. John had not liked the idea of relying on an untested weapon but there had been no time nor opportunity to test it properly. He knew one thing for sure - he trusted Bill's judgement. The soldier seemed very competent and knew exactly what he was doing. If Bill said it would work, John would go on that assumption.

The convoy was driving through the forest, fast approaching the cloud of dissipating gas. It had apparently done its job, as there were no creatures in sight. They drove through into the clearing, Mark could see the castle's drawbridge was down and the gates were open. For a second his heart almost stopped, a sense of panic mounting in him but then he remembered it was all part of the plan. He could see the two helicopters, hovering to the left and right of the castle entrance, ready to offer covering fire if needed. The trucks were racing over the clearing heading for the open doorway, his leading the way, the others close behind. They started driving into the castle, still no sign of trouble. One, two, three, four, five, all six trucks were safely inside, the gates closing and the drawbridge being raised. As soon as everything was secure, the two helicopters landed safely on their pads, their fuel desperately low.

Six trucks safely delivered, John breathed. It had gone pretty well, no real trouble, he thought. They would all learn from the experience, especially him! Next time would be even better. Next time, the thought did not exactly enthral him.

Upon exiting his truck, he saw Stephanie running towards him. They embraced and she kissed him hard on the mouth.

"I heard you nearly got killed!" she almost screamed at him.

"No," John said smiling. "It wasn't even close. Mark was there to look after me. I underestimated how quick they can be. Don't worry, it won't happen again. How are you feeling?"

"A lot better. Especially now," she said, hugging him.

"Congratulations, John," Robert said, suddenly appearing from somewhere. "How was it?" he asked.

"No problems," John replied, sheepishly. "At least, nothing we couldn't handle."

Chapter Twelve - Second Thoughts

Robert asked if they were making a second trip that day, as originally planned, John deciding no. For now, he had had enough. During the next trip they would have to secure the second supermarket and drive the trucks that were parked there back to the castle. In the remaining hours of daylight, there would not be enough time. They would get a fresh start in the morning, at first light.

The team had eaten together, discussing the morning's events. John had praised them all, they had worked well together. He had been the weak link in the chain and with Mark and another soldier having to come back and rescue him, his actions had jeopardised the whole mission. He felt it only right to ask the team if they still wanted him as leader, or whether it would be better for Mark to take over? In his time as an operative with Special Services, his actions had never endangered another member of his team. What had happened that morning in Hadlee was really bothering him. He felt as if they were all already good friends, not just soldiers doing a job. He could not live with himself if his actions resulted, unnecessarily, in the loss of one of those friends. He would understand and totally accept it if the rest of the team all felt that Mark would make the better leader.

Mark himself was the first to loudly reject this notion, followed by every other member of the team. Mark pointed out that John's actions had ensured his team got away first, he had not thought of himself at all. Such an action from an officer leading a mission, was something unusual, at least to him. Mostly it was the enlisted men who were sacrificed to ensure the officer got away. This fact proved to Mark and he was sure to the rest of the men sitting there, that John was exactly the right man to lead them. What had happened on the roof of the supermarket would never happen again. It was all of their jobs to make sure of that. Not just John's!

After they had finished their meal, they went to inspect the freshly liberated trucks. All six were okay and had survived the journey well. In the meantime an unexpected bonus had been discovered, one of the trucks had not been properly unloaded. There was half a load of tinned goods still on board. This meant the four week deadline, John had unofficially set, could be stretched a little.

Work had already begun on modifying the vehicles. The rear doors were being welded shut. New entrances were being cut into the truck roofs and firing ports in the side panels. At some stage the side walls of all the trucks would be armoured. The trucks in which people would be travelling heavily so, the transport vehicles only lightly. On all the roofs steel walls would be built into place, big enough for the soldiers to kneel behind but still be able to fire from. In two corners of the important trucks, heavy calibre machine guns would be mounted, adding extra firepower when needed.

John spoke shortly to Bill, who was confident all modifications would be completed on time, including one or two surprises. He did not want to say what, just in case his plans did not work but felt reasonably sure they would. Stockpiles of ammunition and medical supplies were already packed on board the sixteen tonners. They were well on schedule.

All in all, John and Mark were very impressed with Bill and his team's efforts. They also congratulated them on the success of the modified gas weapons used so effectively that morning.

After saying goodbye to Bill, John and Mark decided to go over the plans for the following day. The reality of what had nearly happened that morning was still worrying John. The creatures had once again almost proved how deadly they could be. Any mistakes the following morning could prove fatal for the whole team. They found a quiet corner, back in the canteen and, together with Stephanie, decided to come up with a few last minute changes. John had meant what he had said about never underestimating the creatures again.

After about two hours brainstorming the following day's battle plan, it was decided that the sixteen-man team needed back up. The helicopters would make two trips. The first time the entry team, consisting of John's men, would be flown in. They would be dropped on to the roof of the second supermarket and, after forming a defensive perimeter, they would wait there. The helicopters would then return to the castle, where they would bring back another sixteen soldiers as back-up. This unit, consisting mostly of snipers, would then take up positions on both of the supermarket roofs. The way the two buildings were situated, they overlooked each other, it would be easy to create a killing zone around the buildings. This would hopefully give the entry team a little more time to secure the inside of the building, without the risk of further attack from creatures coming from the outside. Once the supermarket was secure, the trucks would be commandeered and the entry team would leave. The helicopters would then extract the roof teams and escort the trucks back to the castle again. This time they would take extra fuel along with them, either for the trucks or the helicopters. John felt this plan was a big improvement on the old one and the chance of completing the mission without casualties was greatly improved because of it.

Stephanie was also relieved that John and Mark had, at last, recognised some of the dangers in what they were attempting. She found the macho side of men sometimes very annoying. She had had enough dealings with the creatures herself to realise they were not as stupid as people liked to believe. The next time they returned to Hadlee would be the third time in less than a week. Just as John had anticipated, the heightened activity around the town appeared to be attracting other creatures in the immediate area and their numbers could very quickly swell. With the extra soldiers being flown in, she felt more confident about the end result. The only problem, she realised, was the time the first team would have to spend alone on the roof of the second supermarket. John and Mark both assured her that until the second team arrived they would stay on the roof. John felt confident that the roof was too high for the creatures to reach, the only possible danger for his team was from within the supermarket itself. Both of the buildings had looked similar in design, which would mean small skylights, as on the roof of the other supermarket. If any of the creatures chose to attack that way, they would be limited in number and easy to deal with.

It was early evening and shortly the snipers on the wall would begin to engage any of the creatures that ventured out of the cover of the forest. John had arranged to meet Robert on top of the battlements to observe. Together with Mark and Stephanie, he made his way there. Ever since the attack made on the creatures three nights ago, less and less of them had been seen. John felt that night would not be different.

As they stood next to Robert looking out over the clearing, it was exactly as John had expected. There were no creatures in sight at all.

"What's happening?" Robert asked. "I don't get it. Ever since we took over here, every night we've seen them. Now all of a sudden, they're gone."

"They're still here, Robert," John answered. "We're witnessing something that no one has ever seen before. At least I've never heard or read any reports of it. They are showing us that they're not as stupid as we thought. They've learnt quickly. Think about it, all the times when they've come out at night and nothing has happened, the first time where we react and attack them they suddenly become wary. We've unwittingly changed the rules. The moment we set our plan in motion, they were forced to react. We now know they're intelligent, probably more so than we could have imagined. I would hazard a guess they'll be trying to solve their problem now."

"What problem, John?" Stephanie asked.

"How to get in here. Don't you get it? We were contained, posed no real threat to them. At least, that's how it must have seemed, we couldn't go anywhere. They would have settled for that. Now, through all the activity over the last week, they've probably guessed we want out. Stuck in here, to them at least, we were as good as dead. There was no need to attack, no reason for any of them to die. Eventually, we'd have disappeared without them having to do anything. But now everything's changed. Shit, we are in deep trouble," John answered.

"What do you mean, John?" Mark asked, not really getting John's point.

"They'll be more vigilant now. When we fly out in the morning, they'll know we are coming back, probably with more trucks, just like today. If they have a way to communicate with other groups of creatures and we have no reason to believe they don't, then we may have a warm welcome waiting for us in Hadlee. If not, then when we come back here they'll be waiting for us, more prepared than today! All this 'coming out at night' could just have been a ruse. Up until now they haven't needed to do a lot to keep us guessing, just appear now and then. I've got a feeling we'll find out a lot more about them in the days and weeks to come," John replied, troubled by the latest development.

"What can they do?" Robert asked, not appearing worried. "As far as I know, there's no recorded instance of them using weapons, it's always been brute force. How can they hope to stop us?"

"I have no idea but tomorrow, Robert, you'd better keep an eye on what's going on out there. If they do have a surprise waiting for us, you'll have to deal with it because we won't be able to. How are the repairs on the Apache coming along?" John asked, realising that that particular aircraft could prove very useful in days to come.

"I've got to see Bill about that tonight and the progress on the tanks. As far as I know they are still working on the problems. Bill seemed to think they'd sort it out, it would just take a little time," Robert reported.

"Time's maybe something we haven't got a lot of but, okay, Bill's a good bloke to have and he's got a lot on his plate at the moment but the extra firepower would come in very handy."

"Do you really believe we're in trouble, John? There's no way they can get in here, we discussed that. The castle's secure. Even if they were moderately armed, we could still hold them back indefinitely. Using the gasses we've developed and the helicopters, we can punch right through them, just like this morning, no problem. The fact that they're hiding from us means they're scared, nothing more. We must have nailed quite a few of them three nights ago. They're shitting their pants!"

"They don't have pants, Robert," John said, smiling at the comment.

"You know what I mean," Robert said, laughing. "They are like us in one way, John, they don't want to die. That's the reason why they're hiding now, the only reason - they don't want to die!"

"I hope you're right, Robert, I really do. One thing I know for sure, this morning I underestimated them and it nearly cost me my life. I won't do that again. I suggest none of us does."

Chapter Thirteen - Supermarket 2

After finishing the conversation on the battlement the evening before, they had slept. John had felt tired. As he awoke he decided the episode on the supermarket roof had got to him more than he had realised. He smiled, maybe his beautiful girlfriend had given him the flu. She was still not feeling one hundred percent and had reluctantly agreed to stay in the castle again. He looked at her, thankful that she had seen sense but worried that she had not put up more of a fight. Thankfully, she was sleeping peacefully, her first good night's sleep in several days. He loved her with all his heart. It was clear to him now how lonely he would have been if he had never met her. Why did they have to be alive now he thought? Why not one hundred years before when they would have had a better life together, a house and probably children? Everything that couples had always taken for granted, they could have none of it. He could not offer her anything and she deserved so much. They all deserved something more than the existence that was being forced upon them.

It was 0500 hours. In one hour his team would be assembled and they would, once again, head to Hadlee. He had to shower, get dressed and have some breakfast. Generally before a mission he had never eaten much but a little something in his stomach had always helped him fight his nerves. He had cleaned his weapons the evening before; they at least, were ready. It was slowly time for him to start getting ready. He looked over at Stephanie again, leant over and kissed her gently on the cheek, not wanting to wake her. She stirred, opened her eyes and smiling, asked him what time it was.

"Early," he replied. "Go back to sleep."

"Come back to bed, sexy," she said, teasingly.

"Stop it," he said, playfully pushing her off him. "Unlike some of us, I've got to go to work and I've got to get ready. Besides, you're poorly."

"I'm feeling alright at the moment and they won't leave without you," she insisted and pulled him on top of her.

He was twenty minutes late. He hated un-punctuality and could see his men waiting for him, talking in small groups but it had been worth it. Over by the helicopters he could see Robert and Mark, also deep in conversation, probably about him being late, he thought. As he approached, his men came to attention and saluted.

Robert and Mark asked, obviously teasing, if he had overslept?

"Wankers!" he said, laughing. "Let's go! Robert, see you later."

They boarded the helicopters and took off.

"You guys all ready?" John asked the men in his helicopter. All of them giving the same reply.

"Mark, everything clear?" he asked, using his headset.

"No problems, John. Everything's arranged just as we discussed yesterday and Robert's hoping to have a little surprise ready in time, just in case."

"Okay. I want this to go exactly by the numbers, nobody takes any chances. Is that clear? You need to keep on top of them, Mark, I'm relying on you."

"Clear, John," Mark replied. "We know what's at stake. I'll be watching what we're all doing and that includes you."

After twenty minutes Hadlee was once again below them.

"I'm beginning to hate this town," John whispered to himself. "Pilot, same as last time, please. Hover, if everything looks okay, then land on the roof of the second supermarket. Once we've exited the aircraft, take off and wait for Bravo Two, then proceed back to the castle at best speed. Get those other men back here a.s.a.p., we might need them. Bravo Two, same procedure. Over."

John's helicopter hovered over the building for a minute and, with its pilot not seeing anything suspicious, set down on the roof. They exited the aircraft and took up defensive positions around the roof to cover Bravo Two's descent. After touching down, the other half of John's men joining him on the roof, the second helicopter took off again and together with Bravo One sped off in the direction of the castle.

"We're on our own, at least for a while," John said into his headset. "Stay alert and report anything that looks even remotely suspicious. Mark, take a look down into the store, see if anything looks out of place. You and you," he continued, pointing to two of his men, "cover the intersection over there to the left. You and you, over there to the right."

At that moment Mark came back having checked the store, using the skylights built into the roof. He had also checked the back of the building.

"Everything looks okay, John, no activity at all. The back gates are closed and six trucks are parked there, waiting for us. Should we go for it?" he asked.

"No!" John said with authority. "We wait until the backup arrives. The last time we were here we had visitors, so we know the creatures are in the vicinity. If it was dark now, we'd almost certainly be under attack. Until we know otherwise, we go on the assumption that they're here somewhere. No, we stay put and wait. In about forty minutes unit two will be here and the snipers can watch our backs."

They waited, everything seeming quiet, almost too quiet, John thought. He wondered if maybe he was becoming just a little paranoid. Perhaps Robert was right and John was giving the creatures too much credit but he still felt, if that was the case, it was a healthy thing to do.

At that point, one of his men reported seeing movement at the end of the street to their left. A few seconds later, movement was reported in a wooded area over to their right.

"Mark, I don't like this. They are on at least two sides of us, you can't tell me that's a coincidence. Do it quietly but tell the men to be ready. We're in the shit!"

He could sense something, he was not sure what or how. Up until now, while in combat situations at least, he had always trusted his gut and his gut was telling him to expect trouble. He looked around the rooftop but could see nothing that seemed even remotely suspicious. He looked down over the side of the roof, at the front of the building, nothing. He told Mark to check the sides while he checked the back.

At the back there was nothing that seemed out of place. No fire escape, no ladder in sight, no apparent way up on to the roof. Something was wrong but what? At that moment, movement was seen at the front of the store, in a group of buildings across the street. They were nearly surrounded, only the back of the building seeming secure.

"The back," John whispered.

"What did you say, John?" Mark asked, missing what John had said.

"Come with me quickly," John replied.

They both moved, again to the back of the building re-examining the parking lot there. Everything looked just as it should. The gates appeared shut. There was no way to verify they were locked, at least not without somebody leaving the roof area. That was something John was not about to risk. The trucks were parked, just as they had been the last time they were there. The rear door to the supermarket was closed, again no safe way to see if it was locked. John knew they were missing something. Creatures to the left, right, and now in front of them but no apparent way for them to get up on to the roof. It was a good twenty five feet to the rooftop, he felt sure they could not jump that high. It had to be the back, something he could not see, did not expect. The other creatures had meant to show themselves. Diversion but from what? Gate closed, door closed, trucks intact. It had to be there, whatever it was, he was missing it.

He checked again, then he spotted it. It was subtle, that frightened him somehow but there was no time for that now. They had to escape the trap that was about to be sprung on them. It was the trucks, the six vehicles appeared parked as before but for one. It was parked closer to the building than the others, not much he thought, maybe two yards but that meant that from the back of the truck's roof to the roof of the building, was at most fifteen feet. He had almost missed it. They would be coming that way when they came, the gates appearing closed but almost certainly open, up over the vehicles and on to the rooftop.

"Mark, do you see it? The last truck has been moved and it wasn't driven. You can just make out how the wheels have skidded, it's been pushed. This is a trap and it's about to spring. Get the guys organised quickly, two cover the left side, two the right, two the front, the rest to the back. When they come, they'll be coming this way," John said, rapidly giving out his orders.

"Are you sure, John?" Mark asked. "What if you're wrong? The guys at the front and on the sides won't be able to hold out for very long."

"Believe me, they are coming this way. Think about it for a second, they don't show themselves, you know that, they attack. At least up until now that's how it's always been. Now, we see creatures to the left, the right and in front of us but nothing behind us. Those we see, don't attack. Why not? They attack on sight. For whatever reason they are holding back. Now if that's the case, I bet it's the first time ever!"

At that moment the soldiers watching the left side of the building, reported the creatures were attacking. Almost simultaneously the attacks from the right side and in front of the building also began. John gave the order to open fire.

"Mark, go check how many of them are attacking."

After a minute, Mark came back to report. There were groups of about thirty creatures attacking each side of the building. They were getting closer and the defending soldiers might need help at any second.

"Thirty!" rasped John. "Shit, we are in big trouble. How long until the helicopters are due back?"

Mark checked his watch.

"About ten minutes, maybe."

"Let's hope we can last that long," John said, seriously.

"John, there's still nothing at the back, shouldn't we help the other guys?" Mark asked, slightly flustered.

"We stay here. Trust me, mate," John said calmly.

"You know I do but . . ."

At that second the creatures closed the trap. From behind the supermarket, it seemed out of almost every building, they appeared and charged. John stopped counting at fifty but there were at least twice that many. They stormed through the gates, which had obviously been unlocked and started to climb on to the trucks.

"Fire!" John shouted and started to shoot down into the attackers.

His men obeyed immediately and engaged the advancing mob of creatures. The noise was deafening, the men emptying magazine after magazine into the rapidly approaching enemy.

For every one they killed another seemed to appear. His men were burning hundreds of rounds of ammunition and John realised they could not keep it up for very long. The men from the front of the building now joined in the battle at the back, firing at targets of opportunity, those from the sides doing the same. The creatures that had created the diversion, were also joining the attack at the back of the building.

"Ammunition's going fast, John," Mark shouted, over the noise of the battle.

"Use the grenades!" John shouted back.

"What about the trucks, they'll be destroyed?" Mark asked.

"Sod the trucks, if we can't beat them back we're finished!"

"Grenades!" Mark shouted, the men responding.

Those men carrying them, used them. Explosions erupted all over the parking lot. Debris rained down on the defenders of the rooftop but their supply of the deadly weapons was quickly exhausted and the creatures kept coming. Firing continued but John realised in next to no time they would be fighting hand to hand. He, himself, had only two magazines left for the M-16 plus a few for his two Berettas. It would all go quickly.

Mark appeared next to him.

"Should we run, John?" he asked, desperately.

"Where to?" John answered. "If we leave the rooftop, we're dead! Keep at them."

Some of the men were already down to pistols, their rifles out of ammunition. They were being pushed back from the edge of the roof, the creatures slowly but surely, gaining the upper hand. After another two or three minutes, the leading creatures made it on to the roof.

John shouted to his men.

"Swords."

The men without ammunition now fought their way back into the fight. Swords for everyone. John drew his Samurai, standing next to him Mark, in his hand a short sword. They looked at each other for a second, both realising they could not hold out for long. They sprang into the middle of the fighting. More and more of the creatures were making it on to the rooftop, the fighting desperate.

John's headset suddenly burst into life.

"Entry team, this is Bravo One, do you require assistance? Over."

"You bet your sweet arse we do!" John replied. "Are you armed Bravo One? Over."

"We are, John. Where do you want it? Over"

"Around this building and pour it in here. Over and out."

John shouted into his headset.

"Masks, get your masks on now!"

Still fighting and at the same time pulling on his gas mask, John could hear the helicopters approaching. Suddenly he was blown over by explosions, the complete building and surrounding area immediately enveloped in a gas cloud. If the team that had developed the gas had been right then everything in the area, without a mask, would be asleep in seconds. He waited.

After about thirty seconds, the gas had dissipated enough to reveal the scene on the rooftop. Twelve of his men were still alive, three were dead. They had killed well over one hundred of the creatures, and easily as many again were now sleeping.

He looked for Mark, who was alive and, although slightly injured, well. He told him to get the roof cleared, at least enough that one of the helicopters could land. His men quickly did this, although John was not sure that launching the creatures over the sides of the building was appropriate. Still, he could not blame his men for their reaction. After all, if the helicopters had not turned up when they had, they would all have died.

Bravo One landed, the soldiers inside taking up defensive positions around the roof. They kept the sleeping creatures covered just in case they woke up a little earlier than anticipated. His men reloaded their weapons from the supplies carried by the helicopter.

"Now what?" Mark asked, his wounds cleaned and dressed by the field medic in their unit.

"I don't know," John replied. "How many trucks are still intact?"

"We'll have to go down and check, I don't know," Mark answered.

"The way I see it, these things should sleep for about the next two hours. We can check the trucks and take those that are still okay with us. Get Bravo Two down here, the men inside can help."

"Bravo One, take off and hover. Bravo Two, land at this location, please. Over," Mark ordered, using his headset.

"Copy that. Over and out," came the confident reply.

"Remind me to buy those guys a big drink when we get back. They saved our necks," John told Mark.

"We'll buy them two," Mark replied, sighing out loud.

Once the men were all on the roof, John explained what they were going to do. It was now safe to enter the supermarket, as the gas would have disabled any creatures hiding there. They were going through the building to check the trucks at the back. As soon as they had established how many, if any, were still driveable, they would empty the supermarket of everything they could use. This would then be taken back to the castle. Only four men should stay on the roof to guard the area, the rest of them would load the trucks. That way, the loading would be done as quickly as possible. The two helicopters should constantly patrol the immediate vicinity for signs of approaching creatures but he anticipated they would have no more trouble, at least until the ones sleeping woke up.

They moved quickly down into the building and, just as John had expected, there were no surprises waiting there for them. They moved to the back door, which proved to be locked. Mark asked if he should find the keys? John replied by kicking the door open. There was no point to keys, the supermarket was a loss. They would not be coming back there. Once outside, it was quickly established that three trucks had been destroyed during the attack but three were still driveable. John kept checking his watch, keeping an eye on the time important because of the sleeping beauties lying all around them. In about one hundred minutes, if Bill was right and John had no reason to doubt him, the creatures would be waking up. The men had to work fast.

Bodies were cleared to make room to work. The three trucks that were still operable were backed up to the rear entrance of the building. John spoke to his men informing them that in one hour they were leaving, that was the time they had to load everything useful they could find into the three waiting trucks.

The men worked quickly and in forty five minutes all three trucks were full to bursting.

"Okay, well done, men," John said. "Penetration team stays with me, that means four men per truck, plus me. The rest of you back on the roof for extraction."

He spoke into his headset.

"Bravo One and Two, come in. Over."

"We're here, John. What do you need? Over."

"Bravo One land for pick up. Before you take off again, re-fuel using your on-board supply, we've got plenty. Once you're clear, Bravo Two should do the same. Bravo Two, please pick up the bodies of my men and transport them back to the castle. It will be a squeeze but I won't leave them behind, the trucks are too full. Once you're both airborne, we will leave. Follow us and keep your eyes peeled, the trip home could be interesting. Over and out."

Before he had even finished speaking John could hear Bravo One coming in to land.

"Okay guys, let's get the hell out of here. Mark, what explosives have we got with us?"

"C4," Mark replied, looking a little puzzled. "And plenty of it."

"Where did that suddenly come from?" John asked.

"I just took it off Bravo One when we re-armed, just in case," Mark answered.

John smiled.

"Good, rig the place to blow, thirty minute delay."

"What about the creatures that are sleeping John?" Mark asked, shocked by this request.

"Fuck em!" John replied. "I'm pissed, mate, really pissed. We lost three good men today. We'll send them a message that they can understand. There was no need for this, it's no longer a misunderstanding, their actions today were cold and calculated. Don't misunderstand me, I don't hate them but this has become a fight for survival. I think I finally started to realise that this morning. We have a responsibility to the ones we love, not just ourselves. It's not a moral question anymore. I tried very hard to make it one, almost succeeded but what happened here today gave me a wake up call. If the helicopters had been five minutes later, then things would have turned out differently. I wouldn't have seen Stephanie ever again. That thought really pisses me off, you know what I mean? I think I finally realised this morning just how important she is to me. These things are not going to stop me getting her out of here. Even if it means I have to kill every last one of them to do it!"

Mark stared for a second, then answered.

"You don't have to convince me, mate, like you said, fuck em, fuck em all to hell!"

The charges were set. The helicopters landed and took off again, the trucks were already leaving the town's limits.

Twenty five minutes after the last truck had left, the first creatures that were still alive started to wake up. A couple of seconds later their world was blown to hell.

In the three trucks that were now heading back towards the castle, the mood was mixed. On the one hand, sombre - they had lost three good friends in the battle that morning. On the other hand, a kind of elation because they had survived.

John and Mark were talking in the leading vehicle.

"We did bloody well, John, we only lost three. It could have been a hell of a lot worse," Mark suggested.

"Yeah, right, tell that to the three guys who died," John replied.

"I know it's hard, mate but if we hadn't changed the plan at the last minute, we'd all be dead now. We were supposed to enter the building, remember. That's why they waited so long before attacking, they wanted us inside. If we'd gone in as planned, we'd have been trapped. The second we'd have opened the back door they'd have rushed us. In the confined space we would have been overwhelmed. With us staying put on the roof, they were forced to attack us as they did. That saved us. You saved us by smelling the trap in the first place. If I'd had my way, we would have gone inside. Don't just think about the three we lost, think about the thirteen you saved. Second guessing them and your training with the swords did that."

"I know you're right, Mark. I've lost men before, that's not it. What worries and scares me is how quickly they organised. I think you'll agree, that was a well-planned attack. The distraction, the truck moved just enough, those aren't the actions of mindless animals. They are well thought out and proves they are intelligent, but what scares me the most is how they knew we were coming. What they did wasn't spur of the moment, it was very carefully thought out, that takes time. I can't imagine they've been waiting for us since the last time we were here. That means they received word we were coming this morning. How the hell did they do that? It's seventy miles from the castle to Hadlee. How do you get a message sent seventy miles without radio, telephone or any other means of communication?"

"Runners, maybe?" Mark suggested.

"It took us, what, twenty minutes in the helicopters? Nothing can run seventy miles in twenty minutes. It's something else, something we're missing. Maybe they can communicate telepathically with each other, I don't know. We'll find out soon enough though, because we've got to get back into the castle and I've got a feeling they know we're coming."

"What do we do?" Mark asked.

"Take them head on. Let's hope Robert can help us, that could make the difference."

Chapter Fourteen - Getting Home

"How far, John?" Mark asked.

"About three miles from the forest, six from the castle. Start to slow down," he told the Corporal driving the truck. "I don't want to risk the woods without the helicopters taking a look first," then speaking into his headset, he continued. "Bravo One and Bravo Two, do you copy? Over."

"Bravo One here, John. We copy you. Over."

"Fly on alone over the forest and check the road out, see what's waiting there for us. We'll wait here. Bravo One, you then return to give us cover. Bravo Two, fly on to the castle and report to the Major. Tell him if he can, he should try to back us up."

The helicopters flew off, John told the Corporal to stop the truck. Speaking into his headset, he addressed his men.

"Listen up, guys, we're about four miles from home. I don't know what's waiting for us but they're not going to let us just drive past without trying to stop us. Keep your doors locked and fire through the side windows. Drivers, if anything gets in front of you, mow it down. If any of you get into trouble, stay cool, the rest of us will try to reach you. Bravo One is flying backup and can also pick any of us up if there's trouble. After this morning, expect anything. I've no idea what they could have waiting for us. They've never used weapons, as far as we know but we can't count it out. All we can do is try to finish our mission. Rely on your training and we'll get through. A lot of people are counting on us, let's not let them down."

"Good speech," whispered Mark, a smile on his face.

"Shut up," John replied quietly. "This could be serious," but he was also smiling.

"We'll make it, John, don't worry," Mark assured him.

"John, this is Bravo One. Come in. Over."

"Bravo One, good to hear you again. Give us some good news, please. Over."

"It looks quiet, John. The road seems clear, no apparent difficulties in sight. Over."

John looked at Mark.

"What's going on?" he asked, puzzled.

"Maybe they aren't as clever as we thought. Our imagination was running riot, who knows? If there's nothing in sight John, we should go," replied Mark, hopefully.

"No!" John said firmly. "They are waiting for us to do just that, let our guard down. There's another trap out there waiting for us to walk right into. We have to find it, otherwise we can't prepare for it. Bravo One, take another look, will you? Report anything that looks even remotely suspicious. Over."

"Roger that, on the way. Over and out."

"The longer we stay here the more time we're giving them to prepare. Shouldn't we go?" Mark asked.

"Mark, we've become good friends in a relatively short time but you don't really know me that well or Stephanie, for that matter. God, I wish she was here now. We were both picked to be instructors because we are both bloody good at what we do. During the time we were operatives, we ran into a lot of good men from different departments. One guy I've never forgotten, was Bill Anderson; we became good friends. Bill was a mind guy. He was a Sergeant with the Marines in the two Gulf wars, even did two stints in Afghanistan. His job was always point man, leading the way, watching for danger. In all the fifty two missions he took part in, he never made a mistake. He avoided over twenty ambushes set for the men he was leading, saving lives every time. I asked him how he did it? Do you know what he said? He didn't know. He couldn't explain it. It was a gut thing, you know - the feeling you sometimes get in the pit of your stomach. A lot of people get these feelings but many choose to ignore them, Bill chose to follow them. His job afterwards was training soldiers to listen to and trust these feelings. I spent many hours talking with him and learnt how to trust myself. Stephanie is the same, maybe even better. She's got that whole women's thing working for her as well. What I'm saying, Mark is, I know something's wrong, I can feel it. I trust my gut just like Bill taught me. We wait."

"After what happened back in Hadlee who am I to argue? You say wait, we wait," Mark smiled. "We'll talk more about this gut thing later."

Two minutes later the helicopter was back.

"John, this is Bravo One, do you copy? Over."

"I hear you loud and clear, Bravo One. Anything suspicious. Over."

"We missed it the first time, I apologise. There's a section of the road about two hundred yards from the clearing, it's a different colour. Why, I don't know. From the air it looks as if tree

101

branches have been spread all over the road. That is the only thing that looks out of place. Over."

"That's got to be it. Looks like you found it Bravo One, well done. Any way to circumnavigate that section of the road? Over."

"Negative, John, to the right and left are trees. They could be moved but I don't see any way of doing it safely or quickly enough. Over."

"Using your radio set, can you contact the castle from here? Over."

"No problem, John. My set's powerful enough. What should I tell them? Over."

"Tell Major Jones we can't get through, we suspect an ambush. Ask him if he knows another way for us to reach the castle? Over."

The headsets they all wore were only good for short range. He made a mental note, if they lived through the apparent ambush, then next time they would take along a proper radio.

"John, this is Bravo One. Over."

"Go ahead Bravo One. Over."

He was getting pretty fed up of all this 'Over and Out' nonsense!

"Major Jones said to bring the trucks through. He'll take care of the rest. Over."

He looked at Mark

"What's that supposed to mean?" he asked.

"I've no idea. What does your gut say John?" Mark asked, playfully.

"Let's get going, I trust Robert. He'll have something up his sleeve."

Speaking into his headset, he continued.

"Okay guys, we are moving through the forest. Stay alert."

They started through, not driving too fast, unsure of what was waiting for them. The suspected ambush site was about a mile ahead. John felt sure it was something to do with the road surface being a different colour but exactly what, he didn't know. He was in the leading truck and ordered the driver to slow down as they approached the area of the suspected ambush. He could see the difference in the colour of the road surface but there were no clues as to why. It looked just as if somebody had thrown branches on the road, exactly as the helicopter pilot had reported. To the left and to the right were just trees, no creatures in sight. John noticed that further back in the trees, under cover of the treetops, were piles of earth. They would have been invisible from the air. He had not noticed them the last time they had driven through the forest, indeed the top layer of the mounds looked fresh, as if only just piled there. Where had the earth come from, what did it mean?

"Stop the truck," he shouted, suddenly understanding what it all meant.

"What's up?" Mark asked.

He was sitting next to John but could not see why his friend was getting so excited.

"That's a hole in the road," John said assuredly. "We are supposed to drive into it, then we'd be stuck and they could pick us off at their leisure. Warn the men, Mark, they'll be coming, we'll have to try and back out of here. Get the trucks moving now, or we are dead."

At that moment explosions erupted in the woods to the left and right of them. It was the gas again. Using his headset he very quickly told his men to put on their masks. They all pulled them on and sat there waiting.

Suddenly there was gas all around them, a big cloud of it in front of them but still no sign of creatures anywhere. It had only been a matter of seconds since the gas had been delivered but it seemed like forever just sitting there unable to do anything. John realised if they had been any slower in putting on their masks, they too would have slept like babies. He would have to discuss the art of communication with Robert, once they made it back to the castle. For now he was very interested to see how the Major was going to solve the small problem of the hole blocking their way. He heard a rumbling and could feel the truck's cab start to vibrate. Something was coming through the slowly dispersing gas cloud in front of them.

"What the hell is that?" John asked.

"It's one of the tanks!" Mark shouted, excitedly. "They've got the tanks going again. Alright."

In front of them now rumbled one of the massive tanks John had seen in the castle. They had been out of commission, as far as he knew, this must be Robert's surprise, he thought. The tank was moving menacingly towards them, its machine guns on scatter fire, firing to the left and right into the trees. Every now and then the big turret gun also fired, dishing out death and destruction. The tank drove straight into the hole in front of them, which turned out to be about two feet deep. John realised that if they had not seen it, they would have driven into it and been stuck. The trucks would not have made it back out. The tank, however, had no such problems, it slowly drove back and forth, flattening the sides of the trap that had been laid for them.

Through its considerable weight, the sides were quickly flattened so that the trucks could safely drive through, as long as they took their time doing it.

John's headset came to life.

"Captain Stewart, this is Major Jones. Would you and your men care to join me for dinner?"

"Smart arse!" John replied, playfully and instructed the driver to take them through, carefully.

He looked over at Mark and said, "Nah, gut feeling. What do you say now?"

"Impressive," Mark replied. "Very impressive," and they both laughed.

They had overtaken the tank and entered the castle first, the tank slowly crossing the clearing, occasionally firing behind it, at what John was not sure. One of the helicopters had taken up a covering position above the tank, John thought it looked unfamiliar. He then saw Bravo One and Two were 'parked' in their usual places, this was the Apache attack helicopter giving covering fire. They had fixed that as well.

Appearing next to John, Bill said, "Watch this, you'll be impressed."

At that moment, the Apache assumed an attack posture and demonstrated its firepower. It launched a number of missiles into the trees on both sides of the road, the explosions enormous.

In between time the tank had reached the safety of the castle, the gates were firmly closed, the drawbridge again raised. After the monster tank had parked, Robert appeared on top of its turret, he was waving at John and Mark. They walked over to him.

"Now, guys, what do you reckon? We've been busy," he said, patting his tank like a family pet.

"Thanks, Robert," John said. "You really came through for us."

Robert jumped down from the monstrous machine and embraced the two men.

"I thought it was about time I did something but the real heroes are Bill and his team. They worked right through the night to get everything ready in time."

"That's another drink we owe Bill," John said, looking at Mark, then he turned back to Robert. "Where is Stephanie?"

He was surprised she wasn't there to meet him.

"Nothing's happened to her, has it?" John asked, suddenly worried.

"No, she's fine," Robert said, sheepishly. "Somebody had to fly the Apache, she volunteered, John. I tried to talk her out of it but she wouldn't listen."

"What?" John shouted, seeming annoyed.

He looked over at the landing helicopter, he saw her sitting in the pilot's seat waving at him. She was very beautiful, he thought to himself and, shaking his head, he started to laugh. There would be no stopping her now. She climbed down from the aircraft and ran to him. They hugged and kissed.

"How do you like my new toy?" she asked, teasingly. "It's only a Mark II but it still packs one hell of a punch, don't you think?"

"I thought you were ill," he said, smiling and kissed her again. "You seem to have made a remarkable recovery."

"Anything for my man," she smiled. "Somebody had to watch your back."

Chapter Fifteen - Time to Regroup

They had rested, the morning's work having been harder than they expected. John reported the loss of the three men in Hadlee but Robert already knew. It was still only mid-morning and John wondered if they should return to the town straightaway. He found it difficult to believe the creatures could re-organise that quickly and it would definitely be the last thing they would expect. Mark confirmed the men were willing, the helicopters could be re-fuelled and re-armed within minutes, all John had to do was give the order. Robert argued, successfully that enough was enough for one day. They needed to bury their dead and re-group. It was now obvious that these things were far more intelligent and organised than they had first suspected. Every second they stayed in the castle, longer than they needed to, would make what they were attempting to do more and more difficult. However, now was not the right time for rash decisions. The funerals of the three casualties killed that morning would take place the following afternoon. Up until then, they would use the time to re-think their options. If both John and Mark felt another trip was unavoidable then they would have to plan for every conceivable problem that could arise. The only way to look at that morning's happenings was they now knew and understood far more about the creatures' capabilities. The fact that it had cost three lives was very unfortunate but, Robert argued, better three than thirty! He reminded the both of them that if they could imagine a problem, they could plan a way around it. Putting something quickly together now was just too risky and could cost more lives. With the Apache now airworthy and both tanks repaired they were better armed than before. Any future plans could be formed around that fact if need be. The tanks could travel at upwards of fifty miles an hour on open road, making it more than feasible to take them to Hadlee on future missions. The Apache was, by design, a flying, killing machine, nothing could escape its reach. Whatever was decided, with the additional firepower these mobile weapons could provide, the creatures would be hard-pressed in any forthcoming battles.

John seemed to think at least one more visit to the town would be necessary unless they found an alternative option. They still needed a few more trucks to cover all their needs comfortably. They now had a total of nine, whereas the original plan called for as many as twenty-four. Although nine would probably be enough for transporting everybody, it would greatly limit the amount of supplies they could take with them. Seeing that they had no idea how long they would be travelling, the quantity of supplies they took along could prove to be critical. The more they could take the better, meaning, while on the road at least, they would not have to stick to a schedule. The sixteen tonners were already packed, carrying everything other than food. The trucks they had brought back that morning were full of supplies but, if they could not take them along, it would mean re-supplying on a daily basis. That was a prospect that did not appeal to John as it would be very difficult, probably impossible, to do. Having to move into bigger towns, along their intended route, just to scrounge food was something he felt they should avoid at all costs. He came to the same conclusion as before, they had to go back, the only questions were when and how.

They also had to address the new, very dangerous, question of how the creatures communicated with each other. This was something that both intrigued and frightened him. If the method was as incredible as he suspected, then planning against it would be almost impossible. Robert suggested the creatures had been lucky with the timing of their ambush that morning. John, although agreeing it was a possibility, was still convinced they were missing something. It was probably a piece of the puzzle that they might never find. The only thing that could confirm it either way, were the creatures themselves and they were not about to talk.

Robert and Mark both agreed but insisted that with careful planning they could limit the chances of other surprises. They were both certain that they could at least lower the risk of any more ambushes. They could never be one hundred percent sure they had thought of everything but the three of them together should be able to cover most of the possibilities. John agreed fully but felt that the one or two percent they could not cover would prove to be the most dangerous.

Robert suggested they break for lunch and then rest a while. They could meet again later that afternoon to work out all the details.

John headed for the mess hall together with Stephanie. She told him how they had seen the creatures working in the forest shortly after the helicopters had left that morning. At first they had not understood what they were doing but, after watching them carry large amounts of earth into the trees, they had guessed. The work on the Apache had been quickly finished by Bill's team, in preparation for the return of John and his team. The tanks were already repaired at that time, thanks mostly to Bill and his men working through the night. Together with Robert and Bill she had quickly worked out the little surprise for the creatures that had enabled the trucks to reach the castle unmolested.

She was very proud of her contribution to the whole scenario but not as proud as he was of her. It had been difficult for him to undertake the last two missions in Hadlee without her by his side but he had only been thinking of her health and safety, a fact he was sure she was aware of. She had made it quite clear she was not impressed with being grounded through illness but had, surprisingly, respected his decision nevertheless. The events of the last few hours had made him realise how dangerous it would be for her to take part in any forthcoming missions. He had decided he could not and would not, allow himself to put her at risk again, especially now the creatures had become so unpredictable and dangerous. The only problem with his scenario was telling her. He knew her well enough to know she would normally have fought him tooth and nail. Her participation in the rescue mission had been the perfect answer to his problem and had hopefully got him off the hook. He could use the fact that they needed a third pilot to keep her out of harm's way, at least for most of the time.

They discussed the changes in the creatures, both agreeing the situation had become very dangerous for everybody. With the two traps set by them that morning, they had shown a side that nobody had ever witnessed before. At least no documents pertaining to this new behaviour had ever surfaced during their time with Special Services and John had made it his business to read them all. Things had definitely taken a turn for the worse!

After finishing their meal, John decided to get a few hours sleep. He had never liked sleeping in the daytime but he felt tired and decided, just this once, it was okay. He joked that maybe she had given him the flu after all.

Stephanie was not feeling tired, she was still feeling the buzz from flying the Apache attack helicopter. She had flown one before but not under such circumstances. She was also sure that if she had joined him, he might not have slept a great deal. Although the idea of something other than sleep warmed her, he had seemed really tired and she decided that if the plan for going back to Hadlee was to succeed then John would have to be one hundred percent fit. She told him she would wake him in a few hours and left to inspect her new toy. The Apache! Even the name gave her a thrill.

He smiled. She had seemed excited to be flying again. Up there she would be out of immediate danger, unreachable to the creatures. If he was lucky, he might not even need to make the suggestion that she concentrate on flying. If he was very lucky, she would assume the role of third pilot all by herself without any prompting. He laughed. He had always been lucky. After all, he had met Stephanie in the first place. Eventually, he slept.

Chapter Sixteen - The Tunnel

John was dreaming. It had been so long since he had slept deeply enough to dream, always in the back of his mind the thought of the creatures finding them unprepared and . . . The thought chilled him and he shut it out. He allowed himself to fall back into the dream he had been having, it had been enjoyable.

He was with Stephanie running down a mountain side, covered in wild flowers. It was a beautiful summer's day and she looked gorgeous. She stumbled in the lush grass and lay there laughing. As he caught her up, she pulled him down on top of her and they kissed. He could hear church bells somewhere in the distance but something wasn't right, the church bells were coming closer, getting louder . . . He woke up, but the bells did not stop ringing.

"Shit!" he said, realising they were not church bells but the castle's alarm instead.

He dressed quickly, pulling on the shoulder harness for one of his Berettas, the automatic already in place. He shoved the other one into his waistband and ran outside. There was activity everywhere, soldiers taking up positions on the battlements, helicopters starting, civilians running for cover. He could not see Robert or Mark anywhere, for that matter Stephanie was also missing. For a second he almost panicked but the Apache was still there parked. He decided she must be somewhere inside the castle itself, so he headed for the control room. He could only imagine one reason as to why the alarm bell was ringing, the creatures were attacking! There was only one way the creatures might be able to gain entrance into the castle compound and that was the tunnel. Maybe they had discovered the castle's only weakness. As he reached the control room, he was relieved to find Stephanie already there along with Robert and Mark.

"What's happening?" he demanded to know upon entering the room.

"The outside cameras have just stopped sending a signal, the last pictures showed creatures approaching them. Now it seems they are trying to get through the door," Robert replied, calmly.

"What are their chances of getting through?" John asked, trying to stay equally calm.

"I don't know to be honest," Robert replied. "After today we can't be sure about anything anymore. We know they are strong but that door's solid steel, over twenty inches thick and set into concrete. It must weigh a ton at least. I can't imagine they can get through, even if they do, thirty yards later there is another door equally as strong. Altogether there are five of those doors, after that they'll have to contend with the robot sentries. They are positioned every thirty yards or so, heavy steel doors between them. That's five thousand rounds of armour piercing ammunition they've got to evade. It should be a massacre. If they manage to get through all of that then there is still the last door. It is nearly three feet thick and is set into the castle walls themselves, built to withstand everything. If need be we can blow the C4 charges under the moat but I doubt it will be necessary, John. We should be safe enough."

"Is there any other way to get out there, other than the tunnel?" John asked, not convinced Robert was right.

"No, mate, the area's crawling with the creatures. We could see that before the outer cameras stopped sending a signal," Mark said.

"That means they were looking for the outer entrance," John stated. "That basically confirms our suspicions about how they communicate."

"What makes you say that?" Robert asked, not sure what John was driving at.

"Think about it. All the time you've been here they've never bothered with the tunnel before. Why now? Why today?"

"Bad luck on our part. They just came across it and figured it out," Robert suggested.

"No way, Robert, I don't believe in coincidences. A few days after we capture a creature and bring it in here using the very tunnel they have accidentally discovered, they attack. Can't anybody else see the connection?" John asked.

"It's possible, I suppose. The one we brought in here could have somehow sent a message before it died. But if that's the case why did they wait until now? They could have attacked yesterday or even the day before," Robert argued.

"When we brought it through the tunnel it was drugged. It never actually saw the tunnel itself but it would have recognised the general area where we attacked and captured it. It will have known that we somehow left the confines of the castle. Maybe it just sent a general description of the area and its pals have been looking ever since. Now they've found it, they aren't about to waste any time in trying to utilise it."

One of the soldier's responsible for monitoring the cameras interrupted.

"Sir, we have seen elevated numbers of creatures around the cave system over the last couple of days. We didn't really give it a second thought, it happens from time to time."

"See what I mean?" John said. "They've been systematically searching the area. We are in big trouble!"

At that moment the outer door seemed to buckle and fall outwards. It was gone, creatures pouring through the opening.

"Shit!" Robert shouted. "How the fuck did they do that?"

"No idea, maybe it's all the vitamins. Shit, we should have anticipated something like this after this morning's episode," John said. "If they've made it through the first door, you can be sure they'll make it to the last one. The sentries might slow them down but they won't stop them. By then, there'll be too many of them coming through the tunnel."

"What do you suggest we do, John, blow the moat?" Mark asked, still watching the cameras.

The creatures were at the second door, the cameras installed there suddenly stopping working.

"The cave system where the tunnel entrance was hidden, it's pretty deep and consists of granite. What if we blow it up around their heads? It would seal the way in and trap those creatures already inside. The robot sentries might be able to handle those, if not, then we blow the moat and they drown."

"We can blow the moat anyway," Robert said. "That'll stop them."

"No," John said. "If we blow it while the tunnel is still open, then the moat will empty. There'll be nothing to stop the water. Afterwards the tunnel would still be useable, and the moat would be empty. We've always assumed they can't swim otherwise they'd have stormed here long ago but I bet they can climb. If the moat was empty there would be nothing to stop them climbing the battlements and getting in here. For all we know, that is exactly what they want us to do."

Turning to Stephanie, he stood up.

"Come on, we need to blow up that cave system. Robert, keep watching the cameras. As a very last resort, blow the moat but be ready with everything you've got. Once the moat is empty, they'll attack in force. Mark, get the guys on the battlements ready. Get a team down into the cellar where that last door is, rig the whole room to blow. If it looks like they are getting through, then bring

112

the whole castle down on their heads. We'll have enough to do keeping them out without handing them a back door. Stephanie, come on, we have to be quick."

Without waiting for an answer, they both raced for the helicopter. John was sure in his mind it was the only chance. As they reached the Apache, they could see it had been re-armed since returning from its short adventure that morning.

"Thank God Bill's on the ball," John shouted.

Similar missiles to the ones fired earlier were in place, a complement of six. Hopefully it would be enough. They took off and headed towards the cave system they were about to destroy.

It took them only minutes to locate their target. Hovering overhead Stephanie armed the first two missiles. There were hundreds of the creatures massing in the area and John realised that if this did not work, they were lost.

She fired. The two high explosive missiles only taking a second to reach their intended target. The cliff side, where the cave system had been hidden, shook under the impact. The next two missiles also found their predetermined target, the final two following them in for good measure. After the dust from the explosions had settled, they could both see that the cliffs had been completely destroyed. The once secret entrance into the castle was now buried under thousands of tons of granite. John understood enough about explosions to know that the high temperatures generated by the missile impacts would have melted the rock and reformed it into giant slabs. The creatures could never uncover the entrance. They had stopped the chance of the tunnel ever being used against them again. The only question now was had they stopped it in time?

They raced back to the castle and landed. The moat still seemed intact, they had not blown it yet. As they touched down, no one came to meet them so they both ran for the control room. As they entered, over the microphones, they could hear the robot sentries firing. The noise was deafening.

"How are we doing?" John asked.

"You blocked the entrance, no more creatures are coming through but the ones already in the tunnel aren't finished yet," Robert said, his eyes fixed on the television monitors.

"Where are they?" Stephanie asked.

"They've made it through the first sentry. This is the second one but it's already running low on ammunition."

"How many of them are left?" John asked, looking over at Mark.

"It's hard to tell, maybe fifty. It's too smokey in there to get a clear view," Mark said.

Suddenly the firing stopped.

"That's it," Robert said. "The gun's out of ammo. They're at the next door!"

"How many sentries are left after that one?" John asked.

"Three," Robert replied. "They're working on the door now."

Watching the cameras, John could see the next door already starting to give way. It was obvious these things were enormously powerful. The door buckled under the extreme pressure, the next sentry already opening fire. Would its thousand rounds be enough to stop them?

"Is everything ready in the cellar?" John asked.

"Everything's set. There's about a ton of C4 down there. If it goes up, it will seal the tunnel and destroy most of the castle. We're evacuating the civilians now," Mark said.

"Christ!" John said. "What about the battlements?"

"Everybody that can hold a gun is heading up there now. We're as ready as we can be," Mark said.

"Then pray," John said.

"Been there, done it," Mark smiled.

The gun started firing, the surviving creatures again running into a swarm of projectiles that had a devastating effect on their numbers. After no more than twenty seconds the weapon suddenly stopped firing, but the readout in the control room showed it was not empty, not quite. They all held their breath. The remote weapon carried on keying for several seconds but then settled. They had stopped the attack, everyone was visibly relieved.

"How did you know, John?" Robert asked, realising that John's quick actions had saved them again.

"Mark will explain it to you," John said, heading outside.

Chapter Seventeen - Announcement

The mood at dinner was mixed. On the one hand, they had beaten off the attack by the creatures utilising the tunnel. On the other, everybody now realised that getting away from the castle and finding somewhere safe, where they might have a future, was going to prove very dangerous, very dangerous indeed.

News of the ambush in Hadlee had spread throughout the castle and rumours of the creatures being able to communicate over long distances were spreading. It was being suggested that maybe staying put in the castle was the better option after all?

John, sitting with Stephanie, Robert and Mark, was also feeling mixed emotions, just like everybody else. The one side of him wanted to leave, to run away and find somewhere safe where he could lead a normal life together with Stephanie. No more fighting, no danger of being killed, no risk to Stephanie. The other side of him wanted to attack and kill these creatures, all of them. He had tried to approach the problems they faced logically and without emotion. They had risked their lives capturing one of the monsters, so that they might understand them better. They had attempted to communicate with it, believing there might be a chance for peace. What the creature had said and their actions in the last twenty-four hours had finally convinced John there could never be peace, only war! He had not wanted to accept it and had suggested they fight a different way. The weapons they had used ever since, at least up until the battle at the second supermarket, stunning the creatures instead of killing them, he now realised that tactic had been wrong, however humane it had seemed at the time. The only chance they had was to eliminate the creatures because, given the chance, the creatures would most surely eliminate them.

"You're miles away, John," Stephanie said, squeezing his hand. "What's wrong?"

"Nothing, really," he replied, kissing her gently on the cheek. "I was just thinking about the last few days. Things have changed, our situation here has become desperate. They are on the offensive now and I don't know how long we can hold out. They have vastly superior numbers on their side. We can't send for reinforcements, they obviously can."

"Yes but, John, with the tanks and the Apache again operational, we can also launch a few offensives of our own," remarked Robert.

"We've killed a few thousand of them in the last week, John and lost only three men doing it," added Mark. "At that rate, there'd better be millions of them, otherwise . . ."

John interrupted him.

"The reason being, Mark, we are in the position where we can still use our weapons. It's the technology that's making the difference. Eventually we'll run out of magazines, explosives and fuel. The advantage that's keeping us alive at the moment will disappear. You were in Hadlee, mate, how many rounds did we use on that roof? There were maybe two hundred creatures attacking us. We used thousands of rounds of ammunition and barely survived! At that rate our supplies will soon run out. It may take weeks, even months, but eventually we'll only be able to defend ourselves using our swords. We saw this evening how powerful they really are, the way they handled those doors in the tunnel. I'll be honest, it scared me. If it ever gets down just to hand to hand combat, we'll lose. We couldn't win. The way things are now, it's only a matter of time until we get to that stage. As of then, it's game over!"

This sounded so negative, so final but John honestly believed it.

"John, it seems to me we've had weird conversations like this quite a lot lately. Up until now I've respected your every wish. We risk the entire castle population in capturing one of them to appease your conscience. We accommodate you by developing the gas in an attempt to do the right thing. I've gone out of my way to fulfil your every whim, sometimes without really understanding why. I swear sometimes I don't know whether I'm coming or going. The way it sounds now, you don't think we can even win! If that's the case, then why bother? We can stay here, leave them alone and things will probably quieten down again. If we don't engage them any more, our ammunition supplies would hold out almost indefinitely. We keep flying out for food supplies as long as we can, try growing more of our food here in the castle. We could convert the grounds, build a couple of greenhouses, who knows? We have other options, but John, you came to me, you started this. I know you've had a couple of tough days. Losing your men won't have been easy, it never is. But to have any chance of any kind of existence, whether here or somewhere else, we have to work together, we have to stay the course. You need to get your head together. I respect you and God only knows we need you but sometimes you're a real pain in the arse!" and with that, he stormed out.

"Fuck him!" John said.

"No, John, he's right," Stephanie said, sadly. "We've been together now a long time and I love you, you know that but in the last week it's been a roller coaster ride emotionally. Ups and downs. We have to decide, we have to stick together. I can live here, or we can try to leave, whatever we all decide is fine by me as long as I'm with you but we need you thinking straight. There can't be any doubt that what we're doing is the right thing for everybody. You have to know something? I wanted to find the right moment to tell you but I guess this will have to do. I'm not ill, quite the opposite, actually, I'm pregnant. The doctor confirmed it this morning. In seven months our baby will be born. I'd like to think it had some kind of a chance in this shitty world we've built for it!"

She also stood up, the chair she had been sitting on unintentionally flying backwards and ran out, tears running down her cheek.

John and Mark stared at each other. John asked him if he wanted to have a go as well. Mark saying no but that he was also sure of one thing, they needed John. To stand any kind of a chance of succeeding in their attempt to leave, John had to be part of it. He had developed an understanding of the creatures that nobody else possessed and that could mean the difference between survival and extinction for all of them. Without this small advantage it might not matter what they decided. He then stood up to leave also but before doing so, he turned again to face John and congratulated him on the expected baby.

John sat there alone, unsure. He did not like the feeling. His friends had left him. Stephanie had also run off. Stephanie, he thought, smiling, she was pregnant, he was going to be a father. It was something they had always wanted, often talking about it earlier when the world had been a normal place. Nothing was normal anymore and he could not change that. He could only try to survive and keep his family alive, build a life for them, somewhere, anywhere but not there. He stood up laughing, he was not crazy, his head was clear again. He was going to be a father and he would be damned if his baby would have to grow up in a place where walking through the woods meant certain death. He had to find Stephanie, then talk to Robert. He left the mess hall shouting "I'm going to be a daddy." He felt alive again.

All the doubts were gone, he knew what they had to do. He had known all along, really. He understood it was the right way now, it was the only option!

Chapter Eighteen - The Funeral

He had found her in their room, crying. He had taken her in his arms and kissed her, tears running down his cheeks. He apologised for his outburst and told her how pleased and proud he was to hear her news. To be a father had always been a big part of his dreams. She was making this a reality. He would never be able to thank her enough and promised he would love her forever. They had made love until they both fell asleep exhausted.

After sleeping a full ten hours, John awoke. He felt re-born and realised he had been really tired the last few days, this fact clouding his thinking process and resulting in the negative way he had reacted the evening before. He left her sleeping, she would need her rest now. He was looking forward to all the ways he could use her pregnancy as an excuse to remind her, no matter what she was doing, she was doing it for two. The thought brought a huge smile to his face. He would annoy the hell out of her but it was all part of the adventure they would share together.

He headed for Robert's office, there was another apology he had to make. After making it, Robert told him to forget it and that everything was okay between them. It would take more than a small argument to change that. He was pleased that John and Stephanie were expecting a baby and thankful that John seemed his old self again. He had had enough combat experience himself to realise that the stress of battle affected different men differently. That, combined with lack of sleep, was a cocktail that always caused problems, doubt being a classic symptom. The loss of John's team members had been tragic but Stephanie's pregnancy was again proof that life went on. One life stopped to allow another to start. It was not cold to think this way, it was exactly what war had always done to soldiers. It changed their way of thinking.

"What time's the service?" John asked, sombrely.

"We thought midday," Robert replied. "Everything's organised. The Chaplain has prepared a short requiem. Everybody, apart from the men on duty, will be there."

"I'll see you later then," John said. "I've got a battle plan to work on. Afterwards we can discuss it with Mark, if you've got time."

Robert said he would have time and he would tell Mark to meet them as well.

John had sat down in a quiet corner of the castle, trying to find a way to accomplish their objectives without too much risk but he realised the risk would always be too great. By the time they did what they had to do, the chances were, others would die. This was something he would have to get used to but the better the operations were planned, the less risks there would be.

At 1130 hours he headed for his room, to change for the funeral. The days of dark suits were long gone, it would be either jeans or army issue fatigues, he possessed nothing else. As he entered the room Stephanie was waiting for him. She was already dressed and looked beautiful. They hugged. Smiling, John suggested she sit down. Pulling away from him, a puzzled look on her face, she asked why? He started to explain that because of the extra weight she was now carrying, standing for long periods of time would be uncomfortable for her. The look she gave him frightened him more than any creature ever could. He quickly said he was sorry, he was only joking with her and went to have a shower.

She was pleased he was able to joke again, she had been worried about his behaviour. She felt sorry for him and knew how he must be feeling. They had been his men, his responsibility. It was also clear to her that without John's training more men would have died. She hoped he understood that as well.

He finished dressing and hand in hand, they walked to the small graveyard in the gardens at the back of the castle. It was obviously an area that some of the castle's previous owners had used to bury relatives. It had not been used for hundreds of years, had been very overgrown but some of the killed soldiers friends had worked very hard to tidy it up. It would provide a fitting resting place for the brave men he had lost. This fact comforted John. Everybody was gathered there to pay their last respects and say thank you to the three men who had made the ultimate sacrifice for them all. It seemed strange that he thought that way but John was saddened to hear that they had never had a funeral at the castle before. It had always proved impossible to recover the bodies of fallen comrades, the creatures probably disposing of the remains in their own way. The thought chilled him. At least they had made sure that did not happen this time.

The Army chaplain gave a short service, they all sang hymns, a few of the women cried. It was a very sombre occasion, especially for John, Stephanie and Mark, who had basically picked the men to be part of John's team. Mark was feeling guilty, arguing that if he had picked other soldiers, the three that had died, would still be alive. John told him it was a stupid way to think, the only difference that would have made was that three others would have died in their place. The soldiers fired a salute and the flag, flying above the castle, was lowered to half-mast in respect.

Robert thanked the chaplain, saying the service he had given had been heartfelt and under the circumstances, well received. They all left the graveyard and headed into the mess hall, where tea and sandwiches were being served. It had seemed right to do it that way, even though for the occupants of the castle bread was considered a luxury. Robert wondered how long the mess staff had taken to bake bread for three hundred people?

After a couple of hours most people had left. John, Robert and Mark were still talking. Stephanie had felt tired and had gone to lie down.

"What's the plan, John?" Mark asked, not really sure it was the right time to ask such a question.

"I'm not sure yet," John answered. "I've got a few ideas but we need to iron out the small details. Whatever we decide to do, it will be bloody dangerous. The stakes have been, most definitely, raised. Today should act as a reminder of that to everyone."

"We'll meet first thing in the morning to finalise everything," Robert suggested, then continued. "I'm going to have a few drinks with the men this evening, take my mind off things. Care to join me?"

Mark nodded in agreement but John declined the offer.

"In your office then. 0900 hours okay? I'm going to spend a little quality time with my . . ." and he stopped.

He had almost said wife but they were not married. The whole idea of not being man and wife suddenly seemed very wrong. She deserved at least that, especially now they were going to have a family. He looked at Robert.

"What?" Robert asked, puzzled by John's sudden reaction.

"I need a big favour," John said. "Several in fact. It's time I put something right!"

He carefully explained to the Major what the favours consisted of.

Chapter Nineteen - The Surprise

John had gone back to his room, where Stephanie was resting. He had not really wanted to disturb her but it was necessary for what he now planned. Without it appearing too deliberate, he bumped around the room, making almost too much noise for it to be accidental. Eventually she had awoken.

"What's up, John?" she asked, still half-asleep.

"Sorry, I didn't mean to wake you. I'm a little annoyed, that's all. Robert and Mark are insisting on going over the plans for the precinct mission now. I said we could do it tomorrow but they don't want to wait. They're a right pair of wankers sometimes. It's not as if we haven't been through enough today but, oh no, they just wouldn't listen. I tell you what, I want you there. A woman's perspective could make all the difference. Are you game or do you feel too tired?"

"I'll get dressed straightaway," she answered, almost jumping out of bed.

"Slow down, there's no hurry, take your time. Have a shower first, it'll help you wake up. They decided it's too loud in Robert's office, so Mark suggested we meet in the castle chapel. I swear the boy's getting all religious on me. Anyway, it is probably the most quiet room in the whole place, I suppose it might help us to concentrate. I've got to get some refreshments organised, I'm the bloody tea boy now! It's four o'clock, we've arranged to meet at four thirty, so take your time. I'll get the refreshments and meet you there," and with that John had rushed out of the door.

Shit, he thought, he had not even kissed her. He always kissed her. Hopefully, she would not smell a rat.

She showered, got dressed and started to walk over to the chapel. She did not want to be the first there. What time had John said, four thirty, that was it, it was four twenty five. As she approached the chapel, it was in darkness. John had definitely said four thirty and she was certain he had said the chapel. Maybe she was the first after all, she would go in and wait but if he was messing her about again, she would kill him. She opened the chapel door and went inside, it was pitch black, no candles burning, nothing. She fumbled for the light switch in the darkness. The moment she found and turned the switch, music started playing, the tune somehow familiar. She recognised it, it was a version of the wedding march. Puzzled, she looked around the chapel and to her surprise, found she was not alone after all.

Standing at the altar, she could see John. He was dressed in some kind of uniform, next to him stood Mark, also in full uniform. Behind them stood the chaplain, holding a book, she presumed the bible, in his hands.

Suddenly Robert appeared next to her; he had been hiding behind the door as she had come in. He was also wearing his full uniform.

"What is going on?" she asked him, puzzled.

"I'm here to escort you down the aisle, young lady. If you'll allow me the honour," he said, taking her by the hand.

She started to tremble. He gave her a bunch of flowers, dressed in a pretty bow.

"I'm sorry," he added. "They're only plastic. We couldn't find the real thing in time."

With that he led her down the aisle towards the altar, where everybody else was waiting.

As they approached John and Mark, she started to ask John what the hell was going on but he touched his finger to his lips, as if to say 'be quiet.' They reached them and Robert passed her hand over to John, then playfully punching him on the shoulder, he stepped aside.

She looked at John, suddenly realising what was happening. The chaplain began to speak.

"Dearly beloved . . ."

The rest seemed hazy but at the appropriate time she answered "I do."

The chaplain continued asking John the same questions, he also gave the same answers as she had given, including the 'I do' one.

After about ten minutes, as if in a dream, she heard the words 'pronounce you man and wife, you may kiss the bride'. John turned towards her and gently kissed her on the lips. They were man and wife.

Robert and Mark congratulated them, kissing her and hugging him. The chaplain added his good wishes and hopes that their future together would be long and happy.

"Come on, Mrs. Stewart," John said. "Let's go home."

He led her by the hand back to their room. Upon opening the door they found candles burning all over the place and, on the table, a meal waiting for them. Also on the table, a bottle of wine and a small, but beautifully decorated, wedding cake.

"How, John? How did you do all of this?" she asked, a tear running down her cheek.

Robert did most of it," he replied. "I'm sorry it couldn't have been any better but we don't have a wedding planner."

"It's perfect," she told him. "I love you."

"I love you," he replied. "I'm just sorry it took me so long."

She smiled at him.

"You know, you never actually asked me."

"Asked you what?" he asked, puzzled.

"To marry you, silly," she said, smiling.

"Well it's too bloody late now!" he said, laughing.

They ate the meal that had been so lovingly prepared for them, drank the wine and eventually cut the cake. She had wished for this she did not know how many times. They were married, she was pregnant, if only . . . She let the thought hang.

After they finished their meal, they went to bed and made love. What was it called she thought? They consummated the marriage, that was it. They had made love many times but this time it was different. This time they were man and wife.

Chapter Twenty - Change of Tactics

"Good morning, Mrs. Stewart," John said, happily.

"Good morning, Mr. Stewart," came the cheerful reply.

"I've got to go to work," he said. "This time seriously."

"Should I come with you," she asked, climbing out of bed. "I could make sure nobody picks on you."

"No, you stay here and start cleaning this place up," he said, laughing. "It's filthy! I'll be back around five o'clock and I want my dinner on the table as soon as I come in or there'll be trouble!"

As he left she threw her pillow at him but missed.

He headed for Robert's office, the serious work would begin again that morning. They still had plenty to do before they could leave and, up to now, it was not clear how to do it. As he arrived there, he met Mark in the corridor outside.

"Nah," Mark asked. "Still married then?"

"Going strong, mate," John replied, smiling.

They knocked and entered. Robert was sitting at his desk, obviously deep in thought.

"Hi, guys," he said when they entered. "How's married life treating you, John?"

"Up to now, perfectly, thanks very much," John replied. "Seriously, thanks for yesterday, it meant a hell of a lot to us both. If I can return the favour, you only need to whistle."

"No problem, John. Anytime," Robert answered and they all laughed.

"Shut up, we've got work to do," John said, seriously but he could not help smiling a little more, yesterday evening had been fantastic.

"Okay," Robert said. "What are we doing?"

"We're going back to Hadlee," John answered. "One more time."

"And just how do you suggest we do that with a degree of safety, when we can be certain they're waiting for us?" Robert asked, wondering if he would like the answer.

John began to explain. Robert was right, based on the last time they were there, they had to expect that the creatures would be waiting for them again. This time, probably in even greater numbers than before. They had a couple of choices - they could attempt a similar operation to the one that had resulted in the deaths of his three men or something completely different. The creatures would probably expect the similar action. If that proved to be the case and he was pretty sure it would, they could use the fact to their advantage. The first supermarket was still full of supplies they could use, the precinct even more so. They needed at least fifteen more trucks, realistically, it was probably twenty. If they had to go back which they did, then they would go once more and finish the whole job. That meant they needed enough time to capture the trucks and empty both buildings of anything they could use, without having to fight off the creatures the whole time. It also meant his team could not handle the job on their own, especially now they were not at full strength.

"What exactly does it mean, John?" Robert asked.

"Let me explain what I've got in mind," John replied. "You guys jump in anytime with suggestions, yeah," he continued."As far as I understand it, the trucks we brought back from Hadlee the first time are basically ready, fully modified. Now after seeing the creatures, during their attack using the tunnel, we have to find a way to keep them off the vehicles, otherwise they'll rip them to shreds. Going on the assumption we can do that, then we take three trucks with us. Robert, we are going to need thirty guys per truck, all three helicopters will be coming along and I'd like to take one tank as well. We'd have to drive a little slower because of it but the added protection it will give us is worth that."

"Christ, John, you're basically stripping the castle. If anything were to go seriously wrong, we'd be vulnerable," Robert said, looking worried.

"It's drastic, I know," John continued. "But drastic times, yeah. It's coming down to the wire. The longer we stay here, the worse it's going to get. I'm getting to know how these bastards tick and believe me, they're not going to give us many more chances. One of the main reasons why we have to go all out is the way these things appear to communicate. I know we're not sure and you might think I'm losing it but I seriously believe it's telepathy or at least something similar. It's the only feasible explanation and would explain a few things. The only small hope we have is that there's some kind of range limit to it, otherwise the creatures here could alert their entire population as to what we're doing. That would make our journey down the country even more interesting. That's all speculation, I know but one thing's for certain, the last time there were a lot of those things waiting for us. They organised themselves quickly and did it over great distances. This next time won't be any different and the time after that and the time after that and so on. Eventually, there will be so many of them we won't stand a chance. That's why it's got to be a one shot deal, something so unexpected they won't have a chance. We're going back to Hadlee, gentlemen, to destroy them! Instead of entering the town, as they'll expect, we will stay outside the town limits and draw them out. Exactly how I'm not sure yet, maybe using the tank as bait, I don't know but we'll find a way. If they won't come out to us, then we'll destroy the whole town, bring everything down on their heads apart from our two buildings. We need to take munitions along with us so that the helicopters can re-arm on site. That's another reason why we have to risk the trucks, transport. The gas weapons have worked well up to now but the next time we need a lot more time. Creatures waking up while we are working is something we don't need. I promise it's the last time, Robert but we need to modify the gas again. This time it shouldn't put them to sleep, this time it should kill them outright. The trucks have been modified in such a way that they fit together like a puzzle, that gives our men a solid, defensible position to fight from. After we've drawn them out, the rest of the guys will have to deal with any creatures that reach our base of operations. Come to think of it, the tank would be the ideal bait. It goes in and shoots around a bit, gets their attention, they follow it, out of the town right into our guns. We'll have to modify both of the tank's armour in the same way as the trucks, because I doubt even they could withstand the creatures for long. I know that modifying the helicopter munitions won't be a problem but perhaps we can modify the tank's shells to disperse the gas. Using that in the town would get their attention in a big way. As long as we can get them interested in attacking us, they'll leave the backdoor open. That's why all three helicopters are vital to the mission - the Apache for its firepower, the other two for transporting me and my team into the town to start preparing everything. While the creatures are busy fighting outside the town limits, we get the trucks ready, scrounge some fuel, go through the precinct so that once the creatures have been destroyed, the rest of the men come in, we load up and leave."

"That's one hell of a plan, John. Let's say you're on the right track with them communicating through telepathy or something. What's to stop them sending for reinforcements once we've engaged them? We could be doing okay, then get a nasty surprise and find ourselves up to our necks in it," Robert said.

"The last time we left Hadlee we didn't see any creatures until we reached the forest by the castle, that's a good sixty five miles of basically open terrain. This time won't be any different, they'll be in the town waiting for us. Reinforcements could come up from the south but I doubt it. Just in case, the Apache, being the quickest helicopter by far, can leave us, fly thirty or forty miles down beyond the town and look for large concentrations of the creatures moving northwards. If it can't find any, then we can be pretty confident there aren't any coming. The speed the Apache can maintain, means it can complete its mission and still rendezvous with us to re-fuel and re-arm if necessary, before we reach the town. With its video capabilities it can fly over Hadlee filming, it might provide useful intelligence for our attack. We have two problems to solve, the gas, very important and protecting the vehicles, critical. If you can think of anything else, then now's the time," John said.

Robert and Mark sat quietly for a moment, the gravity of John's plan slowly sinking in, then Mark spoke.

"The gas is no problem, John, we just need to change a couple of ingredients and we can make it lethal. The only trouble is it's lethal to us, so we have to be careful. The tank's shells, no problem there either, we can take out the high explosives, replace them with gas containers and you've got your delivery system. It's no different than firing smoke. The vehicles, I just have no idea. If it's okay with you and Robert, I'd like to bring Bill in on the idea. He's supervising the modifications anyway. If anybody knows a way to do what you want, he does."

Robert and John had nothing against the suggestion and Mark went to fetch Bill.

After a few minutes he arrived and John explained what they needed and why. Bill considered the request for a few minutes and eventually, not really understanding how important his answer was, he made his suggestion. They had several generators, big ones that handled the castle's electricity supplies and smaller ones that were not actually in use at that time. He felt sure that if they insulated the engines enough they could, using the smaller generators, electrify the exteriors of the trucks and the tank, giving them such a charge, that he felt sure the creatures would not be able to grasp anything. The men defending the vehicles would have to be insulated, otherwise the electrical charge could be lethal to them as well. This was the smallest of the problems, as rubber insulating suits were standard equipment for soldiers, and everyone based at the castle had one. The only question was, if he could make his idea with the generators work? He would need at least a day to get it sorted and tested enough before he could be confident of the results. Mark had already explained about the modification of the gas and the delivery system for the tank on their way over there. He anticipated no problems whatsoever regarding those items.

Robert suggested he should try and sort the outstanding questions out as quickly as possible. They would wait for him to report back about the trucks but the changes to the gas and the tank shells should be carried out straightaway. Bill left to assemble his team.

"He's a damn good bloke," Mark said. "Don't worry, mate, he'll sort it out if anybody can."

Robert then made a suggestion.

"John, if the creatures are going to be waiting for us in Hadlee as you suspect, then it's probably safe to say they are there now. Agreed."

John nodded in agreement. Robert continued.

"Then how about paying them a visit tonight?"

"What do you mean?" John asked, puzzled by the suggestion.

"Bill's team can modify the gas today, I'm pretty sure that's no problem. Tonight after dark, the three helicopters can take off, armed with the new gas weapons and pay Hadlee a visit. They can fly off in the opposite direction to the town and then circle back, that should confuse the creatures as to where we're going. The Apache can use it's infra-red capabilities to gather information and then all three can attack targets of opportunity. With it being dark we might get lucky and catch some of them out in the open. The possibility is there, yeah. We've never been near the town at night, they won't expect it."

John looked at Robert and smiled.

"You are definitely learning, mate, that's not bad, not bad at all."

"Mark," Robert continued. "Get back to Bill. I want the modification to the gas and the delivery systems for all three helicopters ready by eighteen hundred hours. Tell the pilots they've got a mission tonight, they need to get some rest beforehand."

John was not sure why but Robert suddenly shouted, "Shit!" He asked why? Robert asked him how many pilots they had. John was not sure, he only knew the two that had always flown them on their missions to Hadlee.

"Exactly," Robert said. "We only have two. That means one helicopter has to stay behind, it limits our firepower."

John interrupted him.

"We have three pilots. Don't forget Stephanie, she's a damn good pilot."

"I didn't want to suggest her, John. She's pregnant, you're married. I wasn't sure how you'd react."

"In the short time we've been married," John said smiling. "I've got to know my wife pretty well and one thing's for sure, if I tried to stop her going on this mission, she'd divorce me in a second."

They could not help it, all three men burst out laughing.

Chapter Twenty One - Night Mission

He told her about the plan to attack the creatures that might be waiting for them in Hadlee that night and the need for a third pilot. She had not hesitated for a second, he had hoped that would be the case. She could not resist the chance to play with her new toy again, her reaction playing right into his hands. As long as he was careful now and did not say anything stupid to jeopardise the situation, he felt confident that Stephanie would accept and relish the position of Apache pilot and continue to fly the exciting machine. This fact would keep her out of harms way, especially in the forthcoming battle.

Although the Apache could be flown by a single pilot, the operation of the camera equipment really needed a second pair of hands, it was obviously better with two people aboard. The co-pilot would operate the sensitive intelligence equipment, leaving the pilot free to concentrate on flying and targeting the enemy. Stephanie asked John if he would fly with her. She had also known what his answer would be.

It was 1700 hours, they were due to take off at 1900 hours. Stephanie was explaining to John how he could control the camera equipment from his seat in the aircraft. The camera feed would also be coming through on her screen, as she needed it to navigate. They could use the cameras to gather information during their flight and also see what was going on in the town once they got there. Using the infra-red technology, fitted as standard to such helicopters, it would almost be as clear as flying in daylight to them. The cameras revealed heat sources, groups of people, vehicles, anything that was warmer than the surrounding air temperature. The creatures would be clearly visible from the air, making it easier to target them. The other two helicopters did not have this advantage but, backed up by compass and radio, they could follow her until they reached Hadlee. If the two pilots took along night vision goggles, they would have no problems in following her or hitting the buildings she picked out for them. If need be they could drop flares on the buildings to be targeted, that way there would be little chance of their missing.

After listening to her explanation, John asked why they could not use the other positional equipment that was packed into the aircraft. The advanced positional technologies aboard all three helicopters would normally have made night flying and target location relatively easy but, because of the amount of fallout in the atmosphere, satellite uplink without the use of powerful equipment was basically impossible. It was exactly the same situation with the helicopters as with the off-road vehicle they had discovered at the farm during their journey to the castle. Neither the Apache's nor the Landrover's systems were powerful enough to punch through the fallout. At least that was the explanation Stephanie had used to explain why she would be flying using the camera technology on board her aircraft and the other two pilots would be following her every move. John had expressed his concerns about missing their intended target in the darkness but Stephanie had assured him they would find it. With the skies free of other traffic, nullifying the risk of collision, nothing could really go wrong.

The new gas had been produced and the weapons modified. It would be lethal to anything coming into contact with it - all three helicopters carried the modified weapons. The Apache, missiles as usual and the other two bombs attached to simple release mechanisms fitted under the aircraft's body between their skids. The bombs were not as accurate as the Apache's missiles but they would be aiming at buildings, big enough, that hitting them should not be a problem.

They had also stored reserve fuel aboard the helicopters, just in case re-fuelling became necessary. The thought of landing to re-fuel in the dark in hostile territory did not appeal to John but Stephanie insisted it would only be in the case of an emergency. It was more of a precautionary measure, the odds of their running out of fuel slim, to say the least.

The three pilots had already talked about the mission and decided amongst themselves that the Apache should fly over the target at higher altitude to gather information first, the others hanging back. Stephanie and John would then decide which buildings they were to target. The three helicopters would then attack in formation.

John reminded all three pilots that it was imperative the precinct and the remaining supermarket remain intact. Any creatures gathered there would have to be dealt with in another way.

At 1845 hours, they gathered at the helicopters, pre-flight checks to be made. Robert and Mark had come to wish them luck. They were hoping that a night-time mission would confuse the creatures so much that they would be slow to react. Just in case they were wrong, they planned on flying off in a northerly direction at first, instead of the usual southwards. After five minutes flying time, they would turn east for three minutes and then south again. With them flying to the north, the hope was that the creatures, based around the castle, would not warn the creatures waiting for them in Hadlee. If they were lucky, they might even catch some of them out in the open.

As they boarded the aircraft, Robert told them to be careful and to come back safely. Giving him a quick wave, they took off.

They were flying northwards, John testing out the camera equipment. Everything was recorded digitally so the amount of time that could be spent gathering intelligence was practically unlimited. Stephanie had felt that, although she had explained everything very carefully to him, time spent practising on the equipment would make the mission over the town more effective. Besides, she needed the digital feed to keep an eye on their course.

They had been in the air for about five minutes, it was time to turn east. She informed the other pilots.

"Bravo One and Bravo Two, this is Bravo Three, let's take it east for three minutes. Copy that. Over."

"Copy that Bravo Three, turning east. Over and out," came the replies.

"Are you okay, John?" she asked.

"No problems," he answered. "I'm just clicking away."

"Just remember what I told you. Don't get carried away, I need the picture to be stable otherwise God knows where we'll end up," she said, trying hard not to laugh.

"Shit! You'd better be joking. I thought you said it wouldn't be a problem," John said, obviously worried.

"If you keep the camera steady, it won't be," she said, smiling.

The three minutes east went quickly, then they turned south. The town of Hadlee was about twenty minutes away. She spoke again to the pilots of the other helicopters.

"Bravo One and Bravo Two, do you copy me? Over."

"Loud and clear Bravo Three. Over."

"Maintain this heading, it takes you straight to the target. In a few minutes I will increase speed and altitude for our pass over the town, you guys hang back. If you take it nice and slowly, that will give me about five minutes over the target before you reach it. We'll rendezvous to the north of Hadlee and then make our attack. Over."

"Copy that Bravo Three. Maintain heading. Over and out."

"John, I am going to increase speed shortly. The cameras will adjust focus and everything will automatically compensate. You just point them where you want to look, okay?"

"Yes, sir," he answered, sarcastically.

"You're on report, mister," she told him, laughing.

"If we accelerate now and leave the others behind, will they be able to find us? What if they get lost?" John asked, thinking back to her remarks earlier.

"They're locked into this heading, John. I'm pretty sure Hadlee is dead ahead, about forty miles away. We'll be fine," she said.

"Pretty sure isn't one hundred percent certain!" John said, a hint of panic in his voice. "Maybe we should stay together?"

Stephanie laughed. He sounded genuinely worried. She considered telling him that she knew exactly where they were and also knew exactly where Hadlee was but decided not to. Him worrying was something that did not seem to happen all that often. She would enjoy the moment while she could.

"Here we go," she said.

The machine suddenly accelerated. John was forced back into his seat a little, it was impressive. He did not know how fast they were travelling but he was thankful that Stephanie was right about any other aircraft flying, the dangers of collision not a problem for them. After what seemed like too little time, Stephanie said they were approaching Hadlee and he should be ready. He started to flip buttons, twitch dials and fine tune the systems. He was as ready as he would ever be. His concerns about the other helicopters finding them were quickly forgotten, his mind concentrating on the job ahead.

They flew over quickly, he had no idea at what altitude but images were coming through on his screen. The precinct and the intact supermarket were both clearly visible. The supermarket they had blown up had been completely destroyed along with a couple of nearby buildings, probably fire damage he realised. Several buildings surrounding the precinct were showing big heat signatures. Large concentrations of the creatures were hiding there, just as they had suspected. Flying over and past the precinct he spotted something he had not expected, a fuel storage depot. He made a mental note, they would have to pay it a visit. There were several large tankers visible. The fuel problems they might at some stage experience would be solved if only one or two of the vehicles in sight were still loaded. He told Stephanie that under no circumstances, should the area around the fuel depot be targeted. They would also have to minimise the risk of secondary damage in that vicinity. He realised, looking further at his screen, there would be targets enough.

They completed their fly-over and were heading back to rendezvous with the other helicopters, targets were marked and locked into the Apache's computers. As long as they had a little luck, the buildings that were important to them would be undamaged. The only real risk, that of fire, was minimal he thought. They would be using the modified gas weapons, the explosive content of the missiles and bombs thereby much smaller than conventional weapons. Smaller explosions, it stood to reason, smaller fires.

There had been several buildings showing a greater heat signature than others, these would be Stephanie's targets, her delivery system obviously much superior to that of their compatriots, thereby guaranteeing accuracy. The other two helicopters, if they managed to find the town, would target smaller buildings, more towards the edge of town, minimising even further the risk of secondary damage to the precinct and surrounding area. To his relief, the other two helicopters were already in position waiting for them. He sighed loudly.

"Sorry, John, did you say something?" Stephanie asked.

"Never doubted you for a second, darling," John said, smiling.

"Yeah, right," Stephanie said.

Both of them laughed.

After rendezvousing with Bravo One and Bravo Two, their targets were designated by Stephanie. She suggested they should at first drop flares to illuminate the area. This would minimise the risk of them missing their allotted targets. Stephanie did not need any help because of her helicopter's capabilities but, for the other two, it would be important because the amount of munitions they carried was limited and the missing of one target could prove fatal to the men who were coming to the town. It was important for them to make the most of this opportunity because, John felt, the creatures would not fall for the same manoeuvre twice. They flew into formation and began the attack.

Bravo One and Bravo Two both launched flares as they hovered over their targets and commenced bombing.

Stephanie flew straight on to the area of the town she had picked to launch her missiles, the buildings she would target showing heavy concentrations of the creatures. She hovered in position and, rotating clockwise, she fired. The missiles, fully laden with poisonous gas, all found their targets. Some creatures could be seen escaping the buildings, where the gas clouds were now doing their work. The Apache's scatter guns made sure they did not get far.

John and Stephanie could see the explosions from where the other two helicopters were hovering, their machine guns also firing, tracer rounds clear to see in the night sky.

After a matter of minutes, it was over. Reports from Bravo One and Bravo Two came over the radio, all targets had been successfully hit and destroyed. The gas clouds were now rolling through the streets of Hadlee, as if they were trying to locate more victims. They flew out of the town and hovered over the outskirts, surveying their work.

"Bravo One and Bravo Two, do you copy? Over."

"We copy, Bravo Three. Over."

"Proceed back to base, at best speed. We want to make another couple of passes over the town using the cameras to confirm casualty counts and damage. We'll be right behind you, over."

"Roger that Bravo Three, see you at home. Over and out."

With that, the two helicopters flew off, heading north again.

"What if they fly the wrong way?" John asked, his panic returning momentarily.

"John, please. Back seat drivers are the worst kind! Trust me, they'll be fine," she said, his concern understandable but nevertheless, annoying.

"I won't say another word about it," John said, realising how he sounded.

Stephanie made another, slower pass over the town, filming with John working the cameras. Satisfied with the job they had done, they headed back towards the castle. Within minutes the Apache had caught up with the other helicopters, the rest of the way again flown in formation.

Twenty minutes later all three helicopters were safely back at the castle. Robert was de-briefing John and Stephanie about the results of the raid, as they were waiting for the photographs John had taken to be printed. There was a knock at Robert's office door.

"Come in," Robert shouted.

A nervous looking Corporal walked in and saluted.

"What is it, Corporal?" Robert asked.

"Sir, Sergeant Major Young's compliments. His team are currently working on the modifications to the trucks. They are at a delicate stage of the proceedings, Sir and cannot stop at the moment. The photographs you requested will not be ready until in the morning, Sir. Sergeant Major Young hopes you will understand," the Corporal said, his report exact.

"Thank you, Corporal. Inform Sergeant Young that's no problem," Robert said.

The Corporal saluted again, Robert returning the salute, before leaving the office. He turned back to face John and Stephanie. John was shaking his head.

"What's all that about, Robert?" he asked. "The poor lad was almost trembling. What was all that shit you told me? 'We play down the rank situation nowadays' my arse!"

Robert laughed. "Discipline is still the backbone of the army, John," he said, barely able to control himself. "It doesn't hurt to make the enlisted men squirm now and then, especially when they make it so easy to do so!"

John smiled, Robert's reaction amusing him. After a good thirty seconds, Robert seemed to compose himself again.

"Anyway, as you heard, the photographs won't be ready until the morning," Robert said. "You might as well get some sleep."

"Alright, mate, see you in the morning," John answered. "We'll discuss the rank thing again, when you've calmed down a bit more."

As they closed the office door behind them, they could hear Robert laughing again. John looked at Stephanie, who was also smiling.

"It wasn't that funny," he said.

"Yes, it was," Stephanie argued, still grinning. "Are we going to bed now? I'm tired."

He was tired as well, granted but more than anything, he was hungry. He would sleep later, first he needed to eat. He suggested they eat first, Stephanie readily agreeing. It seemed to John, her pregnancy was having a definite effect on her eating habits. Walking towards the mess hall, hand in hand, he contemplated saying something but decided against it. There would be time enough over the next months to tease her. Stephanie suddenly let go of his hand and stopped. She looked panicked and afraid.

"What's the matter?" John asked worried.

"What if we can't find the mess hall John? What if we find it but can't find our way back to our room?" she said, trying to appear serious.

"Hey, that's not fair. I'm no pilot, I didn't know," John said.

She started to laugh. For a second he contemplated walking off and leaving her there. Instead he joined in.

Chapter Twenty Two - Final Preparations

The morning after, the photographs were ready, just as Bill had promised. After breakfast, they met in Robert's office to examine the evidence from the raid the night before. They checked the photographs carefully and estimated they had killed at least eighty percent of the creatures that had been waiting in the town. The gas clouds would have killed a few more before the gas settled and became harmless. The quickly thrown together mission had been a great success and would make the battle to come a lot easier.

John told Robert about the fuel depot they had located, although it seemed to be missing from the photographs for some reason. Robert agreed it was important the penetration team paid it a visit. There was also another unexpected bonus found on a few of the earlier photo's John had taken as they had first left the castle. As they had flown north, John had been practising with the equipment. He had not realised it at the time but the cameras had spotted something that could prove very useful indeed. Coming through the forest from the north, finishing about fifty yards before the clearing, was another road! Further to the north, this road linked up with a main road, that led to the road they had always used when leaving or entering the castle. The tanks could be used to clear the fifty or so yards of trees, giving them an alternative way to leave the area, without having to run the gauntlet of the creatures.

They all agreed the mission had been a tremendous success and although luck had played a part, their position seemed stronger. It was time to talk to Bill again, hopefully he had found a way to protect the trucks from attack without risking their lives.

They found Bill and his team working in one of the areas designated to modifications. These areas were sealed off from the civilian population in the castle because some of the work being carried out was very dangerous. The area where they were currently working was walled in, roofed over and acclimatised. As they had entered, John noticed it was a lot cooler inside the temporary building to what it was outside. In fact, it was so cold, as he saw Bill approaching he realised he was wearing an army issue parka.

"Morning, Bill," Robert said. "How's it going?"

"Fine, thank you, Sir," came the reply. "In fact, we are about ready for a test. Would you like to watch?"

"We would but first explain what you've come up with," Robert insisted.

"With your permission, Sir, it will be simpler just to show you."

"Carry on, Sergeant," Robert said.

"John, have you got one of your pistols with you?" Bill asked.

John always carried at least one of his Berettas, even in the castle. He drew it and showed it Bill.

"Good," he said and walking over to one of the trucks parked at the side, he continued. "This is one of the original six trucks that came from Hadlee. John, fire a shot or two at it, please."

John looked at Robert who nodded slightly, so he aimed and fired at the truck twice, as requested.

"Thank you. Now all of you take a look at where the bullets impacted," Bill instructed.

They looked but could find no evidence of impact or damage.

Bill continued. "We have treated this lorry with a compound that was originally discovered about ten years ago. It was designed for military flak jackets. Sprayed thinly over the material, it sets and is more bullet-resistant than Kevlar. Sprayed thinly on the truck's body it didn't have the same effect, so we had to increase the thickness of the layer. The skin on this truck is one centimetre thick and, as you've just seen, it's totally bullet proof. The only problem with the compound for us is to achieve the required thickness and get it to set, it has to be colder than minus five degrees centigrade. Hence, the current temperature in here. I apologise for that, by the way but if it's any warmer the substance degrades. Once it's set, you can't remove it, it's there forever. We've already tested it with M-16s on full automatic, nothing gets through."

John, looking very impressed, told him how well he had done but Bill had not finished yet.

"The problem we then had was complicated. This compound, once dry, is fixed. We can't remove it without chemicals and basically wrecking whatever it's on. It's permanent as far as we are concerned but the creatures are obviously much more powerful than we are. It is feasible they could, given the time at least, damage or even remove it. We wouldn't know for sure, until it was probably too late. Obviously, that is too risky, so we wanted something that would definitely offer enough protection to the men going into Hadlee. The idea of electrifying the truck's bodies seemed to be the way to go but the compound doesn't conduct electricity. That meant the six trucks we'd already modified couldn't be used. Luckily, we hadn't started work on the three you brought back last time. We found a way to electrify the trucks, just as we wanted to but still had the problem of insulating the cab, the engine compartment and, most importantly, the men themselves. The kind of voltage we'd be using, to be certain that it affected the creatures at least, meant that the insulation suits the soldiers are issued, wouldn't take the charge. Then we thought we'd combine both the compound and electric treatment together. What we've come up with is the best of both worlds really. The three trucks have been sprayed with the compound but only inside the bonnet, that isolates the engine, inside the cab, that sorts out the electrics and protects the drivers. Axles and wheels are also sprayed. Inside the actual bodies of the trucks has been sprayed, that protects the men travelling inside and anything else you want to transport. The thought crossed my mind that the extra munitions you plan to take with you would probably cook off as soon as the electrical defences were turned on. This way they'll be safe. The roofs have also been sprayed, including the side panels installed there for the soldiers to fight behind, that insulates the men up top. I've gambled that the creatures can't reach the side panels, because they're too high up from the ground. Everything else will be electrically charged with enough power that it will at least seriously injure, more than likely kill, anything touching it. The tanks have been handled in exactly the same way."

"That's brilliant, Bill, Nobel Prizeworthy," John said, slapping him on the shoulder. "You really know your stuff. When will all three trucks be ready to go?"

"We still need a couple of hours to finish testing. Early this afternoon, probably," Bill replied.

"Then we go tomorrow," John said. "Mark, organise the guys coming with us. We need a meeting called for this afternoon, so we can go through the battle plan with everybody involved."

Chapter Twenty Three - Last Minute

The meeting had been short. All those taking part in the 'Last Battle of Hadlee', as it had come to be known, understood what they had to do and how important the mission was. If they were successful, they would practically be ready to leave the castle and begin their journey to a new home. Originally John had, mentally at least, set a limit of four weeks to achieve what they had set out to do. If everything in Hadlee now went as planned, something he doubted, they would make his unofficial deadline easily. The men taking part in the major operation the following day had been instructed to take it easy for the rest of the afternoon, most of them excused duty because of the gravity of the task that lay before them.

John, Stephanie and Mark were doing just that, playing cards, talking about better times, generally trying to take their minds off the forthcoming dangers. John was having difficulty concentrating on the card game, he could not help wondering if they had prepared everything as well as they could have. He had found in all his years, as both operative and instructor, you could never be too prepared! He now worried that maybe they had missed something that would make the difference. Second guessing the creatures had been, up to that moment at least, his speciality. Could he once again come up with a twist that hedged their bets even further?

Stephanie noticed him, deep in thought and asked what was wrong? John told her he was still concerned about the following morning's major battle plans. Were they good enough? Had they covered all the bases? She said, yes, in her opinion, they were ready, every contingency had been planned for. The attack plan was one of the best she had ever seen or heard. The helicopter mission, the night before, had softened up the creatures and seriously changed the odds in their favour. The defences built into the trucks were formidable, to say the very least! The men were professional soldiers and well trained. The other pilots knew exactly what was expected of them, as did she. They would be better armed than ever, even taking one of the newly repaired tanks with them. She was certain the creatures would be intimidated by it. The tank was equipped with the same modifications as the trucks, making it practically indestructible. It was to be used as bait in drawing the creatures out of the town and she was certain that once it had finished with the creatures, the soldiers would only have to mop up the rest. She was feeling very confident and knew for a fact the other soldiers were as well. She felt he should be too. Mark had agreed with Stephanie and could not understand what was troubling John.

John explained he was not worried. He just wanted to be sure they had done everything they could to ensure the safety of their forces and the success of the mission.

Mark suggested that, without going back to Hadlee again that night, there was not a lot else they could do, apart from stick to the plan.

Suddenly John stood up, that was it. They would go back again that night and attack whatever creatures were still in the town. He told Stephanie to begin pre-flighting the Apache. He would clear the action with Robert and with that, he ran off.

Stephanie looked at Mark, shrugged her shoulders and stood up to leave. Mark told her not to worry, John knew what he was doing. All they had to do was trust him.

"What?" Robert asked, his voice slightly raised.

"We need to go back, tonight."

"John, why? Explain to me why, when last night's operation was such a success."

"Robert, you know I understand these things better than most. My gut tells me we were right to do what we did last night but it was still last night. Let's say you're right, last night we killed over eighty percent of them, that would have been great if we'd attacked today, but we didn't. That means they have had the whole day and tonight to reinforce their positions again. If that is the case, then tomorrow we could run into trouble, big trouble. If we go back tonight, just the Apache, fully armed, we can hit them again and further weaken them. We attack in the morning so they have very little time to re-organise, it makes our job easier."

"I hate to say it but it makes sense. Is there not the possibility we're overestimating them?" Robert asked.

"No, not at all. You're a military man, Robert, think about it for a second. In a war, you are holding a position, the enemy attack you and kills half your men, then they withdraw. You only need to make a radio call and your position is reinforced, without your enemy knowing it. That would give you an advantage. Do you make the call or not?" John asked.

"Yes, I would. Okay, John, it's all right by me. Are you sure just the Apache should go? Wouldn't it be far more effective to take all three again?"

"No. The Apache is a lot faster, we can be there in twelve minutes, that gives them less time to react. After last night's surprise, the creatures here will warn those in Hadlee the minute we take off but the superior speed of the Apache still gives us an edge. We'll fly over once and using infra-red, we'll locate them and destroy them. It will also confuse them. After last night they'll be expecting a ground attack, this way they won't be sure what we are doing. If we attack again tonight, then they'll think twice about sending even more reinforcements tomorrow. That gives us another advantage."

"Okay, John, go for it. Give me a quick report when you get back."

"I will. We'll only be an hour or so. Will you still be up?"

"Get outa here," Robert told him.

It was only six o'clock, he was not that old, not yet anyway. Although, he thought, all the time he had spent with John must have aged him considerably.

As John reached the helicopter pads, Stephanie was already there, the Apache started and idling, fully armed.

"Do we go, John?" she asked.

"We go, come on."

He led her to the cockpit of the small deadly machine she loved to fly. They took off and immediately headed south.

After twelve or thirteen minutes they were once again flying over the town. John could straightaway confirm that all his suspicions were unfortunately true, the creatures had reinforced with considerable numbers. The problem was, as he had always said, they had learnt quickly.

The main target in the next morning's operation was the precinct, and that was exactly where the creatures had chosen to hide! The building appeared full of them. Destroying this building was not an option they had the luxury of possessing.

"Shit!" John shouted. "We are in big trouble. These things are too bloody clever for their own good. It's as if they've guessed we want the precinct. It's the one place we can't attack, either tonight or tomorrow. They're quick, too bloody quick."

"I wouldn't be so sure, John," Stephanie said, sounding hopeful.

"What have you in mind?" John asked his wife.

"Where the precinct is situated and how the wind is blowing tonight, gives me an idea. I know you don't want the precinct damaged but we may have to risk it. The wind is blowing straight up the main street into the precinct entrance. The building is big enough, that at the back it acts as a windbreak. What I've got in mind is risky but, if it works, we achieve what we want with minimal damage. Listen carefully, we have six missiles, full of the new gas. What if we fire five of them in quick succession, right into the precinct steps. The explosions will blow out the big show windows at the front of the building, allowing the wind to blow the gas inside. The creatures will only be able to escape out through the back of the building. We fire our last missile into the gap between the rear entrance and the trucks parked there. With the windbreak effect, the gas should just sit there, blocking their way out. The wind blows the gas from the front through the building. They can't leave through the back without coming into contact with the gas waiting for them there. We get what we want with only a small risk to the plan tomorrow. Building basically intact, trucks basically intact, creatures basically extinct. What do you think?" she asked him.

"Mrs. Stewart, that is brilliant, absolutely brilliant. Now I'm sure marrying you was the right decision. Let's do it," John answered, laughing.

He was very proud of her. Without realising it, she had probably saved the following day's mission. She had most certainly saved a lot of lives.

"You'll pay for that remark, later. Okay, the missiles at the front will have to explode very close to the building. That way, most of the gas will enter through the blown out doors and windows. The one at the back will have to explode as close to the exit as possible, but at the same time not so close that we blow the windows or anything. That way the gas stays in the building longer but we don't damage anything too badly. Anything left in there after all the explosions won't get out. Are you ready, John? It's going to get a little scary for a second."

He confirmed he was ready.

"I'm targeting the steps at the front. I'll have to launch quickly so that we can get around to the back and block the exit before they have a chance to escape. Here we go," she said.

John felt the launch at the front of the building, then the acceleration as the aircraft flew over the building to the back. The machine seemed to twist and turn incredibly in the air. He quietly thanked God she was such a good pilot. Once in position, she fired the last missile and then climbed, the aircraft hovering above the massive gas cloud that hung at the back of the superstore. The front entrance was also blocked by a wall of white death but there the monster was moving into the building. If John had not known better, he would have sworn it was alive and was hunting.

"Now we wait," she said calmly.

They waited for a full ten minutes, monitoring both the front and the rear of the building using the Apache's infra-red cameras. Visual verification was proving impossible because of the amount of gas hanging around the building. From what they could see, it had worked perfectly. Estimated losses to the creatures hiding in the building, one hundred percent. Damage to the building itself, minimal.

"Let's go home," he said, his voice filled with relief.

Twenty minutes later, they touched down in the castle compound. After climbing down from the helicopter's cockpit, John hugged and kissed his wife. It was clear in his mind she had saved the day. Thanks to her quick thinking and skills handling the aircraft, they had turned probable defeat into possible victory. They reported the night's events to Robert, who also congratulated Stephanie on her idea. Robert, looking tired, asked if they could now maybe get some sleep because the main operation was due to begin in just a few hours. John agreed but he was sure that, at least now, they had a good chance of succeeding.

Chapter Twenty Four - Battle for Hadlee

It was time.

The three trucks were tried and tested, the men armed and ready. The tank, which was due to play a key role in the operation, was ready to go. All three helicopters were also fully armed and ready to fly.

Stephanie had a new co-pilot who seemed very capable, despite having very little experience.

John and his team were on board the other two helicopters, ready. Mark was not going with him this time, he had taken charge of the three trucks and the men inside them. John had insisted it was critical that a man with experience stay with the relatively inexperienced soldiers, to organise the defence of the vehicles. If everything went as planned, then the men defending the trucks would probably come under attack from large numbers of the creatures. Having somebody in charge with a cool head at that time would be paramount. Any hesitation or weakness shown at that point would probably prove fatal to some, if not all, of the defenders. Mark, in John's opinion, was the only candidate with the necessary qualifications and experience to get the job done. It was going to be difficult for John without his right hand man at his side but both had agreed it seemed the only logical way to proceed.

John was not looking forward to the battle, because the plan called for him and his team to fly off and leave their friends as they were coming under attack. This was an action that went against his ethics. The thought of leaving anybody in trouble and flying off, something he would not normally have considered but the success of the plan depended partially on his team being able to scout out the deserted town. That was as long as they could persuade the creatures to leave the relative safety of the buildings and attack at all.

Robert had wanted to go along, arguing it was time he got more involved but John had persuaded him otherwise. John had argued successfully that Robert was officially in charge and, on the off chance something should go wrong, it was important that one leader was safe to carry on the fight. This had to be Robert, as both John and Mark were critical figures in the battle plan, their presence not only key to their chances of success but also important to the morale of the men involved. Robert had eventually agreed and, although disappointed, had wished them luck.

As soon as everything was ready John had given the order and the small convoy had moved out of the castle, the tank leading the way. Its first job was to secure the road backed up by the three helicopters, so that the trucks could drive through unmolested. Surprisingly, this proved easier than they had anticipated and the convoy was soon on its way towards Hadlee.

Next, the Apache, piloted by Stephanie, accelerated ahead of the column, its first job to gather intelligence. It would fly over the town and, using its infra-red cameras, locate the creatures hiding there. John was certain that not all the creatures had been in the precinct the night before. They needed an idea of how strong the enemy force was likely to be. She would then continue on south, down past the town, just in case there were other creature reinforcements coming their way. After completing this task, she would rendezvous with the convoy and report her findings. They would then all proceed to the designated point just outside the town limits. Their defences would be set up and activated and then they would wait.

Ninety minutes later, they were exactly at that juncture in the plan. The intelligence mission had been successful, the defences were set up and ready. All three helicopters had been re-fuelled and were ready for immediate take off. Stephanie had checked beyond the town for signs of reinforcing creatures moving up from the south but had found none. The buildings where creatures were still hiding had been marked on a rough map of the town, the map made using the intelligence that was gathered the night before. It was obvious from the latest photographs taken by Stephanie that considerable numbers of the creatures were still waiting for the soldiers to return. If they had entered Hadlee, as the creatures obviously expected, the men involved would have been quickly overwhelmed.

Now, the waiting creatures would have to contend with the tank. Its job was to enter the town, engage the enemy and draw them out into the open, where the rest of the force was waiting to eliminate them. John had told the commander of the massive tank to maintain radio contact at all times and report their progress. If anything unexpected happened and they got into trouble then the soldiers, waiting outside the town, would do everything necessary to extricate them. With that, the tank had rumbled down the road leading directly into Hadlee and had entered the town.

The three man crew worked well together, a well rehearsed team that knew exactly what was expected of them. It did not take long for them to locate the first nest of creatures. One gas shell and the tank's scatter guns made very short work out of the thirty or so monsters hiding in the building. They moved further into the town, seeking out their next target, once found, they only used their scatter guns to engage. The tank commander was well aware that his main objective was to draw the creatures out of their hiding places, so he was gambling that with them not using the gas this time the creatures might think they had run out. This would hopefully encourage the monsters to attack as, up until that point in time, they had always shown little respect for conventional weapons. This tactic seemed to work as some of the creatures in surrounding buildings came out of hiding and attacked the tank but its defences held up well. The 'electric shield', as some of the soldiers playfully called it, actually did kill any of the creatures that came into contact with it, just as Bill had anticipated. Electricity could be counted as another one of their few weaknesses. The fact that their 'friends' seemed to die without apparent cause spurred even more of them to attack. Suddenly, they were coming from everywhere, the streets in the town filling with them. The tank's scatter guns started to fire again as the tank commander gave the order to retreat.

Slowly heading back out of town, the tank would fire its guns and then pull back. Every time they did this, fifty or sixty yards were gained, pulling the creatures further away from the precinct. The creatures suddenly seemed hell-bent on killing the monstrosity in their midst. Their actions reminded the commander of a documentary film he had seen as a young boy. In the film, bees had attempted to protect their hive from an attacker. The way the creatures were now swarming all over his tank, just to be killed by its defences, reminded him of the scenes in the film where the bees had attacked their enemy. The bees must have known that after they had stung only once they would die but they had stung anyway. Their deaths were not as important as the survival of their hive. Watching the dramatic scenes unfolding outside his tank, he wondered if there was a similarity in the creatures behaviour? If so, it would make their job all the more difficult. He remembered that in the film he had watched, the bees had always won!

Another two hundred yards and the tank would be at the town limits again. The commander radioed in their progress to John. Everything was proceeding to plan, he estimated that upwards of five hundred of the creatures were currently attacking or following his tank. He switched the scatter guns to automatic firing, reporting confidently that they could reduce that number before reaching the defensive position set up by the waiting soldiers.

After receiving the message, John decided it was time for his team to leave for the precinct. He told Mark to dig in and, no matter what happened, stick to the plan. If, at any time, his team needed help, he would let Mark know. Nobody else was to enter the town until all the approaching creatures had been killed. As soon as the monsters had cleared the town limits, they should begin using the modified weapons they had brought along. At that point the danger to John's team would be minimal. The last thing they needed was a gas cloud making their lives complicated. He spoke to Stephanie telling her that, no matter what, she was to stay there and give the soldiers fighting from the trucks covering fire. Under no circumstances was she to disengage until all the creatures were dead. He would be fine and she was not to worry.

Bravo One and Bravo Two would fly his team in. They would control the trucks first, making sure enough of them were still driveable, then they would hit the fuel depot and acquire any tankers that still carried fuel. Once all the transport was secure they would move into the precinct, clear it of any creatures still hiding there and start loading. By that time, if everything had gone well, the rest of their men should be able to move up into the town and help. Afterwards, they would all visit the first supermarket and pick up the rest of the supplies that were waiting for them there. It was very important that there be no mistakes, nobody should panic. No matter what seemed to be happening in the town, John and his team were well equipped to deal with it. If, for whatever reason they could not, John would call for help.

The men had boarded the two helicopters, the pilots understanding what they had to do. They would circle around the town and approach from the south, that way hopefully avoiding drawing the creatures back in. The precinct would be approached from that direction, enabling them first to fly over the fuel depot. Without having a greater fuel supply available to them they would need fewer trucks. After visually confirming the presence of at least one fuel tanker, they would continue on to the precinct. If not, then the danger of the precinct could be avoided. He knew he had seen the tankers there but, without the photographs to confirm it, there was always the chance it had been wishful thinking on his part. If fuel was there but all the trucks at the precinct were out of action his team would be picked up again, using the helicopters and flown back to the staging area. Once all the creatures had then been dealt with, the whole column would move into Hadlee and load as many of the supplies as possible into the three trucks they had brought with them. Everything had been carefully thought through so as to minimise the risk to the mission his team was undertaking.

Flying over the fuel depot he spotted the fuel tankers, four of them. Everything looked quiet, there were no creatures in sight but they all understood that did not mean there were not any hiding in the area. Next stop was the precinct car park to the rear of the massive building. The important work there could now begin.

As they approached, the area seemed quiet and John was beginning to believe that maybe their plan had worked perfectly. It appeared that all of the creatures were currently fighting on the outskirts of the town. He knew that might not be true and advised his men accordingly but maybe this time there would not be any surprises waiting for them.

Every man in his team knew exactly what their jobs were once they were on the ground. John and two others would secure the back door, the rest would check all of the trucks for fuel and they would start the engines to ensure they were functional. There was no real reason to be quiet, as the sounds of the battle now raging outside the town would drown out any noise they made. Once this was accomplished, they would know exactly how many trucks were still operational and then head back to the fuel depot, to secure the tankers parked there. There was still the chance that they were empty but John felt the gamble was necessary. From the four tankers they had seen, at least one should be carrying fuel. If not, then they would have to think again but he was sure the odds were in their favour this time.

The helicopters landed, his men immediately taking up a defensive position around the perimeter of the car park. One of the men checked the gates, they were closed but not locked.

John and his two men approached the backdoor carefully, ready to react. The door appeared closed but all the windows were smashed. To begin with John assumed it was a result of the missile detonation from the night before but, after closer inspection, it was obvious the windows had been smashed from the inside. Obviously the creatures that had been hiding inside the building had tried desperately to escape the death trap Stephanie had created but fortunately, for the attacking force, they hadn't succeeded. He looked into the building through the windows and could see the results of Stephanie's handiwork. There were bodies everywhere and lots of them. He whistled. If they had not made the lightning raid with the Apache the night before, then they would have been facing incredible odds at that moment. The thought made him shiver.

"Check the trucks, everything's clear here," he said, using his headset.

His men moved in. There were twenty four trucks to be checked and he wanted to take them all if it proved possible.

"Bravo One, Bravo Two, come in, please. Over," he said, continuing to use the headset.

"We're still here, John. What do you need? Over."

"It looks like we're okay. Head back out over the town limits and support the men fighting there. We'll be moving to the fuel depot shortly on foot. If anything happens and we get into trouble, I will contact you. Over."

"Roger that. Stay in touch and remember your headsets only have a limited range. Don't get too far away. Over and out."

The two helicopters left the area.

"Guys, we're on our own. Keep it tight," John ordered.

The first ten trucks had already been checked. Fuel was turning out to be plentiful and the vehicles still seemed to be in perfect working order, most of their motors starting first time. His men were still working on the others.

The two helicopters had reached the battle ground and contacted Stephanie for instructions.

"Come in low behind them," she ordered. "Machine guns only, I repeat, machine guns only. Do not use your gas weapons, there's too much wind. We're going to have to do this the old fashioned way, gentlemen. Over."

They had descended and were attacking the creatures from behind. The tank could clearly be seen in the creatures midst leading them ever further from the town, the number of attackers starting to dwindle.

The pilot of Bravo One smiled. The picture of these 'monsters' being led away from Hadlee, brought back childhood memories of the children's story 'The Pied Piper' flooding into his mind. The only difference was, these were bloody big rats!

Creatures were now falling to his fire, Bravo Two also taking its toll. The tank was killing more and more of the creatures with every yard it won in the fight to lead them away from John and his men. He still estimated there were over three hundred of the creatures slowly approaching the defensive formation of trucks. By the time they reached them, he thought smiling, there would be a lot less. He continued firing.

John's team had checked all the remaining trucks. Nineteen of them were fully operational, fuelled and ready to go. Five others did not want to join in the party. He was sure that, given the time, his talented men could persuade the unhappy trucks to work but time was something they did not have.

"Okay, leave the others. We move to the fuel depot. Keep it quiet, just in case. Move out. Jenkins and Smith on point, keep your eyes peeled," he said.

Up until that point they had experienced no difficulties at all, he hoped their luck would hold.

Stephanie had, several times, flown down almost in amongst the army of creatures, her scatter guns firing wildly in all directions. She desperately wanted to use the modified weapons her Apache was carrying but a change in wind direction could have proven deadly, either to the men she now defended or to John somewhere in the town. Part of her wanted to leave the battlefield, fly to wherever John was and protect him but he had been very specific about the subject. Her heart had nearly stopped when she had realised the other two helicopters had returned without him or his men. They were now alone, she prayed they would be careful. It was the riskiest part of the whole operation to send just twelve men, without support of any kind, into the town but John had insisted it was the only realistic way to accomplish their mission. Even Mark, somebody she could rely on to watch after John, had not been allowed to go with him. He had saved John's life already on a few occasions, always bringing him back to her. This time . . . She made the chain of thought disappear, it would be alright. They just had to finish their job as quickly as possible and then she could go to him. She continued firing.

Mark had been watching the developing battle through his binoculars at first but the creatures were now so close he did not need them anymore. The monsters would soon be close enough that his eager men could finally engage them. He waited, patience was a virtue. John had taught him that.

John and his team had carefully made their way through the town and were approaching the fuel depot. None of the creatures had been seen in the time it had taken them to reach their target. Everything was still quiet in the town, the noise of the battle raging outside Hadlee the only sounds that reached the men. They moved in slowly and set up a perimeter. The building itself was intact but seemed empty. They quickly checked the four tankers that were parked there, the results more than John could have hoped. Two were fully loaded, one was three quarters full and the last one just under half-full. This was exactly the result they had wished for, fuel would not pose a problem during their journey.

"Perfect," John said, after getting the reports from his men. "Okay, we take all four with us. Get them ready to role, then check around and see if there's anything else we can use."

His men fanned out, looking around the depot. The tankers were started, ready to be moved. Suddenly one of his men called John over to his position, it seemed urgent. John ran over to him. The man had been checking along the back wall, as John reached him he signalled that John should stay down.

"What's up?" John asked, crouching down beside the soldier.

The soldier did not say very much, he just pointed over the wall. Very slowly John raised himself up enough so that he could see over the wall that ringed the depot. Behind the building was an expanse of open ground, John guessed it stretched for about a mile before ending in a thickly wooded area. He saw what was troubling his man so much. Coming out of the tree line were creatures, hundreds of them!

"Shit!" John said, ducking back down. "What the fuck do we do now?"

He called his team in around him. Against so many what could twelve men hope to do? They had no chance, no chance at all. In turn they all took a quick glance over the wall at the slowly approaching army. He could tell by the looks on their faces, they all understood what it probably meant. They all looked to him as leader, he was supposed to find an answer. He had always found one up to now, could he do it again? If not, then it was all over for the men gathered around him, and the men fighting beyond the town limits would be over-run and probably wiped out. He looked again over the wall. He estimated it would take the creatures about six minutes to reach the depot. The helicopters would be at least five minutes away, it was too close to risk it. He had a nasty thought and spoke into his headset.

"Bravo One, come in, please. Over."

No reply came back, he tried again.

"Bravo One, do you copy? Over."

Nothing again, only static. They were out of range. What had the pilot said, he should have checked the range. Now they had one option less. They could run but where to? They could hide but that would not help their comrades.

"Think, John, think," he said, quietly.

They could get in the tankers and attempt to break through the creatures now attacking their friends. The tankers, that was it. They had one chance, maybe it would at least buy them time. He spoke to his men asking how much C4 they had. Ever since the ambush at the second supermarket, the explosives and detonators had become standard equipment. He thanked God they had made such a decision. His men confirmed they had twelve blocks of the powerful explosive and the necessary detonators. He hoped it would be enough. John rattled out his orders, machine gun style. There was not much time.

"You three, plant your explosives in the building. You three, over there along the depot wall. You three, the tanker that is only half full. The rest of us on the pipes over there."

Looking quickly over the wall again, he continued.

"Set your timers to three minutes and get on board the other tankers, we are leaving now."

The men went about their work. He planted his block on some pipe work coming out of the ground in the hope it would create a lot of shrapnel, adding to the explosives destructive power. The men who had planted their explosives on the half-full tanker opened its valves, allowing the fuel to slowly flow out. The liquid cargo was starting to run all over the area, flowing down some of the nearby streets, just as they had hoped. The explosives were all quickly set, the timers ticking down. They quickly climbed on board the remaining tankers and left the depot, heading back towards the precinct. John was looking at his watch, his men doing the same. They had a chance, if he had timed it right.

The creatures were approaching the wall of the fuel depot. They could have climbed over it but instead they started to demolish it, stone by stone.

At that moment something flashed . . .

John and his team had almost reached the precinct when the explosion came. If he had not known better he would have sworn it was a nuclear detonation, the explosion was massive. The resulting shock wave almost blowing over one of the tankers. Whole streets of the town were suddenly gone, buildings were blown over, others were burning, debris was falling everywhere.

Stephanie had just finished another strafing run when the explosion came.
"My God!" she said loudly. "John!"

Mark and his men had finally been able to engage the creatures. They were cutting them down with unwavering accuracy. The tank was still wreaking a massive toll on the surviving monsters. The three helicopters were continuing to attack from above, unrelenting, unforgiving. As the explosion happened, the resulting flash was so bright, the soldiers all shielded their eyes for a second. Mark's first thought was the same as John's, it was nuclear. Even some of the still-fighting creatures had reacted. Mark had quickly recovered and was now spurring his men on. To get to John they had to finish their work quickly.

John and his team had safely reached the precinct car park. Up until that point there had been no sign of surviving creatures following them but it was too early for celebrations. They formed a defensive perimeter around the area and waited, ready for anything that might still be coming their way. John knew the next minutes would be unbearable. Would it be possible life or probable death? They waited quietly.
"Time will tell," John whispered.

Stephanie was near to tears but she still continued to attack the creatures. There were not many of them left now and those that were still alive, seemed more interested in escaping the never ending hail of bullets coming their way.

Mark was also desperate, he had to try to reach his friend, just in case he had survived the massive blast that had rocked the town minutes before. He ordered his men to close with the surviving creatures and finish them. His men, sensing the urgency of the situation, readily left the relative safety of the truck roofs and charged to meet the creatures that were still milling around the battlefield.
"Hold on, John. We're coming," Mark shouted, as he led the charge.

John and his team were very much alive and starting to dare to believe they had been lucky. There was still no sign of any surviving creatures but he did not want to push their luck. He needed intelligence. Where was a helicopter when he needed one?

The battle was over. The last of the creatures falling to a burst from Mark's M-16. They had won and convincingly so. The tactics had been perfect, everybody involved knowing who they had to thank for their victory. The only question now was if that person was still in a position to be thanked or whether he had been wiped from the face of the earth, taken to a place where they could only thank him in their prayers.

As soon as the last creature fell, Stephanie broke off from the battlefield and headed into town. She had to know. Was she still the wife of a wonderful man or the widow of a hero?

John was slowly losing his patience, it was time to move. They still had a lot of work to do before they could leave the town of Hadlee or what was left of the town, forever. He decided he hated the place, however stupid it sounded - once that day was over he was never, ever, ever coming back there. Suddenly his headset came to life.

"John. John, do you read me? Come in, John. Can you hear me? Please come in. Over."

He realised everything had gone quiet, all sounds of battle had stopped. It was suddenly so very quiet. He was not sure what to make of it. His headset interrupted him again.

"John, talk to me. Please, God. John, where are you? Over."

He realised she sounded upset.

"I'm here and everything's alright."

"Oh, God John, I thought you were dead. Are you hurt? God, you scared me. Tell me where you are, I'm coming to get you. Over."

He realised his men could hear everything she was saying and they were finding it quite amusing. He decided enough was enough.

"I'm okay . . . We're all okay. No injuries. Now calm down Stephanie, I need you to fly over the fuel depot and tell me what's going on. Do you copy? Over," he said.

"I copy you, John. I'm sorry. I was scared, that's all. I'll get right on it. Over and out."

His men were still amused, some of them trying to stifle laughs. He also started laughing, finding it strange. Twenty five minutes before they had been facing almost certain death together, now they were practically rolling on the floor, howling with laughter. It was a damn strange world they lived in.

After two or three minutes Stephanie was back. There were no creatures to be seen but she now understood why the explosion had been so massive. Under the fuel depot there had been a storage facility, she presumed for fuel. It had exploded, she could not explain why.

"I'll explain later," John said. "How's the battle going, it's bloody quiet all of a sudden. Over."

"We've won, John. We got them all. Over."

"Great, well done. Okay, we've got work to do. Get back to Mark and get everybody up here. Tell him to take his time coming through the town just in case. We'll go through the precinct and meet you out front. You should land, refuel and re-arm if necessary. Bravo One and Bravo Two likewise. We'll need you in the air watching our backs. Did you copy that? Over," John said.

"Gotcha, John, I'm on my way. I love you! Over and out."

His men started giggling again.

"You bunch of wankers," he said, trying to stay serious but he also started to laugh again.

The trucks were ready, the fuel tankers secure. It was time to go shopping.

John's unit's short journey through the precinct proved to be uneventful as had the short trip through the town for Mark and his force. It appeared, for now at least, there were no more creatures to worry about. Stephanie had landed and, together with Mark, met John on the steps of the building they had all fought so hard to capture. Stephanie hugged and kissed him, tears running down her cheeks. The relief that he was still alive plain to see. Mark went to shake his hand but ended up hugging him instead.

"We've been lucky," John said.

He then went on to explain why the big explosion had taken place.

"Now we need to hurry," he continued. "Two teams, Mark. The first one takes three trucks with them to the first supermarket and loads up everything they think we can use. Twenty men loading, ten go along to watch their backs. The second team stays here with us and empties the precinct. We bring all the trucks around to the front and load here. Once the trucks are full they will be parked and guarded. Don't forget the fuel tankers, they are ready to go. In one hour we are leaving this shitty town and

I, for one, don't ever want to see it again. Stephanie, you and the other pilots patrol the outskirts, watch out for more creatures heading our way. If you spot any then just engage them, that will give us warning enough."

Everybody was moving at once, the orders being carried out. A sense of urgency could be physically felt amongst the men as they organised themselves into groups and went about their business. They had all had enough fighting for one day and if it was possible to complete their mission without having to fire another shot, they would gladly do so. John's original plan called for as many as twenty-four trucks. They already had nine so another fifteen were theoretically needed. Nineteen of the vehicles, now in their possession, were in perfect working order so they decided to take them all and work it out later.

"It's going to be one hell of a convoy, John," Mark said, laughing. "Seriously, getting into the castle might be a problem," he added.

"We'll be okay. The tank and the helicopters will keep the creatures busy while we're getting through with the trucks. Your team will have to provide support fire but I don't see a real problem in that. The main danger is the road. If they've been busy little buggers again, we might have a surprise waiting for us in that department. We need a bit of luck in the mixture but I think we're on a roll, anyway," John said, smiling. "After what's happened here today, I reckon we'll get home alright. The tank can lead the way through the forest, it should be able to deal with anything they've got lined up for us."

It took longer than expected but eventually all the trucks were ready to leave. Almost half of them were loaded with supplies. Another one was full of bottled water, something John realised would be crucial for the journey down the country. He could not believe that nobody from the planning team, including himself, had even considered taking a supply with them. It would have been an interesting trip if nobody had anything to drink for several days! Fortuitously, the potential problem had solved itself. Anything that could at some stage be useful had been taken along, including clothes, building supplies, books, computers, hardware, kitchen equipment, bedding supplies, even toys for the children. The list was endless. John had told his men to take everything. They would sort out what they needed and leave the rest at the castle when they left.

For protection, each truck had three men on board, this fact severely weakening Mark's team but John insisted it was necessary. The tank would lead followed by one of the modified trucks, the other two spread out through the column, one in the middle, one bringing up the rear. The helicopters were also deployed in that way. Bravo One was checking the way ahead, Bravo Two was watching their backs with Stephanie's Apache basically troubleshooting. John and his team, being the better trained, were riding in the lead truck while Mark and what was left of his force were riding in the truck at the rear. They were ready.

"Use the C.B. radios in the cabs," John told the drivers. "No matter what happens we've got to get home. Any problems we come across along the way will be dealt with. If one of the trucks breaks down, we'll evacuate it's crew and leave it. The key now is to keep moving, we can't afford to get stuck at any time. We are spread pretty thin because of the number of trucks but, compared to what we've just accomplished here, the ride home shouldn't provide us with any major problems. Let's go."

With that, they left the town of Hadlee for the very last time.

Chapter Twenty Five - Convoy

John was seated in the leading truck, in constant contact with the rest of the convoy. He knew there would be no problem, at least until they reached the forest road leading to the castle. He spoke to Mark, asking how many of the modified gas weapons were still left? Mark informed him they had not used any at all. They had won the battle the good old fashioned way, bullets and sweat.

This gave John an idea. Using the gas, they might be able to carve a way through the creatures and keep it open long enough for all the vehicles to make it through. He told Stephanie, Mark and the tank commander they would be stopping before entering the forest. The helicopters should land at that time and once again re-fuel.

It would take another hour's travel to reach that point, everybody now rode in silence, the tension mounting. Suddenly, one of the soldier's started singing over the radio, John recognising the song straightaway.

"We've got a great big convoy, trucking through the night."

Others started to join in, John just laughed.

They had reached the point where John had wanted to stop. Mark remarked, sarcastically, that the place looked vaguely familiar. John replied, that with luck it would be the last time. The next time they left the castle and drove through the forest, they would not be coming back, ever.

John explained what he wanted to do. It was quite simple really, they had the gas weapons, they had their masks. Bravo One and Bravo Two should drop their loads to the left of the road, twenty yards inside the tree line, about forty yards before the road left the forest. Stephanie should do the same but on the right. If it were done correctly it would form a corridor for them to drive through. The gas would not dissipate for at least thirty minutes, giving them enough time to get all the vehicles through. Because of the thickness of the woods, the gas should hang in the trees, like a fog, so there would be little danger for the castle's inhabitants. The tank would lead the way, in case any obstacles needed to be removed and then take up a covering position in the clearing. Once clear of the trees, the trucks would make a dash for the castle. If they timed it correctly they would make it. The three helicopters could also offer support fire in case any of the creatures left the cover of the trees. Everything was clear, so they rejoined their vehicles. It was time.

The helicopters took off and headed to target. They would wait two minutes before commencing their attack, giving the convoy time to move up. At the allotted time they dropped their bombs, exactly as John had requested, the gas clouds forming a corridor just as he had hoped. The tank was entering the cloud of poison, searching for trouble.

This time the creatures had not done anything to the road and the trucks quickly started to exit the trees. The castle doors were already open, the second tank had taken up a defensive position next to them. The helicopters were hovering low over the clearing, covering the trucks with their guns but no creatures were to be seen. John was not sure what to make of this, his suspicious mind working overtime as usual.

Within twenty minutes of the helicopters dropping their bombs, all vehicles were safely parked within the castle. They had accomplished their difficult mission successfully and without loss.

And they say miracles never happen, John thought. Apart from the battle and thanks to the bit of luck they had at the fuel depot, it had been easier than he had expected. He hoped their luck would hold, just a little longer.

Chapter Twenty Six - The Party

All the men returning from Hadlee had cheered after dismounting from the trucks, the friends who had been waiting for them joining in. Robert had hugged John, Stephanie and Mark. He had then congratulated every single soldier who had taken part in the action. The excitement within the castle was fever pitched.

They had completed the first and, probably, hardest part of the plan. Their dream of leaving the castle could now become a reality, the hopes of a new life somewhere safe a big step nearer. All of them were tired but at the same time elated. Robert suggested a celebration. They had not had a party for ages, never really having anything to celebrate. That had all changed.

The men who had risked everything for them, deserved at least that. Before the preparations to leave continued, they would really let their hair down. It might be the last chance they would have for a while. Thanks to the supplies from the precinct they had everything they needed to organise a super party. Food and drink were, at least for the next months, in plentiful supply. Indeed, the supplies they had taken would probably last them the best part of a year, if they were careful. So the luxury of such an occasion was something they could well afford.

John felt tired and decided before going to the party, he would get a couple of hours sleep. Stephanie felt the same way and decided to join him. She had nearly lost him already once that day, for the next few days at least, she would not be leaving his side.

Mark had begun to celebrate with his men, a barrel of beer already open. The men were enjoying it for the first time in ages having found six unopened barrels in one of the precinct bars. Robert couldn't help wondering how much of it would be left the following morning. Knowing his men as he did, he already knew the answer. Nothing! He was nevertheless busy organising the food and music, as there would also be dancing. Some of the civilians had often asked if they could organise such nights, sadly, he had always refused. As a military man he had been used to weekend parties and dances, they were a normal part of an officer's life. He had always enjoyed himself on such occasions and considered himself quite a good dancer. That night he intended to prove the fact to some of his men. He would show the enlisted men that an officer could also let his hair down under the right circumstances. He understood that some of his decisions in the past had not sat well with them but that was normal. He had always thought long and hard before making any important decisions, which naturally included the use of castle resources, supplies etc. Tonight he would show them he knew how to party, just like everybody else.

John and Stephanie had slept for a few hours. As they woke it was 1800 hours and they could hear from their room the promised party was in full swing. They each showered and dressed. Although John was not really a partygoer he felt it was right to put in an appearance, at least for a short time. He owed it to his men. They had all done amazingly well and he wanted to show them his appreciation.

They joined the party and after eating, drinking and dancing for about five hours, they decided it was time to retire for the evening. The party would go on into the early hours, so sleeping would prove difficult, but thankfully beds were not just for sleeping in. They would find a way of amusing themselves until they eventually fell asleep.

Robert was beginning to feel the worse for wear. He could not keep up with Mark and his men, although he had had a dammed good go. He felt sure that everybody had enjoyed themselves, soldiers and civilians alike. Even the children had been jigging about for the first few hours. They had all gone to bed at about nine o'clock but the party had continued. Robert felt it was time for him to do the same but Mark was not listening to him. Beer after beer kept appearing on their table, each one always being the last one but they did not stop coming. Robert seriously considered putting him on a charge, for about ten seconds but after drinking the next beer he decided to go with the flow, knowing that eventually his body would reject the never ending supply of beer for him. Whether he would still be able to function as a human being at that point, was debatable.

Mark was finding the whole process funny but he was quietly impressed with the way his boss was handling the beer. It was getting to the stage where even he was struggling with the quantity. All evening long his men had slowly deserted him, the good old days of drinking right through the night apparently something they had grown out of but he had not given up yet. It was now a question of honour. He had to finish off Robert, otherwise it meant an officer out-drinking an enlisted man. That was something, he felt sure that had not happened very often in the history of the army. If he had anything to do with it, it was not going to happen that night. The next two beers were waiting on the table, Robert already reaching for his. Mark gulped, it was going to prove harder than he had expected!

Chapter Twenty Seven - The Day After

John had woken early, showered and dressed and was walking through the castle compound. It appeared as if he was almost the only one awake. The guards on the walls seemed to be the only exceptions.

He headed for Robert's office, knocked but nobody answered. This was strange as the Major was normally always in his office. John decided to find Mark, as he would probably know where Robert was. The only problem, where would Mark be? After the party the night before, John expected Mark would have been drunk. In fact he realised now that is where they would all be, sleeping off their hangovers. He was walking back across the compound when he met Bill, who seemed perfectly all right.

"Morning, John," Bill said. "How's your head this morning?" he asked.

"I'm fine, mate, we didn't stay too long. I'm not much of a party guy and Stephanie needs her rest because of the baby. I presume it was a long night because there's nobody about at the moment. Were they all so drunk?"

"They were all pissed out of their heads! I think they all underestimated the potency of the beer they found, it was the first real shin-dig in at least a year. When you don't drink regularly, it goes straight to your head. I was feeling groggy after my fifth beer, some of them by then, had had almost twice that many. Mark and Robert especially, it turned into a competition between those two. God knows how much they had."

"I've just been to Robert's office, he's not there. Any ideas where he could be?"

"The last time I saw the Major he was dancing with Mark, heading for the kitchens," Bill replied, smirking.

"Robert was drunk and I missed it. Shit!" John said, also smiling.

The picture of the normally dead serious Major dancing with another man flashed into John's mind, he laughed.

"Okay," he continued. "We'll leave the lovebirds alone for now. How do you like all the new toys we brought you yesterday?" John asked.

"I wanted to talk to you about that, there are a few things we need to discuss," Bill replied. "To start with, we don't have enough electrical equipment to modify them all. The modifications are complicated and we need all kinds of cables and connectors. We had a good supply of those items but they were meant for general repair work on the castle's electrical systems, not really for kitting out a load of trucks. I can maybe kit out another two, possibly three more in the same way but all nineteen is just not possible."

"We don't need all of them kitting out, Bill. What we need to do is work out how many people can live in each truck. When I say live, I basically mean sleep, as that's when most room will be needed. Before you modify all of them, it's probably going to be better to finish just one. That way we'll know exactly how many people can sleep per truck. Then we'll know how many trucks we need in total for the civilians. Once that's clear, we'll work out the rest," John suggested.

"I'll get right on it, John. I'll plan it out on paper first, then we'll confer again," and with that, he walked off towards his workshop.

John decided it was too early to wake Stephanie, so he would continue looking for Robert and Mark. He headed towards the kitchens as Bill had suggested the pair were heading in that direction the last time he had seen them. As he entered the kitchen area, it was all quiet, nobody yet working. It must have been one hell of a party, John thought, it was just as well the creatures did not know all of their weaknesses. All they would have to do was deliver a barrel of beer or two, poison it, and by the time the soldiers realised, it would be to late.

He heard something. It sounded like somebody moaning, as if hurt. He reacted straightaway, drawing the Beretta he habitually carried. The noise was coming from behind two steel doors that led to a storage area in the back of the kitchen. He approached the doors carefully, ready for anything.

Suddenly, the doors pushed outwards towards him. He immediately went into a crouch, a classic shooting stance, his gun coming up on line, his eyes searching for the target, then he relaxed. Coming through the doors Robert, holding his head, followed by Mark.

Smiling, John said.

"I won't ask you two what you've been doing in there together."

Robert and Mark both stared at him and almost simultaneously said, "Shut up!"

They had drunk coffee and lots of it, both of them feeling a little better. It had been a super party and exactly what everybody had needed. Now it was time to get back to work, they still had a lot to do. John told them about his conversation with Bill and the possible problems. They all decided another chat with Bill was called for and headed over to his workshop. As they arrived there he was just finishing off his design for the trucks. When he had finished, he began to explain exactly what he had come up with.

"Each of the trucks will be armoured, we have enough of the compound to do that. The problem is the electrical side of the defences, we have enough of the components to completely modify a further four trucks. Together with the three we have already finished, that gives us a total of seven fully modified trucks. I believe the defences held up well during the battle, so it stands to reason the trucks that are fully modified are the safest place for the civilians to sleep. I've estimated at the moment we can sleep thirty people per truck comfortably or forty but cramped. We have no idea at the moment how long we are going to have to spend travelling in the trucks, so I suggest we do it the comfortable way. Thirty people per truck, seven trucks, a total of two hundred and ten people. Because so many of them are children we'll probably be able to squeeze a few more in but we'll have to wait and see for definite," Bill explained.

"That's pretty good," John said. "We have in total three hundred and thirty eight people, of which two hundred and thirteen are civilians, so basically we can protect them all while we're travelling. The soldiers are used to hardship, they can sleep anywhere and anyway. By the time each truck has a driver and guards, we won't need much sleeping space for the soldiers, they'll be mostly on duty. Obviously, we'll have to work out a rota so that they get enough rest but one truck sleeping thirty should be enough. That way, basically a third of our men would always be resting."

"But that one truck wouldn't be as safe as the others," Bill pointed out.

"That's true but with the guards on the roof, the chance of the sleeping men being caught unawares is nil. If we were attacked they'd all be needed anyway, so the risk is minimal. Do you agree, Robert?" John asked.

"Yes. It won't be a problem," Robert said, agreeing with John's argument.

He still looked a little under the weather, John thought - it would take a long time for him to live the party down. The jokes and jibes would very soon begin to surface.

"Good, so we need seven fully modified, one just armoured, that's eight altogether from a possible twenty eight, leaves us twenty to play with. Okay. Next, supplies. How much do we need to take with us?"

"If we are just talking food supplies then, if possible, we should take it all. We have the three trucks from the second supermarket. We now have an additional seven trucks full from the precinct and the first supermarket, that makes ten all told," Mark informed them, he seemed to have recovered a little faster than Robert.

"Where we have to be careful is the size of the convoy," John said. "I'm not sure how big we should allow it to be. Obviously, the more we can take with us the better, makes life easier later but the main problem is protection. We need at least three trucks for carrying spare parts, we need one for cooking in, a mobile kitchen if you like, we now need ten for the supplies. Together with the eight for sleeping, we have a total of twenty-two trucks. The sixteen tonners are already partly loaded, we have six of those. Now we're a convoy of twenty-eight vehicles! Add a couple of tanks and that makes us a target that's about a mile long, difficult to keep safe."

"As long as we keep moving, we'll be alright," Mark said. "If we work out a shift system for the drivers, there'd be no need to stop. We could keep moving basically twenty four hours a day, just stopping to refuel now and then."

"Fuel!" John said. "I almost forgot the fuel tankers. We have five of them, now we're even longer. We've also got the problem, of course, we want to leave the country. That means a ship or something big enough for every vehicle to fit in. That's big!"

"We'd easily fit aboard a car ferry, as we first suggested, we just need to get to the coast and find one. The best bet is still going to be New Hull. As far as we know, it was the only ferry port still working after the war finished anyway. There's bound to be a ferry there. We load everything on board and we are gone," Robert said, still holding his head.

"Okay, we have the beginnings of a plan. Bill, we're going to need two of the truck's modified in such a way that a helicopter can land on their roof. Is that a problem?" John asked.

"No, we'll build a steel frame on the inside and strengthen the roof of each one, the weight won't be a problem," Bill answered confidently.

"Good, how long until everything's ready?"

"If we work around the clock, three or four days and we should be something like," Bill told them.

"Get to it and keep us informed on your progress," Robert ordered. "I need to lie down for a while."

John and Mark both began to laugh, something that Robert did not find very funny.

Chapter Twenty Eight - Nearly Ready

The next three days were action packed, at least within the castle walls. As each truck was finished being modified, it was parked next to the castle gates. This added to the mounting excitement amongst the castle inhabitants. They all knew, with every finished vehicle, the day of leaving their prison was closer.

The trucks designated for transporting food supplies were packed and ready to go, only enough food for the next couple of days had been kept back. Bill and his team had worked wonders again. They had managed to pack everything in such a way that all the supplies were easily accessible but only required five trucks instead of the original ten that had been suggested. John had not quite been able to understand how they had done this but Bill had explained it had proven easier to pack once everything had been removed from the boxes. The packaging had taken up far more space than even he had imagined.

On the trucks set aside for sleeping, Bill had worked extra hard, practically designing the whole idea by himself. He had found a way that forty people could sleep comfortably, where originally only thirty were supposed to fit. This meant two trucks less were required to house the civilians. Instead of the original figure that called for seven, now only five were necessary.

The fuel tankers had been modified, firstly armoured using Bill's magic compound and then firing platforms had been built on to the tankers' bodies, from which soldiers could fire while still being protected. They were ready.

A mobile kitchen had been scraped together, cannibalising parts of the castle kitchens and the mess hall. They would have difficulty preparing a six-course meal but simple hot food would not be a problem.

The two fully modified trucks that were originally meant for civilian transport could now be used differently. One to house the soldiers not on duty, they would then be safe while sleeping and one as a mobile workshop or hospital, if needed. This thought chilled John a little. It was obvious that during their trip it was likely they would have wounded or even worse but, up until that point, he had not given it any thought. He now realised that a hospital facility was something they had completely forgotten about, he was thankful that people like Bill had not. On the roofs of these two vehicles the platforms for the helicopters had been built and safely tested.

Spare parts for the trucks and other vehicles had been packed into one of the sixteen tonners. Bravo Two, the helicopter that had flown his team around on several of the missions, had been dismantled also for spare parts. These were packed on board another one of the sixteen tonners.

To save even more space, the modified trucks had been re-modified, a false floor built into every one. In these hidden compartments they had stored weapons, ammunition and parts that were delicate, meaning that several of the sixteen tonners would no longer be needed. Because these trucks were fully modified and pretty much indestructible, it was felt that transporting important items such as ammunition on board them was far safer. John and Robert had both agreed, apart from food, being able to defend themselves was the most important ingredient in accomplishing their objectives, hence keeping the ammunition safe had to be a priority. Another plus point into the bargain was the size of the convoy had again been reduced.

They were nearly ready and with a total of thirteen trucks, the five fuel tankers and two sixteen tonners. Bill had worked wonders trimming down the convoy's size, just as John had hoped.

The two remaining helicopters had been stripped down, serviced and put back together.

They had discussed the question of rotating drivers in such a way that they could travel twenty-four hours a day but Robert had argued against it. He had reminded John and Mark that they had considerable numbers of women and children amongst the civilians and that, although sleeping in the trucks was very possible, there were unfortunately no toilets. The only option was for the convoy to make rest stops, also the problem with food was to be considered. It could not be expected that the people went without food for days at an end. Seeing as cooking while on the move would prove dangerous and dishing out the food to trucks on the move was impossible, they had to face the fact that stopping was unavoidable. All they had to work out was the safest way to manage it.

Each truck had been assigned crews, consisting of three men in the cab, two of whom would take turns in driving and one to keep guard. Thirteen trucks, thirty-nine men, the same for the sixteen tonners and fuel tankers, bringing the total of men on duty at any one time up to fifty seven. Including helicopter crews and tank crews there would be sixty-seven men required to keep the convoy rolling. The other forty-six would, so long as the convoy was moving, be resting. Their duties would start as soon as the convoy stopped anywhere. It was also suggested that the drivers not driving should rest in the cab's sleeping compartment, this ensuring the drivers were rested enough. John suggested asking the civilian population if any amongst them had experience with the big rigs, as this would also ease the pressure on the soldiers.

Altogether, apart from a few minor details, they were as good as ready. Another few days and they would leave, the only real question now was, where to go?

Chapter Twenty Nine - The Route

Although nearly ready to leave the castle fortress, nobody was really sure where they were heading. Their first thought had been New Hull, the small city being re-built just across the estuary from where the original had stood. The old city of Hull had been bombed during the war but the ferries had continued to sail from there. The new town had just continued the practice. All other ports big enough in the country had been destroyed, in attempts to sink the British fleet. They did not know for sure but anticipated a suitable ship might be found there. It seemed to be the only sensible destination, the big question remaining, how to get there?

John asked if any up-to-date maps of the country were available. Robert sadly confirmed that no maps had been produced since before the war. They had had digital maps at their base and these had been packed amongst the equipment to be flown to the castle along with their uplink equipment. Unfortunately, in the early days of preparing they had experienced problems and one of their helicopters had crashed, killing the crew and destroying it's cargo. On board at the time had been ammunition supplies, computers, other items they thought they would need but most critically, at least as far as they were now concerned, the maps, the uplink equipment and the navigation systems. Without the powerful uplink equipment it was impossible for them to use any of the few surviving satellites that were still in orbit. This sadly meant that all of the equipment in their vehicles and helicopters used for navigation was useless to them. Bill had attempted to remedy the situation but even his talents had limits. The only maps they now possessed were in an old atlas - from the early 1990s - they had found partly burned in the remnants of a car during one of the early food raids. Robert was not sure how much help it would be as the infrastructure of the country had changed considerably since that time. John suggested they take a look nevertheless and that together they would work something out.

They were approximately sixty miles north east of Fort William and they needed to get to New Hull. The major problem for them was the Dead Zone, an area of England shaped in a V, stretching from the south of Edinburgh, down the middle of the country to Derby and back up to York. This area had been designated lethal to all people, because of a nuclear accident involving two high altitude bombers towards the end of war. They did not dare violate this area because of the risk of contamination to the convoy inhabitants.

This meant their journey would have to be much longer than normally necessary. They would have to travel down the country, hugging the west coast as far as the area where Manchester had once been, then move inland. They needed to avoid this area of the North West, because of virus residues. Prolonged exposure was still considered dangerous, even though the war had been over for a few years now. There was a gap between the remnants of Manchester and the rubble of Sheffield where travelling was allowed or, at least, had been. They would then have to head for the ruins of Birmingham, cross the country towards what was left of Leicester and then hug the east coast up to New Hull.

It would be a journey of about six hundred miles, through a country decimated by war and now under siege from a new enemy.

As John had related the proposed route to Robert, he had realised, for the first time, just how close they had been to going under. Nearly all of the population centres had been targeted, many cities wiped from the face of the earth. He thought back to their conversation with the creature they had risked everything to capture and could better understand its arguments. Although in his heart he knew it had been wrong in most of what it had said, it was easy to see why such creatures would come to the conclusions they had. Mankind had proven itself to be very dangerous to anything living, not least itself.

The biggest problem now was finding the safest way to make the journey. The convoy was still pretty big and getting caught or trapped on small country lanes was something that did not appeal to them. They decided it would be better to try and stick to motorways, many of which had still been intact after the war.

Using the motorways would give them the opportunity to travel two abreast. They could even use the other carriageway, normally reserved for vehicles travelling in the opposite direction, and travel four abreast. This would dramatically reduce the size of the convoy, which had still been a problem for John, as defending themselves was for him a top priority.

Another advantage in using the motorways was the bridges they would regularly have to cross. Robert had insisted and rightly so John had decided that they make regular stops, mainly because of the civilians but also because they could not afford to get themselves into the situation where soldiers were tired and could make mistakes. John had seen the sense in this argument and had agreed regular breaks would be necessary. Using the bridges, John felt they could take this idea a step further. It should prove possible to stop for hours, giving everybody the chance to rest properly. Indeed if they planned it right, they could stop long enough that everybody could get some hot food and even a little sleep. He knew how difficult it was to sleep properly while still moving. Whether they travelled by night and rested during the day or did the opposite, he was not sure but he felt it would be possible and present no real risks.

Robert had not quite followed John's chain of thought on this subject and could not understand how they could stay somewhere overnight without the real risk of attack.

John had continued explaining what he had in mind. The modified trucks were built to fit together almost like a puzzle. This meant they could build a wall, using the trucks themselves, across the entire width of a motorway bridge. If they did that on both sides of the bridge, they would have a basically secure position from which to fight. The creatures could attack on one side but, thanks to the modifications fitted to the trucks, the wall would be almost impenetrable. They also had the chance to escape using the other side of the bridge. It was naturally possible that they could be attacked on both sides at the same time but the position they would hold would be very defensible and almost impossible to overrun. Breaking out through attacking creatures, using helicopters and tanks, should not prove too difficult. Inside this secure compound the civilians could leave the trucks, they could cook and eat hot meals, do whatever they normally did, in relative safety. The motorways were mostly built away from the towns, so the number of creatures travelling in those areas should be minimal, at least to start with. They could travel from bridge to bridge until they found one that suited their needs. As long as they did not make any stupid mistakes, the chances of creatures accidentally finding them should be limited. An obvious mistake would be staying around any of the old cities that had existed before the war. They would probably still be crawling with creatures but out in the countryside, between population centres old or new, there would be less danger of attack.

Robert had found this suggestion to be exactly what he had wanted, a way for them to remain civilised. The idea of cowering

175

inside the trucks and running for their lives had not appealed to him. This way, their withdrawal would still be dignified, something he found important as a military man.

They consulted the old atlas, looking for the motorways they would have to use. The motorway numbers they basically needed were all there up until the Birmingham area. The pages thereafter were unfortunately burnt. There was no way they could work out a full route with the information they had at their disposal. John suggested they try for the M9, then link up with the M80. This would take them to the M74, which took them down the west coast and then linked with the M6. That road got them as far down the country as they needed to go with the only problem around Manchester. They would have to stay clear of the old city, he was not sure how. After the M6, they needed to go across country to the east and then back up the east coast but those were the missing pages. They would have to find the way, once they were there. Planning any further was impossible without further intelligence, this they would have to gather while on the road. Any problems route-wise would have to be worked out when they arose.

Robert asked him how long he thought it would take? John was not sure, it was a trip of over six hundred miles across God knows what. The speed of the convoy would be dictated by the two tanks. If they wanted to make stops along the way for food and everything, then maybe two or three days, as long as no problems cropped up. His experience told him they should plan for twice as long, because a thousand things could and, probably, would happen along the way to delay them somehow. If they could manage the trip in about four days, they would have done well.

Robert raised a subject that John considered very dangerous, contact with other survivors while on the road. John explained that in all their time on the road travelling up to the castle, they had only found one person alive. That had been the Sergeant who had told them about the castle and he had died a few minutes later. The chances of finding people alive, at least ordinary people, was at best, slim. He remembered the motorbike tracks they had seen and also Stephanie's dream and suggested there still may be such gangs travelling around. He found it hard to believe that such gangs would bother with a well-armed and well-organised group such as theirs. Normally they were just thieves and bullies who attacked defenceless travellers but they would be prepared just in case he was proven wrong.

Robert suggested the further south they travelled, the more likely it was that people were still alive and fighting. He wanted to know what their stance would be, just on the off-chance. John said he did not know, they would have to play it by ear but they had enough to do providing for their own people as it was. Any extra mouths to feed could be a complication they did not need but Robert was not to worry, they would probably end up doing the right thing if or when the question needed an answer. Their main objective was to get their people safely off the mainland, nothing could be allowed to jeopardise that! Robert had agreed, reservedly.

Chapter Thirty - Just One More

The wrinkles had nearly all been ironed out. Militarily, everything was as ready as it could be.

The civilians had been instructed to pack their belongings and Robert had realised this was something they had completely forgotten. They had not even left yet and already the first problem! This was going to be some trip, he thought.

They could leave some of their personal items behind but he felt the people were risking a hell of a lot and if they did reach somewhere safe, then clean clothes and familiar things would be advantageous in making a new life. The only problem with his thinking was transporting it all. The modified trucks had been fitted out in such a way that forty people could sleep inside one but it left very little space for anything else. Without conferring with anybody else, he made a command decision. They would take one more sixteen tonner with them. It would be big enough to carry all the personal belongings but would not make that much difference to the size of the convoy. He felt it was the right decision and was sure he could convince John the same, although he knew if push came to shove, he was still officially in charge.

The civilians had been organised into groups and assigned to a truck. They had thought long and hard about how to avoid any problems while travelling. It had been decided the groups should be kept simple and the size of each group had worked out just about perfectly. The groups consisted of married couples with children, married couples without children, unmarried couples, single men and single women. The men had all been questioned and thirteen of them found with driving experience on the big rigs. All had agreed to help in any way they could. The women had organised themselves into groups and would take responsibility for cooking duties every time they stopped for a break.

Five men had been chosen per truck and armed. From the truck carrying single women, five had been picked with shooting experience. These twenty-five had, over the last days, undergone extensive training in the use of weapons. This was seen as only precautionary. They would only be needed if it ever got to the stage where all the soldiers were killed or incapacitated. The chances of that happening, Robert argued, were nil.

Robert was convinced they had prepared in every way possible, most of it thanks to John. He found himself wondering sometimes what would have happened to them if John and Stephanie had never reached the castle. They would just slowly have rotted away. He had seen that scenario coming but had not been able to find a way to avoid it. Luckily for everyone, John had. In the meantime, they had become good friends; he considered that a privilege and counted John as somebody whom he could trust with his life. The thought crossed his mind that it might yet get to the stage where John could prove that theory to him.

Chapter Thirty One - Time to Leave

The big day had arrived, they were leaving the castle!

It had been home to most of them for almost two years, to John and Stephanie only the last few weeks. Since they had arrived, life in the castle had changed dramatically. John wondered if the people there thanked him or secretly loathed him. He and he alone had turned their world upside down, suggesting they leave and then coming up with the daring plan to make it possible. He still felt responsible for the three members of his team who had died on the roof in Hadlee. He now had to ensure their deaths had not been in vain. Getting everybody away from the castle safely and finding a place where they could all live in relative safety would go a long way to do that. He would try; all any of them could do was try.

Today would be the first day of a new life for all of them. It was 0800 hours, they were leaving at 0900 hours, the last checks through the castle were already being made. All the civilians were accounted for and on board the trucks. Every soldier, apart from those checking the castle, were at their appointed post. The helicopters were fuelled and armed, the two tanks also prepared. They would be taking part in the very first engagement of the day, enabling the convoy to leave.

Robert came over to John and asked him if he was ready, John replying, yes, it was time to go.

The castle was checked, nothing that could be useful to them had been left behind. Robert asked if they should booby-trap the fortress that had kept them safe for the last two years? John said no. If the creatures wanted it so badly, they should let them have it.

They both climbed into their respective vehicles, John riding in the first truck. Robert had decided to go along in one of the tanks, at least for the time being.

"Let's go!" he shouted, before climbing in and closing the top hatch.

The two helicopters immediately took off and hovered over the clearing, watching the tree line. The doors opened and the first tank rumbled out over the drawbridge for the last time. The men who had opened the doors climbing into the second tank, which followed. Behind them the trucks started to file out over the drawbridge.

The two tanks first job was to clear the trees leading to the road to the north, which was hidden in the forest. They had all felt this was probably the safer route, although a little longer. The creatures would not expect them to go that way, so in doing so, they hoped to win a little time before their enemy could adapt.

The tanks made short work of the trees, leaving the way free for the convoy to move through. The gap that had appeared between the trees, was being flanked by the two helicopters, allowing the trucks to move through unmolested.

The road they now travelled came out of the forest about four miles north of the castle, there it linked with another road that would take them east.

On top of each truck, three men were in position to defend the convoy, in case the creatures chose to attack within the trees but everything remained quiet, almost too quiet.

John's suspicions that the creatures were no longer in a strong enough position to attack them, seemed to be confirmed. He had not shared his suspicions with anybody, apart from Stephanie, feeling that some of the people still opposed to leaving could have argued that with hardly any creatures in the immediate area to threaten them, there was no real reason to leave. He was certain that more creatures would have arrived to continue the siege sooner or later. Their timing in leaving had been perfect.

As if he could read minds, Robert's voice came over the radio.

"What the hell is going on, John? There's not a sign of them anywhere, what do you reckon they are planning for us now? Over."

John smiled.

"I reckon it's going to be a bloody long trip, if we've got to say 'over' every time we use the radio, Robert. Can we drop it, at least when we're just talking like this. It's always got on my nerves."

"Sure, John, it's just a hard habit to break. I guess it's just us anyway, there's no military command to court-martial me," Robert laughed.

"Great," John replied, smiling, then he continued. "I've suspected this ever since we returned from Hadlee the last time but I didn't see any sense in causing unrest. It was weird they didn't try to attack us. In fact, we never saw another creature after leaving the town. The last few nights I've not seen any either, not one. I think we've hurt them more than we realised. With a bit of luck, we killed all of the bastards but I doubt it. I can only imagine reinforcements are already on the way. We picked the perfect time to get out, mate, that's all."

"I hope you're right. Maybe, if they're as intelligent as we think, they'll have a little more respect for us now. Maybe they won't attack us as quickly next time, our reputation might scare them. What do you think?" Robert asked, again laughing.

"I hope you're right, but don't forget we're going to be travelling southwards. Any reinforcements will probably be coming from that direction. I still think their communication skills are limited by distance, so I don't think our reputation will precede us, Robert," and John started to laugh. "We'll have the same old problems if we run into them on the way, they'll attack on sight. We can't have any doubts about that."

They reached the end of the forest road and turned east, basically following the route the helicopters had taken the night of the first bombing raid in Hadlee. At the end of the road, John could see the two helicopters hovering, covering them, ready to pounce on anything that threatened. He suddenly realised it was stupid having both of the aircraft in the air at the same time, and wondered if they could secure one of them on its platform safely enough that they could still drive the truck without risk to either machine or the truck's occupants. He spoke to Stephanie who was flying the Apache.

"Stephanie, can you hear me?"

"Loud and clear John. Over," came the reply.

"Drop the 'over' lark, I've just cleared it with Robert. How long can you guys stay up there without re-fuelling?"

"If we take it easy, about two hours," she informed him. "Why, what have you got in mind? Are you missing me already?"

He smiled. He always missed her when they were separated and she knew it.

"Not at all," he replied, teasing her. "We'll travel for one and a half hours, then we'll make a stop. You guys can re-fuel and we'll discuss a few things. You can make me a cup of coffee," he said, pushing his luck.

"I'm working," she replied. "You can make the bloody coffee!"

He laughed.

"Robert, is that okay with you? Ninety minutes travel time, then we find somewhere for a break. The helicopters have got to re-fuel anyway."

"No problem, John. I'd forgotten how uncomfortable it is riding in one of these tanks. My back's killing me already."

John contacted Mark who was travelling in the last truck and informed him also. He agreed with the suggestion and was also looking forward to being able to stretch.

"Twenty minutes," John thought. "We've been on the road for twenty minutes and they're bitching already."

They turned east and drove about ten miles, then turned south again, heading for John's favourite holiday destination, Hadlee. He really did hate that town but this time they would be driving past and keeping going. However, John felt that stopping between the castle and the town might be a mistake, any creatures that were moving to reinforce those at the castle could be in that general area. Getting caught out in the open could prove fatal.

"Robert, are you asleep?" John asked, the driver of his truck nearly choking.

"No, John, still awake. What's up? Are you bored?" Robert asked.

"Not at all. I don't fancy stopping anywhere near Hadlee. I think we should turn towards the coast as soon as we get the chance. We can then find somewhere to stop."

"I take it you still think Hadlee is dangerous? Maybe you're right. We have to head west at some stage anyway. Okay, there should be a road that heads to the coast in about ten miles, we'll turn there. Alright?"

"Thanks, Robert. I'll inform the helicopters, they can scout ahead for a few miles. Stephanie, do you copy?"

"I'm listening, John. Is my coffee ready?"

"Not quite, the water's just starting to boil. Listen, we'll be heading west in about fifteen minutes. Send Bravo One on alone to check the road ahead of us and find a possible resting place."

"Okay, John, I'll drop back and see if anything is following us," Stephanie replied.

"Good idea. Keep your channel open, just in case. Be careful, don't engage anything, just observe."

"See you soon," and with that she flew off to the north.

She returned after about ten minutes, nothing was on the roads following them. She had spotted no danger behind them at all. John felt this news was not entirely all good, as it meant all the trouble was in front of them.

The other helicopter had also returned, having seen nothing along the road leading west that might prove to be a threat to them. They had also located a suitable area where they could possibly make a short stop. It was an open section of ground about three miles square. They could easily see anything moving towards them and have ample time to evacuate the area.

Robert and John discussed the suggested location and decided it should be safe enough. They would head there and rest, giving everybody time to refresh themselves and change the roof crews, thirty minutes would be long enough. It was about forty miles to the area, it would take them an hour or so to get there. John, using the radios fitted in the cabs, decided to use the time to speak to Bill.

"Bill, are you there."

"I can hear you John, what's up?"

"Can we still keep moving if one of the helicopters is secured on its landing pad or would it be too dangerous?"

Bill answered after a second or two.

"The weight's not a problem. The roofs are so heavily reinforced, three helicopters could land on one at the same time. Securing it is also easy. The only danger is speed. With the additional weight, the truck's speed would have to be limited. We've been averaging about thirty five miles an hour. If we slowed it down to just under thirty, we'd be pretty safe."

"Good, thanks Bill. When we stop, the Apache will be landing on its pad. Get it refuelled and secured as soon as possible, just in case we have to leave quickly. Bravo One needs refuelling but it'll be taking off again. Everybody else is working shifts, it seems to make sense to do the same with the helicopters."

"Got it, John. My guys will be ready."

"Stephanie, do you copy?" John asked.

"Yes, John, I'm still here."

"We'll be stopping in about an hour, Bravo One should land and refuel. Its crew can change, if the guys flying now want a rest. You land on the truck pad you've been assigned. We'll be securing the Apache for now. It's crazy having two helicopters in the air at the same time just for surveillance. If you're needed you can take off again in a matter of seconds anyway, in the mean time you can get some rest."

"Got it, John. Can I ride with you?"

"I don't really have to answer that question, do I?"

"No, see you soon."

Robert came on the radio.

"It must be great to be in love, John," he said, laughing uncontrollably.

John could not think of anything to say really. It was!

Chapter Thirty Two - Rest Break

The hour's ride to the area they had picked to make a stop proved uneventful. John spoke into the digital intercom system, one of these sets built into each truck carrying people. This enabled them to inform their passengers of any developments without having to stop the convoy every time.

"Ladies and Gentlemen, this is one of your Captains speaking."

He had always wanted to be a pilot but never got around to doing anything about it. Maybe one day he would get Stephanie to teach him how to fly the Apache, he thought, then he continued.

"We will be stopping in about five minutes for a thirty minute break. You can walk around outside and have some refreshment. We will organise a toilet area for those that need one," including himself, he thought. "Please do not wander too far from the vehicles. Those with children, please keep them by your sides at all times. We are stopping in a relatively secure area but may need to leave quickly, so please keep your eyes and ears open at all times. The ones amongst you who have been armed should carry their weapons outside the trucks at all times and be especially vigilant. This will be the first of probably many stops but we don't know what to expect. It is daylight so creature activity should be low anyway but please, stay alert. Stewart out."

He then spoke into his headset, ordering the soldiers to be alert, organise a perimeter and watch for signs of attack. The helicopters would be landing to re-fuel, so for a short time they would have no air support, no early warning system other than themselves. He kept it short with the men, they knew exactly what to do anyway.

People started exiting the vehicles as soon as they stopped, the toilet break obviously welcome. The helicopters landed, both were refuelled. The Apache then took off again and landed on its pad on top of the hospital truck where it was secured. The reserve crew for Bravo One replaced the pilots who had flown the helicopter up to then, giving them a chance to rest. If they did this every couple of hours, John realised there would be less chance of anybody getting tired and maybe missing something important.

The tanks were also refuelled, the crew climbing out and stretching. Robert came over to John just as Stephanie joined him.

"Shit, my back's killing me!" he said, stretching himself. "Those things are dammed uncomfortable to ride in."

"Get yourself into one of the trucks. In the cabs you can at least stretch out a bit," John suggested.

"Yeah, I think I will, I'll ride with Mark for a while," Robert said, smiling. "You two lovebirds can be alone for a while then."

"Very funny, ha, ha, ha!" John replied, also smiling. "What do you think?" he asked seriously.

"No problems. Up to now at least, it's going bloody well," Robert answered. "A lot better than I imagined. I expected we would have to fight all the way. I'm so pleased I was wrong."

"So am I, mate, so am I. How far do you think we should try to get today?" John asked. "The first night will be dangerous. We have no idea about possible creature activity or anything else out here, for that matter. We need to find a good defensible position, so that at least some of us can rest easily."

"The first motorway is about two hours away. It's eleven hundred hours now, that should mean we hit the motorway early this afternoon, thirteen hundred hours maybe. We'll need to stop then anyway, so that the helicopter can refuel again. Best suggestion I can make is, we try to get a few hours down the motorway after that and then implement your bridge idea. It will be dark by seventeen hundred hours so we need all the defences set up, at the latest, by then. A couple of hours travelling down fits, we locate a suitable bridge and dig in for the night," Robert suggested.

"Good, I agree. Now I need a toilet and then my wife is going to make me a cup of coffee," John said, smiling at Stephanie.

Stephanie, also smiling, punched him on his arm. "Pig!" she said, playfully but headed towards the makeshift kitchen truck anyway.

"Would you like a cup, Robert?" she called back.

"Yes, please, two sugars," Robert replied, then he followed John, he needed the toilet as well.

They had both relieved themselves and rejoined Stephanie who was talking to Mark and Bill.

"Finished boys?" she asked, as they approached. "Here is your coffee."

The civilians were milling around the area protected by the trucks, some of the children were playing. John watched them,

186

it would not be long until his child was running around with them. As if she could read his mind, Stephanie squeezed his hand. He looked straight into her eyes and mouthed the words 'I love you'. She leant over and kissed him lightly on the lips and whispered that she loved him too, then she walked off to return the now empty coffee cups.

"How's things, Mark?" John asked.

"Okay, mate. I've told the roof teams to come down for now. While we're moving there's no real need to have them up there. They can be rested then for tonight. The tanks and some of the trucks are refuelled, Bravo One is back in the air and Bravo Three is secured. Remember to keep the speed down and we'll be fine," Mark replied.

"How's your end, Bill?"

"No problems at all up to now, everything's working just as it should. We're green, mate," Bill replied.

"We'll be stopping sometime this afternoon, once we have found a suitable location to spend the night, probably a bridge. The area will have to be secured. Have we got any big lights with us?" John asked.

"We have sixteen big searchlights stored on one of the sixteen tonner's, John. The mounting brackets are already fitted on to the modified trucks, so it's just a question of installing the lights and plugging them into the generators. You'll have all the illumination you'll need, no problem," Bill answered, confidently.

"Is there anything you didn't think of, Bill?" John asked, obviously impressed.

"I've got a bloody good team, mate, you should thank them."

"We will but, in the meantime, I'm thanking you. I'm impressed."

Robert also added that the whole unit had worked wonders in the last few weeks and he was proud to command such men and thankful that their time in the castle had not effected their abilities. He had always considered them to be one of the best units in the military remaining after the war and they had proven him right.

John told him to shut up or he would start to cry. They all laughed.

"Okay, we've been here long enough, let's get everybody back on board and get out of here. The tanks should split up now, one leading the convoy, the other bringing up the rear, watching our backs. That takes the pressure of Bravo One, they can then fly on ahead and scout the road in front of us. We'll do exactly what Robert has suggested, we'll head for the motorway and then make a short stop for lunch and let the helicopter refuel. After that, another two, maybe two and a half hours travelling time down the motorway, then we'll stop for the night," John suggested.

"I agree," Robert said. "Let's hustle."

He had always wanted to say that and felt amongst friends, it would be safe to do so. Judging by his 'friends' reaction to the statement, he had been wrong. They were suddenly all laughing at him, saying something about dancing and parties. He laughed with them, realising how stupid he must have sounded.

"You know what I meant."

They all continued laughing, but walked off to get everybody organised.

Chapter Thirty Three - The First Camp

They re-boarded the trucks, everyone accounted for and moved off again. They wanted to reach the first motorway, rest for a short while and then turn south. According to the old atlas they were having to use, somewhere in that general direction was the M9. This led down the west coast, towards the ruins of Glasgow. Bravo One was flying on ahead to confirm this and spot any problems that could delay them.

John and Stephanie were seated in the lead truck. Robert was now sitting with Mark at the back of the column, his back slowly recovering from the short trip in the tank. One of the tanks now led the way, the other bringing up the rear.

Everybody was quiet, John expected this would be normal. He realised just how boring it must have been for the men who had earlier earned their livings driving such trucks, all day, every day. His grandfather had driven for nearly forty years, often away from home for weeks at a time, his grandmother bringing up his father almost alone. This way of life had never appealed to his father, instead he had chosen a career in the military. John now understood that his father's choice had meant a life surrounded by friends and comrades. It certainly seemed to be exactly the opposite of what his grandfather had always done. John wondered if the constant stress between his grandparents over their way of life had influenced his father in his decision to get away from the family trucking business. He had been told by both his father and his grandfather that, after he had left to join the army, things between the two of them were never the same. His father's career had certainly influenced John, he had followed him into the army at the first chance he got. His father had been killed during the war, in a flying accident of all things, his mother dying in a bombing raid in Manchester. John had survived the war, despite a few close calls and had served faithfully up until the day when he had realised the fight against the creatures could not be won. He had convinced Stephanie that the situation was desperate and they had left together, beginning the journey that had ultimately led them to the castle. While he had been a Captain in the Special Services, he had never really had any ambitions to lead, he had always considered the responsibility too great. Now years later, he was considered by many of the convoy's men, indirectly at least, as one of their leaders. He knew this and was also sure that Robert was aware of it but, as far as he was concerned, Robert was still the boss, at least most of the time. He found it funny and strange what fate sometimes had planned for its unsuspecting victims.

Stephanie bumped him with her elbow.

"What are you thinking about?"

"Nothing really, just memories," he answered, seeming a little sad, she thought.

"We'll make a good life for ourselves somewhere, John, we'll make our own good memories in the process. Our life together and then later with our children," she said, looking at him with a twinkle in her eyes, "will be as we've always imagined. We have to believe that or else there's no point to all of this."

He looked at her, his eyes filling with tears. He was not normally so emotional but the last few weeks, especially his time with Stephanie, had changed that.

"I'm going to have a nervous breakdown if this trip stays boring," he said, laughing.

"I wouldn't worry about that," she told him, also laughing. "There'll be enough surprises along the way to keep us busy, of that I'm certain."

"I'm going to get some sleep, while it's still quiet. I probably won't sleep much tonight. Would you care to join me?" he asked her, trying to sound seductive.

She looked quickly over her shoulder at the soldier driving the truck and then back to John.

"I don't think so, stud," she replied, smiling. "You get some rest, I'll wake you if anything happens."

John climbed into the sleeping compartment at the back of the cab. He had not really meant what he had said in the way she had taken it. He hoped she realised that. He was not sure she did, he would have to explain later but for now he slept.

It had only been about an hour, short but it had done him good. Stephanie had awoken him, gently.

"John, the helicopter's coming back, wake up. They're on the radio."

He had awoken and climbed into the front seat again.

"Bravo One this is John. Robert must be asleep. What have you seen?" he asked.

The radio suddenly got quite loud. They could only catch the odd word but it was obvious Robert had not been asleep. John told him to calm down, he had only been joking. Bravo One answered John over the ruckus.

"The road's clear, John, right up to the motorway. We followed the carriageway south for about fifty miles and saw nothing, no creatures, no blockages on the road itself. Everything is okay."

"Well done. How's your fuel?" John asked, concerned.

"We are okay for at least another hour, maybe a little longer," the pilot reported back, unconcerned.

"How long until we reach the motorway?" John asked.

"You're about twenty miles away from the on-ramp. It should take you about forty minutes at your current speed to get there."

"Okay, keep your eyes open. We'll take a short break when we reach the motorway, so you guys can re-fuel. How is the helicopter doing, it's not getting too hot or anything?" John asked.

Stephanie almost choked, trying hard not to laugh.

"They don't get hot, John. Everything's in the green," the pilot answered, laughing.

"Okay, clever git, I was just trying to be nice," John replied, realising he must have sounded stupid but he was also laughing, as was Stephanie. She had not been able to hold it back any longer.

"Keep in touch, guys. See you later," John said, slightly embarrassed.

He turned to Stephanie. She was still smiling, obviously at his expense.

"Ha ha," he said, playfully punching her. "We'll get to this on-ramp that cocky git's on about, drive down the motorway a couple of miles, then stop for a break. That will allow the helicopter to land and re-fuel. What do you think?"

She tried to stay serious but failed miserably. She burst out laughing again.

"Ah, bollocks!" John said, shaking his head.

He used the radio to inform Robert and Mark, then he settled back in his chair again.

"Sorry," Stephanie said. "It was funny."

"I know," John said seriously. "Maybe that's what I'll do when this is all over, I'll become a professional comedian. I can entertain all of you then!"

He stared at her, trying to keep an angry look on his face but couldn't manage it. He laughed with her. She hugged him, still laughing. He sat there smiling, holding her close. Despite all their troubles, life was good. There was just one small problem. His body was starting to react to the time being spent in the cab,

191

doing nothing. He could now understand what Robert had meant about his back. In another hour or so he could thankfully stretch his legs. The time could not go quickly enough, but somehow he knew it would drag.

After forty five minutes of uneventful driving, they had reached the on-ramp and were heading south on the motorway.

Apart from the odd abandoned car, there was nothing even remotely interesting on the road. They were driving two abreast on the southbound carriageway, the helicopter again giving them forewarning of anything threatening in front of them. After another twenty minutes, they stopped, allowing the helicopter to land and refuel. The crew was again replaced, giving the pilots a chance to rest. John was speaking to the new pilot.

"It's now two o'clock," he said. "We need to set up camp, before it gets dark. We'll be here for about half an hour, then we'll be leaving again. Fly on ahead checking out the bridges, we need something big enough, maybe an overpass. Try to find something within the next forty odd miles, we don't want to travel much further than that today. Good hunting."

With that the helicopter had taken off. The women had been preparing a light lunch for the convoy inhabitants, they would all have something a bit more substantial once they had stopped for the night. After a little over a half an hour, the convoy got underway again, they were making slow but steady progress southwards.

It had not taken the helicopter long to find a suitable bridge, one that seemed to fit their requirements perfectly. It was forty miles away. At their current speed they would be there in about seventy minutes. By then it would only be about four o'clock so they would have plenty of time to set up their defences for the night. John could not help wondering what surprises their first night away from the castle might bring. He suspected a lot of people were probably asking the same question. The answer would be known soon enough.

They had reached the bridge and were parked right in the middle of it. It was about two hundred yards across, four carriageways wide and exactly what they had been looking for.

John was standing together with Robert and Mark, discussing how best they should set up their defences. They needed to block both sides of the bridge with the fully modified trucks, leaving an area between, where they could park the rest of their vehicles. John suggested they leave an area of thirty or forty yards clear at both sides of the bridge. This area could then be booby-trapped with trip-wires, or mined in such a way as to warn them if any creatures tried to sneak up on them in the darkness. As soon as one of these traps was sprung, they could turn on the searchlights for illumination, giving a clear field of fire to the men on the truck roofs. He did not like the idea of using the big lights otherwise, as it may attract creatures from further afield, something they did not need. Although it was a little risky blocking off both sides of the bridge, John felt that the chance of their being attacked from both directions was unlikely. From the evidence at that moment, he doubted they would be attacked at all.

What he had suggested, seemed to cover all the angles and they decided to carry out the plan exactly as he had proposed. It would take a little time to set everything up but afterwards they would be quite secure.

The civilians had remained in their trucks until the defences had been set up but as everything was now finished, they were out and about preparing the evening meal.

It was arranged that the soldiers now on watch would be relieved at midnight, allowing them to rest. The men replacing them would then rest as they were travelling the next morning.

John and Robert felt that everything that could be done had been done to ensure their safety. Now it was time to eat a hot meal and try to relax. They would soon learn what the night had in store for them. All they could do was wait and see.

Chapter Thirty Four - Second Morning

The first night passed without incident.

There had been no sign of creatures, no real evidence of any in the area at all. John wondered how long it would stay that way.

The defences were being dismantled, so they could use them again. The civilians and those soldiers not on duty were finishing breakfast. It was eight o'clock, they would be leaving within the hour. Robert had estimated their position to be somewhere north of Glasgow, they would pass by the ruins of the city later that morning. Their aim that day was to travel down past Carlisle or at least the area where the city had been built and find somewhere north of the Manchester ruins to spend the night.

John, Stephanie and Robert were eating breakfast together, a meal consisting of tinned meat, tinned potatoes and baked beans. There was also fruit available - tinned, of course and, for those craving a slice of normality, slightly stale breakfast cereals with powdered milk.

Although the meal was tasty enough and John was impressed at the women's ability to keep the menu even remotely interesting, he could not help wondering if things would ever get back to normal, where breakfast consisted of real bacon and fresh eggs. He could not remember the last time he had had real eggs.

"The first night was very uneventful," Robert said, interrupting John's dream of fresh food.

He said it in such a way that he sounded almost disappointed.

"Let's hope they all are," John replied. "I would imagine we'll have some company soon enough. In a way we should be thankful, it's perfect really. The last thing we needed is a running gun battle all the way down the country. That would delay us considerably and likely cost us supplies we might need later. It would also scare the civilians to death. This way, while there's no trouble, they remain confident that leaving the castle was the right decision and what we're doing is correct. You know as well as I do, at some stage, we'll run into the creatures again. There'll be time enough for being scared and doubting we are doing the right thing. The first few days were important. We are all settled now into the new routine and in a position to deal with any trouble that comes our way. We stay vigilant and keep them all as safe as possible. The longer they stay happy, the better it's going to be."

"Yeah, you're right," Robert said, then added. "I guess it's the soldier in me, not knowing where they are or what they are doing. It could drive you mad. In the castle we always knew they were outside, waiting for a chance to get us. Out here, I've no idea. I imagined all kinds of scenarios, I never imagined we wouldn't see any of them at all."

"Don't worry, mate, we'll see enough action before we're finished," John assured him.

"Okay, another subject. We'll be passing the ruins of Glasgow at some time today. Is it worth us taking a look-see?" Robert asked.

"It might be worth flying over in the Apache but we shouldn't stop in the area. I know the place is in ruins but it could still be crawling with creatures. We'll see how we are doing for time when we get in the area," John replied.

Stephanie was interested to know how flying over the destroyed city could possibly help them. Anybody left there alive would be hiding. They did not need any provisions, so what good would it do?

John's only answer was intelligence, it could give them an idea of how many creatures were in the general vicinity, plus he was basically curious.

"You mean nosy," she said, smiling.

"How well you know me," he replied, laughing.

"John, we'll decide later. Maybe you're right, attracting attention is something we shouldn't do. You know how I hate unnecessary risks," Robert said.

They finished eating breakfast and got ready to leave, everything was packed away on the trucks and everybody accounted for.

Bravo One had already taken off and was following the road, looking for trouble that might be waiting for them. John and Stephanie were again sitting in the lead truck, following the tank that was leading the way. They planned to travel for three hours, before taking a break again. John, on the one hand, was very pleased with their unchallenged progress but on the other, he was bored. He was already at the stage where he would welcome a little bit of action, he had got used to it. He settled into his seat; if this carried on he might have to start reading or something, maybe one of the Apache manuals.

It had been almost an hour and John was starting to doze off, when suddenly the radio came to life.

"Convoy, come in. This is Bravo One."

John sat bolt upright, something in the pilot's voice catching his attention.

"Bravo One, this is the convoy. What's up?"

"We have a problem. We have found a section of the carriageway that is blocked off."

"Blocked by what? Can you be more specific, please?" John asked.

"It looks like somebody or something has pushed all the abandoned vehicles together to form a roadblock. It's massive, twenty five yards wide, a good twenty yards deep and maybe five yards high."

John looked at Stephanie.

"Shit that's big! Could it be man-made?"

"Looks too big to be man-made, John. We flew down pretty low and couldn't make out any tracks from heavy machinery or anything that could have been used to build it. Looks like it was done by hand, that's a lot of weight for people to lift."

"Okay, it sounds like an ambush, get back to us as soon as possible."

"On our way, John."

"Robert, were you listening? It sounds like we've got trouble. We'd better stop until Bravo One gets back," John said.

"I heard it all, John, what do you think?" Robert asked.

"It smells like an ambush. We can't be sure but something's not right. Blocking the carriageway in the way it's blocked, without using machinery, has to be the creatures' handiwork. Whatever it turns out to be, we'd better be ready for anything," John said, also sounding unsure.

"Pick a spot, John and pull over," Robert said.

John radioed the leading tank and, at the next suitable location, the convoy pulled over. They would wait for the helicopter to come back and devise a way to beat the roadblock and possible ambush waiting for them.

The helicopter was coming in to land. As it touched down, Robert and Mark came running up to join John and Stephanie.

"What's the situation?" Robert asked, slightly out of breath.

"We're not sure yet, the helicopter's just landed," John informed him.

The pilot of Bravo One came running up to them and, seeing that the Major was standing there, he started to salute. Robert told him to report, after giving a short salute back.

"It's exactly as we reported, Sir, the carriageway is blocked, about ten miles down the road. No idea who or what has done it. There's no way to tell how old the roadblock is. It could be years old, it might have been built yesterday. We looked for signs of the creatures, we found none. Either they have learnt to hide their tracks or the blockage is really years old and all tracks have been washed away by the weather. It's strange, where the roadblock is situated, is just beyond the point we reached yesterday while checking the route. If we'd flown a couple of miles further we'd have passed over it then."

"I don't think so," John said. "It's them, I can feel it. The scary thing is, it doesn't make any sense. They have to realise that we'll just move the blockage out of the way, it won't do them any good. The tanks will have no difficulty in shifting a few cars, it wouldn't even delay us for very long. You're absolutely sure that you didn't see any creatures at all?"

"No, John, no sign whatsoever. The only trouble is, on both sides of the motorway, there are woods lining the road. If they were hiding there, standing still, we wouldn't see them anyway," the pilot argued.

"Of course not," John said, agreeing with the observation. "Describe the area exactly to us, maybe we're missing something."

"It's a stretch of road about five hundred yards long, between an off-ramp and an on-ramp. The roadblock is about fifty yards after the off-ramp, trees and cover on both sides of the road. That's about it," explained the pilot again.

"It's almost as if they want us to take the off-ramp," Robert suggested.

"Could be, maybe the ambush is waiting for us there. It doesn't matter either way, we have to get through it," John said, emphatically.

"We could bypass it," Mark suggested, emphasising the word bypass.

"What do you mean?" John asked.

"Simple. We use the tanks to remove the central reservation, and take the convoy down the northbound carriageway. We give it plenty of welly, and fly right by. They couldn't stop us, even if they wanted to," Mark explained.

"Brilliant, mate," John said, congratulating him on the idea. "The only trouble is, I'm still not seeing it. I find it strange that only the one lane is blocked. They must realise we'd think of using the off ramp or the other carriageway, they've left us an obvious way out, at least this time. Next time they might block both carriageways, forcing us to fight. Shit, second guessing them this time is a bloody nightmare."

Robert asked if they were not making it a little bit too complicated. They had always assumed that, for whatever reason, the creatures did not like direct sunlight. They had mostly attacked under cover of darkness. Was it possible the creatures had expected the convoy to reach this spot the night before, they could not have known that they would stop for the night. If that was the case, then there might not be that many of them in the area at that moment. The fact that the convoy was coming through now might have caught them by surprise.

John agreed that was a possibility, although he reminded Robert that the last few attacks, made by the creatures in Hadlee, had been day attacks. They had not been bothered by sunlight then and he doubted they would be now. He suggested it could have to do with how they communicated again. Maybe the creatures had the equivalent of communities. With them now travelling down the country, maybe they had passed from one community into another. It was possible that the two groups did not communicate with each other. In that case the creatures would not have known they were coming. They could have seen the helicopter possibly, maybe the convoy had been spotted en route. It was possible these creatures had only dealt with unorganised groups of people up to now, helicopters and the like, not really being normal equipment for civilians. They would have no idea about the convoy's capabilities and probably thought a simple roadblock would be enough to trap them. Robert had asked once if John thought their reputation would precede them, this appeared to be the proof that it hadn't. They could speculate as much as they wanted to but it would not help them decide which way was best to avoid the probable ambush waiting for them.

Mark reminded them that they only had a couple of ways to remove such a roadblock. They could push it out of the way using the tanks or blow it out of the way using high explosives. If they decided to blow it up, it was likely the road surface would be damaged. It could even be impassable afterwards. Taking the size of the roadblock into consideration, even using the tanks to remove it, would take a lot longer than John was anticipating. It was not a five minute job. They would have to move tons and tons of awkwardly shaped car wrecks, far enough out of the way that the convoy had enough room to pass through. In the time it would take to do this, any hidden forces in the area could obviously attack. They definitely needed to bypass the problem.

John and Robert both agreed with Mark's prognosis. The off-ramp seemed to be the obvious choice to make, so they would avoid it. That left the other carriageway as the only real option. The tanks would remove enough of the central reservation to allow the convoy to cross through onto the other side of the motorway. They would travel down that road and hopefully avoid the roadblock and any other problems that were waiting for them.

"It's time to unpack the Apache again," John suggested. "Bravo One can lead you through the area. I want to fly with Stephanie and take a look at what they had planned for us. As soon as you're clear we'll deliver a message to them, let them know we're not as stupid as they believe. It might make them think twice about attacking us again. It will at least help us if they try anything similar again."

"Good," Robert said. "I'll ride with the first tank, at least until we're through. My back will stand it that long."

John smiled, telling Mark to get some men back up on the truck roofs, just in case. Half of the fully modified trucks, especially those carrying civilians, should be at the front of the convoy, the others bringing up the rear. The fuel tankers and the sixteen tonners should be positioned in the middle. One tank leading, one bringing up the rear. He would stay behind with Stephanie in the Apache and take a look at what appeared from above, then deliver the message. If they were wrong and nothing happened, then at least it would prepare them for the time when something did.

The tanks had made short work of the barrier dividing the two carriageways. The convoy was now parked on the northbound side, but pointing to the south.

John was sitting behind Stephanie in the Apache, everything prepared. He spoke to Robert, one last time, before the convoy started to move again.

"Robert, keep them moving, no matter what. We'll watch your backs. Good luck."

The convoy slowly picked up speed, it would take them about twenty minutes to reach the point where the southbound carriageway was blocked. Bravo One would keep an eye on the road they were travelling down, in case of other surprises. John and Stephanie in Bravo Three would hang back, at altitude, to see what happened after the trucks passed by. John was not sure just exactly what they should expect.

They stayed in constant contact, using the radios. The convoy was picking up speed, Bravo One reporting no problems ahead.

Two hundred yards before they were level with the roadblock, the tank that was leading the way fired its machine guns into the woods on the left of the carriageway. This was precautionary and did not necessarily mean that any creatures had been sighted. It was more of a deterrent to discourage any of the monsters that might be hiding within the tree line from leaving the cover of the trees.

The tank had slowed and stopped. It was level with the blockage, standing guard, its guns trained on the trees. The leading trucks were already beyond the roadblock, the rest following quickly. John and Stephanie could still see no evidence of anything suspicious. It appeared as if they had totally misread the situation, the roadblock probably man-made after all.

The last truck had passed the roadblock, they were clear. The two tanks were now bringing up the rear, still watching for signs of hostility.

Suddenly, there was movement in the woods to the right of the southbound carriageway, they could not see what or how many but something was definitely coming through the trees. Both of them understood straightaway what it had to be. John told the tanks to speed up and re-join the convoy as soon as possible, just in case. They would wait there and greet whatever it was rushing towards them.

Stephanie reduced altitude, armed her weapons and prepared to attack what was about to leave the cover of the trees. They waited. The convoy was safe, that was all that mattered. Now it was time to reward the creatures for all their efforts. As they watched, it seemed to them that the whole area of trees was moving in some way.

"There are a hell of a lot of them, John," Stephanie said, sounding slightly panicked.

"Don't worry," John told her. "We'll deliver our presents, then get the hell out of here. Be cool, okay."

The first creatures were clearing the woods. Stephanie had been right, there were a lot of them.

"Get ready to fire," John told her, calmly.

Suddenly, something else appeared, it also cleared the tree line. It was similar to the creatures, but much bigger and a lot uglier!

"What the fuck is that?" Stephanie shouted, obviously shocked.

"I don't know," John said, trying to stay calm. "Fire. Everything we've got."

She fired six missiles, all of them finding their targets, releasing the gas they carried. It had an almost immediate effect, as usual, the creatures dropping down dead. They pulled back a little and climbed, preparing to dive down and use the scatter guns on any of the creatures that had managed to avoid the gas. Suddenly, Stephanie screamed, something had scared her. John was struggling to see what was going on in front of them, so she rotated the helicopter slightly, giving him a clear view. He spotted what had scared her, and for a second it terrified him.

The big creature was not alone. There were several of them standing in the open, the gas having had no apparent effect on them whatsoever.

"Use your guns, Stephanie, we have to know if we can kill them," John shouted.

She opened fire straightaway, bullets from her scatter guns hammering into the creatures, the new monsters screaming with rage. Despite the withering fire, one of the creatures picked up a piece of one of the cars, John thought at first it was a whole car and threw it with incredible force at the helicopter. Luckily they were too high to be in any real danger.

"Why won't they die, John?" Stephanie asked, again sounding slightly panicked.

"Just keep pouring lead into them," John shouted, over the noise of the guns.

After what seemed like minutes but in reality was only seconds, the creatures left alive disappeared back into the trees. As John and Stephanie watched them retreat, they noticed that three of the enormous creatures were lying on the ground, not moving. It appeared they were dead.

John sighed, loudly.

"At least we can kill them," he said, obviously relieved.

"But it took nearly all our ammunition. Why are they so much harder to kill? Why didn't the gas effect them in any way?" Stephanie asked, still shaken.

"I don't know. We need to take a closer look at one of them. Take us down and hover," John told her.

"No way, John! What if they're not dead?" she asked, the panic mounting again.

"They're dead, the others are gone. We need to know what we are fighting, so we can work out a way to kill them more efficiently. I need to have a closer look. Take us down, Stephanie and relax," he told her, trying to re-assure her.

She flew the helicopter slowly down and hovered about twenty feet above the dead creatures on the ground. John was staring through his side window, examining the bodies as best he could from that height.

They were at least ten feet tall, massively built, their bodies rippling with muscles. At first glance, John thought they were wearing some kind of body armour, the thought of which scared him to death. If they had started using such things as body armour, then it would only be a matter of time until they were using weapons as well. At that moment the war would be over, for mankind. Upon closer inspection he realised the armour plating or whatever it was, appeared to be part of the creature, a type of exo-skeleton. It looked to consist of a bone type material and, judging by the number of bullet holes in the body, it seemed to be highly resistant to projectiles. He could see the creature had been hit in the head area on numerous occasions. Around the eyes, there appeared to be a weakness in the armour. The armour around the lower extremities also appeared susceptible to damage. However, only the wounds to the head area appeared fatal.

Shit, he thought, the calibre of the helicopter's machine guns was far greater than their normal assault rifles. If the weapons used by the Apache were only just powerful enough to kill the new creatures then, with the M-16s they would not really stand a chance. They would have to develop some new weapons and quickly, if they were going to stand a chance of combating this new threat.

"Can we get out of here now?" Stephanie asked, urgently.

"Yes, we can go," John answered. "I've seen enough."

Suddenly, Stephanie screamed in panic and the helicopter seemed to lurch to the right.

"What the hell?" John said, suddenly unsure what was going on.

"John, do something quickly, or we are dead!" she shouted, almost hysterical.

He looked out of his window and saw what had made the helicopter suddenly bank to the right. Firmly attached to the right-hand skid, was one of the enormous creatures. It was pulling itself up, in an attempt to reach them. He realised the monster must have run from cover and jumped nearly twenty feet in the air to be able to have grabbed the skid. That showed incredible speed and strength on the creature's part and confirmed his suspicions. The new enemy was very dangerous indeed.

"Don't just sit there, John, do something or we're dead!" Stephanie screamed at him again.

John realised she was close to losing it.

He opened the co-pilot's door and, with his Beretta already in his hand, told Stephanie to climb. He aimed and fired, concentrating on the head area of the creature. He emptied his first magazine, unbuttoned the spent one and inserted a new one up the well, then continued firing. The bullets just seemed to deflect off the creature's head. They were at about sixty feet and still climbing, the helicopter starting to struggle under the creature's massive weight. John guessed it weighed at least six hundred pounds. He had one magazine left, reloaded his pistol and aimed again, this time at the creature's eyes. After the third shot, he got the desired effect. The creature was not dead but it let go, holding its face. As it fell, it screamed, an agonising noise that made John almost feel sorry for it but only almost.

They were at eighty feet as the creature let go and the fall did not help the creature's appearance at all. It impacted the motorway's surface and lay still, obviously dead.

"Shit, that was close! Are you okay, Stephanie?" he asked.

She was shaking visibly and obviously panicked. He tried to calm her down, telling her everything was now alright. They should fly back to the convoy and report this little development. She was calming down slowly, still quietly sobbing but coming to terms with what had just happened. It had been a big shock, he realised. She had seen the monster jump for the helicopter before he had even known something was wrong. She had still managed to keep control of the Apache, even though she was panicking. That showed remarkable control. She would be fine despite the harrowing experience.

"Stephanie, are you okay?" he asked her again.

"Yes, but don't ever do that again, you idiot. We almost died!"

"I'm sorry but at least we know we can kill them. It was important to know that; we can then plan against them."

"I understand that but next time do it some other way. Okay."

"Okay. Take us home."

They caught the rest of the convoy up, after about ten minutes flying time, landed and packed the Apache away again. John, Stephanie, Robert, Mark and Bill were sitting in the truck they had brought along as a workshop or hospital, going over what had happened. John thought it best, for the time being at least, to keep the news of these fearsome new creatures secret. At least until they found a way to deal with them, thus the meeting in the workshop truck, alone.

"What happened, John?" Robert asked, staring at Stephanie, who was still visibly shaken.

"We've got trouble, big trouble," John replied. Then he told them of their encounter and near escape.

"Where the hell did they come from?" Mark asked, worried.

"Remember when we captured the creature at the castle, it said something about them changing or something, I can't remember exactly," John said.

"It said that some of them had been changed," Robert informed them. "I remember because it seemed a weird thing to say. I've always wondered what it meant. I guess we know now."

"I guess we do," John confirmed. "That was their big brother, and we've got problems."

"I don't get it, how can they have changed?" Mark asked.

"Mutation, accelerated evolution, take your pick. It's probably a combination of both, brought on by nuclear fallout, I don't know. A scientist could probably explain it. One of the theories regarding the creatures was that they had evolved from the same slime bucket as we did but in a different direction. When we are exposed to radiation we mutate. Why shouldn't they?"

"So basically, we've done it to ourselves again. We have through indirect action, created the very things that could end up destroying us. Shit, John, will we ever learn?" Robert asked.

"Our problem isn't why or how? It's whether we can kill them. They're immune to the gas, it didn't even make them sneeze. The normal ones died as usual but these monstrosities walked right through it. No effect. There were six or seven of them and we basically emptied the helicopter's whole magazine into them. We killed only three! The rest moved off as if unhurt; that makes our life very difficult. Their only apparent weak spot appears to be the head, even then, you need a lot of luck to do them any real damage. I emptied two magazines into the one on the helicopter, at point blank range but I'm pretty sure I only wounded it at best. The fall from eighty feet killed it. They are bigger, a lot stronger and probably smarter. I'd say we were meant to take the off-ramp, they were waiting for us. It was only luck on our part that we used the other carriageway. Otherwise we would have been in big trouble because I'm not sure our modified defences will stop them. We need suggestions and quick," John said, seriously.

Robert looked at Bill.

"What can you do, Bill? You've solved every problem up to now, don't let me down."

"I need some time," Bill replied. "I've got some ideas. We had a lot going on towards the end of the war, a lot of experimental stuff. I've still got the files and some of the prototypes we developed. We should be able to come up with something useful. How many of them are there, John?"

"Maybe not too many, that's something that could play out in our favour. We never saw any around the castle or in Hadlee. It could be this is their territory and they never ventured up north. It could be they are just spread thinly but one of these things is a threat to us, four or five a disaster, more and, well, you get the picture. We need an answer and quick."

"Okay, leave it with me. I'll get my team together, we'll be travelling in here for the next few hours," Bill told them.

They stopped but only for a short time. John, Robert, Stephanie and Mark returned to their normal vehicles while Bill got his team organised and moved into the workshop truck.

After only a matter of minutes the convoy was moving again, southwards towards Manchester. An hour later they passed the ruins of Glasgow, nobody really paying any attention to it. There were other problems, other questions to be answered.

John and Stephanie were sitting together in the leading truck, she was still quiet. He asked her if she was okay, she said yes but she felt a little ashamed. She had never panicked so much before, had never been so afraid of anything but the big creature had taken her completely by surprise. John explained it was normal and very much okay to be scared. Anybody who said they had never been afraid was a liar! Being afraid and having other emotions, such as love, understanding and compassion was the difference between the creatures and them. That was what made them human beings and not cold blooded monsters. They had hugged and she had slept lying on his lap. Afterwards she felt better.

Chapter Thirty Five - Mission to Hull

"Where are we?" John asked, just waking up.

He had slept for a good two hours. Stephanie, sitting next to him, answered, "We're between the ruins of Glasgow and Manchester, still travelling south. Everything's quiet, no problems since . . ."

She did not manage to finish the sentence, still not completely recovered from the shock of their close encounter.

"We need a break, they'll be going crazy, What time is it?" he asked, trying to wake himself up.

"It's two o'clock," she replied. "Do you think it's a good idea to stop? What if there are more of 'them' in the area?"

"We'll have to risk it sooner or later, we've all got to refuel anyway. If we don't stop now while it's light, then we'll be forced to stop somewhere that is not of our choosing and maybe at night. I'd feel better facing those things when I can see them, rather than have them sneaking around under cover of darkness. Driver, pull over."

The convoy had stopped at the next suitable spot. It was not very secure but they were not stopping for long. All of the passengers used the time to go to the toilet and get some refreshment. Although nobody, apart from the leadership team, knew about the new deadly enemy, the convoy inhabitants could tell by the heightened activity of the soldiers that something was wrong. John and Robert managed to avoid a few awkward questions, just explaining everything was precautionary.

The helicopter landed, refuelled and took off again straightaway, without the pilots taking a break. This added to the speculation that something had or was, going to happen.

The leadership team were again sitting alone in the workshop truck, Bill having told them he had a few ideas to report. This meeting, in apparent secrecy, fuelled the rumours that serious developments had occurred. The civilian passengers were suspicious and frightened.

After only a few minutes the convoy was once again moving. All drivers had received explicit instructions to alert John and Robert at the slightest sign that trouble was looming. The helicopter had also been instructed to stay close to the convoy, keeping constant watch. John had suggested that the creatures would probably not use the roadblock scenario again, seeing as it had not worked. If they were as intelligent as the creatures had been around the castle and in Hadlee, then they would learn from the attempt and try something different. Watching the road in front of them was therefore, not as important as watching the surrounding countryside.

"Bill, what have you come up with? I know we've been putting you and your team under pressure to deliver over the last few weeks but if we ever needed some good news, it's now."

"We are still working on a few ideas, John but I seriously think we've got to the stage where we'll struggle to develop any of them. We didn't bring all that much equipment with us, because of space and keeping the convoy small. If we were still in the castle and had a little more time, then we could come up with a safer way of dealing with the big boys. As it is, we've done what we can. It should give us an advantage. First we've come up with a way to re-tip some of our existing ammunition supplies with titanium, the bullets destroy Kevlar. They are similar to the old police killers but even more powerful. I haven't seen any of our new friends but these should make a mess of their armour. They will at least be more effective than our normal rounds. We'll have five thousand rounds ready by tomorrow morning. I suggest we load magazines with them but only use them when one of these things turns up. The next item isn't new but it will put them away, of that I'm sure. R.P.Gs, Rocket Propelled Grenades. We've got plenty of them, stored all over the place, there are fifty of them waiting for you, ready. They aren't always accurate but if one of them hits one of these things, it's dead! It doesn't matter what their armour is made of, it won't be able to withstand the impact. We have enough guys who know how to use the weapons effectively. I suggest one soldier per truck. We still have the gas weapons and we are trying to convert grenades at the moment. If we manage it, then every soldier could carry them and use them anywhere but it will take time. The work is delicate, and we can't afford a mistake, so I doubt they'll be ready any time soon. Eventually we'll get it sorted, something for later maybe. A new development is and you'd better not laugh, bows and arrows."

John looked at Bill as if he had suddenly grown another head.

"Yeah, I know how it sounds but during the war these high tech. bows were developed. It was considered a good weapon when silence was required. The idea has been around for years, our only difference is the arrow heads. They are explosive and tipped with a nutrium tip. This stuff's state of the art, it's harder than diamonds, very new. The arrows will pierce steel plate that's six inches thick, then the head explodes. I'm pretty certain they'd take out our trucks, even though they are armoured. Against the creatures, they'll be very effective. They are a kill every time and very accurate, the only problem is quantity. We have forty of the heads, no chance of any more at all but it's an advantage. We've still got the newer versions of Bazookas, they'll more than likely hurt them and tank shells or normal missiles from the Apache will take them out. All in all, things could be worse."

"Very good, Bill, it gives us a fighting chance, at least," Robert told him. "John, any thoughts?"

"At the moment? I'm hungry, that's about the sum of it. As usual Bill has managed to impress me. I owe him about six bottles of Scotch now. We'd better get some of these weapons distributed to the men. We don't tell the civilians but we'd better inform the men otherwise, when these things appear again, it will be a shock and the resulting panic could be fatal for all of us. The less the civilians know the better. They'll find out eventually anyway but, for the time being, we'll keep it on a need to know basis. Do we know where we are at the moment?"

"Exactly, John?" Robert asked.

"Yes, exactly," John replied, seriously.

"No," came the short reply.

"We are about fifty miles north of Manchester," Mark said, smiling.

"Okay. It's nearly three o'clock, we need to find a bridge for the night, the best bet is a big one. We can use the same routine as last night, only this time we leave more space at both ends, just in case any of our new and improved friends come to visit. Bill, issue the weapons to the men. We'll need everything you've got, trip wires, anti-personnel, flares. I want it so tight out there, nothing can get through without tripping something. I really am hungry. Let's get the convoy stopped somewhere and get set up, then we can eat."

Using the radio, the pilot of Bravo One was instructed to locate a suitable bridge as soon as possible. The driver of the tank leading the convoy, was instructed to stop as soon as the convoy reached the location. Within thirty minutes, they were parked and the defences were being set up, some of the civilians again asking awkward questions but, with clever answers, a panic was avoided.

The evening meal was being prepared in the kitchen truck. John, still hungry, was talking to Stephanie, eagerly awaiting his meal. To kill time, he was drinking his third cup of coffee in less than an hour. He had hoped the coffee would convince his stomach that he was not as hungry as he really was but all it was doing was reminding him he had to pee.

"You've been quiet all afternoon, what's the matter? I thought we'd talked about what happened this morning," he said, worried that Stephanie was still upset about the incident with the new creature.

"I don't know, John, it's different now. Before it was just you and me. It was dangerous, sometimes it was even life-threatening but the risk to us was always manageable. I somehow knew we'd get through, no matter what. Now I'm pregnant. Now it's the three of us! The stress and tension can't be good for the baby. I don't want to risk our baby, John," she was crying.

"You won't - we won't," he corrected himself. "I'm sorry about all the shit at the moment, especially this morning. But you've got to understand, I need you in that helicopter. I know it's hard to understand but, up there, at least I know you're safe. If things are going badly for us and we're getting hammered, then at least I know you're okay. You could get away, fly off somewhere, I don't know but I need to know that you're not in danger. Down here, I can't guarantee your safety anymore, not with these new creatures attacking us!"

"Yes, John, I know what you mean," and she kissed him, smiling for the first time that afternoon.

They ate, the meal yet another concoction of tinned foods but John's stomach was at last starting to quieten down. Everybody was feeling a little more confident about the situation since the talks with Bill. The weapons had been distributed amongst the men, they had been given specific instructions on how and when to use them. It was now dark but John did not expect any visitors that night, because of the distance they had put between them and their attackers that morning. He felt it unlikely that the creatures could organise any kind of attack quickly enough. They should be safe for the night. John decided he needed to speak with Robert again; he had had an idea that might save them time in the long run. Robert was talking to Mark about the day's events, as John found him.

"Robert, I need your permission to take one of the helicopters and fly to New Hull," John said, quietly.

"Sorry, John, what did you say?" Robert asked, sure he had heard wrong.

"I want to go to New Hull now."

"You're joking. What's got into you?" Robert quizzed.

"I've been thinking, that's all. We are currently heading down to Birmingham, then across the country and back up the coast to New Hull. From here it is still the best part of four hundred miles but we have no idea whether a big enough ship is there waiting for us. From where we are now it can only be about eighty miles to the city as the crow flies. We can't drive through the dead zone but we can sure as hell fly over it. We make the trip, check for a ship and fly straight back. It's two hours tops in the Apache. Using its cameras we can gather intelligence over the city, get a lay of the land. It could save us having to make an unnecessary journey. Just imagine for a second, we fight our way from here to there and there's no ship. We'd be fucked because we'd have to come all the way back. This way, if there's no ship visible, we still have time to think again, maybe keep going down past Birmingham to the south coast and try and find one there. It could not only save us a lot of time but probably keep more of us alive."

"The idea's good, John but what about the Dead Zone? Are you sure you can fly over it?" Robert asked, obviously concerned.

"Yes, I've flown over it before, just after the war. We were still working with Special Forces and were sent to control the area. It was only possible from the air. It's only ground level that's lethal."

"As long as you're sure there is no risk to you or whoever is flying the helicopter, then it's fine by me. Just don't take all night, we might need you at some time. Who is flying? Stephanie?" Robert asked.

"No. What happened this morning freaked her a little, understandably. I'd rather she slept. I'll ask one of the other guys to do it," John answered.

"You will not!" somebody said, from behind him.

He recognised the voice straight away, turning to face her. She looked angry.

"I'll fly you. I'm all right and you know it! When do we leave?"

"In ten minutes, okay," he answered.

"Fine by me. I'll check the helicopter is fuelled and armed. See you there," she said walking off in the direction of the Apache.

"Oop's, it could be a chilly flight, John," Robert said, noticing that Stephanie was not very friendly.

210

"She'll be fine, I hope," John said, then continuing. "You guys stay sharp, just in case. Mark, keep on their backs, we can't afford any mistakes. I'll see you in two hours."

He walked off to join Stephanie, who was pre-flighting the helicopter. As he approached the aircraft she climbed out and stood waiting for him, hands on hips. He wasn't sure but he had the distinct impression she was angry.

"What the hell was that bullshit, John?" she asked.

He had been right, she was angry.

"I wasn't sure you'd want to go after what happened this morning. I didn't think you needed anymore pressure. I was only thinking of what you said about the baby. I didn't want to take any unnecessary risks. I was worried about you, that's all. Sorry."

She smiled.

"Okay, I believe you. Let's go."

With a final wave to Robert and Mark, they took off and headed east.

Robert looked at Mark and, shaking his head, said, "That guy never quits. Thank God he's on our side."

"You're sure about this, John, flying over the Dead Zone is safe?" Stephanie asked, suddenly thinking about the baby inside her.

"It's safe. I wouldn't risk our baby. You can believe that."

"Should I redline it? If I do, the eighty miles will only take about twenty minutes. Ten minutes looking around, then another twenty minutes back. Everything sorted in less than an hour. What do you think?" she asked.

"Redline it," he answered, softly.

She powered out, the normally quiet-sounding engine becoming a little louder, the aircraft picking up speed.

"I'm sorry about before," she said into the headset. "Don't treat me any differently, John, not yet anyway. There'll be time for that later. I'm still perfectly capable of pulling my weight you know, being pregnant is not an illness, it's a gift."

"I know and I'll try not to but if I do, you just kick my arse. Okay?"

"Yes. I love you, you know that don't you?" she asked him.

"I know and I love you more than anything," he replied. "Now, fly the dammed helicopter, we'll get mushy later."

John had turned the cameras on and was constantly watching his screens. Flying over the Dead Zone, he could see nothing, nothing at all.

"What do you think it's like down there, John?" she asked.

"Basically, it's dead. There's nothing left, everything is covered in contamination. If we entered the area, then one or two weeks later we'd be ill. A short time after that we'd die, a painful and horrible death. They estimated the area would be that way for at least one hundred and fifty years. I tell you that nuclear shit is a nightmare. Why we ever thought it would benefit us, I don't know. Every discovery we've ever made, the first thought was always using it as a weapon. All the viruses and diseases we've unleashed on our planet over the years. Ebola, Aids, Bird Flu. It always turned out we did it, we took the lid off the bottle then blamed something else. The billions who have died because of our need to know. What do we know now?"

"You're being a little hard on us, John. We discovered worthwhile things as well, medicines, vaccines. Look at antibiotics. How many people were saved over the years because of that one discovery? " she argued.

"You were with the military just like I was, you were privy to the same information. You know such products were sidelines, they were discovered accidentally. We weren't looking for them, we were trying to find other things. Everything that was ever found that did any good, only came about because we were trying to find something else. Sure, they always had cover stories, scapegoats, somebody who would claim responsibility, even take the credit but it was mostly smoke. Only very few of them knew where the real fire was."

"Married life has made you cynical, John Stewart," she told him, trying to lighten the conversation.

"Yeah, you're right. I do get a little carried away sometimes but looking at the world today, as it now is, it's hard not to," he answered.

They had reached the east coast and were closing in on New Hull, the moment of truth fast approaching. John wondered what they could do if there was no ship? What other options did they really have?

"We are coming up on the harbour, John," Stephanie warned him.

Watching his screen he could see the city was dead. Nothing moved, there weren't even any creatures in sight! They flew over the first half of the harbour, John assumed from the north but there weren't any ships big enough to suit their needs. A few fishing trawlers were visible but they would need a fleet of those. She flew on, the second part of the harbour coming into view.

John felt that this was the moment that would decide their future, he closed his eyes and prayed.

"John, do you see them?" she asked, excitedly.

He opened his eyes and looked. He could see what had made her so excited. Tied up at the dockside there were two enormous, beautiful-looking car ferries. For a second he thanked God.

"We're going to be okay, John, we're going to make it," she said, the relief in her voice obvious.

They took some photographs of the two ships and the surrounding area, then decided it was time to head back and report the great news to the rest of the convoy. Stephanie banked the aircraft to the west and throttled out again. She was happy and really excited, the trip had been a slight risk but it had paid off.

Twenty minutes later they landed back at the campsite, thankfully everything was still quiet. There had been no visitors while they were away. As they landed, Robert ran up to meet them; he had been concerned about the dangers of flying over the Dead Zone. After making sure they were both okay, he asked if they had seen anything, Stephanie answering him before John could. Two ships were ready and waiting. They had a chance, a good chance.

News of the sighting spread rapidly through the encampment. After the photographs had been quickly printed, these too were passed around, adding to the excitement.

People were celebrating, at least quietly. It was not the right time for a party, that would yet come but at least now they were all sure the trip was not being risked for nothing. The fights and battles they had fought up to then, the sacrifices everybody was making were not in vain. It might just pay off after all.

In the morning they would continue down the motorway, heading south, their aim perhaps north of Birmingham. Once there they would turn east and then back up the east coast. Two, maybe three days, John thought and they would be there. Maybe then they would be free of the creatures, at least for a little while.

Chapter Thirty Six - The Observers

"Vinny, take a look at this," Snake said, excitedly.

"What yer got Snake? It'd better be important, I'm starving," Vinny replied, sounding agitated.

He had noticed over the last weeks that Snake was getting more and more impatient with him. It was becoming harder to keep his men under control because of it.

"There on the bridge, take a look."

"Shit, there's people moving around," Vinny exclaimed.

They had not seen anybody for weeks, at least not alive. Just creatures, they had seen enough of them, especially the bigger ones. They had taken their toll on the number of riders in his gang over the last few months. He could not remember exactly how many men they had lost to the big monsters but it was definitely more than to the normal ones.

"What are they doing?" Vinny asked, thinking out loud. "Where did they come from?"

"I don't know," Snake answered. "But they got a sweet set up."

"Yeah, we could sure use some of that gear ourselves," Vinny said, watching through his binoculars and knowing exactly what would be going through Snake's twisted mind.

"What do yer reckon they're carrying in those trucks, food maybe or what?" Snake asked, obviously thinking of his stomach.

"Probably, maybe other goodies as well. How many men have they got?" Vinny asked.

As soon as he asked the question he realised in the dark it would be impossible to tell. This fact could use to his advantage. He knew straightaway he would have to find a good reason this time to stop them attacking. It had become very difficult to keep certain members of the gang under control. He had been thankful of every day they had not seen anybody alive. The last few occasions they had, it had proved very difficult to hold his men back. He had managed it – just - even though some of his decisions had been questioned, mostly by Snake and his friends.

"It's hard to see, it's bloody dark you pratt," Snake replied, more than a hint of conceit in his voice.

Vinny scuffed him across his head.

"Watch it, you gobshite. I still run the show, don't ever forget that."

"I was only messing with you, Vinny. Shit, you'll give me a headache," Snake moaned but Vinny knew it was only his reputation as a fighter that was keeping Snake from trying to take over the gang.

"Okay, we camp here and take a look at first light," Vinny told him.

"Are we gonna take 'em Vinny?" Snake asked, barely able to hide his excitement.

"Yeah, I reckon so. The boys need feeding, we need more supplies of everything. We'll decide in the morning, after we've taken a good look at them," Vinny answered, secretly hoping the morning would give him the excuse to leave the people on the bridge alone.

"The guys are pretty pissed off, mate. We've had no decent food since the run through Manchester. It'd be good to take their minds off their bellies, a good fight'll do it," Snake remarked, still trying to watch the activity on the bridge.

"I'll handle the men, no problem," Vinny told him, menacingly and they walked back down into their camp.

The 'boys' were there waiting for them.

"How's it looking, Vinny?" one of them asked.

"We'll know more in the morning but it looks promising. Now get some sleep, that goes for all of you. You'll need to be fit for tomorrow," Vinny told them.

The sixty bikers who were all members of his gang started to settle down for the night, dividing off into smaller groups. Some were trying to sleep straightaway, some starting to play cards, some were just talking. Vinny noticed Snake sitting with his pals, talking quietly, Vinny could guess about what. He would have to watch Snake in the morning, no matter what he decided. His conflict with Snake had become a powder keg that could erupt at any time, he needed a victory to prove his position as leader. Whatever or whoever it was camped on the bridge, would not be that victory, he would make sure of that. He would have to see in the morning how his men took the news but it was clear in his mind that attacking fellow human beings was not an option.

"Snake, wake me at four. Don't fucking oversleep," he barked, in Snake's direction.

He was awoken at four o'clock, just as he had instructed. In a couple of hours, it would be light enough to see what exactly was going on. He drank a cup of the coffee they had made the day before, it was too valuable to waste but it still tasted like piss. He wondered if he would ever have fresh coffee again. He waited, soon he would know more.

It was getting light enough to be able to see. He could make out the people on the bridge quite clearly now. He realised they were preparing to break camp. It was obvious to him he would not need to find an excuse not to attack them, the truth of the matter would be enough reason to leave them well alone. It was clear to him now this was a military unit, far more organised than he had first thought, militarily superior in every way. They had air support, tanks and more men who all seemed to bristle with weapons. He guessed ammunition would not be a problem for the unit he was staring at, unlike his own men who had very little left of this precious commodity. It was quite clear to him they could not hope to win a confrontation against such a force. He was glad because any of his men could see for themselves that he was right. Besides, the guys on the bridge were probably one of the last chances for mankind in the struggle against the creatures.

"Fuck it!" he said, trying to sound disappointed. "We've no chance against them. They are way too strong for us to even think about it."

Snake stared at him.

"We can take 'em, Vinny. With what they've got in those trucks, we could live for months. Some of those trucks have got to be carrying food, tons of it."

"Snake, you're a good man in a fight but you're thicker than shit. We're sixty guys on bikes. We've all got guns but only a few assault rifles. Mostly we've got shotguns and the like. We don't have that much ammunition as it is, so we can't afford to waste it in a futile attempt at taking them on. Take a real good look. They are transporting civilians, that's obvious but the soldiers are heavily armed. Most of the vehicles are armed. They have got tanks, air support, the full monty. You don't have to be a fucking genius to work out what would happen if we attacked them. They'd wipe us out, probably wouldn't take more than ten minutes. We'd have no fucking chance at all," he said, dejectedly.

"The boys ain't gonna like this, Vinny, they want blood," Snake warned him.

"They'll have to lump it then, won't they? The idiots will get killed before they get close enough to see what's killing them. Those guys on the bridge are professionals, we are strictly amateurs. Forget it," and he headed back to their makeshift camp.

Back at the camp the men were waiting for news. They had had enough of empty bellies, running battles with these monsters and freezing nights sleeping on cold wet floors. They wanted more and were intent on getting it.

As Vinny explained they would have no chance, certain members of the gang became very violent. Everybody was suddenly speaking at once. The general belief was obvious, they could take the arseholes on the bridge but Vinny was not the one to lead them in doing it.

Vinny was slowly reaching for the pistol tucked into his belt, he recognised how serious his situation was becoming. While facing the men in front of him, he had forgotten Snake who was standing just behind him. With Vinny's attention focused elsewhere, Snake took advantage of the situation. He grabbed Vinny around the neck and, using his eight inch blade, stabbed him in the back. Vinny struggled shortly then crumpled to the ground, apparently dead.

Snake stood there in front of the gang, his knife dripping blood.

"Now I'm the leader. Any of you wankers got a problem with that?"

The gang stood there quietly. After Vinny, Snake had always been one of the best fighters. Because of that, nobody trusted themselves enough to object. Besides, to a lot of the bikers, Vinny had shown himself to be a coward, backing away from easy fights on numerous occasions. He had always had some cock and bull story to justify doing it. Maybe with Snake leading them, they would have more luck.

As had become custom with certain members of the gang, they raised their weapons in the air and fired to show their approval of Snake's leadership. They momentarily forgot that the sound of gunshots carried over great distances, Snake telling them to lower their guns quickly.

"You fucking idiots, they'll hear you on the bridge," he shouted.

At least he was intelligent enough to realise the danger of what they were doing.

"We gonna take 'em, Snake?" one of his friends asked him.

"Why not? We'll follow 'em for a while, pick our moment. Yeah, we're gonna take 'em and get all their gear for ourselves. We'll kill 'em all, every last one of the fuckers! Now mount up, we're leaving. We'll follow the motorway, keep ahead of them and when the time's right, nail the bastards."

His men were breaking camp, mounting their bikes, getting ready to travel. He liked being leader already, liked it a lot.

Chapter Thirty Seven - The Patient

"What the hell?" John said, looking out over the surrounding countryside. "Where did those shots come from?"

"Over to the east, John," Robert replied. "It sounded like a short battle but it's stopped now. Weird."

"Shit, Robert, that means other people are still alive. We should try and help them, we said we probably would. What do you think?" John asked, expectantly.

Robert stared at him. He had broached the subject of finding survivors back in the castle during one of their planning sessions. At that time, John had reacted negatively against the idea of taking on strays, arguing that they had enough to do looking after their own people. Now, all of a sudden, it seemed he was keen to do just the opposite. It was another one of the situations where Robert felt confused by John's actions.

"I'm not sure. We're almost ready to leave, besides we have no real idea of where the shots came from. They have stopped now anyway, whoever was shooting is probably dead already. How do you expect to find anybody out there, they could be anywhere?"

"We've at least got to try. The people who were shooting could still be alive. What if I take six men and fly over the area in Bravo One? We'll just have a quick look. It might make a difference. What do you say?" John asked, knowing it would prove difficult to find anything in the thick woods surrounding the bridge but certain they had to try.

"John, sometimes I don't understand you. When we broached this subject back in the castle, you weren't exactly keen on the idea of taking in stragglers. Now you want to fly off, on what will probably be, a wild goose chase. You're a real pain in the arse sometimes but you already know that, don't you?" Robert said, smiling. He then continued, "The stupid thing is, I wouldn't want you to be any other way. Pick your guys, go and have a look around. We'll be ready in case you need back up."

"We'll just fly around over the general area, fifteen minutes tops. If we don't find anything in that time, we'll come back and we can get underway," John said, backing away from Robert.

He started to run towards the truck where most of his men were stationed but turned back to Robert saying thanks.

After quickly organising his six men, they boarded Bravo One and took off. What were the odds, he thought, of finding somebody? He decided pretty slim but the chance of finding somebody from that general area who might be able to help them, was too good to pass up. People who had survived the conflict with the creatures this long, deserved a helping hand. Besides, it beat sitting in the damn truck!

Robert told the men still guarding the campsite to be alert. The civilians were all on board the trucks and would stay there until they had made sure there was no threat to them. The Apache was being readied again, just in case John and his team required assistance and to provide air support for the parked trucks until Bravo One returned. He watched the helicopter, carrying John's team, fly off over the surrounding countryside in the general direction of where the shots had come from. He doubted they would find anything, not now anyway.

Bravo One had flown over the hilltop, just to the east of the bridge where they had stayed the night. John was certain the gunfire had originated there. They could not see anything, no smoke, nothing that was normally visible after a battle. He had promised Robert that after fifteen minutes searching, they would head back. He hoped it would prove long enough.

It had been twenty minutes since they had left to search the area, Robert could see the helicopter returning. Only five minutes overdue, that was good for John, Robert thought. Mark came running over to him. John was on the radio and it was urgent. Robert ran to the nearest truck and answered.

"What's up, John?" he asked, expecting trouble.

"We're coming back with a survivor. He's badly wounded, it looks like a knife wound. We'll need the med. team alerted."

"We're on it, John," Robert answered, sending Mark to get everything organised. "Just one survivor, how many were killed?"

"That's the weird part, Robert, none. He was all we could find, nothing else was in the area but we found tracks. Motorbikes and a lot of them. It would appear we've got problems other than the creatures. It looks like they are shadowing us, purpose unknown but I bet we can guess. If this guy makes it, maybe he can tell us more. We'll be landing in less than two minutes, we can talk more then."

"Good. John, we'll be ready."

The helicopter landed, the medical team meeting it. John explained again where the man was wounded, stab wound in the lower back area. Whoever had stabbed him had probably assumed he was dead and had left him lying there. The doctor examined the man and immediately turned to Robert.

"We need to operate straightaway. He's bleeding internally. If we can't stop it, he'll die. It appears he's been lucky. From what I can see, there are no major organs damaged. If I can stop the bleeding quickly, he should make it," the doctor reported.

"What do you need, doctor?" Robert asked.

"I need the hospital truck cleaned and sterilised - and quickly. We don't have a great deal of time, he has lost a lot of blood. I need to type him and then we'll need donors, four maybe five pints to be safe. Then I need maybe two hours without bumps and surprises. We can travel but slowly. I'll let you know when we are finished. Now if you'll excuse me, I have work to do," and he walked off with his team leading the patient.

"He's a bossy git!" John said, looking at Robert.

"Bloody good doctor," Robert said, looking around. "Mark, get the hospital truck scrubbed up. Tell Bill he'll have to finish his work somewhere else for now."

Bill had been using the hospital truck as a workshop, to develop the weapons they would be using against the new creatures. Robert continued talking to Mark.

"Talk to the doctor and get him some blood donors organised, the guys who give blood are excused duty for today. We can travel, but tell everybody to keep the speed down until further notice. Let me know when you're finished."

Mark ran off, barking orders.

"What do you think, John?" Robert asked.

"I think we've got a problem. There were at least fifty sets of tracks. If we go on the assumption there's only one rider per bike, then we have at least fifty guys out for our blood. Probably more than fifty. That could be a problem for us. I think we'll have more than an edge weapon-wise, but desperate bikers will do stupid things. They were obviously spying on us, more than likely with a view to attacking. To consider attacking a well armed, well organised unit such as ours, they must be bloody desperate. If our friend makes it, he can tell us more about them, fill in the blanks, so to speak. For the moment we keep going, slowly, until the doc gives the all clear, carefully afterwards. At some stage they'll make their move but we've got the edge on them."

"How do you work that out?" Robert asked him, puzzled by the remark.

"Easy," John replied. "We know about them but they don't know it. We have time to prepare, plus, they can't know how strong we are. It's enough to make a difference."

"They were watching us, John, they'll know exactly how many men we've got," Robert stated.

"Yeah, but when they were watching us, nearly half of our men were sleeping. We keep those guys hidden, they'll be our insurance. Good, eh?"

"Now, John, don't get cocky on me," Robert said, realising John was right. "Let's move out," he shouted to his men.

The convoy started to roll. They had wanted to make it as far as Birmingham that day but they were late starting. Robert had joined John and Stephanie in the lead truck. They were filling the time discussing some of the missions the now married couple had undertaken as operatives with special services.

After about an hour of travelling slowly, the doctor, using one of the radios, reported that the operation was finished. They could pick up the pace again.

"How's our patient?" Robert asked, sounding genuinely concerned.

"He will be fine. He is weak due to the loss of blood but he will pull through," came the reply.

"Can he talk?" John asked.

"Not yet, he is resting. In a couple of hours, perhaps. Not before," the doctor told him, quite clearly.

"Thanks, doctor, well done," Robert said, signalling to John he should keep quiet.

"Who the hell does he think he is?" John asked, obviously angry, just as Robert had guessed.

"John, he is probably the most important person here. He can keep you alive and, although he is a real pain in the arse sometimes, he's bloody good at his job. Don't let him get to you. Eventually you'll get used to his ways. Don't forget, we might unfortunately need him."

"I never did like doctors, they can be so bloody abrupt. They always seem to rub me up the wrong way. But I guess you're right, I'll cut him some slack."

"He's afraid of them really, Robert!" Stephanie said smiling.

"I am not," John argued. "Doctors are just wankers who think they know everything!"

Robert smiled until he saw the look on John's face.

"We'll keep going, have a break early this afternoon and talk to our new friend then. Do you agree?" Robert asked.

John nodded.

He hoped the situation between the doctor and John would not escalate any further. He had also found the doctor's bedside manner to be downright rude sometimes but he had got used to it over the years he had served with him. It would take John a little longer.

"Yeah. Let's try and make up some lost time. Our friend can wait, after all, he's not going anywhere, is he?" John answered.

After three hours driving, without signs of the creatures or the bikers now stalking them, they found a suitable spot to stop. John and Robert, after making sure the defences were organised and sending Bravo One on ahead to check the route, headed for the now converted hospital truck. After speaking shortly with the doctor about his patient's condition, they approached the only cot in the mobile hospital. John could not help wondering how long it would be before more would appear. He found it amazing that up to then at least, they had suffered so few casualties.

They stood over the dozing biker they had rescued and saved. The biker, perhaps sensing they were there, opened his eyes.

"Who the hell are you guys? Where am I?" he asked trying to sit up but flinching with pain at the attempt.

"Lie still, relax. You're okay now," Robert said, trying to calm the man. "You've had an operation which saved your life, by the way but the doctor says you will be fine. You'll be weak and sore for a couple of days."

As if he remembered suddenly what had happened to him, he cursed.

"Snake, that fucking bastard! He got me from behind. I should have known better than to take my eyes off him."

"Woah, slow down. Who the hell is Snake?" John asked.

"First of all, who the hell are you?" he countered.

"Sorry, we should have introduced ourselves first," Robert said, apologetically. "My name is Major Robert Jones and this is Major John Stewart."

John looked at Robert and started to say something but Robert interrupted him, saying something about a field promotion and smiling, then he continued.

"We are the commanding officers of the convoy you and your friends were spying on."

"And just how the hell did I get here?" the biker asked puzzled.

"We heard gunfire and John went to investigate. He found you dying and brought you back. Our doctor saved your life and here we are," Robert explained.

"Am I a prisoner?" the biker asked, seeming agitated.

"Of course not. You're free to leave as soon as you are well enough. We can't spare you any transport though and it would seem your friends took your motorbike with them. Exactly how and where you'd go, I don't know," Robert said.

"Fucking bollocks!" the biker exclaimed.

"You're welcome to stay," Robert suggested. "We can always use an extra man around here."

This statement seemed to confuse the biker, he was not sure what to make of the suggestion.

"You'd let me stay, even though I was part of a gang of idiots that wanted to attack you," he said, not believing what he had heard.

"You don't seem to fit the normal picture of a blood-crazed biker, something is different about you," John said. "What's your story?"

After staring at John for a second, as if weighing him up, the biker seemed to relax a little.

"Yes, you're right. Before the war I was a normal guy, working all over the place, lot of different jobs. I had a small flat, Sunday lunches with my Mum and Dad, the usual bog-standard member of the community. Christ, I even had a cat called Benny. I had a Hog, but only because I enjoyed riding one. I had nothing to do with biker gangs or any of that crap. During the war I did my bit, home defence, Merchant Navy for a while, a lot of things. I managed to survive the War and settled back into a normal life, then this shit with these fucking things happened."

John presumed he was talking about the creatures.

"I lived in a little town in Shropshire. I had a girlfriend at the time. We were talking about getting married and having a load of kids. You know, re-populating the planet and all that shit. Anyway, I was away working when a gang of these fucking monsters attacked the town. When I got back everyone was dead, including my girl! I buried what was left of her, it wasn't easy. I still had my bike and a few guns left over from the war, so I hit the road. I kept moving, killing these bastards every chance I got. The situation changed me, I started to enjoy killing them, you know. I got real good at it. I lost count of how many I killed but it was never enough. I fell in with this gang of bikers eventually because they were doing the same thing at first. We found other bikers along the way and our numbers grew. We got bloody good at killing the fuckers. Hit and run, the stupid fucking things didn't know how to deal with us. Then we started hearing reports that we were losing the war against them and everything changed. Instead of hunting them, the gang started raiding towns and communities, killing to take what we needed to stay alive. A lot of people were killed trying to defend their homes against us. The leader at that time was a real wanker, he argued we'd done our share of killing the monsters and that we deserved our share of the spoils. Fucking pillock! That wasn't my thing, so eventually I challenged him. I managed to kill him and I became leader. I then spent all my time finding reasons not to kill any more people but concentrate on wiping out the bloody monsters. It was a fucking nightmare because a lot of the gang had got used to the easy life by then. Killing people was a lot easier than killing the monsters and a lot safer. Luckily for me, the gang members were mostly dumb bikers and I could nearly always justify my reasons for leaving people alone. Nearly always. Eventually there weren't any more people left. That meant we could take what we wanted without having to kill anybody. You're the first things we've seen, other than fucking monsters, in months. I reckon everybody else is dead. At one stage we numbered over ninety but in the last few months we've run into more and more of the monsters, including the bigger fuckers. It seemed almost as if they were hunting us. We lost a lot of guys. We were beginning to think we were the only ones left alive and then last night we spotted you sitting on that bridge. The gang is desperate for supplies, so they wanted to attack you straightaway. I tried to persuade them otherwise but they wouldn't listen. Snake, he was second to me, he must have got me from behind, left me for dead. He'll be the leader now, he'll think they can take you. You'd better watch your backs."

"How many bikers are there altogether?" John asked. "We found tracks but couldn't really work out how many bikes there were."

"There's sixty guys on bikes, all armed but mostly shotguns and the like. They have a few automatic rifles but little ammunition for them. They have no explosives or anything like that but they are desperate. I don't suppose they'd stand a cat in hell's chance against you but that won't stop them trying," the biker said.

"Okay, thanks. Hey," John said, "we don't know your name."

"Vincent Peterson. If you laugh, I'll kick your fucking arse when I'm better," he said, smiling for the first time. "My friends call me Vinny."

"Okay, Vinny," John said, without hesitation. "We'll get some food sent into you. Rest now, we can talk more later."

Chapter Thirty Eight - The Third Night

Once outside, Robert turned to John.

"What do you think?" he asked.

"I reckon you're round the bloody twist," John said. "What's all this shit about a field promotion, you berk?"

"John, we both lead here! You're not stupid. Well, neither am I. The men look to you, I know that, so I figured it's the best way for everybody. We both have the same rank now, that way there won't be any problems with the chain of command. You know I'm old-fashioned at heart. The military way of life might be dead, thanks to what's happening all around us but it is still important to me that we have, at least on paper, a disciplined order in the ranks. I cannot continue to be ordered around by a Captain! That goes against the grain. If you are a Major as well then, at least mentally, I have no problems when you get on your high horse and take over," Robert said, smiling.

John stared at him for a second, a smile appearing slowly on his face. Robert was being as diplomatic as he could be under the circumstances.

"I don't want to lead, Robert. I thought we'd already talked about that," John argued.

"Some people don't have a choice, John. You're a born leader and I'd be a fool to ignore that. Now shut up, Major. Accept the fact and tell me what you think about Vinny."

John shook his head. It seemed he had little choice but to accept the situation.

"I think he's on the level. It had crossed my mind that we might have been set up. I was supposed to find him and then, well who knows, but that wound was definitely life-threatening. Another ten minutes or so and he would have died. They couldn't have known we'd bother to investigate and they couldn't have been sure we'd find him if we did. I think he's telling the truth about his past and everything, he seems okay. Just another victim of circumstance."

"We can trust him then," Robert said, relieved.

"Hell no! Don't be stupid," John said, smiling. "For the moment he's definitely on a need to know basis and he doesn't need to know anything. Tell Mark to put a couple of shadows on him when he's finally up and about. Our forces that are resting at the moment should be kept hidden from him, just in case I'm wrong. If we were meant to find him and he's here to spy on us, we'll find out soon enough. In the meantime we keep him in the dark about everything."

"I'll tell Mark," Robert said. "According to the doctor, Vinny could be up and about as early as tomorrow. We'll keep him away from anything delicate."

"Good. Let's go and get some food, I'm starving again."

The two of them had met Stephanie and they had eaten together. The pilots of Bravo One had reported in, the road was clear, no signs of creatures or the bikers. The convoy left after one hour's break. They wanted to get as far down the motorway as possible before stopping for the night. Because of their late start that day, they had at most only two hours of daylight left. They still considered travelling at night too dangerous but John wondered now, with the additional threat of the biker gang, whether they should risk it. He remembered back to the last time he had taken a similar risk. It had almost backfired then. If they had not had their share of luck that night back in Churchtown, he and Stephanie might have been killed. He decided to discuss the subject with Robert later, when they camped for the night.

He was sitting with Stephanie talking. She had not been feeling too well for the last few days but the doctor had confirmed it was nothing to worry about, just the effects of her condition. She was further along in her pregnancy than they had first suspected, the doctor confirming she was ten weeks. He had told her to take it easy for the next few days, John insisting the same. After that, they would hopefully be on the ship. The only problem now was the Apache. She was not the only pilot capable of flying the deadly aircraft but it turned out she was the best qualified. With the added danger of the biker gang that was now stalking them, the air support they had could and probably would, prove invaluable. Both of the aircraft were now armed with both conventional and modified weapons, Bill's team again working wonders. Stephanie agreed, begrudgingly, no flying or over-exertion unless it was absolutely necessary. She was not over the moon about it but realised it was sensible and safer for the baby she now carried inside her.

John was secretly pleased the last twenty four hours had been reasonably quiet, that way his wife did not need to feel so left out. Ever since their journey up the country to the castle, she had always been in the thick of things, helping him every step of the way. On several occasions she had saved his life. To have to sit around while others were fighting and maybe dying, would have been a nightmare for her and he knew she would have struggled mentally. He knew he could not have dealt with such a scenario, he would have been forced to act, as would she. The short time where they had not had to fight had done her good. He leant over and kissed her lovingly on the cheek. He felt very proud of her.

The helicopter returned having located a suitable night stop for the convoy. It was thirty miles further down the motorway, about twenty miles north of Birmingham but only one mile north of the road they would have to take to travel east across the country. The road in front of them was clear of both creatures and bikers, as far as the helicopter crew could tell. They had spent a little time looking for signs of the gang, now shadowing the convoy but with no success. Wherever they were at that exact moment, it was going to be difficult to find them. This worried John, even more so than the lack of creature activity, so Stephanie suggested they should go and have another talk with their 'new found friend' Vinny, as it might prove helpful. John agreed and informed Robert that as soon as they stopped and the defences were set up, he would be heading to the hospital truck again. Robert agreed to join him there.

Another hour passed by and the convoy reached its objective for the night. Mark was left to organise the defences, as John and Robert, together with Stephanie, went to the hospital truck to see Vinny again. As they entered, they were surprised to find the biker was already up and about. The doctor had not recommended it but his curiosity had been too great for him to remain in bed.

"How are you feeling, Vinny?" John asked.

"Yeah, better thanks, eh, John wasn't it?" he answered.

"Right. This is Stephanie, my wife," John said, introducing her.

"I'm so glad you're going to be okay," Stephanie said, as diplomatically as ever.

"You up to a bit of fresh air, Vinny?" John asked, guessing the answer before it came.

"You betcha. I'm sick of lying down. I haven't slept so much for years," he laughed. "That okay with you, doc?"

"I wouldn't recommend it," the doctor said. "But I don't suppose that bothers you, does it?

Vinny shook his head.

"It might be different if you were blond and good looking," Vinny said, laughing.

"Come on," John said. "We'll give you the guided tour, then we'll get a coffee. Nothing too exhausting to start with. We've stopped for the night now, another hour or so and the evening meal will be ready, if you're hungry," John said.

"I could eat a scabby cat, mate," Vinny replied smiling.

"We'll see if we can arrange that for you then," John said, laughing.

He had heard the saying many times before but could still not imagine why anybody, in their right minds, would want to do anything so disgusting. No matter how hungry they were! They led Vinny outside into the encampment. After about twenty yards he needed to sit down. It was obvious he was not quite as strong as he had thought. They all sat down together around a small fire, Stephanie fetching coffee for them all. John needed more information about the new threat facing them. He hoped he had not misjudged Vinny and the information would be forthcoming. Vinny was drinking his third cup of coffee and looking around, a bewildered look on his face. He turned to face John.

"I was right," he said.

"About what?" John asked, unsure about what was meant.

"As I was spying on you on that bridge, I realised you're probably the most well equipped military unit left in the country. I tried telling those fucking pratts but they weren't having it, said we could take you, anyway. Everything went black at around that point. Now I know I was right. Where the fuck have you guys been hiding?" he asked, genuinely interested.

"We were based in Scotland. When things started getting out of hand, we took over a castle up there. Altogether we were there for about two years," Robert said. "We decided there was no future in staying there, so we left. We've been on the road now for three days."

"Where are you heading? You know the whole country is gone. There's nothing left, anywhere. We've been travelling around for months, on the run if the truth was known but these things always turned up, no matter where we went," Vinny said.

Before Robert had a chance to answer Vinny's question about their planned destination, John butted in.

"We're not sure yet. At the moment we are just heading south, maybe to the coast. Once we get there, we'll play it by ear."

Vinny smiled. "I get it, you don't trust me. I don't blame you. I'd probably be the same way. Look, don't worry about me, I'm finished with those wankers. They left me for dead! You don't forget something like that so quickly. In time, I'll prove that you can trust me."

Shit, John thought, this guy is no fool, he saw right through me.

"You've got to understand, Vinny, we have to be sure. At the moment we can't afford to lose our advantage. We are pretty sure we can trust you but until we are certain, we have to be careful. We're not in the habit of taking too many risks and we aren't going to start now," John said.

"I understand, John, no problem. Honestly."

"What can we expect from your friends?" Robert asked.

"They're no friends of mine," Vinny answered, sounding agitated by the question. "I've no idea. They aren't too bright, at least from a military point of view. They are used to all-out fights, nothing too clever. I would imagine they will wait somewhere and ambush you as you're passing by."

"Would they be prepared to join us?" John asked.

"What?" Robert asked. "Why would we want that, John?"

"Think about it. The way things stand, we've got the creatures to contend with and now the possibility of a running gun battle with these bikers. It's a complication we don't need. If we offered them the chance of joining us and they accepted, we've one problem less. Plus, we would be considerably stronger because of it."

"Makes sense," Robert agreed, but Vinny put the dampers on the idea.

"No chance," he said. "They'll want it all, everything you've got. Sharing with others is something they don't do well, believe me. Quite a few of the guys are really okay but Snake, the leader now, is a born again Nazi. He'll kill you for your fucking socks! No, I'm sorry, John, that's not the way to go."

"What do you suggest we do?" Robert asked.

"For the time being, wait. Keep your heads down, sooner or later they'll make their move. All you can do is try to work around them but don't be mistaken, you'll have to take them. They won't leave you any other choice."

"Thanks for your honesty. What are you going to do? Stay with us or do you still want to leave?" John asked.

"I might have been one of them for a while but I'm not bloody stupid. I'll stick around if that's still alright with you guys," Vinny said.

"It's alright with us," John said, stretching out his hand. "Welcome aboard."

Robert and Stephanie also shook his hand, both saying they were convinced he had made the right decision.

"Come on, let's get something to eat. Afterwards we can show you around a little more, work on that trust thing," John suggested, smiling.

"Great, but can we take it easy? I don't want to sound like a baby but my back is killing me," Vinny said.

"Don't worry about that, I'm use to babies," John said, staring at Robert.

He was remembering how Robert had constantly moaned about riding in the tank and how his back had hurt him. Robert, realising what John was implying, started to say something but just ended up laughing out loud.

"Am I missing something?" Vinny asked.

"I'll tell you about it sometime," John laughed.

As they were eating, the conversation got around to how Vinny and his gang had dealt with the creatures all the time they had been on the road. The ex-biker explained that they had had no real problems at all, that is until the bigger ones started to appear. These bigger versions only seemed to be in the middle of the country. The bikers had travelled down as far as the south coast but had not come across any there. They had always used hit and run tactics to avoid getting cornered but the new monsters were stronger and faster. This fact had allowed them, on several occasions, to corner the biker's gang by blocking roads with heavy objects. These instances had resulted in the gang losing quite a few of their men. John also asked how the gang had managed to kill the bigger creatures. Vinny had confirmed the usual ways, guns, bullets and knives! This fact had amazed even John, who found it hard to believe it would be possible. Vinny had confirmed that they were harder to kill than their smaller brothers but not impossible. He had noticed, on more than one occasion, that as soon as all of the smaller ones were dead, the bigger ones just seemed to mill around as if not knowing what to do. He was certain that the smaller ones were the brains, the bigger ones the muscle. John felt that this information was very useful, as the problems they were anticipating might not be as serious as they had first thought.

After they finished eating, they led Vinny back to the hospital truck, where he would again spend the night. The doctor examined him, deciding everything was alright. In fact the exertion had apparently done him good, the pain he had experienced in his back just stiffness. They said goodnight and left him there resting but promised to rescue him in the morning.

Outside the hospital truck John told Robert that Vinny's experience in dealing with the creatures, both big and small, might prove valuable to them. It could be lucky that they had found him when they did. They decided to get some sleep while everything was still quiet and retired to their respective trucks. Nobody was sure how long it would stay quiet, only time would tell.

Chapter Thirty Nine - Night Attack

John had been asleep for several hours when Mark woke him up.

"We're getting something on the radio, John, Robert sent me to fetch you. Sorry I had to wake you."

"No problem, mate. I'll get dressed but keep it quiet. I'd rather Stephanie slept a bit longer, she needs her rest at the moment. It's hard enough trying to sleep in one of these truck cabs. God knows how the men who used to drive the damn things for a living ever managed it night after night."

Without waking her, he quickly dressed. They had not had a good night's sleep for a while now, this was the first night she had slept well for ages and was exactly what the doctor had ordered. He headed, together with Mark, over to the truck where Robert was standing. As he reached there, he could hear why Robert had thought it important enough to wake him.

"Hey, you guys in the convoy, we know you can hear us. We just want to talk."

John started to whisper, he was not sure why because nobody, apart from Robert and Mark, could hear him anyway.

"Who is it? Have they said anything else?" he asked.

"We don't know for sure," Robert answered. "And we haven't answered yet but I think we can have a pretty good idea who it is."

The voice on the radio spoke again.

"Come on, you can talk to us. What are you afraid of?"

In the background noise, during the brief transmission, it was clear other men were laughing, obviously finding the whole thing funny.

"What do we do?" Robert asked, looking at John. "Should we answer?"

"No, for the moment we do nothing. Keep them guessing. You're right, it can only be the bikers. There's no real other possibility and we know exactly what they want," John answered. "The best bet is we wake Vinny, see if he can recognise any of the voices. Maybe he can talk some sense into them and save us all a load of trouble," John suggested.

Mark was sent to fetch Vinny from the hospital truck. After a few minutes he came hobbling up. The radio was chattering again.

"How many of you are there? There's twenty of us. We could sure use some food. Can you spare us any?"

John signalled to the radio operator, not a word, not yet.

"Oh come on, this is fucking stupid. We know you can hear us, we promise we won't hurt any of you, honestly."

Just before the signal cut off, laughter could clearly be heard in the background again.

John turned to Vinny, apologised for waking him and asked if the gang of bikers he had ridden with had had a radio set?

"Yes, a small short wave set," Vinny told him. "I'm surprised at this though, John, I don't know what they are playing at. They are definitely in this general area though because the radio that we had didn't have much of a range. You'd better be ready for anything."

At that moment the radio spoke again.

"Yo! Soldier boys, I'm getting fucking annoyed slowly. Why won't you speak to us, we don't want any trouble, we just want to talk?"

After listening carefully to the voice, Vinny said, "That's Snake."

"Are you sure?" John asked, although he had suspected it would be.

"Dead sure. I don't have a clue what his game is though. It's definitely Snake. Should I speak to him?" Vinny asked.

The question made John feel nervous, he was not sure why. He looked at Robert who nodded slightly.

"Okay, Vinny, see what he wants," John instructed.

"Yo soldier boys. Come on, this is getting boring, say hello," Snake said.

Vinny took the radio and spoke.

"Snake, why are you bothering my new friends?"

For a second nothing happened. The radio that had been noisy for the last ten minutes was suddenly quiet. John imagined the look of surprise on Snake's face. He pictured the scene as the radio had spoken back to him, even calling him by his name. He would not be so cocky now. After nearly a minute the radio came back to life.

"Who the fuck is this? How do you know my name?"

"Now Snake, don't tell me you've forgotten your old pal already," Vinny answered, smirking.

He was obviously enjoying himself.

"My old pal? I don't have any fucking pals, mate! Who are you?"

"It's me, Snake. It's your old pal Vinny."

"Vinny's dead. Who are you, you wanker?"

"You left me for dead but you were too stupid to check I was really dead. Well, surprise, I wasn't. Now you're the leader, I'll bet the guys are thrilled with the prospect," Vinny said, goading him.

"Vinny, it is you. Next time I'll make sure, I'll cut your fucking head off!" Snake screamed.

"Now that's not very nice, is it? I've called for a chat about the good old days and all you can do is shout stupid threats at me. It hurts!" Vinny said, really getting into his role.

John almost choked trying not to laugh.

"Just stop fucking about and listen, Vinny. Tell your soldier friends to give up. We want their supplies and their women. If they are good boys, we might even let them go."

"Don't be a wanker, Snake. These guys will kick your arses, you've no chance. These people are okay, they've even suggested you could all join them, share the food and supplies with them," Vinny suggested.

"We don't want to share, we want it all. If they won't give it us then we'll just take it and kill every last one of the fuckers!"

"Snake, be reasonable. Forget our differences for the moment. This is a fight you can't hope to win. You're outnumbered and outgunned. Tell the men the truth, let them decide for themselves," Vinny asked, almost pleading.

"Don't be so fucking stupid, this isn't a democracy. I'm the fucking boss now. So fuck you and fuck all your friends!"

The radio went dead.

"Good try, mate," John said. "Do you think it made any difference?"

As if answering John's question, shots rang out in the darkness.

"Shit!" John shouted. "It's a night attack. The bloody idiots."

Telling Vinny to stay put where he was, John and Robert ran from the cover of the truck to see exactly what was happening. Their men were quickly taking cover, Mark running over to them.

"What's the story, Mark, where are the idiots?" John asked, agitated.

"They're in the trees, over to the left of the bridge, on the slope of the hill. They're firing blind at us. They can't see anything, as long as we keep our heads down we'll be okay," Mark reported.

"They might not be able to hit us but the constant firing will alert any creatures in the area to our presence. If they continue for long, we'll soon have company. We can't afford to get dragged into a battle just because these pratts won't listen to reason," John argued.

"Should I take a platoon and go in after them?" Mark asked.

"No, I won't risk one of our men on these fucking bullies. Get four or five mortars set up and blast them out. Tell the men on the mortars to watch out for rifle flashes and home in on them. They'll soon get the message and piss off."

Mark barked a few orders and mortars were hastily set up. After only a few minutes, they commenced firing. Explosions erupted on the hillside, where the bikers were hiding but the gunfire continued.

"They don't give up easily, do they?" Robert remarked.

"Pour it in there," John shouted to Mark, over the noise of the gunfire.

The mortar fire increased in quantity, starting to prove effective, the gunfire decreasing slowly. The bikers were either pulling back or falling to the withering explosions raining down all around them. After another five minutes all gunfire had ceased, John telling the mortar crews to cease fire.

It was quiet again, John still could not believe how stupid the bikers had been. To attack a well-defended position at night, without air support, without night vision technology at least, was suicide. He told Mark to check for casualties or damage.

"Pratts!" Robert said, annoyed.

"Yeah. I doubt they'll try it again in a hurry. Nobody is that stupid but just in case they do, we'd better be ready. Issue the guys up on the truck roofs night vision scopes. If there's a next time, we'll be able to pick them off. Shit, we should have expected a dumb move like this and prepared for it," John said, also angry.

"We can't be prepared for everything, mate, especially being attacked by crazy bastards like these. Don't knock yourself, you can't second guess anything like this," Robert said, patting John on the shoulder.

Mark came walking up, he looked shocked.

"What's up, mate, have we got wounded?" John asked, suddenly worried.

Mark nodded.

"Three wounded, two of them seriously John. Just flukes really, nobody could have known," he hesitated.

"What's up, mate?" John asked.

"John, one of them is Stephanie. She got hit leaving the truck where she was sleeping. I'm sorry, mate, she's in a bad way!"

John Stewart started to run.

Chapter Forty - The Operation

John ran to the converted hospital truck. Where was she? Was she still alive? The questions were racing through his mind. He needed answers, otherwise he would explode.

As he entered the truck, he found the doctor already inside. He was scrubbing up, as if getting ready to operate on somebody.

"Where's my wife, doctor? How is she? Why are you just standing around doing nothing?"

He sounded really panicked. Robert, who was two paces behind him, could understand why.

"She's alive at the moment. I need to operate and remove the bullet. I'll know more into the procedure. I'm sorry John but you can't be here, I need the truck sealed and clean. I'll let you know as soon as possible how she's doing. Now get out!"

John, tears running down his cheeks, shouted.

"No, I won't leave her and you can't fucking make me!"

The doctor turned to Robert.

"Major, get him out of here, please. He can't do anything at the moment, apart from stop me trying to save her. The longer he stays, the less time I have to operate. She is losing a lot of blood, I don't know for sure how long she can hold on. Do something for Christ's sake, otherwise your friend's wife will most surely die!"

Robert and Mark both grabbed John and dragged him out, he was almost hysterical. Once outside, Robert took him by the shoulders and turning him around, he slapped him hard across the face. John just stared for a second, Robert almost panicking himself, the look so intimidating but John simply said, "Thank you. "He sat down and buried his head in his hands, still sobbing but basically back in control.

"John, come on. You can't stay here. She's in good hands. The doctor will fetch us when there's any news, you have to believe she'll be fine," Robert said quietly.

"I can't leave her, Robert, I love her. Without her, I'm finished. What would I do without her, what?"

They led him slowly away from the hospital truck towards the centre of the campsite.

"Come on, let's find you a drink. I'm sure we can find a bottle of Scotch or something similar. Those pratts may yet come back for another go," Robert suggested.

"Those bastards! If she dies, I'll hunt every last fucking one of them down and kill them with my bare hands!" John said, the threat sounding more like a promise.

"If that's the case then we'll all help you, mate but don't think like that. She's going to make it, she's strong. You have to believe that, you have to," Robert said.

They led him further into the camp. Robert decided he needed a drink as well. His best friend's wife, maybe dying after such a stupid stunt pulled by bikers, it was not fair. After all they had been through to get where they were, if she were to die, John would probably never recover. It was still a shitty world in a shitty mess and they were stuck right in the middle of it.

They were all sitting with John, drinking coffee. He had refused anything else. His need to keep his head clear, the excuse for not opening the bottle of Scotch. Nobody really knew what to say, how could they? None of them was married, not even close.

Although they had warned against it, Vinny had come over to speak to John. Nobody was really sure how John, in his current frame of mind, would react to this as Vinny had played his part as catalyst in the night's tragic events.

"John," Vinny said, wary of what might happen.

"What do you want, Vinny?" John asked. "It's not a good time."

"I just wanted to say how sorry I am. If there's anything I can do?"

"Thanks but, at the moment, only two powers can help me. One is God who is hopefully on our side today. The other is the doctor, who has the power to save her in his hands. The rest of you should leave me the fuck alone!" John said deliberately.

"It's best you go, Vinny. He'll be okay, we'll stay with him," Robert said, gesturing to Vinny that he should leave. "Okay, John?" he asked, timidly.

"I'm fine, Robert but I won't be okay again until she's okay. Now leave me alone, please."

They left him alone but sat nearby waiting for news. It had already been over an hour and, as far as they knew, the doctor was still operating. How long, they all wondered, how long before John Stewart exploded?

The minutes felt like days, the wait agonising for them, so for John it must have been almost unbearable. After what seemed like forever, the doctor appeared, looking exhausted.

"How is she, doctor?" John asked, jumping up.

"She should make it," the doctor announced. "There is always the chance of secondary infection but I think she'll be okay. She's strong."

"Thank God," John said, sinking to his knees.

"Oh, John," Robert sighed. "We told you she'd be fine."

"When can I see her?" John asked, a sense of urgency in his voice.

"It'll be a while. John, there were complications, we did everything we could but . . ." the doctor said.

He paused, suddenly seeming more upset than before.

"What is it, what's happened, doctor?" John asked, the panic returning.

"She's lost the baby, John! There was nothing we could do, no way to stop it. The trauma, the blood loss, it brought on a miscarriage. I'm so very sorry, John."

"Shit!" John whispered, the tears flowing again.

Robert and Mark went to console him, both of them crying.

"Does she know?" John asked, sobbing.

"She hasn't regained consciousness yet, she doesn't know. It might be better if you told her. There were no complications with the miscarriage, that happens sometimes, so she can still have children. John, do you understand me? Be sure to tell her that, it will help," the doctor said.

"Yes. When can I see her?"

"Maybe this afternoon, she needs to rest. At the moment she's on medication to prevent infection but by this afternoon she should be feeling better, at least medically. I have to get back, we have other patients. One of them is unfortunately critical. John, come and see me later, I'll tell you when you can see her," the doctor said, then turning to Robert he continued. "Make sure he comes to me first, Major, I don't want any risk of infection. Alright?"

"Okay, doctor, thanks. Get back to your patients, we'll stay with him."

As the doctor left, Robert sat down next to John.

"She's alive, mate, that's the main thing," he said.

"How am I going to tell her, Robert? How?" John asked.

"I don't know, mate, I don't know."

Chapter Forty One - The Visit

Robert organised the convoy and they left the area where the surprise attack had taken place that night. John, still shocked over the news of his and Stephanie's loss, had not spoken to anybody since the doctor had left. Robert thoroughly understanding the terrible situation, had not pressed him. He could not imagine what John was going through. On the one hand, his wife's life had been saved, on the other, his unborn child had died during the life saving procedure! The mixture of such emotions was a dangerous combination. Now it was down to John to find a way to tell Stephanie the terrible news. As far as he was aware she had no idea that her baby had died during the operation. Robert wondered what effect it would have on her. He did not envy John the task at all.

Vinny had wanted to talk to John again but Robert had persuaded him otherwise, still not sure how John would react to the ex-gang member. He suggested Vinny wait until John had had the chance to talk to Stephanie.

The whole convoy had been shocked by the attack. They were especially saddened to find out the attack had been made by fellow human beings only after what they could get. That three people were wounded as a result had deepened the shock but when the news spread about John and Stephanie's loss, a lot of people had wept openly. The closeness of the small community an established fact, everyone sharing their loss.

Although a lot of people sympathised with John, it was not to be forgotten that two other people had been wounded during the attack. One of Robert's Corporals had been lightly wounded in the shoulder but was expected to make a full recovery. The other casualty was sadly a civilian member of the population. As far as Robert could remember, it was the first time ever, at least since they had taken over the castle complex that a civilian had been injured. He found it sadly ironic that the man in question had been shot by other survivors of the war with the creatures. To survive so long, during which time thousands if not millions of people had fallen prey to the unyielding creatures, only to be shot by a gang of cut-throats. It seemed so unfair. The casualty in question had been shot in the head area and was reported to be in a critical condition. His name, Robert had swallowed hard as he had been told, was Smythe. He was the retired car ferry owner who was supposed to help them once they had acquired a ship. It appeared that would now be unlikely and Robert could not help wondering how they would get around the problem.

All the fights and major battles they had fought against the creatures, they had had no serious casualties, with the exception of the supermarket in Hadlee where unfortunately three men had died. It was hard to believe that a minor scuffle with a gang of idiots could have been so devastating.

They had made good time since leaving the campsite, experiencing no further problems that morning. Robert estimated they were east of Birmingham heading towards the ruins of Coventry, still on the M6. He had decided they should take a break. The night before they had nearly all gone without sleep and he could tell a lot of people were tired. He ordered the stop, instructing Mark over the truck's radio, an hour's break would do everybody some good.

The mood amongst the convoy residents was subdued. They were sitting around in small groups discussing the events of the previous night but, although upset by everything that had happened, they were still resolved to carry on and try to finish their journey. Robert wondered how many more times their resolve would be tested before they reached safety.

Suddenly, he caught sight of John apparently heading towards the hospital. Robert caught him up and asked him where he was going?

"Where do you think? I'm going to see my wife and tell her we've lost our child!" John answered, deliberately.

Robert tried to stop him but John was not having it; he shoved Robert up against one of the nearby trucks. For a second it looked as if he would get violent, Robert worried John was going to hit him. Instead, John let him go and stood there, his head hanging.

"If I don't do it now, I won't be able to, Robert. I won't have the nerve again, don't you understand? It has to be now while I'm still able to do it," John babbled.

"Okay, John," Robert said, realising John was on the edge. "We'll have to check with the doctor first. As long as he agrees, you can see her. Okay?"

"Alright," John agreed.

They had checked with the doctor, he had said yes but not for too long. She still needed a lot of rest. Robert asked if he should go with him, John saying thanks but no thanks. It was something he had to do alone. He climbed into the hospital truck and saw her for the first time since the night attack. She was lying on a cot, motionless, hooked up to all types of monitors, drips and with all kinds of tubes protruding out of her body. At first he was shocked, he had not been prepared for the scene that greeted him. With tears again running down his cheeks, he walked the few steps up to her bedside. She appeared to be sleeping. He took her hand in his and whispered.

"Stephanie, can you hear me?"

There was no reaction at all, he tried again.

"Stephanie, wake up, it's John."

This time her eyelids fluttered and she slowly opened her eyes.

"John. John, is it really you?"

"Yes, my darling. I'm here."

"John. I'm so sorry. I heard shooting and I wanted to find you, to make sure you were safe."

"Don't worry now. The doctor says you're going to be fine. In a couple of days you'll be as good as new," he was crying again.

"John, I'm sorry."

"You've nothing to be sorry about, the main thing is you get well. I need you, you know that, my life's not worth shit without you looking after me."

"I lost our baby, John, I felt it die inside me!"

He just stared for a second. Nothing could have prepared him for what she had just said. She already knew. How could she know?

"I know but it wasn't your fault, it was mine. I should have . . ."

She interrupted him.

"No! It wasn't your fault, just stop it. You blame yourself for everything that goes wrong. You've got to stop it, John. Without you, I would have died months ago. You're my reason to live."

"I love you. It's probably not the right time to tell you this but the doctor says we can still have children. There weren't any complications, so as soon as you're well enough, if you want, we can try again," John said, not sure it was the right thing to say.

"I'd like that but not here. When we are safe, away from those things, then we can try," she answered.

"Once we're safe, we'll have all the children you want. I promise," he told her, squeezing her hand.

"Once we're safe. We'll make it, John, won't we?"

"You bet. I'll get you out of here, no matter what. Nothing can stop me. You just get well. I love you."

"I'm tired, John, I want to sleep," she said, barely able to keep her eyes open.

"Then sleep. I'll come back later when you're feeling better."

She closed her eyes and in a few seconds was asleep again. He checked the monitors, for a second almost panicking but she was fine. He left her, after kissing her gently on the forehead and went outside where Robert was still waiting for him. He felt so relieved he hugged Robert, the emotion of the visit getting to him.

"How is she, John?" Robert asked.

"She's okay, mate, she's going to be fine," John said, tears again welling up in his eyes.

"Thank God, John. I'm so happy for you," Robert said, this time he hugged John.

"We've got to get away from this crazy place. I promised her we'd make it and we will," John stated, renewed determination in his voice.

"We will, John, we will, but we have a problem," Robert informed him.

"What?" John asked.

"Mr Smythe died ten minutes ago, he never regained consciousness."

"Shit, I heard a commotion in there but didn't take any notice. I was too involved with Stephanie. Those fucking bikers, they've got a lot to answer for. If I ever come across them again . . ." he left the sentence hanging but Robert understood what he meant.

"John, we have nobody who can sail the ferry now, we're knackered."

"No, mate, we'll find a way," John reassured him. "How hard can it be?"

"Maybe you're right, we've managed to achieve so many things I thought were impossible. We'll manage that as well, somehow."

John suggested they go and console the wife of the deceased, they would have time later to discuss other problems. They had a funeral to organise, something that would prove difficult standing on a road bridge, situated on a motorway. They could also expect the biker gang, that had instigated the last few hours tragic events, to return and try again. John had the opinion they would not give up so easily and they needed to prepare certain measures to combat the threat. However this time, if they wanted a fight they would get one, a fight they would not forget in a hurry, that is, if they even survived it.

244

Chapter Forty Two - The Rescue

John and Robert both expressed their condolences to Mrs. Smythe who was obviously very distraught at the loss of her husband. John felt responsible for the man's death, as it had been his idea to leave the castle. If they had stayed put, the old man would still have been alive.

Mrs. Smythe told him not to think that way. Although her husband had argued against leaving at first, he had quickly realised it was the right thing to do for everybody. He had expressed his admiration for John, on numerous occasions, having witnessed several times how John had risked his life for all of them. John had made a lasting impression on him and he had been proud to be able to play a small part in the adventure, especially with his part involving his beloved ferries. They had provided him with a good lifestyle and he was exceptionally thrilled when he had realised they would play such a key role in their survival. It had given him another lease of life and she was thankful for that. Her only regret about the whole situation was that her husband had always wanted to be buried at sea, this would now be impossible. John turned to Robert and, after a short discussion, they decided to honour the man's last request. They would take his body along with them and, once safely at sea, carry out his wish. She thanked them both for their compassion and retired to the truck where she had been sleeping, to get some rest.

Both John and Robert let out great sighs after Mrs. Smythe left, the responsibility of leadership never more apparent than now. They were both certain they had done the right thing. The body of Mr. Smythe would be transported, for now at least, in the hospital truck. With a little bit of luck, in another day or so, they would reach the ship and be in a position to keep their promise. John looked at Robert, saying this was one of the reasons why he never wanted to lead, had always fought against the idea. Robert agreed it was a hard part of the job but it was something that needed doing every now and then. They had been lucky up to now. During the Third World War, he had delivered sad news to relatives on almost a daily basis. It was a duty he would not wish on anyone. The sadness of such occasions, something he could never forget. He could fully understand John's point of view but, as he had said before, some people were born to lead. He was certain John was one of these gifted people and not to use the ability would be wrong. However difficult it became, they would succeed in leading together. As for now, it was time for a strong coffee. Caffeine had always helped, it would help now.

They sat with Mark, discussing the danger of the gang coming back. They decided extra measures should be organised to counteract another attack, whether at night or in the daytime. Afterwards they had eaten. John, knowing Stephanie was now going to be all right, was returning to his old self. He had two helpings.

Vinny appeared and once again apologised for the gang's actions. He felt responsible for the attack, feeling he had pushed Snake too far. John, back to thinking clearly, told him he was wrong. The gang members had already been in position to attack, before Vinny had even said a word. Only one idiot was responsible and that was Snake. John now apologised to Vinny. Because he had been so concerned about Stephanie, he had treated him badly. He had not meant to. He knew the whole episode had basically nothing to do with him, he had just been in the wrong place at the wrong time. Vinny accepted John's apology, telling him it was not necessary. He was pleased Stephanie would be fine but was sorry they had lost their child. He told John if there was anything he could ever do to make up for the gang's actions, he had only to ask. John told him to forget it - friends did not need to think that way.

The convoy got underway again. To be sure of clearing the Dead Zone, they needed to travel past the pre-war town of Leicester and then turn north. John suggested they travel beyond the point chosen for that night's stop and try to get as far as possible, stopping somewhere between Coventry and Leicester. This might throw the bikers off and disrupt any plans they may have made. To get that far, they would have to risk travelling at night, at least for a short time but it would mean they were probably less than a day's travel from New Hull and their goal.

Robert agreed it was worth the risk and suggested organising the men accordingly. As they were already moving, it was all done using the radios and intercom systems, the civilians being told they would have to wait a little longer than normal for their evening meal that day. The Apache helicopter was already in the air and was sent on ahead to check for signs of trouble, Bravo One was riding on it's platform. They felt that the Apache, using the advanced technology it possessed, might have more luck locating the bikers or any creatures in the area. The pilots, although not as talented as Stephanie, were very capable of flying the deadly machine and its added firepower in any combat situation would prove valuable. Until she was well enough to fly again, the other two pilots would take turns patrolling in the attack aircraft.

John, using the radio, checked with the doctor regarding Stephanie's condition. The doctor was pleased to tell him she was steadily improving and over the worst. He could relax and get back to protecting the convoy. This had cheered John up even more and with lack of sleep finally catching up with him, he had slept for the first time in nearly twenty-four hours. He had only been asleep for about an hour when Robert suddenly woke him.

"John, wake up. The Apache pilot is on the radio, there's trouble ahead."

John quickly realised the convoy was not moving anymore. He was puzzled at first but then Robert carried on explaining.

"The Apache is about ten minutes ahead of us. It was returning to refuel when it spotted our biker friends or what's left of them, at least. They are on a bridge overlooking the motorway. It appears they were planning a little ambush for us but unfortunately for them, they've been ambushed themselves. On both sides of the bridge, the pilot can see creatures attacking. He's reporting a number of the bigger ones are amongst the attackers. The bikers are trapped and heavily outnumbered, he's not sure how long they can hold out. What do you want to do?"

"Why have we stopped?" John asked, seeming remarkably calm to Robert.

"I didn't want to run into a gunfight," Robert answered. "John, what should we do? The Apache pilot is requesting permission to engage the creatures. What should I tell him?"

"Tell him no!" John said, coldly.

"What about the bikers?" Robert asked, puzzled at John's reaction.

"Fuck 'em!" John said. "They've made their bed, let them lie in it."

"What? I know you don't mean that. Think about what you're saying. We can't just leave them and not do anything. I can understand that you're still upset but that's not the way and you know it," Robert argued.

"They can fight the creatures and keep them of our backs. We can just drive right past. Perfect for us, bad luck for them," John stated, he had had enough of the bikers to last a lifetime.

"John, I'm sorry but I can't and, what's more, I won't just drive past and leave them to their fate. No matter what they've done. It strikes me this Snake character is the black sheep, the rest of them are just soldiers following orders. They do what they are told or else they have to answer to him. You can't condemn them all because of one idiot."

John appeared to think about what Robert had said for a minute, then spoke again.

"Yeah, okay, you're right," he said, coming to his senses. "We should help them if we can but, after we've risked our lives for them, they'd better prove to me it was worth it otherwise they won't enjoy the consequences."

"Good, I'll tell the Apache to attack," Robert said.

"No," John said. "There's a better way. Get Bravo One ready for take off. Tell Mark to pick another six guys out of my team. They need to be well armed, we'll need to take plenty of ammunition with us. We'll need some of the newer weapons, especially if the big boys are about. Bravo One can fly us in and drop us behind the creatures to the west of the bridge, then together with the Apache, it should attack the creatures on the east side. We'll attack the creatures on the west side from behind. If any of the bikers are still alive and fighting, we'll get the monsters in a crossfire. Tell the Apache to wait for our arrival, we'll be there in a few minutes. In the meantime you get the convoy rolling again. I want you through and away, just in case things go wrong."

"We're better waiting here, what if you need back up? If you run into trouble we won't be in a position to help you," Robert argued.

"By the time you hit the bridge, Robert, either it'll all be over or they'll all be dead. You keep going, we'll catch up. I won't risk any more men or waste any more time on these pratts."

"I don't like it, John, it's bloody dangerous for your team," Robert said, unsure.

"Robert, it's this way or the highway. Every minute we stand here arguing, there's less chance of any of those wankers still being alive. Now make up your mind, please."

"Okay, John, we do it your way."

"Good. Tell Mark to pick the men and meet me by the helicopter in two minutes. I'll get my gear," and he ran off.

Robert found Mark and told him. He moved off quickly, shouting names and instructions.

The group of men was sitting in the helicopter, together with John, three minutes later. They were heavily armed, with both their normal weaponry and some of the recently modified weapons. These were to be used specifically on any of the big creatures they came across. The helicopter took off and sped down the motorway towards the bridge, where the bikers were fighting for their lives.

Robert saw them off, then started to get the convoy moving again. His job was to ensure the convoy got through the battlefield without being molested. As he was shouting orders, he bumped into Vinny.

"What's going on, Robert?" he asked.

"We're trying to save what's left of your ex-friends. They are under attack from creatures a little further down the road. John's leading a rescue mission now."

"After what they did last night? I hope you know what you're doing," Vinny told him.

Robert boarded his truck. He still had to tell the Apache pilot what was happening, then they would leave.

In Bravo One John was briefing his men.

"This has all been thrown together quickly, so we have to be bloody careful. I can't afford to lose any of you, so be advised, if we run into difficulties we'll be leaving quickly. As of that moment, the bikers are on their own. Now listen up. We'll be dropped behind the creatures to the west of the bridge. The two helicopters will then attack the east side. We'll attempt to break through to the bikers and get any of them that are still alive out. There aren't many of us but we've had bad odds before. There are apparently several of the big creatures in the area, use the new weapons on them. They shouldn't be a problem. Because we are attacking them from behind, we should have the advantage of surprise on our side for a change. Hit them hard. I'd rather not get down to swordplay, so make your shots count. As soon as we've subdued the creatures enough that the bikers can leave, we'll be getting out again via Bravo One. Whether the survivors come with us or not will be their decision. Everything clear, check your weapons and get ready. Good luck."

The helicopter was approaching the bridge, the Apache pilot reporting that a number of bikers was still alive and fighting. John checked his weapons, apart from his normal rifle, pistols and sword, he was also carrying one of the high tech. bows and several of the explosive heads. Although his heart was not really interested in rescuing any of the men who had nearly killed

Stephanie and cost them the life of their unborn baby, he was interested in testing the bow's ability to deal with the bigger monsters. Looking at their current situation as a way to test their abilities in direct conflict against the big creatures, was the only way he could mentally justify being there. A part of him felt he was betraying Stephanie, in attempting to rescue the arseholes who were responsible for her injuries but he knew her well enough to realise she would have insisted on his taking part in the rescue mission, no matter what had happened. She would have made him realise it was the right thing to do.

"Okay, pilot, drop us off behind the attacking creatures to the west of the bridge, then rendezvous with the Apache and commence your attack. Stay on channel in case we need immediate pick up, clear?" John told the pilot of Bravo One.

The pilot nodded. John had learnt in his time at the castle how well he could trust the helicopter pilots, they had saved his life on numerous occasions. He suddenly realised he did not even know their names. It seemed stupid to know the call sign of a helicopter, and not know its pilot's name. He would have to remedy the situation at some time.

The helicopter was in position behind the creatures, hovering low enough for them to be able to jump out. After they exited the aircraft, it flew off to join up with the Apache and carry out their part of the mission.

John checked his weapons one more time. He looked at his men, they were ready.

"Okay, let's move in. Fire at your first opportunity. Let's get them."

They attacked, shooting the creatures in the backs, not hesitating for a second. Some of the creatures turning to meet them but their fire was so accurate that many of the creatures, so taken by surprise, never stood a chance.

Suddenly, one of the bigger monsters appeared in front of them, John ordering the use of R.P.Gs. Two of these were used simultaneously. The resulting explosion died and it started to rain pieces of the creature that had just been annihilated. There was nothing left of it, his men letting out a cheer.

"Close with them, finish them off," John shouted.

On the other side of the bridge the explosions were dying out but the scatter guns from the two helicopters were still firing.

Back on John's side, the remaining creatures were trying to escape the unceasing rain of bullets but John and his men weren't prepared to allow that. They closed in, killing anything that moved.

Another one of the big monsters appeared but it seemed lost and confused. It was just as Vinny had said, without the smaller ones to control them, they were not as frightening after all. John took the bow off his back and reached for one of the explosive heads. The creature was basically just standing there, John almost felt sorry for it but he knew at any time it could turn into a killing machine, nearly unstoppable. He took careful aim and whispering 'Bite my ass' to himself, he fired. The arrow struck home and a second later it was raining again.

Suddenly, the firing on his side of the bridge stopped. All the creatures were either dead or dying. He could see the bikers, at least what was left of them, coming out from behind their bikes. There were eleven of them left alive. He approached them.

"You guys, get on your bikes and split, fast. There'll be more of them coming. I'm not sure how long you've got," he told them.

One of the younger bikers asked, "Where should we go?"

"You've got two choices, you can come with us or you can go where you want. I warn you now, if you leave and I ever see you again, I'll kill you! Those of you who decide to come with us will be welcome. It's up to you."

He contacted Bravo One, telling the pilot to land and pick them up. The Apache should finish off any creatures that were still left in the fight. Although, judging by the amount of firing that was still going on, he assumed the fight was almost over.

The convoy had passed under the bridge a good five minutes ago, basically unnoticed by the creatures or indeed the bikers. Both elements were so intent on staying alive, they had not noticed the passing trucks.

His men were back on board the helicopter. Two of them were slightly injured but only cuts and bruises. They had performed superbly again. Even the bigger creatures had been unable to withstand their attack. Things were turning around, he could feel it.

The bikers made the only decision they could have made. They were following the convoy down the motorway. John was interested what Vinny would say when he saw them. He had a feeling it would prove to be a very interesting reunion.

Chapter Forty Three - The Reunion

The convoy had stopped again to allow the helicopters to land and refuel. The men who had just been involved in the rescue of what was left of the biker gang disembarking and returning to their trucks.

John and Mark walked up to Robert, reporting the mission had been successful. Robert asked how many of the bikers had survived and where they were? John told him eleven had survived the battle and they should be catching the convoy up at any second.

"Are they going to join us or can we expect more trouble?" Robert asked, on the one hand sure they had done the right thing rescuing the bikers, on the other realising there would, more than likely, be difficulties until the bikers settled in.

"Probably both," John answered, his opinion of the biker gang had not changed. They were scum!

He had been against rescuing the remaining gang members, feeling they were not worth the risk.

"What do you mean?" Robert asked him.

"Well to start with, it's going to be interesting to see how they react when Vinny appears, alive and well. I can't imagine that pratt, Snake told many of them about his radio conversation with him. He didn't seem the type to share information like that. The fact that Vinny is still alive would have weakened his hold on the gang members. Theoretically, you could say Vinny is still the leader. He's not dead, is he? All in all, the first meeting could prove to be exciting."

"That's true. It might be an idea to keep them all apart, at least until we stop for the night. We can control the situation better then, we don't need a confrontation now. What do you think?" Robert asked.

"I agree. We're out in the open here, we've no time for theatricals. Our best bet is to keep them moving. Tonight, when we eventually stop, maybe they'll be too tired to cause trouble . . ." John suggested.

At that moment the surviving bikers arrived. John looked at Robert.

"They're your problem now, I've done my bit. You explain it to them," and he walked off with Mark towards the truck, where his men were being treated by the doctor.

He wanted to check on them and then pay Stephanie a quick visit - there would be time enough to worry about the bikers later. He smelt trouble and hoped Robert would not, at any time, regret his decision to help them.

Stephanie was feeling much better and listened intently to his descriptions of the battle on the bridge. She asked him what he thought might happen when Vinny and the bikers were reunited. He told her he had no idea but of one thing he was certain, he would not stand for any of their shit. They would either fit in or fly, one way or another. She asked him to be careful and at least give them a chance. She knew the bikers were directly responsible for her being injured and the loss of their baby but she did not feel any hostility towards them. She could not explain why but in her opinion everything happened for a reason. It had not been the right time for them to have children, their situation too dangerous at the moment. She had felt this right from the beginning but had been happy and excited about the pregnancy nevertheless. Ever since she had woken up, after her operation, she had tried to think rationally about everything that had happened. She had come to the conclusion that, for whatever reason, God had wanted it this way. He had brought them together. He had kept John safe up to then. She thanked Him everyday for that. If the price of all that was losing her unborn child, then she could accept it. She loved John with all her heart, he gave her the strength to carry on and made her happy. Given the choice between losing him or anything else, no matter what it was, then she knew exactly what she would choose every time. John said he understood what she meant and promised her that everything would work out for the best. They would soon be safe, away from the creatures for good, somewhere where a normal life could be possible again. He was thankful he would be sharing his with her. He told her he would come and see her again once they stopped for the night. After kissing her, he left to join Robert in the lead truck.

In the meantime, Robert had instructed the remaining bikers to follow them, they were all filling their bikes with fuel as John walked up. He caught one of them, he seemed to be the biggest, staring at him, the biker's face filled with contempt. John did not feel like any trouble so he looked away, deciding to do what

Stephanie had asked, at least for now. When he looked back, the biker was gone, already moving off down the motorway.

"How do they seem?" he asked Robert who had walked over to him.

"They seem alright, a little wary of us. I don't think they believe we mean what we're saying about letting them come along. We'll watch them closely, just in case you're right. I've told Mark to alert the men. Don't worry, John, until we're sure, they'll get special attention, even if they don't realise it," Robert informed him, proudly.

"Well done, mate. We'll sort them out," John said, telling him Stephanie's reaction to the situation.

On the one hand, he found it unbelievable that his wife was so forgiving, on the other, it made him so proud. He was not quite as far down the road of forgiveness as she was. He would respect her wishes and give them a chance but he would scrutinise the bikers' actions until he felt sure they could be trusted.

"Where's Vinny?" he asked Robert.

"He's resting in the soldiers' truck. He's apparently had enough of the hospital and the doctor. He's still having a little pain but the doctor says it's normal, something to do with muscle damage in the area of his wound, nothing to worry about. A few hours sleep and he should feel better. As far as I know, he's heard about our biker friends but he's had the good sense to keep out of the way. Later tonight, he'll be up and about, then we'll see how he and they react," Robert explained.

"I'm not bothered about Vinny's reaction, he's one of us now. If any of those pratts cause agro with him, they'll have us to answer too," John said.

"It was still the right thing to do, John, you know that, don't you?" Robert stated, referring to the rescue.

"Yeah, I suppose so. Only trouble is, I've got a feeling it's not a done deal, not yet anyway. Time will tell. Anyway, I'm tired. I'm going to try and get a couple of hours sleep. Keep 'em moving. It would be nice to get past Coventry, somewhere close to the ruins of Leicester. It's nearly four o'clock now, aim to stop about sevenish. Wake me if there's a problem," John said.

"Don't worry, everything's under control. I'll wake you when we're stopping for the night," Robert told him.

John climbed into the bunk at the back of the cab. He felt terrible. The strain of the last twenty-four hours had almost been too much for him. He had been uncomfortably close to losing

Stephanie. He had lost their unborn child! Then the battle on the bridge. Within a few minutes he was sleeping deeply.

He was not sure how long he had been asleep but it was dark outside and the convoy had stopped. Looking out from the truck's cab, it appeared as if they were already camped on another bridge. He was beginning to dislike bridges. Climbing down from the cab, he could hear a commotion somewhere over to his left. He walked over that way to investigate.

The raised voices were coming from the centre of the camp. He could see a group of figures standing there, apparently locked in a hefty discussion about something. As he got nearer, he could see one of the figures was Robert, standing next to him was Mark. They were arguing with several of the bikers, one of whom seemed to be doing all the shouting. He approached Robert, asking what the problem was? Robert suggested he should ask the big biker making all the noise. He did.

"What's your problem?" John asked bluntly.

"We want our share of the gear now," demanded the big biker. "Then we'll decide if we stay or leave."

"Your share of the gear? You don't have a share," John told him, trying to stay calm.

He noticed that most of the other bikers were not getting involved in the argument, they were staying out of the way. This one guy seemed to be causing all the trouble on his own. John recognised him, he was the biker who had stared at him so funnily, earlier that afternoon.

"I reckon we're entitled," the big biker argued.

"You're entitled to shit!" John told him, slowly starting to get annoyed.

"Who the fuck are you?" the biker asked, menacingly.

"My name's John. I'm the pratt who led the team to rescue you wankers! Who the hell are you?" John asked back.

From behind him, a voice came out of the darkness.

"John, say hello to Snake. Just don't turn your back on him!"

It was Vinny, he had heard the commotion.

"Well, fuck me, if it isn't Vinny, still alive and on their side now," Snake said, his tone hostile.

Some of the other gang members seemed pleased to see Vinny but were obviously afraid to say so because of their fear of Snake. John could tell this guy would be a threat to the convoy and a danger to their success chances.

Vinny walked towards Snake.

"You're a prick, Snake, you always were. I should have known you'd stab me in the back the first chance you got. That's all you're capable of. You're just muscle, no brains at all! These people are giving you all a chance, one you don't deserve."

He turned to the other bikers who were all murmuring in the background.

"You guys need to think for yourselves for once. I know all of you and most of you are okay. This wanker shouldn't have the right to decide your future. Here, with us, you're a lot safer than out there on your own. You can't ignore that. This gorilla will get you all killed."

There were cries of agreement from most of the other bikers.

"Vinny's right."

"Yeah, listen to Vinny, he always steered us right."

This annoyed Snake even more.

"Shut your fucking mouths! As long as I'm leader, you'll do exactly what I tell you and you'll like it," he growled.

"Then maybe it's time for them to choose a new leader," Vinny said, deliberately.

Snake laughed. "You dozy bastard. You know dammed well this has never been a democracy. Nobody chooses shit! They want a new leader, somebody is going to have to grow some big balls quickly and fight me," Snake stated, obviously confident nobody would.

"I'll fight you, you prick!" John said, coolly.

"You! Why?" Snake asked.

"Because as their leader, you ordered that stupid night attack. My wife was hurt badly and we lost our baby because of it. That gives me reason enough," John told him

Snake smiled. "Ain't life a bitch!" he said coldly.

"Give me a second," John said.

He took off his jacket and handed it to Robert, saying if he lost Robert should shoot the big ape because he would cause trouble as long as he stayed with them. Mark suggested shooting him straightaway and drew his pistol. John saying no, he wanted the chance to beat the guy fairly and in front of the other bikers. He suspected that once Snake's hold on them was broken, the rest of them would fit in fine. Vinny came over warning John that Snake was powerful and fast. He should not underestimate him and to watch out for tricks. John told Vinny not to worry but thanked him for the advice.

He turned to face Snake. He was ready.

Chapter Forty Four - The Fight

They stood facing each other.

Snake had also removed his jacket, revealing a body rippling with muscle.

"I'm going to break your fucking neck, soldier boy," he goaded.

John smiled at him telling him to go for it.

The two circled each other, looking for an opening. Snake was taunting John the whole time about his wife's injuries.

"It's a pity she didn't die, boy. Then again, if she was dead, I wouldn't be able to show her what a real man can do."

"You gonna fight or talk me to death," John said, still smiling.

John snapped his left fist out towards the biker's jawbone, his hand connecting squarely with the big man's jaw.

Snake did not react, he just brushed the blow off and flicked his own right out. John jerked his head back from it but not quickly enough. The biker's fist impacted John's jaw on the left side, near the base. He stumbled backwards, his balance gone.

He started to recover but Snake was already beside him, his hand grabbing at him but John's right fist hammered forward into Snake's abdomen. Snake's body did not seem to react to the blow and he hurled himself forward.

John side-stepped but not fast enough to get in a kick to the groin or anywhere else vital, instead he twisted half right, his left fist hammering down, as the biker's body lurched past him.

Snake hit the concrete, waited there for an instant, then pushed himself back up. John realised the biker was strong and fast, he would have to be careful.

Screaming, the biker threw himself forward again, his huge fist rocketing towards John, who tried to block the punch but missed. John felt the impact against his abdomen and doubled forward.

Snake's left foot snapped out but John looked up just in time. He caught the biker's foot and went with its direction of motion, rolling, dragging the man down. But Snake was fast. He got to his knees, his right fist hammering out, John taking the impact, falling back.

Snake hurled himself from his knees, John twisting his body left across the road surface. John realised if the big man crashed down on him, he would never get up again. He snapped his left leg out, impacting the right side of Snake's face. He kicked again and heard a groaning sound. He kicked again, missing as the biker rolled away, blood streaming from his mouth.

The big biker swung his left, John dodging back, the biker's left fist just glancing off his chin. John hammered out his own left against the right temple of the biker, the man's head snapping back. John's right, hooking up under the chin, the head snapping back again.

John drew his right back again, lacing it across the biker's mouth, then his left, then his right, his left, his right. His knuckles were bleeding, his fists numbing as he hammered at the man again and again.

Snake's head sagged, lolling to the left side.

John stumbled to his feet, starting to walk away but Snake was not finished. The biker charged again from behind but John side-stepped. He shifted his balance, wheeled and hammered his left foot into the biker's chest, the man's body rocking, swaying. John balling both fists together, crossed the biker's jaw again.

The big man was down, eyes closed, blood washing down his jaw and on to the road surface.

John stood there for an instant and said 'Done' to himself. He started towards Robert and Mark, the fight was over.

Suddenly, shots rang out. He looked for the source. It was Vinny. The gun was aiming behind John. He turned to see why Vinny had fired. He was quick enough to see Snake falling, two red blotches showing on his chest, a pistol in his right hand. Snake had not been finished. He was now!

He looked at Vinny.

"Thanks," he said.

"No problem, John. I owed you both," Vinny replied.

Vinny then turned to the other bikers telling them they had a choice to make. They could stay and follow Robert and John's orders, just like everybody else or leave now and take their chances outside the protection of the convoy.

The bikers made their decision quickly, agreeing to stay. They seemed unconcerned with Snake's demise. It turned out that since taking over the gang, he had made their lives hell. They had all been against his idea of attacking the convoy but no-one amongst them had been willing to cross him.

It was done.

Vinny assured Robert and John they would not have any more grounds for concern. He would take responsibility for the remaining bikers but there would be no further problems.

"What should we do with the body?" Robert asked.

"He should be buried," John said. "We'll find a spot tomorrow, a bit nearer to New Hull."

"Good, John. Now go and see the doctor, make sure you're okay," Robert suggested.

"I'm fine, thanks, the guy never touched me," John replied, smiling.

"Yeah, right," Robert said smiling.

He knew better.

Chapter Forty Five - The Discussion

He used the visit to the doctor as an excuse to visit Stephanie again. This had been a mistake, he thought, she had already heard about the fight with Snake.

"You could have been killed! Shit, John, why's it always got to be you?"

"I'm sorry, it was something I had to do. It never crossed my mind that I could lose," John answered.

"You nearly died! If it weren't for Vinny you would be dead," she argued.

"Yeah, all right, it was stupid but the guy really got to me. He ordered the attack on us, he was responsible for . . ." he let it hang.

"You macho! Don't you get it? Our own choices make us responsible. Our decision to join the people at the castle. Our decision to leave there. My decision to leave the truck cab. Your decision to fight Snake. We have to make better decisions, John. I'm sorry we lost our baby but we still have each other, that's important to me. You getting yourself killed because of some stupid biker winding you up, after everything we've been through, is crazy. Can't you see that?" she asked.

"You're right but we are so close now, another day and we should be in New Hull. I promise I won't take anymore unnecessary risks," he told her but he knew inside that might not be possible.

As if she could read his mind, she asked him to at least try to be more careful. She knew he could not promise anything of the sort.

He kissed her goodnight and told her to get some sleep, he would see her in the morning, then he left. He wanted to talk to Robert. He found him chatting to Mark and Vinny. Everybody else in the convoy was already getting ready to settle down for the night. Some were discussing what had happened over the last twenty-four hours, others finishing off their evening meals and planning for their future, a future somewhere without the constant threat of attack by the creatures. They were close, that much was certain. It was common knowledge amongst the convoy's inhabitants that New Hull was less than a day's journey away. The ship that would take them to freedom was there waiting for them. John hoped the final hours of their journey would prove easier than the last twenty-four but somehow he doubted it.

Robert saw him. "How's Stephanie?" he asked.

"She's almost her old self again," John replied, smiling. "She even bollocked me! Thanks for telling her about the fight."

"Hey, I didn't tell her. Word spreads quickly around here. She must have heard about it from one of the civilians. Besides, she's right to bollock you: that was unnecessary with Snake. We could have dealt with him another way."

"No we couldn't have, he wouldn't have stopped. If he'd have stayed, he would have made trouble at every opportunity. If he'd left, he would have continued harassing us any way he could. Eventually we would have had to sort him, one way or the other. He wasn't the type to fit in, go along, he was too full of himself for that. No, sorry, Robert, it was the only way," Vinny stated.

"Vinny's right," John agreed. "He wouldn't have followed orders, he wouldn't have fought for us. It would have been a constant struggle to keep him under control. If he had remained leader of the gang, we'd have had a potential time bomb ticking in our midst. I don't know about you, but I like sleeping with both my eyes shut."

"Yeah, okay, I get the picture. I still find it hard to accept there are pricks out there who'll kill you for the fun of it. I would have hoped that once everybody realised what was happening with the creatures, we would have banded together to fight them, not kill each other. You never see them killing each other. It's tragic, I mean, how many of us can there be left? We've nothing better to do than fight amongst ourselves."

"It's classic paranoia, Robert," John told him.

"How do you mean?" Vinny asked.

"How can I explain it?" John thought for a second, then continued. "Okay, we have always had the problems of not trusting each other. Throw jealousy or envy or greed into the cocktail and you've got potential problems. Every conflict throughout our history has happened because one or more persons wanted something that was unrealistic or they imagined some crazy scenario and reacted against it. Other people listen and get involved, it then becomes a movement. If it continues to escalate, it then becomes a conflict. Eventually, if nobody intercedes, you'd have yourselves a war! Your basic problem is paranoia. The human mind is complicated and everybody at some stage has experienced the phenomenon, whether they realise it or not. The only difference is, for nearly everybody, it's just a short and basically harmless experience. Unfortunately for some, they get so involved in the paranoia, it takes over their lives. It starts to control their way of thinking and their actions. As of that moment they are lost to it, prisoners if you like, caught in a never-ending cycle of negative thoughts and horror. They imagine all kinds of things, most of which aren't true but they can't tell the difference anymore. They want what their neighbours have got but without having to work for it. They imagine certain groups of people are plotting against them, conspiring to undermine everything they consider important. Look at the second world war. Hitler's stand against the Jewish race. Many have tried to explain it but nobody really understood it apart from Hitler himself. Nobody could have done. It was his paranoia that fed the fire until the blaze got out of control. Our history is full of such actions from leader-type dictators who have appeared from nowhere and have caused tremendous amounts of suffering for others, solely because of a belief they had. On a different level, Snake was no better. He believed he was entitled to anything that anybody had and it was his God-given right to get it. If anybody disagreed with his way of thinking, there could only be one course of action open to him. Kill them and take it!"

"What the hell are you on about, John?" Robert asked.

"Okay, we'll try it another way. When I was young, I used to love going fishing. Every chance I got, I'd get my gear and head off around the countryside looking for pits or lakes where I could spend a few hours fishing and relaxing. I had a friend who used to come with me, his name was Nick. He was a little older and had a car, that meant we could go further afield. We found a small pit, in the middle of nowhere; the next house was three or four miles away. It was the farmhouse where the man who owned the land the pit was on lived. There were big tench in this pit, bloody big, so we decided to go night fishing. Everybody knows the best time to catch big tench is early morning, so we asked the farmer if it was okay if we stayed all night. He said yes no problem, even allowed us to park the car in one of his fields. We set our gear up and started fishing. It got to about midnight and was very dark – scary, if you like. We heard a noise, it sounded like somebody breathing but heavily, you know - the typical horror movie breathing. Where we were sitting, we were surrounded by a thick hedge. There was just a small hole we'd crawled through, so we couldn't see anything behind us but hey, we were two big strong guys, frightened of nothing. The breathing continued, even seemed to get louder, it was unnerving to say the least. After about an hour of listening to the noise, we were getting edgy and nervous, that's when the paranoia really kicks in. I asked Nick what he thought it was. He didn't have a clue but suggested it might be the farmer pissing us about. We even shouted that we didn't think it was funny but the noise continued. After a few minutes discussing what we should do, we decided to leave and come back at first light. We left all our fishing gear there and headed to the car across the fields. It was pitch black and, although we would never have admitted it, we were scared. We reached the car and I opened the gate so that Nick could reverse out. He turned on the car's lights while reversing out of the field. You could just make out the pit from where we'd just come. I was waiting to close the gate and watching the area where the pit was at the same time. In the glare of the car lights, I swear I saw something run away from the pit! I couldn't see what it was but it was low to the ground and moving fast. I closed the gate, got in the car and told Nick what I'd seen. He'd seen the same thing! We drove off not knowing what to do."

"What did you do?" Robert asked, totally enthralled in John's story.

John realised all three of them were listening intently, he could not help smiling at their reactions.

"We waited until it got light. In the meantime we talked about what it could have been we saw. Our paranoia was growing with every second. We imagined everything from murderers to werewolves."

"Werewolves? You were crazy!" Mark told him.

"That's what happens, mate. Once this shit kicks in, you lose all track of reality. Your mind plays funny tricks on you. You're stuck in the nightmare you are generating. The only way to end it is to find a rational explanation for what's happening or do something about it. Although, if ten years ago somebody had told any of you you'd end up fighting for your lives against monsters such as these, you'd have said he was mad but here we are," John told him.

"What happened next?" Vinny asked.

"As soon as it was light, we went back. We checked everywhere but found nothing. There was nothing to indicate anything had been there, our fishing tackle was just as we'd left it, nothing. We carried on fishing and even caught a couple of nice tench."

"That was it. Nothing?" Robert asked, thinking the story was over.

"That should have been it, Robert. Because we could find no reason to feed the paranoia that had been in our heads, it died. We quickly forgot what had happened and settled back into our normal uneventful lives. The week after we went again. Same place, same story. Everything was quiet until about midnight, then the same breathing noise came again. As soon as we heard the noise, the paranoia started again, only it was worse. This time we were really scared from the beginning. Whatever it was, it was back. We didn't wait long that second time, we left. Again our minds were working overtime, imagining all kinds of shit. At first light we went back, we had armed ourselves with knives and axes, this time we were going to kill whatever it was. There was nothing there again, no signs, apart from what looked to be a trail through the long grass, leading to and away from the pit. This was enough for us, we were certain something was stalking us. We'd convinced ourselves of this, our minds again, working overtime. The difference this time, we reacted aggressively. We decided to go back the week after but this time we'd be ready. We took another friend with us, Kevin. He had a rifle. Me and Nick were both armed again and determined this time not to run. Whatever it was that was theoretically hunting us would be in trouble if it showed up again because we were determined now to hunt whatever it was and kill it! Shortly before midnight the heavy breathing started again. This time we stood our ground. We shouted a warning to whatever it was that we were armed and it should leave us alone but the breathing continued. After five minutes of shouted warnings, Kevin opened fire. We were standing next to him, ready for anything."

"Did you kill it, John?" Mark asked.

"There was nothing to kill, mate. We didn't leave, we stayed the whole night. Just as it was light enough to see, we heard another noise. It was the sound of beating wings. Smack bang in the middle of the pit there was an old tree stump. In the top of it there was an owl's nest. The breathing noise that had driven us nearly insane for the last three weeks was the noise the baby owls made while their mother was feeding them. There were no monsters stalking us, nothing dangerous about the situation at all. It was just our paranoia!"

"You wanker!" Robert said, obviously disappointed with the story's ending.

264

"What did you expect, Robert? Monsters? Ghosts? You see how you got sucked in, your mind was running away with you. Paranoia, mate, you'd better be careful," John said, smiling.

"What you're saying is, Snake couldn't have changed even if he'd wanted to?" Mark asked.

"No, he didn't want to change. As far as he was concerned, we owed him. The only way we could have helped him, was to show him his beliefs were false. That's something we couldn't have done, not without a qualified psychiatrist helping us and not without hurting ourselves," John argued.

"So you're saying that our fighting amongst ourselves all the time is because of a mental illness! That proves the creatures are right about us, doesn't it?" Robert asked, seeming confused.

"No, Robert, they're wrong. Sure, some people like Snake don't deserve a second chance. The pratts who caused the war don't either. Dictators and leaders who have put their own needs before the needs of others and have risked millions of lives because of it, don't deserve a second chance. Those who have tried to change peoples' religions just because of their own beliefs, don't either. There are probably numerous examples we could take but it's pointless. All of the idiots involved were so far gone, the real world didn't exist any more, just their version of how it should be. The normal everyday person deserves a chance at a normal everyday life. We are fighting to stay alive, that's different than fighting for gain or some stupid belief. The creatures have built a picture of us in their minds, based upon certain events in our history. It's obvious they've used times of conflict and nothing else - not really fair when forming an opinion. Other times of peace have been ignored. The times when our actions have saved lives, again ignored. Their opinion of us is as one-sided as it could be, it's keeping their paranoia alive. Allowing any other thoughts into their way of thinking would be dangerous to their way of life now," John said.

"Shit, John, you should have been a psychiatrist," Mark said, grinning

"Shut up," John replied, laughing. "It's just that as long as we say we tried everything, we can justify any of our actions. We mustn't fall into the trap Robert just fell into, it's dangerous," he smiled at Robert, then continued. "As long as we do that, we are better than them and we deserve a second chance of living free of them."

"Then why won't they give us that chance, why do they keep trying to stop us?" Robert asked, still not clear what John meant.

"Because their experiences of us won't allow it. Their paranoia keeps telling them the war was aimed just at them. God knows how many of them we must have killed without knowing. Ask yourself, Robert, if somebody killed all your family and friends and nobody did anything about it, what would you do?" John asked.

"I don't know, I guess I'd sort it myself," Robert answered.

"Exactly. Now, once you'd come to the decision and you were stuck in your version of events, nothing would stop you doing what you thought was right. Even if that person said he was sorry or came up with some lame excuse, you wouldn't suddenly be able to forgive him and forget your family were dead. You'd finish what you'd started. Afterwards, when it was too late, then you'd wonder if you'd done the right thing but by then, it'd be too late anyway. That's were they are, stuck in their version of events. They won't listen to us anymore, we tried it, it's gone too far. Snake couldn't back down, he didn't dare lose. That's why he went for his gun at the end. The creatures are no different, they can't back down, they have to finish us or die trying," John explained.

"Shit, John, we brought it on ourselves," Robert stated.

"We always do, mate. We always have!" John replied.

Chapter Forty Six - The Last Leg

After they had finished their discussion, they had eaten their evening meal and retired for the night, which had passed without incident.

With travelling longer the evening before, the point had been reached where New Hull was less than a day away. Robert and John both agreed that getting off the mainland that day would be their aim. To stand a good chance of achieving this, an early start was necessary. It was four thirty a.m. Those who were up and about were dismantling the convoy's defences and helping to prepare the breakfast, hopefully their last on the road. For many it had proven to be too early, they were still sleeping.

John estimated it was still about one hundred and twenty miles to New Hull, a distance they could theoretically manage in a day. The only problem that could slow them down was another attack from the creatures. Seeing that they were now travelling northwards, parallel to the Dead Zone, John anticipated they would have no problems until the outskirts of the small city were reached. No creatures could live inside the Dead Zone for long, the radiation there as fatal for them as it was for humans. He suggested the chances of their being attacked from the west were basically non-existent. To the east it had been sparsely populated after the war, so John suspected the creature population would also be sparse in that area. The creatures had mostly lived in and around population centres, the countryside did not seem to appeal to them. Robert suspected there was maybe not enough food. It was certainly a possibility they should not ignore. All the evidence seemed to indicate the trip up to the small city might prove uneventful but, once they reached the city itself, they could probably expect a warm welcome.

John walked over to the hospital truck and spoke briefly to Stephanie. She was feeling fine, the doctor had even suggested she could be up and about later that day. Her wound was healing very well and would have no long-term effects on her health or mobility.

After leaving her to try to get back to sleep, John bumped into Vinny who was also up. He had been discharged from the doctor's care, his wound as good as healed. He could even begin light duties. Vinny was wondering what he could do to help the convoy. John suggested they discuss it with Robert and Mark.

They headed over to the mess truck together to get some breakfast. After picking up enough for themselves, Robert and Mark, they went to find them both. They found them supervising the dismantling of the defences.

They sat together and ate, John telling Robert that Vinny needed a job. The Major did not know what to suggest, so he asked Mark if he could suggest anything. Unfortunately for Vinny, all duties involved with the convoy's security were currently detailed to soldiers who had years of experience. Mark felt that for Vinny, who had practically no experience in such matters, the day to day setting up of explosive devices and the like, could prove to be dangerous, if not fatal. He suggested Vinny should fit in, wherever he wanted. Vinny appeared disappointed with the situation, he had obviously looked forward to playing a more important role. Just fitting in, did not seem to appeal to him.

John suggested that they could make better use of Vinny's talents and at the same time, find something for all of the other bikers to do. Something that would hopefully appeal to all of them. Robert was interested to know what John had in mind.

John explained that, including Vinny, there were in total eleven bikers. They had proven they could fight. It was obvious they could handle their bikes well. Why not combine the two? He suggested they could be 'The Cavalry', a unit that concentrated on hit and run tactics. With the speed of their bikes, they could get anywhere fast, fight and get out before the creatures had a chance to react. If they rearmed them with some of the newly modified weapons as well as more up to date conventional weapons, they would make a formidable fighting unit, able to defend the convoy anywhere along its length or a first strike unit in a conflict. With Snake's death, a bike was available for Vinny to ride, so he was the obvious choice to lead the unit. The idea appealed to Vinny and he felt sure the other bikers would also find the idea super. He would ask them but anticipated no problems. He went off straightaway to talk to them and Mark went off to organise the weapons they would need, leaving John and Robert sitting there.

"How do you do it, John?" Robert asked.

"Do what?" John questioned.

"Keep coming up with good ideas. The cavalry!" Robert said, a wry smile on his face.

"It's a gift, mate," John said, smiling back.

"Thank God, you've got it," Robert added. "It's a great idea. It makes us stronger and more flexible to deal with anything those things throw at us."

"One step ahead, Robert, that's the key. Always one step ahead."

The bikers had found the idea brilliant, having Vinny as their leader was also readily accepted. They had been rearmed with the newer weapons and Vinny was already discussing tactics with them. They were taking their new roles very seriously, just as John had hoped. The idea would give them a purpose and bring them together, making a better fighting unit out of them. Their abilities gave the convoy the added security of a very mobile fighting force, a force that could spot something at ground level that might possibly be missed from the air and be in a position to deal with it.

The convoy, in the meantime, was ready to leave. The bikers took up positions in two units, one at the front, one at the back. The distance between them no problem because of the acceleration of the machines they rode. John felt it was almost like having a shield around them, able to react against anything in seconds.

They were more ready than ever, the last leg of their journey could begin. At six thirty a.m., the convoy started to roll.

Chapter Forty Seven - New Hull

They made good time all morning. They had already passed the bombed-out skeleton of Nottingham and were about forty miles from New Hull.

Robert ordered a stop for lunch, he felt it wise to discuss their plans for the final push into the city. John agreed but did not want to hang around too long, he wanted to be on the ship by nightfall.

A quick meal had been organised, which had tasted awful. John had left his, using the excuse he was too excited to eat. They sat together in one of the truck cabs discussing the safest way to achieve their aim.

"Do you think we'll hit trouble in the city, John?" Robert asked.

"Honestly? Yes," John answered, without hesitation.

"Shit, I've got the same feeling. It's almost as if they've left us alone too long, hoping we'd drop our guard maybe, I don't know," Robert said, then continuing. "Where do you think they'll hit us?"

"New Hull. At least if I were them, I'd be waiting there. They've probably guessed where we're heading, they might not be sure why but, yeah, the logical choice is the city itself," John answered.

"What do we do?" Robert asked.

"Prepare for it," John answered, as coolly as ever. "What we need is intelligence."

"Then we send the Apache in ahead of us. It can tell us if they are there waiting for us, even if they are hiding," Robert suggested.

"Yeah, normally I'd agree but this time that tactic alone might not tell us enough. There are old tunnels and shelters from the war all over the place, built under the old and new city. The Apache's camera technology won't help us there. We need eyes on the ground, as well as in the air," John said.

"What are you suggesting?" Robert asked.

"Send the cavalry," John answered.

"The bikers, John? Are they ready?"

"They just need their speed, they don't engage anything. Just in and out. The Apache's going as well, so it can cover their backs if necessary," John suggested.

"I suppose so, if you're sure it's the only way," Robert agreed.

"It's the only way," John confirmed.

"I'll fetch Vinny and we'll brief him," Robert said and he left to find the leader of the newly formed unit.

Five minutes later, they both returned.

"What's up, John?" Vinny asked, cheerfully.

"We've got a small job for you and your guys, mate. It could be dangerous and I'm sorry you don't have more time to prepare for it but we can't see any other way of getting the information we need," John explained.

"No problem, John. We're ready to earn our keep," he replied, confidently.

"Okay, listen. We're approaching the city of New Hull. Because the creatures are leaving us alone at the moment, we suspect they are planning something big in the city. We need intelligence; that means a reconnaissance mission. We could send the Apache on its own but couldn't be sure of the situation on the ground. There are probably lots of hiding places in the area left over from the war. If the creatures are hiding there, the helicopter won't be able to detect them. To be sure, we need eyes on the ground. That's where you guys come in. The Apache will fly over the area at altitude; it might catch them unawares if we're lucky. Your unit covers the area at street level, in and out using your speed. Don't, under any circumstances, get dragged into a fight. First signs of trouble, get the hell out. Any questions?" John asked.

"Yeah, why the hell are we going to New Hull?" Vinny asked, puzzled.

"We are hoping to capture a car ferry, load everything on board and sail somewhere, maybe the Med. Find us a little island where there aren't any creatures and live happily ever after. Only problem is, our expert on ferries, Mr. Smythe, was killed during the attack by Snake and his gang. We'll have to work out how to sail the dammed thing once we're on board. How difficult can it be?" John asked.

"Sailing one isn't that difficult but docking one can be a bitch!" Vinny stated, sounding as if he was speaking from experience.

"Have you sailed one?" John asked, hopefully.

"Yes, many times. Some of my guys have also worked on one, it's not a problem, John."

"You're a life saver, Vinny. That was our only problem," John stated, excitedly.

"That's not exactly true," Vinny started. "Your problem's not how to sail one but where to sail it to. Sailing to the Med. in a car ferry isn't really possible. That's not to say we shouldn't do it but it's bloody dangerous. The first major bollocks is fuel. These things don't average forty miles per gallon. They need to refuel, both ways, when they just cross the channel. From New Hull to the Med. we'll have to refuel six or seven times. That means putting in to six or seven ports along the way. Each time we'll need luck in finding fuel and every time we'll run the risk of being attacked by creatures. The second and probably the worst problem, is the route we'd have to take. Down through the channel, no problem but the weather there is never that bad. The few days a year it gets really bad, the ferries didn't normally sail. Your real big problem starts when you leave the channel and enter the Atlantic. The weather there makes the channel look like a pond in a field. It can be a nightmare for the real big ships. A ferry isn't built to take that kind of punishment and could sink in a heartbeat. What you're suggesting is bloody dangerous. To say the least, it could prove fatal to everybody."

"That's not the kind of news we needed after we've come all this way," John said, sounding a little demoralised.

"Hey, the plan's sound. As I see it, we have to leave here, a ship's the only way. We might just have to re-think where we're going, that's all," Vinny said, cheerfully.

"Okay, first thing's first. We have to capture a ship before we can use one. We still need to get through to the port; that means intelligence. You still game, Vinny?" John asked.

"Sure, we'll go and take a look."

"Good. We'll travel to within ten miles of the city together, then you can move in and have a nosy. We'll wait for you and the helicopter to return before we decide how to proceed. With the speed of your bikes, you should be able to cover the distance to the city in no time. Just in and out, watch out for ambushes but I don't think you'll have any problems. If they are waiting for us, they'll want us all, not just a few scouts. That'd blow their cover. Get your team ready, take plenty of ammo along just in case. We'll move up into position," John instructed.

It had taken another hour to finish their lunch break, the convoy then moved to within ten miles of the city. It was early afternoon, John hoped there would be enough time to do what needed to be done.

Vinny and his men were ready to leave, John reminding him once more, just to go in and out, no heroics. The Apache would watch their backs but could only do so much. They needed to be as careful as possible.

They rode off, Vinny leading the way. John anticipated they would know more in about thirty minutes. In the meantime, they would bury Snake, the biker who had been killed the day before. They had brought his body along, waiting for an opportunity to bury it; this might be the last chance they would have.

Robert organised the burial detail and the chaplain said a few words. All in all, it was far more than the biker had deserved.

Vinny and his men had moved to within visual range of the city. The helicopter was flying somewhere above them at a higher than normal altitude, hoping to avoid detection and catch some of the creatures unaware.

Using his binoculars, Vinny scanned the outer limits of the now deserted city, looking for signs of creature activity. He could see nothing that indicated their presence. The old city of Hull had been built over the bridge on the other side of the river. The new city was before the river. It was nowhere near as big as the old one but had probably been a nice place to live after the war had ended. The ferry terminal was on the harbour front. To get to it, you had to basically drive straight through the middle of the city.

"Okay, we're moving in. Keep your eyes open, first sign of trouble, get the hell out. Understood?" he said into his headset.

All his men were now wearing one, part of their new equipment. They all signalled that everything was understood.

They rode slowly into the city, half expecting to be attacked at every turn they made. After a couple of minutes they reached the main street, everything up to that point seeming quiet. They had seen nothing that aroused their suspicions. The only evidence that people had ever had anything to do with the city were the houses and deserted shops. Vinny had seen abandoned towns and cities before, something seemed wrong but he could not put his finger on it, not yet anyway. The streets were just too clean, almost tidy, not the normal picture of a place quickly abandoned.

They started down the main street, riding slowly, everything again quiet. Nothing seemed even remotely out of place. If Vinny had not known better, he would have thought the town was sleeping; its inhabitants not yet awake. Something inside him was telling him that if he waited long enough, the town would eventually come back to life. The only problem with his scenario was, he did know better.

As they continued down the street, the first thing that looked out of place since they had entered the city appeared. In one of the side streets to their left, some kind of barrier had been erected, put together using old vehicles. A little further down the main street, this time on their right was the next street, again blocked with abandoned vehicles. They continued on, only to find the next blocked street, this time the street leading off to the left again. Vinny was now suspicious. John had been right, something was wrong, very wrong but what? The street ahead of them leading down to the harbour was clear. No vehicles, no debris, nothing, none of the normal clutter you could expect to see in an abandoned city. This fact was beginning to intrigue Vinny. What had happened there? They were three quarters of the way down the main street and could see the waterfront ahead of them. There was still no evidence of creatures in the town but Vinny sensed they were there.

As they reached the end of the main street, they could see the ferry terminal straight in front of them. The two ferries everybody in the convoy had talked about could clearly be seen docked at the quayside, along with a couple of smaller vessels. Everything there was again quiet, no apparent sign of their enemies. The terminal buildings seemed intact but, because they were relatively small, they did not offer a lot of cover for hiding creatures. The yard itself was clear of debris and surrounded by a stout-looking steel fence, the two big gates leading in open and inviting. Again there was nothing to get in their way.

Vinny considered entering and checking out the two ships but remembered what John had said, in and out, no heroics. They stopped before the big gates and turned their bikes around.

The trip back along the main street proved to be as uneventful as the trip down it. Nothing, just the weird roadblocks to either side. Vinny was not sure what they meant. Maybe the old residents of the city had built them while fighting the creatures, he did not know. There were no unexplained sounds, no shadows seen at the windows of the buildings, nothing to indicate something might be there watching them. He felt as if they had failed, they had been sent to gather information but all they could report back was that everything was quiet. He hoped the helicopter had experienced more luck. He gunned his bike forwards, rapidly accelerating. It was time to be getting back. As they left the city, he opened the throttle out. He was riding Snake's old Harley, the ride exhilarating. Surrounded by his men, he realised that John had been right, they would be a formidable fighting unit. It was just a pity their intelligence gathering skills were not up to much.

At eighty miles an hour, it took less than seven minutes to reach the convoy. John and Robert were there waiting for them. Vinny stopped his machine next to them and dismounted.

"How's it looking, mate?" John asked.

"Quiet," Vinny answered. "I'm sorry, John, there's nothing. We didn't see a dammed thing!"

"How far did you go?" John asked, puzzled by the news.

"We got to the ferry terminal. I even considered checking out the two ferries but decided against it. We saw nothing, we heard nothing, nothing at all," Vinny told him.

"Shit, I don't get it," John said. "They're out there, I know it. What have they got planned for us?"

Vinny asked if the helicopter had returned yet, John saying no but it was expected at any minute. Maybe they would know more then.

The helicopter returned to share its information which turned out to be very little. The pilots had seen a few creatures but basically not enough of them to threaten the convoy in any serious way. Nothing else seemed out of place at all, except there was something strange about the building tops. They were covered in all kinds of rubble and other household junk. It appeared the ex-inhabitants of the city had dumped most of their unwanted rubbish on the flat roofs of the buildings. There were fridges and cookers plainly visible on most of the rooftops. It also appeared as if many of the house owners had been renovating, chunks of walls and big pieces of rubble also visible. They had no explanation for the phenomena.

John again turned to Vinny.

"Are you sure there was nothing out of place? It might have seemed weird to you at the time, not worth mentioning but it could be bloody important to us," he said, trying to make sure they had missed nothing.

"No, John, there was nothing. A few of the streets leading off the main street were blocked off but I presume the people who had been fighting there did that. One thing did strike me as odd, the place was tidy, as if it had just been cleaned for our visit," Vinny told him.

Robert suddenly shouted. "Gauntlet!"

John looked at him, not understanding what he meant.

"What did you say, Robert?" he asked.

"Don't you see it? They've created a gauntlet. One street leads to where we want to go, the streets leading off it are blocked. That gives us nowhere to go but down the street. Everything is tidy because they have taken everything they can use against us up on to the rooftops. What did the pilot say, rubble and junk? Everything that is normally abandoned in the street when people leave is on the rooftops waiting to be thrown down on us when we attempt to drive through. Some of that stuff must weigh quite a lot. Thrown from such a height, it'll be like a bomb landing on us. It's going to make a mess of the trucks, that's for certain. It's a gauntlet and, if we want to leave, we've got to try and run it!" Robert told them, certain he was right.

John nodded in agreement, now it was obvious.

"Jackpot!" he said. "Well done, mate."

Chapter Forty Eight - The Gauntlet

"What the fuck do we do now, then?" Vinny asked.

"We try to work out a way of getting through the surprise they've got waiting for us," John told him.

The pilot of the Apache suggested that the bigger pieces of rubble, gathered on the building rooftops, were probably too heavy for the normal creatures. That meant the bigger ones were more than likely involved. If this were true, then it offered a possible explanation as to why the helicopter's infra-red camera technology had not been able to spot many creatures. He suggested the creature's armour shielded their bodies somehow, making it difficult to detect, in which case there could be a lot of them waiting in the city. John and Robert both agreed this prognosis was likely and made their task of beating the gauntlet even more complicated. If the convoy was stalled at any time, the bigger and more powerful creatures would be quick to press their advantage and probably attack in force.

"Shit!" John said. "We've got problems. We need Mark and Bill in on the planning. This is serious, we need to come up with a way to beat this trap and quickly. It'll be getting dark in a few hours and we can't stay here. It's too open."

The pilot went to find the two men and fetch them. They duly appeared and Robert explained the situation, telling them to get their thinking caps on. They had precious little time to come up with a solution.

Vinny came up with a direct approach, suggesting they use the helicopters to blow up the buildings and bring them down on the creature's heads.

Although the idea itself appealed to John, he pointed out it would probably end up blocking the only street left leading to the ferries with rubble. They would not be able to get the convoy through afterwards.

Bill was asked if he thought the trucks could withstand the barrage of heavy objects that would apparently be raining down on them. He was not sure for how long but felt confident the modified trucks would withstand most of it, at least for a short time. The tanks would not have a problem, their normal armour, combined with the modifications, making them practically indestructible. In his opinion the weak link would be the fuel tankers. They were partly modified but their general construction was not very strong. They would struggle against the bombardment. The only other problem would be if, during the attempt to get through, the street became blocked by all the debris. That would stall the convoy for sure.

Robert suggested they should just run it, get through as quickly as possible and not give the creatures enough time to react. John agreed their only chance was to run the gauntlet waiting for them but they needed some kind of insurance to keep them from getting bogged down until everybody was safely on the ship.

After about twenty minutes discussing the problem, John suggested that Bravo One should fly him and a small team of men in over the city to the ferry terminal. They would secure the area and the gates and be in position to fight a rearguard action once the convoy got through. Vinny and his unit should lead the way through the city. They were most vulnerable because they would be riding their bikes but, being at the front of the convoy, the speed of their bikes should get them through. They would then secure and prepare the ferry to leave. The truck carrying the soldiers should be next, just in case there were creatures waiting on the ship. They could then assist Vinny and his men. The civilian trucks followed by the supply trucks next, then the sixteen tonners, bringing up the rear the fuel tankers just in case Bill was proven right about them being the weak link. The two tanks should cover the rear of the convoy, engaging any of the creatures leaving the buildings to follow and give support fire to John's team. Both of the helicopters should engage any creatures visible on the rooftops but as soon as the sixteen tonners were through, they should land and somehow be taken on board. Bill would have to assist in making that possible. The two aircraft would be needed again, whenever they reached their destination. By the time the helicopters were on board, the fuel tankers should also have made it through, the two tanks should then follow them. As soon as the whole convoy was safely on board, the ferry should leave, it was not to wait for the rearguard. As soon as the ferry had cleared the dock, they should be safe. John's team would join them as soon as it was possible to do so. If necessary, they would have to swim!

Robert argued it was dangerous, especially for John's team and Vinny's men. He suggested they all break through together but John countered, saying that if the convoy got through, the creatures would attack them while they were loading. At that stage, they needed all their time to secure the vehicles and get the helicopters stowed away, not fight off an attack. No, in his opinion, the rearguard was the only option that might give them enough time.

Robert had eventually agreed but insisted on riding in one of the tanks. He wanted to stay behind as long as possible to try to make sure nothing happened to John or his team.

Mark would go with John, the two friends having developed such an understanding of the creatures and how to combat them, that together, they were a formidable fighting team, and, if anybody could hold the creatures back long enough for the ferry to escape, Robert felt sure they could.

Vinny and his team would be in charge of the ferry until they had cleared the dock and were underway. They were the only ones with any kind of experience with the big ships anyway and John realised that if they would have had to work out how to sail the ferry themselves, it would have taken too long. The creatures would have had ample time to overrun them. He said a silent prayer, thankful they had found Vinny and thankful that the other bikers had joined them.

Bill would supervise the loading of the ferry, some of Vinny's men helping with weight distribution and the securing of all vehicles.

"Okay, Robert, we leave in fifteen minutes," John said. "Tell the men what to expect. Tell the civilians to stay in the trucks until we're safely on board the ferry. Bravo One should get ready to fly us in. Mark, ask the pilot how many men he can transport safely if he pushes it and then pick them. Take plenty of ammunition along, explosives and some of the new weapons for our big friends. I'll meet you in five minutes at the helicopter."

Mark ran off to organise everything and get his gear. John continued.

"After Bravo One has dropped us off, they'll pull back and, together with the Apache, give you guys covering fire. Vinny, you get your guys on the ferry as quickly as you can. Expect anything but get it ready as soon as you can. The minute the tanks are on board, get it away from the dock. Don't wait any longer, no matter what! Is that clear?" John asked.

"Crystal," Vinny replied, looking at Robert.

"Alright, let's move," John said and he went to get the rest of his weapons.

He had to tell Stephanie and get her to move into one of the civilian trucks until they were safely on board. He wondered how she would react, somehow he knew.

She had reacted just as he had expected, flipping out but he had managed to calm her down, arguing it was hopefully the last time they would be facing such a threat. With luck they would board the ferry and be free of the creatures, at least for a while. She kissed him, telling him to be careful, she would be waiting for him.

He had joined Mark at the helicopter. They were taking eight men with them, the pilot had said that would be the maximum number he was able to carry safely. Ten men against God knows how many creatures. It would be dangerous but John was still convinced it was the only way.

They were flying over the city towards the terminal. There was still no sign of the creatures but they knew they were there. Another two minutes and the small unit would be in position, twenty minutes later the convoy would reach the main street and the fun would begin. As they flew over the buildings, John could see what the pilot had seen on the rooftops. There was rubble, huge slabs of concrete, fridges, all kinds of heavy rubbish, everything piled up, ready to be used as weapons against the approaching convoy.

As the helicopter touched down inside the ferry terminal, he could see the two ships tied up at the dock. There were still unanswered questions, fuel quantities and the like but no time to check. If ever they needed a little bit of luck, it was today. Still, he thought, that would be Vinny's problem. He would be otherwise engaged.

They had worked out their tactics while flying over the city. Mark and half of the men would concentrate on the normal creatures, John and his men would take out the bigger ones. They moved to the fence line, fixing explosives every fifty feet to the fence. These would be detonated by remote control, their last option to win enough time for the convoy to get through and for themselves to make the ferry. They were ready, another ten minutes or so and it would start.

A few minutes had passed and the lead elements of the convoy were approaching the main street. Vinny and his men were out in front, they would be first through. Already Vinny could make out shapes and shadows moving on the rooftops, they had guessed right. It would be a gauntlet, the likes of which had never been seen before!

He gunned his bike forwards, accelerating, they needed to get the ferry ready. His men were briefed, clear on what they had to do. He hoped there would be enough time. They sped ahead of the convoy, the sooner they got started the better.

Bill was in the lead truck, just about to enter the main street. Figures were now appearing on all the rooftops, carrying huge objects, preparing to launch them downwards on to the passing trucks. He hoped the men on the truck's roofs had taken cover inside the trucks but there was no time to check.

Robert was in one of the tanks bringing up the rear, he was in a relatively safe position, the tank's armour able to withstand anything the creatures could throw at it but he would have to watch as the rest of the vehicles under his command were rocked and battered.

Vinny and his men had already raced past John's position, throwing him a quick wave. They had ridden straight on to the right hand ferry, its rear door already open for loading. They were gambling on it having a full load of fuel. He would soon know if the gamble had paid off.

John and Mark's teams were ready, another five minutes or so and the fun would begin. John told them all to make their shots count, they had no way of knowing how many creatures would be coming against their position. They had to hold out as long as possible to give the convoy a good chance of getting away. Once the ferry had left, they would attempt to reach it any way they could, even if it meant swimming! He wished them all luck, telling them how proud he was to have known them. Mark had told him to shut up, they weren't dead yet. Most of the men had laughed but John was sure they all realised the chances of their getting away, once the ferry had left, were slim to say the least.

The lead trucks were about a quarter of the way down the main street when the attack finally came. Rubble and masonry rained down on the convoy, the impacts on the trucks making a hell of a noise, the trucks rocking but staying in one piece. The drivers had been instructed to increase speed as soon as the attack came. The quicker they now boarded the ferry the less time the creatures would have to react and attack otherwise. The trucks all accelerated.

More and more debris rained down on them, the street gradually filling with the makeshift bombs. It would have been impossible to drive along the street, if the convoy had not stuck to the middle of the road. This fact, plus the trucks were driving very close to one another, kept the middle lane pretty free of debris, most of the 'bombs' bouncing off and landing to either side of the convoy.

Robert could see that most of the modified trucks were clearing the buildings and driving into the ferry terminal, some of the supply trucks, the sixteen tonners and the fuel tankers were still in the line of fire. He had witnessed a fridge bounce off one of the fuel tankers and fly through a shop window on the other side of the street. He laughed as the saying 'throwing everything into the attack' popped into his head but the fuel tanker had visibly rocked, the driver just managing to keep control of the vehicle.

Now, behind them, creatures were coming out of the buildings they had already passed. He ordered both tanks to open fire. Using high explosive shells, they blew up the buildings behind them, bringing rubble and debris crashing down on the creatures. Talk about turning the tables, he thought and smiled again.

John had watched the first trucks fly by; now he could hear the explosions following the convoy. He presumed the two tanks had opened fire. Things were starting to heat up. He looked to his men and told them to be ready; it would start any time.

Vinny had reached the control room on the ferry without much trouble. There had been five creatures hiding on board up to that point, his men taking care of them easily. The moment of truth had arrived. Vinny checked the fuel gauges. They were lucky, the ferry's tanks were full. Now, as long as the engines started, they would be fine. He checked everything that needed checking and pushed the starter. The engines coughed and spluttered but did not start. He fiddled with a few more knobs, regulating the mix, and tried again, they coughed and spluttered again but came to life. Using his headset, he told his men to start loading and be ready to cast off as soon as the last of the vehicles were loaded.

John heard the engines start, could see the water at the stern of the boat churning now through the propellers' activity. He informed Bravo One and the Apache. They should land and prepare for loading. He had seen Bill in the first truck and knew he would be supervising the complicated task of getting everything on board; he would see the helicopters land and act accordingly. The first trucks were already loaded, he could see soldiers milling around the ship's decks, taking up firing positions. The scene was hectic, everywhere he looked, activity. The sixteen tonners were driving past his position, the helicopters had already landed, men wheeling them towards the belly of the boat. He could see Bill supervising the procedure, just as he had expected.

The five fuel tankers and the two tanks were the only vehicles still left to board. They were making slow but steady progress towards the ferry terminal, the last two hundred yards of the street barely passable now. The first tanker was through, then the second and the third, followed by the fourth. Suddenly, the last one seemed to lurch, then it broad sided, obviously out of control. It ploughed into a building on the left side of the street and stopped. Some of John's men started to leave their positions and move towards the tanker wreck, John telling them to hold. Using his headset, he asked Robert if he had seen what had happened? Robert explained how a chunk of rubble, the size of a car engine, had crashed through the windscreen of the tanker, killing the driver and his guard. With control of the tanker lost, it had jack-knifed. There was nothing they could do!

John told him to bring the tanks through and to board the ferry as quickly as they could. The surviving fuel tankers were already boarding as the two tanks rolled past John's position, still firing.

"It's up to us now, guys," John told his men. "We need to buy five minutes, then we're gone, so keep cool. You all know the drill. Fire as soon as you're ready."

They commenced firing, creatures big and small were already advancing on them. John quickly realised there were too many, they were in danger of being overrun. He looked at the fuel tanker across the street.

"Mark," he shouted over the noise of weapons firing. "Put a few rounds into the tanker."

The answering fire from Mark coming almost instantaneously, pouring into the tanker's body but it had been armoured by Bill's magic spray. The bullets were having no effect, they just bounced off. John, angry with himself for forgetting the modifications, turned to one of his team, the man carrying R.P.Gs. One was quickly aimed and fired, straight into the tanker's body. The resulting explosion was massive! It killed many of the creatures heading John's way.

Robert spoke to John using his headset.

"John, we're ready to leave, pull your team in now!"

"No!" John answered. "We'll catch up, get out of here, Robert."

"Sorry, mate, I promised Stephanie we wouldn't leave without you."

Still firing, John shouted into his headset.

"Bullshit! You never spoke to her! Stick to the plan, Robert, leave. We'll be okay."

Looking at the number of creatures that were slowly advancing towards them, he somehow doubted it.

"Sorry, John, no go. Either you all come now or nobody gets to leave. I'm still officially in command, so take it as an order, soldier. Now, move it!" Robert shouted.

"Ah, fuck!" John said quietly. He spoke into his headset. "Pull back towards the ferry, keep pouring lead into them guys. Mark, be ready to blow the charges. Let's go."

They retreated back towards the waiting ferry which was cast off and ready to leave. Forty yards, thirty yards to go, the creatures coming through the big steel gates ready to charge. John shouted.

"Mark, now!"

Mark hit the switch and the explosives blew. They all turned and ran under the cover of the explosions.

They reached the relative safety of the ferry's deck, turned and carried on firing at the creatures that were already coming through the smoke. The men positioned there on the deck, John presumed by Robert, firing also but the ship was already moving. A minute later all firing stopped. They had made it!

Chapter Forty Nine - Where To?

Robert was standing on the deck, hands on hips, smiling.

"Nah? It worked out fine after all," he said, conceitedly.

"You pratt!" John shouted. "It was an unnecessary risk. You could have got us all killed. We'd have made it, somehow."

"I didn't want you all catching colds, the water is freezing at this time of year," Robert said, laughing.

"Yeah, alright smart arse, it was dangerous all the same," John said. "How did we do?"

"We just lost the two men and the fuel tanker, everything else made it safely. We did bloody well!" Robert answered.

"We're a good team, mate," John said agreeing.

"We should go and see Vinny, he's on the bridge," Robert suggested.

"I don't know," John said, shaking his head. "Five minutes on a ship and you're coming out with all the nautical terms. Bloody bridge! Okay, lead the way, you can manage to do that right, can't you?" he asked, trying not to smile.

Robert went to punch him playfully, John starting to cover his face. Instead they shook hands and hugged. They had successfully achieved what they had set out to do and with minimum losses. It was a military marvel, to say the least.

Robert led the way through the newly acquired ship to the bridge. All the way there, civilians were coming up, congratulating and thanking them. The excitement generated by their situation was something that was impossible to ignore. As they reached the bridge they could hear Vinny singing some stupid song about pirates. He was sat in the Captain's chair, shouting out the occasional order.

"It's good to see you're having a nice time," John said, smiling.

"Sorry, John," Vinny said, jumping up out of the chair. "I've always wanted to do that. I'll behave myself from now on. How did we do?"

"We lost two men and a fuel tanker, not bad I suppose. It could have been far worse," John answered.

"I take it that was the explosion we heard," Vinny said.

"Yes. In a way it saved us, it took a lot of them with it!" John confirmed. "How's it looking in here?"

"Good, couldn't be better really. We have a full load of fuel, the ship is handling well, everything is in the green. Everything is sorted out down below, all the vehicles are secure. On a personal note, sleeping arrangements are currently being sorted out. I've reserved you and Robert a cabin in first class," Vinny said, smiling.

"What, together?" Robert asked, smiling.

"It can be arranged, Robert, if that's what turns you on!" Vinny laughed.

"Wanker!" John said. "Thanks, anyway. Now let's get serious for a moment, where are we going?"

"Well, I don't know how you guys are feeling but I'm knackered and so are my men. The last couple of days have been hard on everybody. So, what if we sail out a couple of miles from shore, anchor, and sleep on it? We'll be safe, we could even party a little. Or maybe even a lot! This ship's got everything, from disco bar to casino. What do you say?" Vinny asked. "Come on, gentlemen, you know it makes sense. One night of normality, then tomorrow we'll decide where we want to go."

John looked at Robert.

"Sounds like a plan, mate, we've earned a day off. Well, a night at least. What do you think?"

"I agree, we've all earned it," Robert said. "The civilians will also get a sense that the risk we all took was worth it. Yes, why not?"

"Okay, pick your spot to anchor, Captain and get a celebration going," John said. "I'll see you later. I'm going to make sure Stephanie is alright."

The doctor had promised he would release her from hospital that day and John wondered if she would feel up to a party or whether she fancied doing something else the ship had to offer. It would do them good to really relax for a few hours.

He found her relaxing in one of the ship's lounges, sitting together with a group of women she had befriended. As she saw him enter the lounge her face lit up; she stood and quickly walked to meet him. They embraced and kissed. He was so relieved to see her up and about. She introduced him to all her new friends who, like everybody else, thanked him for giving them a new chance at life. He was embarrassed by all the attention but stayed and talked with the group of women for about fifteen minutes before dragging Stephanie away. He spoke to Vinny, using the ship's intercom system, asking where their cabin was? It turned out Vinny had not been joking about the cabin arrangements and they were soon sitting in a relatively luxurious first class cabin with a sea view.

The ship's amenities appeared to be all in working order, so they both even managed to have a shower. Stephanie hinted that she wanted John to make love to her but he declined. He felt it was too early and was worried about the effect love-making might have on her wounds. Now she was free of the hospital, he was not going to do anything that might mean her going back! He suggested they wait a day or two, until she regained her strength fully, then they would make love for hours. He had missed making love to her terribly but was convinced it was the right thing to do. At first she seemed disappointed but, after hearing his arguments, quickly realised he was only thinking of her, a quality she loved about him. Eventually she had kissed him, saying, thank you. They had both slept for a few hours, the relief in being free of the mainland giving them both the chance to sleep deeply again. As they awoke, it was apparent the party was in full swing, music could be heard playing throughout the whole ship. They decided to join the on-going celebration, John promising they would not stay long, just show their faces.

People were dancing all over the ship, children running around playing, everybody was laughing and having fun.

They bumped into Robert who straightaway said what John had been thinking ever since leaving their cabin. Seeing the smiling and happy faces was proof that the decision to leave the castle had been the right one. If anybody had ever doubted that, they would not anymore. It had been worth it. Robert was dragged away by five or six women, towards one of the numerous dance floors. The look on his face was something John would not forget in a hurry.

They had seen Mark who was also surrounded by women, Stephanie confirming they were all single and available. It appeared that, with the threat of the creatures momentarily forgotten, life was getting very quickly back to normal.

The party had gone on into the early hours. John and Stephanie left early because she was feeling a little tired. John was secretly pleased to get away. The bed in their cabin again proved to be very comfortable, both of them sleeping late for the first time in ages.

Awaking mid-morning, they both showered, dressed and made their way to one of the ship's restaurants where a brunch-type meal was being served.

The room was still full of excitement, the party doing nothing to change that. A few of the men were looking the worse for wear, alcohol obviously having played a part. After finishing eating, John left Stephanie there talking with her friends and headed for the bridge. He was supposed to meet Robert, Mark and Vinny there at midday to discuss their destination. As he got there, it was obvious he was the last, a fact that did not happen all that often.

"Morning," he said, cheerfully.

"How'd you sleep, John?" Vinny asked. "How's my ship treating you?"

"I slept fine, thank you, Captain Igloo! Any thoughts on where we are heading?" John asked.

"Yeah, several actually. As I explained yesterday, the Med. isn't a good idea. What we need is somewhere not too far away and, until we really get the hang of handling this tub, somewhere that's not too difficult to find."

"Where do you suggest?" Robert asked.

"Well, I've heard the Isle of Wight is lovely at this time of year!" Vinny answered, smiling.

"You've got to be bloody kidding!" Mark blurted out.

"No. Dead serious, mate and here's why," Vinny said. "First we can reach it without having to refuel, that's a major plus in its favour. Second finding it won't be a problem, we can hug the coastline and sail straight there. The next reason is the killer, pay attention. There has always been a ferry service from there to the mainland, that means fuel! We'll need to refuel anyway if we decide to sail on but just think for a moment. The actual island is not that big, its pretty flat, the weather's generally okay and we can easily reach the mainland from there. That gives us numerous small settlements and towns, even a couple of pretty big cities, all within reach of the helicopters. That makes re-supplying a lot easier, plus it would be English food and that wins points on my scale! We will have to refuel there anyway, so it's got to be worth a look, at least."

"Your arguments are sound, mate, we'll head there and take a look," John said. "How long will it take to get there?"

"We're talking about three hundred miles by sea. We'll be there sometime tomorrow," Vinny said.

"Then get us underway as soon as you're ready, Captain," John said, then turning to Robert and Mark, he continued. "Would you care to join me on the sundeck, gentlemen?"

"Certainly, John," Robert replied.

288

"Yeah, the sea air will do us good," Mark added, smiling.

The next twenty-four hours went quickly, the excitement amongst the ship's passengers continuing to grow. It was the first time in months they had all felt totally safe. The children played on deck, went to the ship's cinema complex and watched films, they played games in the game room, whatever they wanted and, for the first time in years, nobody had to watch them constantly. The adults were also finding ways to enjoy themselves, the general atmosphere very relaxed. The soldiers also took time off, their first real opportunity in a long, long time. It all worked wonders for morale and everybody seemed genuinely happy. Another night was spent on the ship. It turned out to be similar to the one before, they partied a little more. The whole atmosphere reminded Robert more of a cruise liner, not a car ferry that was trying to escape certain death at the hands of marauding monsters!

The next morning, Vinny spoke over the ship's intercom system, reporting that the Isle of Wight had been sighted. The whole ship seemed to vibrate, as everybody screamed their delight at the news. Most of the passengers rushed on deck to get a first glimpse of their potential new home.

John, Mark, Robert and Vinny met on the ship's bridge to discuss their next move. Vinny reported that the ferry did not have enough fuel left to enable it to circle the island and he suggested that stopping there to refuel without first checking the area would be too dangerous. John suggested that a small group of his men could take one of the rescue launches and go ashore. They could check out the immediate area for signs of creatures or anything else that might prove to be a danger to the ship. Everyone agreed this was the logical step to take. From where they were now anchored, they could see quite a lot of the island and, from that vantage point, everything looked quiet. John and his men would hopefully have little trouble while scouting the area.

Thirty minutes later, one of the ferry's launches was heading for a beached area on the east side of the island. Beyond the beach was a wooded area and beyond that in the distance, a village could be seen. It seemed like a good spot for a scouting mission. On board the launch were John, Mark and ten of their team. They were taking no chances, so they were well armed and prepared for anything.

The small motor launch fought its way through the surf and landed on the beach, John starting to step out on to the sand. He was halfway out, when he stopped. Coming out of the trees were creatures, big and small. There were lots of them!

"Fuck!" John said. "Here we go again!"

The End?

Printed in the United Kingdom
by Lightning Source UK Ltd.
129037UK00002B/7-12/P